# PROMISE

ALSO BY MINROSE GWIN

*The Queen of Palmyra*

*Wishing for Snow*

# PROMISE

## MINROSE GWIN

WILLIAM MORROW

*An Imprint of* HarperCollins*Publishers*

PROMISE. Copyright © 2018 by Minrose Gwin. All rights reserved. Printed in the United States of America. No part of this book may be used or reproduced in any manner whatsoever without written permission except in the case of brief quotations embodied in critical articles and reviews. For information, address HarperCollins Publishers, 195 Broadway, New York, NY 10007.

HarperCollins books may be purchased for educational, business, or sales promotional use. For information, please email the Special Markets Department at SPsales@harpercollins.com.

FIRST EDITION

*Designed by Bonni Leon-Berman*

Library of Congress Cataloging-in-Publication Data has been applied for.

ISBN 978-0-06-247171-0

18  19  20  21  22    LSC    10  9  8  7  6  5  4  3  2  1

For the uncounted, but not unmourned.

And for Anna, in memory.

# THE OTHER STORM STORY

## AUTHOR'S NOTE

*A few minutes after 9 P.M. on Palm Sunday, April 5, 1936, a massive funnel cloud flashing a giant fireball and roaring like a runaway train careened into the thriving cotton-mill town of Tupelo, in northeastern Mississippi. The tornado was measured as an F5, the highest level on the Fujita scale. Winds were estimated at 261 to 318 miles per hour, leveling 48 city blocks, about half the town.*

*The Tupelo tornado wreaked havoc. The dead and dying were strewn about the town, dangling in the sheared limbs of leafless trees, buried under debris, pinned to the bottom of a small lake called Gum Pond, laid out in alleyways and makeshift morgues. Members of a family of thirteen, including a newborn baby, were blown in all directions; none survived. My grandmother found a dead baby girl in a crepe myrtle bush and wrapped her in a dish towel and laid her on the kitchen counter. There are at least five published accounts of flying children, including a girl around eight years old, who was blown from her own home on the black side of town, miraculously sailing through a window and landing dazed* but unhurt in the attic of a white family a mile away. Featherless chickens and hornless steers wandered the city streets. Debris from Tupelo was found in the neighboring state of Tennessee.

The official death toll ranged from 216 to 233; between 700 and 1,000 townspeople were listed as injured, many of them having lost limbs. Based on these figures, the Tupelo tornado of 1936 remains today the fourth most deadly tornado in the history of the United States.

Growing up in my grandparents' sturdy four-square house, one of the few left standing on their side of town, I heard these stories and many more. I thought I knew everything there was to know, truth or lore, about the Tupelo tornado of 1936.

I was wrong.

What I did not know was that the casualty records for the Tupelo tornado were incomplete and therefore inaccurate: members of the African-American community, one-third of the town's population, many of whom lived in ramshackle housing on a northeastern ridge called the Hill, were, quite simply, not counted. The death and injury tolls were much higher than records show.

We will never know those numbers. We will never know the names of all the uncounted.

A STORY can sometimes tread where history fails to clear a path or when that path has been made too tidy, obscuring a fractured landscape. It is that fractured landscape that I've tried to decipher in this work of fiction.

Events and place names in this story of the Tupelo tornado and its immediate aftermath are from newspaper accounts, oral narratives, and memorabilia: the characters and their stories are entirely fictitious.

# PALM SUNDAY,
## APRIL 5, 1936

# 1

## 8 P.M.

Too still out there. Dark coming on and no birds singing good night lady. No squirrels rummaging for last year's acorns under the big oak out front. The sky bruised, yellow and green with streaks of plum.

Peculiar smell in the air too: sour, vinegary. Downright peculiar. She knew it but couldn't place it. Something to eat, maybe? But what?

Now the wind kicked up in wicked little bursts. Rain or worse. Maybe hail.

And there it all was, an entire day's work, flapping on the line like some big white fell-from-the-sky bird: the McNabb wash. Sheets, towels, underwear, diapers, what have you. One sheet wrapped around the line, snagged. The Judge's upside-down dress shirts white as the driven snow, that much less skin on her knuckles. Her fingertips still burned, slick from the bleach.

She stood on her tiptoes and peered out the open window over the kitchen sink. Her neck rose in cords above the buttoned collar of her wash dress, which was pocked with pulls and stains and gaping where the button under her breasts had long since popped off and been lost. She wiped her hands down the sides of her dress to dry them and touched her head the way she used to do when she was little and her people got around the table and started telling about how she came into the world with a little cap of hair that looked for all the world like the feathers of a baby bird. She'd had trouble catching her first few breaths and so was a grayish color when her father first saw her. He called her his Dovey, insisted on the name. Her mother had sat straight up in bed, labor sweat still wet on her face. Naming her firstborn after a bird? What you going to name the next one, she'd asked. Pigeon? Crow?

But Dovey had always liked her name. When she was a girl, she studied doves: the maternal bulk of their bodies, the way they bobbed their small heads and cooed full-throatedly and stayed low to the ground. How they fussed when she got too near and flushed them. They seemed to her more human than other birds, more willing to stay close, less afraid of a human hand, downright companionable. Sometimes, now, on winter nights when she slept deep and still under a pile of quilts, she dreamed she was one. She fluttered on the edge of something brown and warm, and then, cooing, she flapped her arms, and then, oh glory! She took off into the wide blue yonder, riding the wind. Up Main Street, past Crosstown where the two train tracks made an X like a bull's-eye in the middle of town, over the churches and steeples, the fancy columned houses up and down Church Street, Pegues Funeral Home, TKE Drug Store, People's Bank and Trust, Reed's and Black's department stores: Whitetown.

Then, to the southeast, Milltown: a different set of white folks. Skinny as rails and so paper-thin white they looked like you could poke a finger through them. They lived in rowed-up shotguns that sagged and leaned like a stack of dominoes about to go over. They worked twelve hours a day six days a week at the mill, even the children, who were scrawnier than any black child up on the Hill or even down in Shake Rag. Looked like they'd never sat down to a meal of fatback and greens and corn bread. Wormy.

Then she would turn back north, swoop and flutter up Green Street, rising with the landscape, toward home: Elephant Hill, where her own people lived. She wasn't sure why they called it that—some called it Park Hill—but the Hill it was, a humped bluff overlooking muddy Gum Pond, also called Park Lake. Perched on top: Carver High, Springhill Cemetery, the faded old school bus where the Davises packed in three large children and a pair of twin babies. St. John the Baptist Church, J. W. Porter Undertaker. Houses that snaked in all directions, having been built onto bit by bit as they filled up with babies and old folks to take care of. Lucille Jones's garden with its splash of daylilies and black-eyed Susans. At the highest point, the water tower, a monster on stilts, cast a shadow over the whole community.

NOW IT was coming on dark sure enough. Out beyond the wash on the line, to the southwest side of North Green, where the paved street turned to rutted dirt, stretched Glenwood Cemetery, the chalky gravestones bent over like the broken-down, mostly old white people who now rested beneath them. To the east, Gum Pond, swampy and crawling with muskrats and snakes, not to speak of all manner of no-count lowlifes, black and white, hanging around out there under those big gum trees all hours of the day and night, smoking that Mexican hemp they sold up at Blue Mountain, up to no possible good. And back to the north, Springhill Cemetery, where her Mother and Daddy lay, with Janesy and Uldine and Blue. Her whole family long gone from the typhoid, leaving her an orphan at eight, forced to live with an aunt who put her to work at the washboard, where she'd been ever since.

That afternoon when the wash was done, she'd walked over to Springhill, her white head rag bobbing up and down over the high ridge and rolling hills, over the indentions where the graves, marked and unmarked, lay. She sat down next to her family, all five of them there together in an impossibly small piece of ground. The late day sun flooded the western ridge in gold and turned the grass and moss to green velvet. The sun's rays came in over the graves like the points of a spear, showing up the telltale scallops in the ground where each grave had been dug. When it reached her lap, it fired the faded roses on her housedress to hot coals. There was an old cedar tree at the top of the ridge. Next to it an old-man sycamore bent eastward from years of wind. She pushed herself backward into their shade, sweating a little. Her dead ones, were they at peace? Hadn't they wanted more of this dear sweet earth? The smells, the birdcalls, the way the light turned slant in the fall? Hadn't they wanted all that?

There was a place in the cemetery where she didn't go. A far corner, backed up to some scrub pines. The small stone she and Virgil had bought now mottled with moss and mold, covered over in pine needles and broken branches. There was a disturbance in the needles; some animal had made its bed there.

NOW, AS she stood at the kitchen sink, that old whistle shattered the odd quieter-than-quiet, making her jump. Once, twice, three, four, five times. The eight o'clock M&O, its tracks to the northeast, just the other side of Gum Pond. When she was a girl, after she'd lost her family, she used to lie in bed and listen for the eight o'clock, her little chest a turtle's shell, grown hard from the slow crawl of grief.

Now she felt the old rumble in her throat, something between a growl and a song that came from a low place, calling back to the train, saying she was sad, sad, she wanted her brother and sisters back. Saying what that McNabb boy did to her Dreama deserved a killing. She would relish it. But how to kill a white man? Well, poison, for one thing. Was there a poison a person might use on clothes? Sprinkle it on like starch and, one two three, Bogeyman's dead as meat and nobody knows why. Ha!

Dovey didn't study white folks unless forced to. Bad enough dealing with their peculiar odors and stains that lingered on sheets and handkerchiefs and underwear. (Did they ever bathe?) Bad enough the scrubbing and bleaching those stains out, only to have them returned to you the next week, nastier than ever. But what that devil did to Dreama was like a tiger sashaying through the front door. You couldn't *not* study it or it would eat you alive. She and Virgil had gone to the sheriff and then to the boy's daddy, the Judge. Nothing was done, nor, she knew in the pit of her stomach, would it ever be, white folks being white folks.

It *would* have to be the McNabbs' laundry out there. She couldn't help herself, she flat-out detested the whole family, even the little baby, which she knew was wrong, wrong, wrong. But she couldn't help herself. She knew the McNabbs in the most intimate ways, in ways they did not know one another. She knew that the Mrs. had not once ceased to bleed since that baby was born four months ago, that she perspired so much she wore underarm pads with even her everyday dresses. She knew the girl had broken her left arm; the left sleeve of several of her blouses had been cut off and hemmed. She knew the Judge ate tomato salad every Thursday at TKE Drugs because he splattered it all over his white shirt. She knew that boy didn't keep himself clean in the private ways a decent person should, which didn't surprise her in the least. He was lower than low.

At the sink she shifted from one foot to the other. Her feet, tiny and swollen and gnarled as the bark of an old tree trunk, her legs like a bird's. You one scrawny little woman, Virgil would say. You near about a midget, girl. He'd come up behind her while she was doing the wash and say, what you know good, girl? Then lift her off her feet and kiss the back of her neck where her scarf was knotted and the hair poked through.

Tonight her pelvis ached. She'd been at the washtub all day, beating and scrubbing and pushing that roller round and round to wring out the clothes. Her right shoulder felt off in the socket, as though it'd been knocked out and put back wrong. She reached up and rubbed it. Now, thanks to this mess of weather, she was going to have to get in the whole shooting match and be quick about it from the looks of that sky. She would have to bring the McNabbs back into her house; her hands would have to touch their clothing yet again. Everything would still be damp, given the mugginess in the air, maybe even dripping wet. She would have to iron every blasted piece of it dry, the wet starch coating her iron. It would take half the night. She'd have to fire the stove back up to heat the iron, and in this weather. Here it was barely the first week of April and hot as blue blazes. As the train passed through, wheels click-clacking, she went from sad to mad. She

could barely catch her breath she was so furious. Pure aggravation, this weather. She'd be up until midnight. What a humbug!

Some nights she lay in bed and the laundry of the whole town,
a grayish mound of white people's dirt, rose up before her. Then
something in the pile of clothes would shift and it would start to
slide and bury her, smother her. From time to time she considered maiding, but there was no money to speak of in it, just a lot
of leftovers, and working in some white woman's house, under
her thumb. It didn't appeal, not even on a night like tonight. At
least she could stretch her legs, rest when she wanted, go out
in the yard and watch the mockingbirds fight. No persnickety
Miss Lady breathing down her neck. Saying, day in and day out,
now you come, now you go. No good Christian husband and
father coming at her from behind, whispering filth in her ear.

All through supper, some corn bread and beans and buttermilk, and then the washing of the dishes, she'd looked forward
to the moment when she could put on her nightgown and sink
into bed, pull the quilt just so over her aching legs, turn her
body to curl around Virgil's, taking on his shape, adjusting the
timing of her breath to his. She looked across the room at him,
already in bed in the corner and dead to the world. Flat tuckered
out, like always. Millwork, but not really millwork. That was
left to the whites—mostly Milltown women, and the girls and
boys who rode the looms with their bare feet like monkeys. The
adults made twelve dollars a week, good money. He made less
than a quarter of that sweeping the cotton lint up and down
the long aisles, the only Negro allowed in the mill. White fluff,
mountains of it. He brought some of it home in a croker sack for
stuffing the mattress when it got beaten down, and sometimes
for pillows or a new quilt. The rest of the time he was glad to

be shuck of it. He never stopped sweeping, he told Dovey; he swept in his dreams, woke up every morning with the broom in his hand. Nights he'd come home with aching shoulders and a crotchety back, all covered in white fuzz. Look like Old Saint Nick, he'd say. The joke got old fast. Better let up, she'd say, you no spring chicken. No old man neither, he'd say back, then come for her to prove it.

The cotton compress was the largest in the state so the mill flourished, producing "Tupelo Cheviots, the cloth with a million friends." The work was steady. When the bales were spun into fabric, the fuzz went every which way. It's snowing every day over there, snowing white money for white folks, Virgil would say, just one big old snowstorm. When he'd get home at night he'd go around back and take off his shirt and overalls and hand them over to Dovey on the back stoop. She'd shake them off and pin them to the line. Every Saturday night she put them in her washtub for a good soak. He'd stand behind the house in his underwear, white from Dovey's bleach, and run his hands through his hair and over the hair on his arms. He kept his handkerchief to blow the fibers out of his nose. Dovey would come back out and hand him what they called his house clothes, a soft flannel shirt and some old cast-off pants. He'd take a few swipes at his shoes and come on into the house where she had him a cup of warmed-up breakfast coffee waiting on the kitchen table. He'd have his coffee, complain it was strong enough to walk out the door. Then he'd take off his shoes and read the paper while Dovey got their supper on.

He sneezed and sneezed. Sometimes, in bed at night, he woke up gasping for air and she would have to get out the Mentholatum and rub down his chest.

On Sundays, when the mill was quiet and Dovey busy, like she was today, with the never-ending wash, Virgil worked on the house. He'd built the house himself, a dogtrot on top of one of the Hill's several ridges. He'd gotten only one side finished by the time they moved in as a young couple and he was always working on the other half, a task that seemed more pressing now that the baby was almost ready to sit up. It wouldn't be long until that one was on the move. Then, Katy bar the door, Promise would need more room, and so would the rest of them. The work had taken years because Virgil used wood scrap he gathered piecemeal around town, usually behind Leake & Goodlett Lumber, plus he was busy with other business. He was big in the Negro Elks, always going to meetings and fixing things at other folks' houses. People came to him for advice and favors. He never turned anybody down. You always got to be the busiest man in town? Dovey would complain, but secretly she was proud of the way folks counted on him, proud that he was a man who couldn't say no.

AFTER THE eight o'clock rumbled through, Dovey got her basket and started out the back door. She stopped at the door to take off her sweater. It had been chilly this morning on the porch when she started on the day's wash, but now it was like an oven outside, the sky still moving into dark. And, Dreama and Promise, where'd those two get off to? They ought to be home from church by now. Dreama went to church every time the doors opened, not what you'd expect from a sixteen-year-old girl. Virgil said she got more religion than God Himself got.

But really, Dreama went because the Heroines of Jericho held a nursery for the babies every time the church doors opened. It wasn't God she was after, it was a few minutes' peace and quiet. Promise was a pistol. When he was the size of a newborn pup and waking up and crying every few hours, Dreama would drop him off with the Heroines of Jericho and hole up in the last pew and sleep through the service. Sometimes she forgot to wake up when the service was over and everybody else got up to leave. Then one of the nursery ladies would have to bring Promise to her. But nobody cast aspersions on Dreama. What had happened to her was a crime. If she wanted to sleep in church all day, well, let her do it. Maybe a piece of the good Lord would seep in through the skin, buck her up. She was too young for any of this, she was just a baby herself. It was a miracle she'd taken to the child at all. Truth be told, it was reported to Dovey, some of the nursery ladies let Promise cry longer than the other babies, let him cry a little too much; some cringed when they had to change him. Some, nobody'd mentioned names, gave him his bottle in his bed instead of holding him close like they held the others.

Before Promise clawed his way into the world, Dreama had spent all her time hating the thing inside her, had, in fact, sat on the edge of the bed with her legs crossed after her water broke and pronounced she wasn't going to have it, it could just go back where it came from. Gertrude Fisher, who delivered babies up on the Hill and down in Shake Rag and who, like everyone, knew what had happened to Dreama, told the girl to push and get it over with, but Dreama wouldn't. After a good long time, all that day and most of the night, so long that Dovey was about to send Virgil for the doctor, Promise pushed himself out, landing on the bed slam-bam facedown and crying his first mad where's-my-ma'am cry into the old sheet Dovey had put under her grand-daughter.

Dreama delivered the afterbirth and turned her face to the wall, told Dovey to take that screaming thing out of there, she couldn't stand the sight of it.

The baby, pink as a piglet and still gelatinous, looked more like the expulsion of a foreign body, a tumor, than a child.

"Lord," Gertrude Fisher said quietly. She gave Dovey a long look, then got a washcloth and began to wipe him clean.

Dovey took a deep breath and looked away. Not the child's doing, she told herself. He didn't ask to get born.

A week passed, then two. He grew into a pretty baby. Sweet like Dreama. Cooing and whapping the air, a whisper of a smile. The light brown hair, just slightly curled. Skin the color of may-onnaise. Those gold eyes, where did *they* come from?

Those first weeks Dreama flat-out refused to name him. The first day she refused her breasts to the snuffling creature, said he reminded her of a toad. Finally Dovey brought him in to her and held him aloft screaming and kicking. "You want this baby to die because you starved him to death?" she demanded of her granddaughter. "Ain't you got some act-right in you, girl? Where's your heart?"

Then she placed him on the bed beside Dreama and walked out.

She stood behind the doorway and listened. After awhile, a shift of weight on the bed and the cries suddenly hushed.

For weeks, though, Dreama wouldn't get out of the bed or leave her room except to relieve herself out back. The baby slept in an old laundry basket next to Dovey and Virgil's mattress in the main room of the house, and Dovey took care of all his needs except for the feedings. Even then she had to bring the child to the mother, who took him indifferently, staring into space as he fed, holding him just enough to get him to the breast. At night Dovey and Virgil could hear Dreama lying up in bed crying. Who the baby now—the child or the mother? asked Virgil.

It was Virgil who'd come up with the name Promise, though the child was hardly that. Dovey thought the name a bit much, nobody having made any promises in the getting of this baby, quite the opposite, actually. But they were all suffering, no need to cause more by quarreling over a name.

Before Dreama had Promise, Dovey and Virgil moved out of the one bedroom in the dogtrot into the main room, hoping that when the baby came Dreama would take one look and see something that could be loved, a dimple, a fingernail, an eyelash. And after awhile, miracle of all miracles, she did. One night, when Dovey went to retrieve him from nursing, she found Dreama sitting up in bed with him in her lap. She was holding both of his feet in the palm of her hand. She wasn't smiling but she wasn't crying either. Look how pretty his feet are, she said to her grandmother, look how regular his toes go down.

After that they brought the basket into the bedroom and Dreama got up on her own to clean him up and feed him. In the weeks that followed she made up for lost time in getting acquainted. She couldn't get enough of her son. Every inch of him from head to toe interested her: his hair, his buttercup mouth, those delicious jelly rolls of fat on his thighs. In his right armpit he had a small red birthmark that looked like a cloud, and she would pull up his arm and kiss him there again and again, making his milky eyes wobble in his head. She started dressing him in little outfits and taking him with her on errands.

By then the money had started coming. A crisp twenty, folded inside a blank piece of paper, arrived like clockwork the first of every month. A small fortune.

They never spoke of it. Dovey could barely stand to touch the cream-colored envelope, which came with no return address. Each month she took it out of the mailbox, handling it by the edge like it was hot, and laid it on Dreama's bed. Sometimes Dreama bought herself a new outfit from what was inside. Last month she'd gone down and bought them all a Silver 155 radio at Hall's Electric, a rounded rectangle made of walnut. Dovey frowned when Dreama presented it to her—she should be saving that money, not spending it on trifles—but Dovey loved to run her hand up and down its curved sides while she listened every week to the President talk about hardship and tribulation and courage and how they were all in this together and citizens needed to have faith that better days were at hand.

Dovey liked the word *citizen*. She rolled it around on her tongue like a caramel. Two years ago, when the President had come to town, *her* town, she'd gone down to Robins Field and stood at the back of the crowd with the other Negroes to hear him talk about progress and jobs and cheap power. He was in the wheelchair so she only got a glimpse of him, but she liked the way his voice rang out, presidential yet intimate, the way he didn't talk down to regular folks like herself. She pictured him sitting at her own kitchen table, his leg braces propped on the chair, his eyepiece sliding down his nose, bow tie askew, sipping a cup of warmed-up coffee and having a good heart-to-heart with her about hard times, her own up close and personal fireside chat. She'd cut his picture out of the paper and tacked it to the wall.

Mostly, though, the money went for Promise, his extra milk

and clothes, his medicine when he got that cold last month. Even so, when the baby reached three months, Virgil asked Dreama about the money, how much of it she'd been holding back, hiding God knows where, and what she intended to do with it. Thirty dollars, as it turned out, too much to have hanging around the house. He told Dreama they needed to get that kind of money into the bank, or the word would get out and no telling what kind of trash would come calling in the dead of night. Plus Dreama needed to get back to school come September; she'd been out long enough. No grandchild of his, no matter how unlucky, was going without a high school diploma. The money would pay for somebody to take care of Promise while Dovey made her rounds. The money was Dreama's future, her ticket to that college up in Holly Springs.

So just that past week, Dovey and Dreama had put Promise in Dovey's laundry cart and walked into downtown to the People's Bank and Trust Company on the corner of Main and Broadway. That morning Dovey had put on her good dress with the climbing rose print, long sleeved and high collared, and a round-brimmed felt hat that so dwarfed her head she had to tie it on with one of Virgil's old belts. Dreama wore a new polka-dotted skirt and blouse, which hung on her because she'd not been allowed to try it on in the store and of course couldn't return it for a smaller size.

In the cart, Promise brimmed with goodwill. When Dreama pulled him from the cart and they came into the bank, struggling with the heavy door, he smiled that gummy smile of his, lighting up the whole place. They stood uncertainly in the middle of the floor under the gleaming chandelier, waiting for the line of white people to go up and do their business. A woman in line reached over and touched Promise's head, twirled a curl the color of lightly browned toast. Promise turned and looked up at her, swatted at her hand, and grinned from ear to ear. The woman smiled back and looked at Dovey. "Whose baby y'all taking care of? Never seen this one before."

Dovey's mouth opened and closed. Dreama glared at the woman. "This is *my* baby."

The woman's eyes widened, the hand came away. She faced forward again and began to whisper into the ear of the woman ahead of her in line, who turned to look.

Dreama drew herself up and said, again, "*My* baby." Louder this time, causing Dovey to frown at her granddaughter, move between her and the white women as though she were herding the girl, shake her head at Dreama, touch her lightly on the hip.

They waited a good long time. When there were no more white customers in line and they got up to the bank window, the cashier sucked her teeth. Dreama looked too young to be opening a savings account. How old was she? Where, pray tell, had all that money come from?

Dovey stepped forward. "Come from my laundry money. This girl's my granddaughter and I got a mind to give it to her."

Dreama giggled. Dovey shot her a look.

The woman had a long chin ending in several white curly whiskers. "Well, you'll have to put your name on the account too."

When they finally left with nothing but a little book with $30.00 written in it, Dreama stopped on the corner outside the bank and told her grandmother she wanted to go back inside and get her money back from the goat lady. She had a bad feeling about letting white people get hold of her money.

Dovey put a hand on her granddaughter's shoulder. "Wait a while, baby." Dreama was changeable, flighty. She was only a girl, after all. Tomorrow it would be something else.

On the way home, Promise grinned and reached for the strands of forsythia that lined the street. Dovey couldn't help but smile at him. He had the same goofy grin Dreama had had when she came to them. She'd come on the eleven o'clock M&O from way down in New Orleans almost two years to the day that Dovey and Virgil's only child, Charlesetta, named after his father's father, had jumped a boxcar and ridden as far south as the M&O traveled. Before she left she didn't make any bones about the fact that she wasn't staying in this podunk town, living up on the Hill or, worse yet down in Shake Rag, the rest of her life, cleaning up white folks' dirt, cooking their food. She was good with numbers, Dovey had seen to that, and she could sing. She got it in her head that, in New Orleans, she could wait tables and get tips and eventually, with that voice of hers, sing in bars.

Charlesetta was eighteen by then, a grown woman, but Virgil had all but hog-tied her to keep her from leaving. New Orleans was nothing but a dream somebody thought up, he told her. People starving down there in that den of iniquity, white trash thick as thieves. She'd buy herself trouble she couldn't even conjure; she'd end up in Storyville gyrating around in nothing but her underwear. They'd pick over her like garbage, use her up, and toss her out on the street. Virgil knew what he was talking about too. His father, a Creole man named George Grand'homme, had come to Tupelo from New Orleans to work as a porter on the Frisco railroad. He told Virgil stories about the too-much honkytonking that liked to have ruined him if he hadn't wised up and moved north. He told Virgil he never wanted to hear tell of him heading down there.

One night, Virgil and Charlesetta fought it out. He begged her to go to Memphis if she had to leave. Virgil and Dovey could visit her, she could come home for Christmas. "Memphis is one big old Mississippi," she'd said. "I'm looking to get out of Mississippi. I'm looking to get away from white folks' laundry."

"That laundry put food in your mouth, girl." Virgil took her by the shoulders then and shoved her. It was the only time he'd ever laid hands on her, but it landed her on the floor.

When Dovey tried to pull her up, Charlesetta snarled, "Get your hands off me."

The next morning she was gone. Dovey cried and cried. "You run off my baby," she told Virgil.

After awhile they started getting letters about the heat in New Orleans and gravy sandwiches and juke joints and shotgun houses. Charlesetta was eating good and feeling good. She didn't mention how she was making a living or where she was staying. Important, necessary things. She didn't offer an address they could write back to.

The baby girl came to Dovey and Virgil in the arms of a sourfaced nun wearing an astonishing hat that looked like a big white bird had landed on her head. Charlesetta came on the same train but in a box, which was taken from a freight car at Crosstown and rushed to Porter's Funeral Home. When they got the telegram—the death in childbirth, the baby girl they were to expect shortly—Dovey and Virgil, who'd paid fifty cents a week to a policy man named Fred Holcomb, a white man with a big red pocked nose, tried to cash in but were told that Charlesetta was too old to still be on the policy. They went ahead and bought the burial plot in a far corner of Springhill Cemetery under the scrub pine and took back the baby bed they'd long ago turned over to the church nursery.

When the train came in, Dovey took one long look at the baby in the nun's arms and burst into tears. She'd been crying nonstop for Charlesetta but a little voice in her head had whispered, *At least there's the baby.* When she saw Dreama for the first time, her hand went to her mouth but not before something between a gasp and a curse came out. *Now this! Charlesetta, what you gone and done?*

It opened a door that couldn't be closed. Weeks later Dovey was still crying, her tears dripping into the wash and onto the baby's chest as she changed her. She woke up crying and went to sleep crying; she cried in her sleep. The word about Charlesetta's baby spread. There was a constant procession of Heroines of Jericho bearing flowers, fresh-cut from gardens up and down the street, and plates of chicken and potato salad. Some came out of kindness, some out of curiosity. There were cobblers, peach and apple. Lloyd Pickens from up the street brought Dovey one of his hams. She could barely eat a bite. She thought of her namesakes, the doves, who took flight only when things got too bad on the ground, how they cried out as they scattered. All the fluid seemed to be leaving her body; she grew shriveled and light. Her hair turned gray almost overnight.

She laid it all at Virgil's feet. He'd driven her child away. When he came in at night, she exchanged his work clothes for his house clothes without saying a word. She didn't heat up his coffee or make small talk with him over supper. Some nights she tended Dreama instead of sitting down at the table with him.

One morning, as she was diapering her dead daughter's baby,

the child's hand, light as the cotton on Virgil's work clothes, touched her cheek, and the tears, shed and unshed, froze into a chunk of ice.

Virgil meanwhile had named the baby Dreama because, for him, given the situation, she was a dream come true, a way to start over, to make good on the promise he somehow felt he'd broken to their daughter, to keep her safe, to make her happy with what she had. He built Dreama a little bed on the side of Dovey's laundry cart, the same cart she would use to take Promise to the bank sixteen years later. Dovey took Dreama on her rounds—what else could she do with her?—gathering the dirty and delivering the clean. When folks up on the Hill would bend over the laundry cart and their eyes widen when they took in the baby's color, the straight hair and freckles, the green eyes, Dovey would glare at them, her eyes flashing, defying them to roll their eyes or make a noise under their breath.

The years went by, and little Dreama lived up to her name. She was sweet and pliant where her mother had been sassy and stubborn. She loved school and went willingly, joyfully. Weekends she helped Dovey with the ironing. She stayed after school to help some of the slower ones learn to read, going over their lessons with them on the board since they had no books. She leapfrogged over two grades and decided she was going to go to college and be a teacher, come back to Carver High and teach English. At night, instead of running off to Shake Rag to hear Lonnie Williams or Nap Hayes play in the juke joints the way her mother had done, she moved the iron back and forth over the men's shirts in Dovey's laundry basket—arms and cuffs first, then backs and sides, finally the collar—and went on and on about literacy being the key to Negro advancement in the professions. Smart as a whip, her English teacher, Etherene Johnson, told Dovey and Virgil; they needed to start putting money away to send Dreama up to Holly Springs to Rust College, where Ida B. Wells had gone. Etherene said the teachers at Carver, some of whom had gone to Rust, were bound and determined that girl was going to get a scholarship.

Dreama's other talent was gathering strays: dogs with ridges for backbones and wormy half-dead kittens, wall-eyed children from over in Shake Rag, broken-winged sparrows that hopped around the yard, pecking at the dirt like chickens. One Saturday morning Dreama went out to take back some clean laundry to the McNabbs and showed up at home carrying something with a pink pointy snout. Dovey, rolling some wet clothes through the wringer, jumped halfway across the porch.

"What you doing, girl, carrying around a rat like it was a baby? Bite your fingers off, make you sick. Ain't you got good sense?"

"It's a guinea pig, Granny," Dreama said. "I found him in a ditch over on Church Street. Must have been somebody's pet got loose. Named him Henry."

Dreama always made sure to have her animals named by the time she presented them to her grandmother.

"No rats coming up here on my porch."

"Please, Granny. Look, he's cold. Can't he just live in a box up there? He won't be trouble. They don't eat anything but grass."

Dreama had just turned nine. Her hair fell in loose curls around her face. The morning sun cast her in bronze. She took Dovey's breath away. Her legs, like Dovey's, were sticks; her silhouette looked like one of those birds all the time walking around at the scummy edge of Gum Pond seining for fish. Girl needed some meat on those legs.

"That thing ain't setting foot in my house and no table scraps," Dovey said finally, and Dreama rushed off to find a box in the shed.

Seven years later Henry still lived on the porch when he wasn't out in the yard grazing. He stayed close, returning to his box at night. Dovey had gotten used to him under her feet. Sometimes, in the summer when she was making jam, she slipped him peach pits and overripe muscadines.

NOW, ALMOST time for the nine o'clock Frisco. A flash of lightning, then another. The sky suddenly the color of soot. Whatever it was was coming right this minute. She better hurry. She looked around the room for her basket. On the window sill a movement caught her eye. A yellow jacket.

A yellow jacket in April? It made no sense. But there it was, the ugly thing. It twitched and pulsated, pushing its stinger up and down, just looking for something soft to dig into. Normally she would have opened the kitchen window and shooed it out; she didn't like to kill innocent things. But tonight she was so aggravated about the coming storm and all those clothes on the line that she reached into the dish drain and picked up the jelly jar Virgil drank his tea from and brought it down hard, crushing the wasp with a satisfying crunch. She rinsed the bottom of the jar. When she opened the window to brush out the crushed yellow jacket, a gust of wind caught its pieces and blew them back at her, scattering them in the sink.

Through the open window the wind blew in that peculiar

smell. She still couldn't place it. She closed her eyes and sniffed, once, then again. Then a good whiff hit her dead-on, so strong it about knocked her off her feet. Horseradish! Virgil liked it with the catfish he'd catch sometimes down at the river. Horseradish, for sure. She never liked the stuff. It reminded her of piss.

She looked out the open window. Below her in the street, children were dancing in the wind barefoot, their clothes billowing this way and that. She hollered down at them to get on home, a storm was coming.

It was coming now, for sure. Her ears popped and she yawned to unplug them. She headed out the front door to get the clothes in. Once in the yard she couldn't get her breath; the air was like cotton lint, clogging her nose and throat, making her gag a little.

Dreama and Promise, why weren't they back? St. John was usually out by now, though this was Palm Sunday, which could run long. That morning she and Dreama had cut the low-lying new branches from the mimosa out front for the children's procession down the aisle. "Hosanna in the Highest" in those high, pretty voices. (How her Charlesetta had loved to sing! How pretty she'd looked in her navy-blue choir robe with the white collar Dovey had crocheted.) The Heroines of Jericho's big day, they'd be decked out in full regalia, white all over, head to toe. Dovey had been too busy to go.

Now she reached up and began to take the McNabb wash off the line. She knew what things were that boy's. It made her gorge rise to touch them after they'd come into contact with his flesh. Every week she wished him dead, and if not dead, then gone. At the very least gone. She tied a small knot in the toes of his socks and muttered curses she didn't know she knew. When she prayed, which wasn't often these days, she prayed for justice.

Tonight the church service should have been quieter and, more to the point, shorter, heavy with the sense of foreboding, Jesus having been sent on his way to what was to come. And for what good reason? It seemed silly and on God's part mean-spirited, when there was so much suffering in the world to make more.

The wind had stopped. The remaining clothes hung limp now on the line. They looked painted there, white patches against the sudden slide into dark, as motionless as the gravestones across the street.

Now a long moment of stillness. Long enough for Dovey to pause and wonder whether the rain was going to pass them by. The house faced west, and as she stood there in the yard, suddenly hopeful, her basket on her hip, the last of the sun, which had slipped under a soot-colored cloud, emerged at the horizon. There were children twirling around in the street below the house. In that moment she knew, suddenly, that she was about to witness something strange, something miraculous. She remembered her grandmother talking about the night the stars fell. It was Alabama and her grandmother a barely walking girl. Her mother held her up to see and told her that deliverance had come, the stars falling out of the sky was a sign from God. He was setting them free.

Dovey knew she was being greedy, greedy, having already had herself one good time that day, to ask for more. Early that morning, she'd taken Promise outside on the porch while she did the McNabb wash. She'd gotten a fork from the kitchen. As the early sun crept around the corners of the house behind them, they'd sat together on the porch, Dovey behind the laundry tub, Promise on her lap. Every so often she picked up the fork, dipped it into the soapy water in the washtub and blew, and the bubbles drifted up against the blue blue sky, catching the sun's rays and separating into color. Pink and yellow and green. Looking out, Promise had made a sound in his throat, almost a purr, and Dovey had gazed down at him. *This is what the heart looks like,* she'd thought, *it looks like him with them bubbles.*

She'd wanted to see Charlesetta in him. Now that would be the true miracle. Charlesetta's chocolate-drop eyes and tight curls, the dimple in her right cheek. None of it in this one.

**NOW DOVEY** put her hand to her temple. The morning and its vision seemed like days ago. Her head had begun to throb; it felt like it had been caught in a vise. One of her headaches for sure, coming on strong. She loosened the top button of her collar, touched the cords of her neck.

Below her in the street, the children, bereft of wind, stopped twirling and looked up at her. There was a little girl on the edge of the group who resembled Charlesetta at that age. The girl poked a finger in her ear, shook her head like a dog with mites. Her ears must be popping too. The setting sun, cut in half by the horizon, flared. Dovey, now wreathed in gold, looked down at the top of her own right hand, which held the basket against her hip, and saw painted over its ridges and rough spots an unearthly yellow. Then a crack, the sound of a massive limb falling, and she looked up and saw the ball of fire in the sky. Below her, in the neon light, the children, now frozen in place, looked as though they'd just been torched.

In the distance and getting nearer, gathering and gathering, the sound of a freight train, though it wasn't time yet for the

Frisco to come through. Now, it was louder than a train, much louder, the sound of a dozen trains, a roar and a clatter and a shriek and a groan.

Then, through the slap of blackness that in the still-long-and-getting-longer moment had just veiled the sky, lightning flashed again, bright as day. Then she saw it coming. The funnel, spewing debris, huge shards of wood and metal, an easy chair, something large with hair and four upside-down legs.

She dropped her basket and hollered for Virgil. She began to run, down the hill toward the little girl, to snatch her up and get her inside. Dreama and Promise, where *were* they?

But now it was upon her, roaring and screaming, a tiger, a train, a monster from hell shrieking and flailing, and she felt her bare, swollen, exhausted feet leave the red clay dirt she stood on—the good sweet earth she loved—and she felt it take her, and she felt herself begin to fly.

# 2

## 9:03 P.M.

When the first shard of lightning cracked open the sky, Jo had just opened up a coat hanger and pushed it down between her left arm and the plaster cast that encased it. She was standing next to the house, in the backyard. The end of the coat hanger was jagged and it tore at her flesh, drawing blood she felt sure. She didn't care. The itch itched. It had itched all last night and all this morning and afternoon. In the early morning hours she had awoken to a whole colony of fire ants drilling holes into the mound of flesh that covered her broken arm. They bit and stung, again and again. Then, as the day had turned hot and muggy and her arm swelled inside the cast, the itch had progressed from simply irritating to unbearable. Damn that horse of Bill Kelly's. Whatever had possessed her to get on the blasted thing? The minute she'd pulled herself up into the saddle and situated her feet in the stirrups, before she even had gotten a good grip on the reins, it had started up galloping hell-bent for leather, and then stopped on a dime like it'd run over a patch of glue, lowering its head to a few sprigs of grass as if bowing to some unseen deity. All of which had somersaulted her into the air with a sickening lurch. She did one full rotation and after what seemed like an eternity, she came down on her left shoulder and heard the crack, felt the stab of bone tear flesh and (horror!) emerge through it. She took one look, saw cotton fluffs in the air around her, vomited up her breakfast, and passed out.

At Sunday school this morning she'd taken her arm out of the sling and cradled it in her lap like a baby. She'd tapped the surface of the cast with her fingers, trying to scatter the ants, but the tapping just seemed to aggravate them and they drilled in deeper, as if they were boring into the bowels of the earth to make a permanent mound. They kept it up all through church, where she prayed, in rapid succession, to God, Jesus, and finally the Holy Ghost to give her some relief, a supplication that had no effect whatsoever. The ants kept it up all through Sunday dinner's chicken and dumplings (her favorite dish) plus collards, not a bite of which she could enjoy. At the table she resumed tapping her cast, more out of frustration than any hope of relief. Her father told her to stop that; it was irritating, nobody could talk over it, and she snapped at him, asking him what he'd do if his arm felt like it was getting stung by fire ants. He told her to buck up; it was common for a cast to itch. Think about something else. Get it off her mind. She had two more weeks in that thing. She'd stormed from the table, before her mother had dished out the raspberry sherbet, the latter long awaited each spring and just in at Nesbitt's Grocery.

Then came the still-as-death afternoon and early evening. She tiptoed around the dim, blind-drawn house so as not to disturb her mother, who was napping while the baby, Tommy, now four months old and the crankiest baby alive, was down. Jo's mother, Alice, who taught English at the high school, had named her second and third children after literary figures, Jo after the character in Alice's favorite girlhood book *Little Women* and little Tommy

after Tom Sawyer. One family name, she said, was enough, refer-
ring to Jo's older brother, Morton McNabb III, called Son, who,
to everyone's dismay, was anything but filial. Now, though, Alice
was stuck at home with Tommy, having taken the year off. Her
substitute, a younger woman named Myrtle Crisp, was wildly
popular at school, knew all the latest writers, and rumors were
flying that Mr. O'Reilly, the principal, might prefer her over
Alice, none of which Jo had told her mother.

Alice McNabb had bigger fish to fry than worrying about
keeping her job. After Tommy was born, she'd gone into a sadness that had descended like a dense fog over the household,
then crept out into the town itself. It gathered intensity in
whispered talk at church and the Curb Market and Lil's Beauty
Parlor. At home, when she wasn't in her room sleeping or tending to the baby, Alice took up her post on the front porch, in
the big swing, the outline of her slumped body generating something akin to hysteria among the town women. Jo sat beside
her mother, watching the ongoing parade of Junior Auxiliary
ladies and Bible study ladies and bridge club ladies, and even
some of the town's working women—Lil, who did Alice's hair
and painted her nails Dusty Rose; Marge, the dry cleaning
clerk who for years had taken in Jo's father's dress suits and ties.
They brought her banana pudding, potato salad, even a chuck
roast with carrots and potatoes floating in grease. They sat in
the swing with Alice and took her soft pink hands in theirs and
gave advice. She had a beautiful new boy; she had responsibil-
ities. Alice, for her part, would listen and smile a little and nod
her head and say, gently so as not to hurt their feelings, that
she just needed some peace and quiet, she would be all right.
When they left, she would resume her swinging and staring,

pushing the swing higher and higher to the point at which it would squeak and creak alarmingly. When the baby began to cry, she would sigh and drag her feet and slow the swing to a stop and go inside to tend to him, leaving Jo sitting motionless.

EARLIER THAT afternoon as she paced the dark hallway in the hot wet blanket of afternoon, Jo had begun to think of her flesh as being shredded like hamburger in a meat grinder, pieces of her skin actually sticking to the inside of the cast. By the time she ran through the back door onto the screen porch and then out through the screen door and down the back steps, she'd worked herself into a state. Once outside, she set her shoulders and marched up to the massive pecan tree in the backyard and slammed the cast against its trunk, an act which sent such waves of pain through her arm that she saw cotton again. She collapsed onto the ground and leaned up against the tree trunk while the pain subsided. When it did, the busy, vicious ants started right back up again, now in even more of a frenzy, a seething, infuriated mass. She wanted to chop the arm right off, ship it to Siberia. Instead she decided to go back inside and stick it in the icebox and was headed for the back door when her father emerged from the house and told her it was 5:30, time to get ready for Young People. She gagged at the thought. The food at Young People was horrible, usually some form of odious sandwich, a gelatinous olive loaf or liverwurst or a watery egg salad, all of which she detested. Then Bible study, which she was in no mood for. The church basement, with its painted-shut windows and one small rotating fan, was bound to be stifling. (Why was it so hot today? More like July than early April.)

Shading her eyes with her right hand, the shaft of afternoon light almost blinding her now, she looked up at her father and said she wasn't going, her arm was itching so bad she couldn't think straight. She waved her casted arm at him, making her point.

"Stop doing that," said her father. "You'll reinjure the arm. Young People will take your mind off it. It's Palm Sunday. Go on in now and get yourself dressed. It feels like rain. Grab an umbrella."

Jo kept scratching. "If Son's not going, neither am I."

It was a mean-spirited thing to say, and silly to boot. Son had just turned nineteen, for one thing. He hadn't been to Young People for at least five years. Her words buzzed in the still hot air like angry wasps. She wished she could reach out and catch them in a jar, put a lid on it, hide it behind her back. Her poor father was doing the best he could with her brother. Of course Mort McNabb Jr. would have liked to have made Son go too, but Son, as everyone knew, now commanded a rough crowd of boys over at Milltown and was out running wild out in the county, despite Alice and Mort's best efforts to corral him and return him to the sweet-faced baby boy of his early pictures, a boy Jo, three years his junior, had never known. They treated their firstborn son as if he'd developed a malignancy, an illness caused by "bad influences," which if they were kind enough, firm enough, *parental* enough, would eventually be excised. He was their failure, a failure that had stooped Mort's shoulders, plowed a furrow between Alice's brows.

The final straw was when Son came home one day in a sportster, a red Alfa Romeo, which he said a friend had loaned him for the time being and which cost more than his father had made in

the last three years in his law practice and time on the bench.
Mort had gone into the bedroom and, without even shutting the
door behind him, begun almost immediately to pull at his hair
and pace. "We have failed that boy! How did we let this happen? This is our fault," he thundered at Alice, then eight months
pregnant, who had been sitting there staring out the window.
After he stormed out, Jo hovered by the open door, wanting to
tell her mother she wasn't to blame; there'd always been something wrong with Son. His hazel eyes, light and wide and empty
of whatever it was that should be in eyes—a spark, a softness,
a luminosity? You could see right through those eyes of his, like
they weren't there at all, like they were nothing but clear yellowish water, or ice, and the person behind them wasn't there
either. Jo never looked directly into Son's eyes. They frightened
her in some deep way.

Then there was the trick. A Friday afternoon in October, how
old was she by then? Seven? A delicious chill in the air, leaves
everywhere, reds and oranges mostly, maple and gum. She'd just
gotten home from her piano lessons with Miss Edwina Edwards
next door and had done well. Miss Edwina, as her pupils called
her, was said to be unaccountably nervous (though Jo saw no evidence of this), having long ago been abandoned by her husband.
He'd hightailed it for Houston, where he'd made a fortune, first
in cotton and then oil, leaving Miss Edwina to knock around by
herself in the big white wedding-cake house next door. It had
enormous columns and a long, narrow screen porch down the
side. Some late summer afternoons, when the frogs and katydids
revved up and the swallows and bats swooped for mosquitoes,
Miss Edwina would throw open her doors and windows and
take to her piano. The crashing chords of Rachmaninoff would

burst forth from next door and echo up and down Church Street as though Miss E's heart were being beaten against the cliffs of some rocky shore.

Miss Edwina was blind. Her eyes were watery and blue with what looked like little white puffy clouds sailing across the pupils. She sometimes wasn't buttoned or zipped properly or she appeared at the door with crumbs on her cheek and then Jo, who couldn't bear to see her like that, would whisper in her ear and help her readjust. Throughout the years Miss Edwina's arthritic collie dog, Major, regally escorted each of her pupils into the house. That fall afternoon, Jo had walked back to the fence line between Miss Edwina's and her own house, escorted by Major, and then opened the gate to enter her own backyard, giving the dog a farewell pat on the head. She still had on her school clothes: a white blouse and plaid pleated skirt and knee socks. It was an outfit she particularly liked. The morning had been chilly and her mother had gotten out her favorite blue sweater from the cedar chest. It still smelled like mothballs.

That day, there were leaves everywhere and black moldy pecan shells scattered on the ground among them. They crunched under her feet.

Her brother had some friends hanging around in the backyard. They told her there was a stray kitten out behind the garage, which was true. When she rounded the corner, one boy had the kitten by the scruff of the neck. It was white and dirty with green eyes that oozed. It was crying and hissing and twisting, its little legs bicycling the air. When she ran to the poor thing's rescue, Son reached out and grabbed the tail end of her blue sweater.

He did it all, her own brother. He took her down to the ground and pulled off her underpants and held her legs open for his friends to see. She fought, then froze like a rabbit in the field, large-eyed and quivering, as their faces closed in. There was more, but she couldn't now recall the rest, only that she was a door to a house they wanted to enter. She'd gone somewhere else in her mind, somewhere where there were green trees and mountains and little trickling streams moving over rocks. There was a picture of this place in the dentist's office, on the ceiling right above her head as she sat in the dentist's chair, and she'd come to think of it as a place she'd actually been. In the distance she heard birdcalls and Miss Edwina playing Rachmaninoff. She had just lost her two front teeth and when she tried to scream only a whistle came out, causing Major to come to the fence line and paw the ground frantically, bark his high-pitched bark, then run back and forth. Son and his friends were going on ten, still in knickers, large for their size.

Now that she was sixteen, what was left of Major was only a bump in the ground under the giant sycamore in Miss Edwina's backyard and Miss Edwina herself long gone to a first cousin in Meridian, the wedding-cake house sitting empty behind closed venetian blinds. Jo didn't think about the trick much at all and when she did, she did her dead-level best to think of it as just that, a prank, one big fat joke on her. Jo liked to think of herself as an ordinary girl; she had a nice family and nice friends and she lived in a nice town. Her father was a lawyer and a judge (more precisely a referee in bankruptcy), her mother a schoolteacher. What could be more respectable? The most exciting thing that had happened to her to date was falling off Bill Kelly's horse and breaking her arm.

That day of the trick, after the boys had run off, she had gathered her things and walked around to the front of the garage and made her way inside to a dark corner at the back, squatting down behind a spare tire her father kept there. Her mother was still at school, her father at the courthouse downtown. While she waited for one of them to get home, she'd drawn pictures in the dirt of the garage floor. A sun with twelve rays, one for each month. When she got up, there was a bit of blood, which she covered with an old greasy rag.

Later that night, she took a bath. She even sang in the tub as she watched the water turn pink, behind the locked bathroom door, just so her brother would know she wasn't bothered by his silliness. The next day she took her time getting home from school, stopping by to visit with her great-aunts, Fan and Sister, in their musty house farther down Church Street, toward Main, and having peppermints and tea with them, the late afternoon sun filtering through the drawn drapes, letting their old-lady smells descend on her like the clouds of mosquito repellent the town wagons sprayed on alternating Monday nights during the summer. In the months ahead she became quite fond of Aunt Fan and Aunt Sister, taking pleasure in their little squabbles, the way their nails were always perfectly done and their fingers dripped rings from long-gone McNabb matriarchs. She absorbed their parsed pleasures as her own, the way they brought her into their circle, talked of miscarriages and legal squabbles and the price of black-eyed peas at the Curb Market. She liked their independence, the way they lived lean as the meat they ate, how they washed out their own personal laundry and hung it on their side porch, not caring who saw what. The washwoman picked up their sheets and towels, but only once a month.

By the time she climbed the steps to the back door that afternoon of the trick, her mother was at the stove stirring a pot of leftover soup, and Son long gone. The black stains from the molded pecans on the ground never came out of her blue sweater despite the washwoman's best efforts, and so it was donated to the First Presbyterian Church to send abroad for an orphan child, who wouldn't care, Alice said, that Jo had been careless enough to dirty her best sweater. The orphan, who didn't have the advantages Jo had, would be *happy* to have such a pretty sweater.

The kitten came back the next day. It followed Jo up Church Street to school, a little white ghost with emerald eyes, dingy and silent, with a sprinkle of gray on the top of its head. It always seemed to be walking on tiptoes. When school was out that afternoon, it reappeared about halfway back to her house and followed her home. It was thin and there was a scab on its nose. As they grew close to the house, it began to call out to her. *You, you, you.* For reasons she wasn't clear about, Jo was a little afraid of it. It followed her into the kitchen and she put down some milk in a saucer. It lapped it up and called out to her again. She went to the icebox and got out some leftover ham, which it gobbled down and then jumped up onto a kitchen chair and went to sleep. Later, Alice came into the kitchen and took one look and said it had to stay outside. Did Jo remember that guinea pig she'd insisted on getting, how it used the whole house for its bathroom? Pellets in the cooking pots, pellets in Jo's underwear drawer, pellets here, there, and everywhere. The kitten could live in the garage.

Jo got an old towel and made it a bed on a shelf. When she carried it out to its bed, it hissed and ran off into the night. She was worried that it had run away the way the guinea pig had. One minute Piggy was grazing in the front yard, the next he was gone forever. (It was assumed that he'd strayed into Miss Edwina's yard and Major had dispatched him, though no one ever brought up this probability to Jo.)

The next morning, though, Jo found the kitten curled up nice as you please on the towel. It stretched and offered her its belly. When she rubbed it, it tapped her hand as if to say hello. She named it Snowball, a silly name she knew, but in truth it resembled a ball of old snow, dirty and refrozen. Mort McNabb had gone to Harvard Law School and he talked about how the snow up north lingered until May, freezing and refreezing and piled up on the sides of streets until it was the color of soot. Jo had loved the idea of snow, which she was always wishing for and which had only come twice in her lifetime and then, in the blink of an eye, had melted.

NOW, A decade later, Son was the talk of Tupelo. Why couldn't Mort McNabb control his own boy? His failure to do so was a source of deep embarrassment; Jo had heard her father telling her mother he'd never be elected an elder in the First Presbyterian Church and they both knew why; his father and his father before him had been elders, Mort had been a deacon for a decade now.

At first, the boy's actions had seemed like high jinks. Four years ago, when he was fifteen, there was the trouble at Reed's Department Store when he grabbed not one, not two, but *three* fedoras off the hatstands, piled them on top of his head, and sailed out the side door on a busy Saturday morning, leaving the clerks gaping. Just a prank, he'd told his father, he was going to bring them back.

Then, a little more than a year ago, there was something about
that colored girl, the washwoman's granddaughter. When the
washwoman, so skinny and little she looked like a child herself,
and her husband, a tall, wiry man, came to the back door one day
during the noon meal, not on a Saturday morning the way she
normally did, and asked to see Jo's father, Jo knew it had to do
with Son. Mort was aggravated by their sudden, silent appearance at the back door. They hadn't knocked or made a sound.
How long they'd been standing there like two statues nobody
knew. Mort was still at the table, enjoying his after-dinner
favorite, a slice of corn bread in a glass of ice-cold buttermilk.
He'd just dropped the corn bread into the glass and broken it
up with a spoon when Essie, the McNabbs' cook, called to him.
He had gone out and stood on the top step looking down at the
two of them, his napkin still tucked into his collar, his hand on
the screen door. Mort was a tall man and, standing several steps
higher, he dwarfed the two of them. This didn't seem to bother
him in the least, Jo observed through the kitchen window. He
was used to looking down at people from the bench. The two of
them looked up at him from the driveway, talking and talking in
low agitated voices, their hands shading their eyes, which were
full of trouble and sadness and something else: an accusation,
an old rage. Tears rolled down the washwoman's gaunt cheeks.
Her husband, who looked like he'd come straight from the mill
and had cotton fluff all over his overalls, had his arm around his
wife. Jo had drawn close to the open window to hear.

"He *bothered* her, he hurt her bad," said the washwoman.
(What was her name? Jo couldn't remember.) "No telling what
going to happen to her now. Won't go to school. Won't even get
herself up off that bed, just lays there and not a mumbling word.

Doctor had to stitch her up. Smart girl. Dead set on going up to Holly Springs to that school up there."

Jo's father snatched the napkin from his collar and wiped his mouth with it. "Dovey, you sure it was Son? Is *she* sure? Your granddaughter. What's her name again?"

The washwoman's husband stepped forward, his eyes flashing. "This woman here been washing that boy's diapers since the day he come into this world. Been doing his laundry ever since. Dreama been delivering it clean to this house every week for the past four years. You think that girl such a fool she don't know what he look like?"

The washwoman pushed on her husband and shot him a look.

Jo's father didn't seem to notice. He shook his head, his face opening to the bone underneath. "Damn that boy's hide."

"May not be the worst of it," said the washwoman. "I got me a bad feeling."

"I'll make it right," Mort said. "Count on it. I'll make it right." He wiped his mouth again.

The washwoman raised her knuckled hand and pointed one finger at him. "No making it right. Not enough bleach in this whole wide world to make it right."

AT YOUNG People the church ladies served fried catfish in a pool of bacon grease and potato salad. Jo didn't bother to get any food, just sat dumbly in her chair, a lock of hair, heavy with oil and dirt, over one eye. She hadn't washed her hair thoroughly since the accident a month ago. It was hard to keep the cast dry in the tub; she had to sit up straight as a board and hold her left arm above her head. Her mother had instructed her to take

sponge baths, but the hair washing, with her mother preoccu-
pied with little Tommy and her new sadness, had gone by the
board. Jo had tried to help her mother with the baby, but little
Tommy was a handful; Jo thought him a most unpleasant baby.
When he was newborn, the town pediatrician, Dr. P. D. Campbell, said he had the colic and they just had to live through the
screaming (blood-curdling screams, as if someone were pricking
him with pins) until his insides straightened out. Now that he
was presumably teething, Dr. Campbell's nurse said to rub paregoric on his bottom gums, and sure enough, that took the wind
out of his sails. Now he gave halfhearted yelps every so often
during the night. Alice would feed him his bottle, then rub some
more paregoric, sometimes sipping a bit too, just to calm her
own self down. Last week Jo had been looking for some aspirin
in the back of the bathroom closet and had come upon a dozen
empty paregoric bottles, pushed into a back corner.

After supper at Young People, one of the deacons, Mr. Lump-
kin, a skeletal fellow with monstrous ears, talked about Jesus
making a decision, a *conscious* decision, to be crucified. Why
had he let himself be talked into getting nailed up on a cross?
He could have headed back home up to Heaven and told God
the Heavenly Father to just flat forget it, he didn't cotton to the
idea of nails being driven into his hands and feet and hanging up
there on a splintery cross for days on end, he didn't appreciate
having to wear a crown of thorns. He did it, Mr. L said, pointing at each of them in turn, for you and you and you. When he
pointed at Jo, she wanted to bite off his hairy forefinger. Did her
sins amount to all that?

Just as Mr. L was winding down, Jo's father came into Young
People without his coat and tie and told Jo to come on, they

weren't going to go to the evening service. Odd, since he was a churchgoing man and believed in the necessity of giving God one's undivided attention as often as possible. He earnestly lectured Jo on right behavior: that faith without works is no faith at all, just as mercy without justice is no mercy (though Jo wondered whether he'd gotten the latter statement turned around). Alice McNabb had avoided churchgoing like the plague since the baby, so Mort had come to count on Jo to sit on the hard cold pew beside him, the third on the left, where his grandparents and parents had sat for umpteen years. He would put his hand on Jo's shoulder and belt out the hymns in his cracked voice, the way he'd done at night when she was little and he put her to sleep singing, not lullabies, but, for her, worrisome hymns. In the sweet by-and-by they would meet on that beautiful shore or fall into a fountain filled with blood, drawn from Emmanuel's veins. (For years Jo thought it was Emmanuel's *brains*.) She had a soft spot for her father's bad singing and she admired him generally. Despite some inconsistencies, which she tried to overlook (she'd found a jar of moonshine and a well-worn copy of what she would later come to know as the *Kama Sutra* behind his law books in his glassed-in bookcase), she appreciated how he worried about doing the right thing as a judge: weighing all the evidence and handing down fair judgments. On summer nights they would sit alone together in the big porch swing. He would tell her about his job of judging other people's promises. Bankruptcy, he explained, happened when people broke their promises. His cheeks flared pink, and sweat collected on his forehead as he talked on. He would push the swing faster and faster until her stomach did flips and he would explain to her about justice, the necessity of justice. Opinion, politics, prejudice: they all dissolved in the face of justice.

Her father had his ways. He was particular about his clothes and he believed in schedules. On Mondays nights, he went to the Tupelo Elks Club meeting; on Wednesday, it was Prayer Meeting. On Thursday nights for as long as she could remember, he would return to work after supper and put in a good long evening at the office, just to keep up, he said. She'd once begged to go with him, she wanted to help him, she thought she might file his law papers. She liked to put things in order. Her blouses were on the left side of her closet, her skirts on the right, with dresses between. Each night before she went to bed she stacked her school notebooks in the chronological order of her classes. But he said no, he needed to concentrate; filing was too complicated for her to manage. Sunday, of course, was church from morning to night. But tonight, much to her relief, Mort said he didn't like the look of the sky; he wanted to get on back home, batten down the hatches. He didn't want the two of them getting caught in a big rainstorm; he didn't want Jo's mother left alone with the baby. The lights might go off.

Back at home, Jo changed into her nightgown, brushed her teeth, and washed her face; all the while the ants were still having a field day. She had a test the next morning on Poe's "The Gold Bug." Plagued as she was by the ants, she didn't like the idea of a bug biting anyone; she rather generally hated the story, the idiocy of the colored man (she couldn't believe anyone was that stupid), everyone going crazy over buried treasure. But she was a conscientious student so she sat down at the little desk in her room and reread the story and took some notes in her English notebook. Then, for Latin, she translated a chapter on Caesar's conquests, which she cared not a flip about (and really, how could anyone expect her to study while she was being tortured by this eternal itching?). She disliked the idea of men on horses with swords, hitting at one another, all in a frenzy of self-righteousness and greed. Except for *amo, amas, amat,* which she liked the sound of, she generally detested Latin with its eternal conjunctions and declensions.

As she put up her books, she heard a scratching at the screen door out back, then a series of bumps and bangs. The back door from the downstairs hall to the screen porch had been propped open to let in some air, though the air outside was hotter and muggier than it was inside the house. She went to the door and there was Snowball, something wet and wriggling in her mouth. A kitten. It looked like it had just been born. Snowball had gone and done it again. Over the course of the years, she'd had a zillion kittens. Some of them still hung around, taking care of the mice in the garage, but most were long gone. And now a new litter! But why was Snowball carrying this one to the house? She always kept her kittens well hidden until they were so lively they couldn't be contained and came tumbling out of whatever hiding place she'd stashed them in.

When Jo opened the door, Snowball ran in and dropped the kitten under the table on the screen porch, where it lurched about blindly, and then went back to the door leading out to the backyard and cried for Jo to open it. Jo let her out and a minute later she was back with another bedraggled kitten, which she put alongside the first. Jo went back inside and got several towels from the bathroom and put the kittens on it. When Snowball came back with number three, she stayed, placing the last on the wood floor of the porch. She dragged the towel with the first two kittens on it farther back under the table to the back wall, then picked up the last one and placed it alongside the rest and settled down beside them. Jo hoped her mother wouldn't notice. The screen porch held a haphazard assortment of things: the table with its oilcloth tablecloth was covered in pots and gardening supplies and canning jars; there was a clothesline for her mother's stockings; in the corner, mops and brooms, a large crock for pickled peaches, a chair for Essie to sit in when she needed to take a break from the heat in the kitchen, though now they no longer employed Essie full time in an effort to cut costs, which was all the pity since Alice McNabb was not gifted in the kitchen, and between the baby and the cleaning, she was always late with the midday dinner. This made Mort McNabb grumpy when he walked home from his law office down on Jefferson to eat and have his midday nap. But money didn't grow on trees, and without Alice's salary, Essie had become a luxury, not a necessity. Now all she did was the heavy cleaning and Saturday dinner, muttering under her breath about how she was now having to peck around like a chicken all over town to piece together a living wage, how this arrangement couldn't go on.


NOW THE train's whistle cried out in the distance. It was getting late. Would she ever sleep a wink with this itch? *No no no no no*, moaned the train. The M&O ran north-south, the Frisco northwest-southeast, the track lines at Crosstown going catty-cornered by the compass. At 9:03 every night, including apparently Palm Sunday, the Frisco Accommodation with its fancy passenger cars came in. You could set your watch by it. A few travelers, usually Memphis businessmen with the cotton mill or garment factory or fertilizer plant or government officials with the fishery, would get off. Charlie, the porter from the Kinney

Hotel, would meet them at the depot with his double cart for their luggage and then he'd walk them over to the hotel for the night. Once, one of the train conductors had let her peek inside the Accommodation. Its velvet seats and tables for eating hot food were nothing short of splendid; she imagined herself going to Memphis on it, and maybe beyond Memphis, out into the real world. Chicago or St. Louis. She imagined herself on a bunk in a sleeping car, knees tucked to chest, listening to the *shellac shellac shellac* of the wheels hitting the tracks.

Train tracks: how firm and straight they were, how purposeful. That's when the idea of the coat hanger popped into her head. A coat hanger! Why hadn't she thought of it? The day before, she'd stuck a bread knife part of the way down the cast, but, long as it was, it was too wide to go far and only made matters worse by tickling the area right above the ants, causing them to dig in with even more zeal and determination. Her mother had suggested talcum powder, but she couldn't get it to go down far enough.

As she struggled to open the coat hanger, bruising her fingertips as she unwound it, she thought this must be what hell was like: flaming flesh, tormenting itches (she imagined her arm now, at this very moment, covered in little red blisters like the ones real fire ants leave), hot as Hades. She'd been pouring sweat all day. She should have taken another bath before putting on her nightgown. The air hadn't cooled as evening had come on; it had, in fact, gotten worse, murky and motionless as a swamp. When she stood up from her chair, her gown stuck to the seat. Now, as she worked to open the coat hanger, it occurred to her that God might be punishing her for something. She'd not been altogether good. Last week, she'd snubbed Doris Grissom, who'd snubbed

her the week before but, to Doris's credit, had said she was sorry
and wanted to make up. Forgiveness was not one of Jo's strong
points. The horse that threw her she still wished dead, though
it was just a poor dumb creature. She must be a better girl, try
harder not to think mean thoughts or do mean things. She must
resist her natural inclination toward impatience (this she got
from her father). She must be kinder to little Tommy, help her
mother with him (if she could ever get this miserable cast off)
when he screamed to high heaven for no good reason. She must
try to rise above (but never to forgive) Son.

Another twist and the coat hanger swung free. She headed
outside and took up a brick from the border of one of the flower
beds. She lay the hanger on the ground and began to beat it
straight, holding the thick wire in place with her foot as she
banged away.

Something—was it a rumbling?—caused her to look up and
pause. In the near dark, everything seemed suddenly luminous,
pulsing with possibility. The world, it seemed to her in that
moment, had stopped in mid-rotation and said, *Get aboard, it's
your time, your time is now.* Her life, she knew suddenly, in that
instant, was too small. She would need to leave this place. Now,
as the sky gathered itself, she was afraid of this awful knowledge. The house, the town, her parents, her friends: was she
anything without them? Was there a *she* who stood apart from
history and place? Or was what she thought of as herself just
a reflection of what other people thought of her? A mirror of a
mirrored image.

She looked around at the house behind her. It seemed to look
back. She and the house had come into the world together, in
1921. Before the furniture was even in, she'd scooted on her

baby bottom across its newly varnished oak floors; her first memory was of their shine, their slickness. The sense of possibility and wide open space. The house sat at the corner of Church and Walnut; soon after they moved, her mother had spent hours planting crepe myrtle bushes along the L-shaped perimeter between the sidewalk and the street, singing, under her breath, little snatches of "Look for the Silver Lining." By the time Jo was five, she'd ridden the curving banister, whipping around the two landings, from top floor to bottom. On the long front porch, Son had pushed her down when she was just learning to walk, breaking open her forehead on the tile, leaving a jagged scar descending her forehead from the scalp to the top of her left eyebrow, which she hid by scalloping her hair to that side and fastening it with a barrette. The house was a four-square, and everything about it was solid, every exterior—brick, trim, roof—the color of the red clay dirt it sat on. The front porch, with its square brick columns, now covered in ivy, ran the length of the house. There was clover in the front yard and a concrete and brick ledge around the top of the porch. One warm autumn day, she'd jumped from the ledge onto the lawn and had the misfortune of getting stung by four honeybees, one under each hand and one under each knee she landed on. On the farthest corner of the ledge, on the uncovered part of the porch, was a giant concrete pot with small succulents growing inside, never quite reaching the top of the pot. Jo would sit beside it and peer into the massive pot, imagining that the tiny plants were trees and the ants (tiny black ones, not the red monsters now running amuck on her arm) were lost souls trying to make their way through the Amazon jungle.

In the yard, spring had come early. The jonquils had turned to paper; the iris had already set buds. After Tommy's birth, the only thing Alice seemed to enjoy was her garden. The spade work had been done by the yardman, Lamar, who shoveled dirt and weeded and put in the bulbs and petunias and fall mums and pansies. Alice said Lamar Henry had as much of a green thumb as she did. When she won the Kiwanis Most Beautiful Garden prize the first time, she sent him home with a batch of molasses and a bushel of pecans. The second time it was some pickled peaches from the previous year's batch and a sack of Mort's old clothes.

This spring, though, the yard had gone to seed. Lamar Henry had been let go over the winter. Crabgrass dotted the flower beds, elm seedlings had set down roots in the hedges, the yarrow was suffocating the tender new iris shoots. Now, when the baby cried, Alice cried too. When Jo broke her arm and her mother sobbed by her bedside at the hospital, Jo knew it wasn't for her she was crying, but for the loss of her help with little Tommy, who, if truth be told, Jo was beginning to detest: his unpleasant cabbage face, his bloody-murder shrieks that made her mother bite her lip until it bled. He had been a great big surprise to everybody. Jo had heard her mother upchucking in the early mornings before school; she'd heard Alice tell Mort it was all his fault. His big you-know-what again. She'd seen her father's countenance turn to stone. Then, after little Tommy was born, Mort's eyes brightened with some other feeling: had it been joy? Relief? Second chances seldom came along, but here one was, red-faced and furious and colicky. Another (thank God!) son. This one surely a gem.

NOW, ALICE'S forsythia had burst into bloom. The bushes clustered in one corner of the yard; the weight of the blossoms bent the branches to the ground. Over everything, a yellowish cast, the sun low and intense. Yellow on yellow. Beautiful really. Jo wanted to call to her mother to come and see. Beauty was the only thing these days that brought even a half-smile to her mother's face; now Alice spent most of her waking hours, when she wasn't caring for the baby or clanging about glumly in the kitchen, staring out the front window of her bedroom, watching the street as if someone important was expected.

But the room upstairs was still dark.

What Jo missed most since Tommy had been born were her Words to Keep. When she was five, Alice had given her the first one, which was *articulation*. Alice had pointed to her own mouth and said the word, then touched Jo's throat. Alice had pulled out a thick, lined notebook, on the front of which was written *Jo's Words to Keep*, and had written the word *articulation* in it, along with the date. Since then, Alice would call Jo to her several times a week, and Jo would bring the notebook. Sometimes, when she was doing something else, she would groan inwardly—the words had grown increasingly more difficult, well beyond the limits of her own vocabulary—but she always went to her room and opened the top drawer to her dresser and pulled out the notebook. Alice would be waiting. She would say the word once and then a second time, and then spell it. Jo would write it into the notebook. Later, it would be her job to look it up in the four-inch-thick unabridged *Webster's* her mother had given her for her seventh birthday. As this interchange had developed over the years, Jo had come to notice that, more often than not, her mother's chosen Word to Keep would reflect some event or predicament of the moment. One blistering day in July when the water tower ran dry and water out of the faucet made a red-clay stain in the kitchen sink, it was *petrifac-tion*. The December morning after some of Alice's students had come by with a platter of Christmas cookies, it was *plenitude*.

USUALLY, IN spring, swallows and bats came out this time of the evening to swoop and feed. Now, all Jo saw were moving clouds of small gray birds silently circling, so high they looked like pepper, darkening the sky. Jo imagined herself taking flight, in one of those planes from the airshows, landing far away, over the ocean.

Where would her golden life take root in this large, large world?

The itch called her back. She began to fit the coat hanger wire at the point the cast began, where her arm met the shoulder. It didn't go down easily; in fact, she worried a bit about it getting stuck, but then she pushed and the ants scattered before it, giving way to something else, a tearing of flesh. Exquisite, delicious, heavenly pain.

Maybe, before the crucifixion, God gave Jesus an itch that couldn't be scratched so the pain came as a blessed relief.

Looking down at her arm, relishing the pain, she barely noticed the lightning. She didn't see the sky crack open like a giant egg.

Now someone called to her from the screen porch, her father. She hoped he hadn't found Snowball and her brood on the porch. The sky had grown suddenly dark. Half hidden by the pecan tree, she squeezed her eyes shut and ignored her father, scraping the skin under the cast even harder; maybe if she cut the skin of her arm to ribbons it would stop itching and just hurt, just burn and sting and smart. That would be delicious, a crown of thorns she'd gladly wear.

Mort burst through the screen door. "Jo! Didn't you hear me? Get inside. There's a storm coming." Then he spotted her across the yard. "What's that you're doing to your arm?"

But he wasn't interested in her arm. He came on down the back steps and looked up at the sky. "Get in the house right now. Get your mother up, tell her to get the baby down to the cellar. Now. Move!"

Jo jerked the hanger wire up. It stuck about halfway.

"What's wrong with you, girl? Get in there. Tell your mother to get the baby to the basement! Where the hell is Son?"

He searched the sky again and then turned back toward her. In that moment the lightning flashed again, and Jo saw the look on her father's face and began to run.

As she ran toward the screen porch, toward her father, the lights went off in the house. She stopped in her tracks, peered out down the street. No lights anywhere.

Her father hollered again. "Somebody downtown's cut the electricity! Means it's going to be bad!"

Jo took off running toward the house, the coat hanger still under the cast, half in and half out. In mid-stride she gave it a final jerk. It came, tearing the flesh, a white-hot pain. It came out dark, with a bit of something (was it bloody skin?) dangling from the tip. She held on to the coat hanger and ran toward the house. As she ran she felt as though she were swimming through the sloshing air, the hideously warm wet air: that what was supposed to be air had liquefied and grown strains of ivy that clutched at her, that pulled her back into the deep dark, the just-fallen dark. The house rose up before her like a large animal. Square and tall and not at all pretty. Nor, even before the electricity was cut, had it been lit up like a regular house should be this time of night, little Tommy upstairs in his crib in the still-dark back bedroom facing west, her mother probably in bed across the hall. Was her mother still asleep? She'd been in bed since early afternoon. Was she having one of her cries? And Tommy? She must have dosed him up good. He never slept this long.

Her father shouted again from the backyard, his voice in an upper register she'd never heard. "Jo, get inside!" Then a deafening crash, the sound of a tree falling, then a roar, getting louder. Now a train was coming, coming fast, shrieking, flying through the air at them. *No no no no.* How could a train fly?

She burst into the house. "May-May! May-May!" Her childish name for her mother, the one she'd given up years ago.

Alice called back to her from upstairs, but the roaring was so loud Jo couldn't hear what her mother was saying. Then there was the sickening sound of glass shattering upstairs, then another crash. A bang. Her mother called out to her again. Where *was* her mother? Why wasn't she running downstairs?

"Basement!" Jo screamed. "Get down to the basement!" She turned around and looked behind her. Her father! Why wasn't he coming inside? And Snowball and her poor little kittens! She turned to run back onto the porch to snatch them up.

In that moment, though, the train was upon her. It came at her as if she were a car stalled on the tracks, pushing her back into the house. There it turned her around one full rotation and took her up like a piece of cotton fluff and blew her from the back door, where she had been standing, down the hall toward the front of the house and into the living room.

Through it all she held on to the straightened coat hanger with her one good arm. As the storm pushed her forward, the hanger extended before her like a saber. And then, and how impossible this was in retrospect, that at that very moment she was half-running, half-flying down the hall, into the living room, right up to the front door, Son, her brother, would push open that very door and rush into the house shouting something (What had he been shouting? Was he coming home to save the day? What a joke.) and that, in that same instant, the coat hanger she held out before her, as though she were Joan of Arc leading her army into battle, would drive straight through his shirt and then his lower chest and even come out his back, even as Jo's fist remained closed around it so that she looked, as he fell, as if she were knocking on the closed door of his breast-bone.

Before her brother went down, there was a ball of fire that lit up the whole world, or so it seemed to Jo, and their eyes locked in that moment of illumination and the something that should have been in her brother's eyes all along suddenly, for just a second or two, flared and burned, and, before the wind blew her onward, she saw him in a way she'd never seen him before: a little boy, lost and alone. "It's all right," she shouted as she slammed into him and then deflected toward the back of the room. "Don't worry."

She landed up against the fireplace. Then a piece of something sharp flew toward her and lodged in her forehead. She felt around and crawled inside the hearth and crouched there, her hands over her head. The wind shrieked through the house, knocking a china cabinet on its side, dishes clattering and breaking. It slammed the dining room table up against the wall, shattering the plaster. It tore the front door off its hinges and sent it flying onto the front porch and out into the darkness beyond. There was a popping noise as the nails from the boards in the woodwork shot across the room like bullets. Overhead, Jo heard the crash of something large, then something else that sounded like a gunshot.

The last thing she heard before everything went black was a woman (her mother?) wailing, but that too might have been the sound of the train.

# 3

## 9:32 P.M.

No up, no down.

Nothing but black-as-coal water. No air nowhere. Something alive, in a tearing hurry, scratchy little feet, brushing her cheek. Got to be a rat.

It was the first time Dovey had been in water over her head.

She banged into something hard and big and slick. Under the slime it was rough and round. What? Felt like a tree, but what was a tree doing in water? She dug in her nails and climbed it, trying not to breathe, knowing that any second now she would have to draw in the breath that would kill her, trying to reach the top. If she breathed in water, that'd be it, she'd be dead sure enough, if she wasn't already. Maybe she had already passed and this was hell. Maybe hell was being almost dead.

*Old storm, you ain't got me yet.*

No air. All of a sudden she understood somewhere deep in her body that she wasn't moving up or down but sideways. How could a tree grow sideways, and in the water? Then she figured it out. The storm had blown her from up on the ridge clear down into Gum Pond. This old tree, she'd seen it a hundred times, sitting jay-wonky, dead as a doornail, in the middle of the pond. Gum Pond was shallow. All she had to do was grab hold of it, steady herself, put her feet down.

She did it, let herself sink. Hit bottom. Pushed. Came up, took in air. Gasped, coughed, spit. The bottom was slimy and muddy. She slipped and down she went again. Something sharp sliced her bare foot. It stung, the skin flapped as she moved it in the water. But, oh my, she wasn't drowning no more. She pushed a few more times, moving along with the tree trunk. Then, as the tree rose from the water toward the pond's edge, she was able to stand on her own two feet and make her way to the side, the water first at chin level, then shoulder high.

Her foot touched something slick and soft. She reached down and slippery fingers snatched at her. She went under and pulled but she couldn't budge the one attached to the fingers. She groped around under the water and felt a naked man, his skin slick like he'd been greased. Then she touched his middle and found out why she couldn't move him: a piece of wood—felt like a two-by-four—had gone straight through him. Pinned him to the bottom. She pulled on the wood, but it kept slipping out of her hands. Then she pulled on the man's arm, which was even slicker. She kept hold of his hand, but the fingers didn't move now. She shuddered, left the hand to float then sink, and kept on moving.

Now she was up to her knees, now emerging, her sodden, muddy dress, still covered in the apron, clinging to her, heavy and cold, reminding her of a wet sheet on the line. She hurt all over, touched herself here and there: her belly and breasts, her head. She swung her arms, kicked out her legs. All moved. The cut on the bottom of her foot she couldn't see.

Get on home, that's what she needed to do, find Virgil and them. Her arm grazed something with feathers that floated on the surface of the pond.

Dreama and Promise. Were they in church when this thing

hit, or on the way home? Outside like her? Dear Lord. She imagined little Promise sailing through the night sky, then plummeting down and down, his little head bouncing on something
hard—a rooftop or one of the newly paved streets—and burst-
ing open like a cantaloupe. If the storm had managed to blow her
all the way from her house up on the Hill down into Gum Pond
along with the rats and chickens and dead folks, if she could see
(she *did* see it!) an upside-down cow coming toward her in that
monster funnel, it sure enough could have blown that child all
the way to Tennessee.

Everything pitch-black. Tangled shapes all she could see.

And here came the rain, hard, stinging her skin like bleach,
and with it a whistling wind and a deep chill in the air. She shivered and shook and hugged herself, looking around to get her
bearings. No trees, no houses neither. Just piles of lumber and
tree trunks and what was that before her? Dark and metallic,
with sharp jagged edges. A hunk of the water tower from the
crest above her house, or where her house had been.

She staggered on in the dark, heading back up the ridge
toward home. She put her feet down carefully. Broken glass all
over. The bottom of her right foot already cut, don't need no
more. All around her, folks cried out for help and dug at piles of
wood as tall as houses. Moans came from underneath. People
pulled at her, begged her to help them find this one or that one.
She kept on, stumbling right into an almost-dead horse, lying on
its side. She felt its head, flung back at an impossible tilt. Against
its warm belly, she could feel its heart gallop, heading, heading
down that long lonely road. The rain had by now chilled her
to the bone; she trembled and shook. More than anything she
wanted to stay and warm herself against the animal while it

was still alive. The horse's heart was slowing now. It wouldn't be long. Maybe she should stay until then. She drew closer to the animal's belly, her hands folded across her chest so that she could feel her own little heart, clickety-clack across the track, four beats to the horse's one. Her eyes closed against the blistering rain. She took a long shuddering breath.

Somewhere, off in the distance, a woman moaned.

NOW SOMETHING startled her awake. The horse was ice cold and so was she. *How long had she been asleep?*

Her first thought was Virgil. Just today a cold spell had come over her and she'd turned away when he went to kiss her good night. His shoulders had slumped and he'd gone on off to bed, not saying a word.

She got up and began to make her way through the dark. Buckets of rain and darkest dark. There was no finding the street and without the street, there was no finding the house. Or where it had been. There were no markers, and she couldn't have seen them even if they were there. Not a single house left standing. Not Martha Johnson's front porch with her pretty colored pots, not the Davises' rusted school bus, children popping in and out of windows every hour of the day and night. Not a single measly tree neither, just big old holes filled with water where their roots had been. She caught herself just before falling into one.

She climbed higher, then turned in a circle to try to get her bearings. Through the downpour she caught sight of the white tombstones across the way in Glenwood Cemetery. Most scattered here and there, but some still upright. *Dead white folks good for something.* From the location of the cemetery, she paced out where she judged the dogtrot should be. When she'd found the place, she stopped, stood there in the downpour, and peered at what looked like a towering pile of kindling.

She ran toward it. *Virgil.* Had she called out his name aloud or only in her head? She went up to where the pile of wood began and started pulling on it, hollering for help. The rain poured, drowning her out. How could anybody be alive under this here? She was panting like a dog, couldn't draw enough air. She began to claw at the pieces of wood, splinters gouging her hands. Some of the pieces of lumber bigger than her.

The rain came on harder, little needles on her arms. Then it was sleet.

A man lurched toward her out of the dark. He wove from side to side like he was drunk, his face bright as a fresh handkerchief against the darkness.

She ran and snatched at his sleeve, pulling him toward the pile of rubble that had been her house.

"Whoa, horse," the man said. He started pulling up the lumber, two and three pieces at a time.

She tried to help, moving the smaller pieces to let the man get at the larger ones. After awhile he said, "Move over, auntie, you in the way." So she ran from side to side of the pile, wringing her hands, crying out to the man to, please mister, hurry. He didn't answer, just kept on pulling at the lumber, the freezing rain pouring off his shoulders. As he dug down, the pieces of wood seemed more thickly embedded one into the other, like the pickup sticks Virgil had whittled for Charlesetta to play with when she was a girl.

Was her Virgil still drawing breath under all that? And if he was, what kind of shape would he be in? Virgil crippled? Better dead.

At long last, the man got it down to where they could see the shattered bed. It was flattened, nothing but a little pile of lumber with Dovey's quilt, soaked and clotted, underneath, along with Virgil's shoes.

Dovey jumped in to help the man pull the last of the boards away. *Virgil, Virgil, Virgil.* She'd steeled herself, expecting to feel a foot, a hand, limp and bloody and deader than dead. How could anybody not be, under all this?

Nothing there. Nobody there.

The white man stopped pulling away the boards. "Nobody under here," he hollered at her over the downpour. "He done got hisself blowed clear away."

Dovey put her apron to her face, collapsed into the mud, sobbing.

The man patted her head and then turned and trudged on, through the black and the rain and the sound of somebody down the street wailing.

The wailing grew louder, closer: a woman's voice, high pitched and constant, coming from the direction of the church. The woman almost tripped over her before Dovey got a good look. Poor thing had hardly a stitch on, only a thin slip, once white, soaked and plastered to her body. You could see right through it. It was a moment before Dovey recognized the woman, saw the face and realized it was Etherene Johnson, Dreama's English teacher. She'd been snatched bald-headed by the storm, her piece and the hair that held it peeled back like a boiled egg.

Dovey snatched off her apron and put it over Etherene's front side, tying the soaked ties with numb fingers.

Over the downpour, Dovey hollered, "Where you coming from, Etherene?"

Once, not too long ago, she wouldn't speak to Etherene. And for good reason. When Dreama turned up pregnant from that Devil McNabb boy, Etherene had gotten into it. She'd come to her door, sat down at Dovey's kitchen table, and said there was a white man, a sure-enough doctor, out in the county. *She'd* take Dreama there. She'd *already* talked to Dreama's other teachers. A collection had been taken up. It was all settled. Etherene always dressed to kill, and her stockings swished as she crossed and recrossed her legs.

"You got your business, I got mine," Dovey had told her. "I lost one child, ain't going to lose one more to some dumb peckerwood with a coat hanger. Stay out of it."

Now Etherene put her lips to Dovey's ear. "Church. Coming from church."

"Y'all in church when this thing hit? You see Dreama and the baby?"

The warm breath from Etherene's lips tickled her frozen ear. "Last I saw, both of them on the ground. Just leaving church and we heard it coming. She put the baby down in the street and threw herself on top. Sounded like a freight train going ninety miles an hour. I jumped in a ditch next to the Horton place. Got blown across the street, old thing whipped my dress right over my head. When I crawled out, no sight of them. Nobody else either. A whole bunch of us walking home when it hit. Did you see the water tower fly apart?"

"So they was out in it?"

"Afraid so."

"Then no telling."

"No."

"I'm going looking for them. Them and Virgil."

"Can't see your hand in front of your face, much less find any-body. Here you are shaking like a leaf. Here I am with nothing on but a slip and an apron. I'm heading back for the church."

"You heading the wrong way then."

"You sure about that? Seems like it's this way." Etherene pointed toward downtown.

Dovey turned her around toward the cemetery. "That's Glen-wood over there. Church is back the other way."

Etherene wiped her face with Dovey's apron. "Oh Lord, noth-ing looks the same."

"You see Dreama and them, tell them I'm looking for them. Tell them I'm all right."

"If the storm blew them, it blew them same direction it blew me. Maybe somebody's taking care of them down in town."

Dovey peered through the night at Etherene. "You think white folks going to be taking care of us in this mess? You think they'll put *us* in their hospital longside them?"

Etherene didn't hear. She had turned around and started back the way she'd come, melting into the downpour. Dovey wanted to follow her, she did; now that their spat was over, she felt sorry for Etherene. There was something about her that folks didn't cotton to. Was it her bright skin, her pride, her little piece perched on top of her head like a watchful nest? The fact that she was a busybody where her pupils were concerned, Dreama being a prime example? But those were only pebbles; there was a boulder there somewhere. Dovey didn't go around talking, so she didn't know what it was, but it was specific, that much she knew, specific enough to make people move slightly over in a pew when she settled next to them, as if Etherene carried an odor or some contagious sickness.

THE SLEET had turned to hail. Dovey touched her hair and felt shards of ice. She heard sirens coming from downtown. She stood in what she thought was the road and looked around her. If she'd gotten blown clear down to Gum Pond, maybe Virgil had too. She couldn't stand to think about what had happened to Dreama and Promise. She turned and headed back down the ridge to the pond, slipping and sliding in the mud and, here and there, something oily she assumed was gasoline, given the smell. *Nobody better strike a match*, she thought, then began to laugh out loud, a crazy high-pitched laugh that turned into something else. It was easier to go down the hill than it had been to come up. She slipped and slid past the moaning and crying out for help. All around her bedlam. Folks hollered back and forth, digging through the rubble, throwing wood every which way, toward the voices underneath. *Where are you? Here, no, over here.*

At Gum Pond an old woman was coaxing a bonfire along. Hail the size of eggs sputtered into the fire. Then the hail turned back to sleet. Men were walking up to hip level in the pond, poking at the bottom with the branches from trees. Dovey stumbled over a dead man, then saw the row of bodies. They were laid out uncovered, their faces flung upward, receiving the sleet without flinching so that they seemed to be weeping silently. Dovey walked among them, bent down to try to see their faces, hoping she wouldn't find Virgil or Dreama or Promise. Some she recognized. Luther Johnson, Etherene's husband who'd moved out in a huff over a decade ago. Beulah Winson, one of the Heroines of Jericho who worked in the church nursery. Essie Lee Miller, who used to work for the McNabbs, each week preparing the laundry for Dovey to pick up. Essie Lee had put a sheet on the floor, then put all the dirty clothes and linens in it and tied it neatly in a knot for Dovey to grab on to.

*Lord, all these folks. Decent folks. Lord, what You gone and done here? What You trying to accomplish?*

Looking down at Essie Lee's streaked, impassive face, Dovey began to tremble.

She walked along and peered at the other faces. No Virgil. No Dreama. No baby boy.

Somebody in the pond called out, "Got one over here," and her heart stopped. Some men went to help.

It was covered in mud. But thank you, Jesus (and Lord forgive her for being thankful for somebody else's misery), it was large and had on a skirt.

Now, as if they'd planned it this way, all the men came out of the pond and made a circle around the fire. Bent over with the cold, they shivered and shook, looking as if they were doing some strange dance. One of them announced to those who hovered close by, "Can't do no more tonight. Feet and hands numb. Can't feel nothing."

Dovey went all the way around the pond, looking. She climbed through furniture and dead animals, and God knows what else. Nobody else that she could see, though for all she knew, there could have been dozens flung about in the mud.

She felt her bladder tighten and she squatted. What if Virgil and Dreama and the baby were hurt and somebody had found them? If they didn't take colored at the hospital, they still must have them someplace downtown. Having delivered laundry for umpteen years, she knew Whitetown like the back of her hand. She rose and headed back toward Green Street. Once she came to the roadway she took a left, threading her way as best she could around downed trees and giant shards of wood and metal. No sizzling wires, and for that she was thankful. Somebody had turned off the power. The sleet stopped; then it began to hail again. The stones bounced off the top of her head, burning and stinging. She walked on, nothing around her except debris. She knew she'd moved from black to white when the dirt turned to pavement. She crossed Jackson, or what she thought was Jackson, heading south toward downtown, picking her way around flipped cars and wagons and tree limbs and whole trees. People swept by her, hollering names. A man staggered by, mumbling something about a cow, how it was there one minute and gone the next. Dovey wondered if that was the upside-down animal she'd seen sailing along in the funnel.

On the corner of Green and Franklin, a house came up to the left, the first she'd seen upright. She went up onto the porch and stood there shivering, thankful to be under cover.

A lady with white hair opened the door. She had a flashlight and shined it in Dovey's face, blinding her. "What you doing up on my porch?"

"Just looking to get out of the weather."

The woman shot the flashlight around and behind Dovey. "Got anybody with you?"

"No, ma'am."

"All right then. Come on inside. Take your shoes off."

"Ain't got no shoes."

The house was dry but tomb-cold. There was a fireplace in the living room and some wood beside it.

The woman stood with her flashlight pointed at Dovey. She didn't ask Dovey to sit.

"You dripping on my rug."

Dovey's teeth were chattering. The shaking, now that she was inside, had grown worse. "Sorry, ma'am. You got something I can dry off with?"

The woman ignored the request and drew closer. "Was that a tornado just came through?"

"Yes, ma'am. Blew me all the way down to Gum Pond. My house is plumb gone. Nothing left of it. Can't find my people."

"Lord. Did everybody up on the Hill get hit?"

"I think so."

Dovey stood just inside the front door, her wash dress clinging to her. The woman had a shawl over her shoulders. Dovey briefly considered snatching it and running. Had she ever wanted anything as much in her life as she wanted that shawl? The more she tried not to shake, the harder she shook.

"You ain't going to up and have a fit on me, are you, girl?"

"No, ma'am, just cold. Reckon I could build a fire for us to warm up?"

"Wouldn't mind if you did. My husband usually lights it, but he went over to see about our daughter. Don't go burning down the house."

Dovey went over to the fireplace and knelt down. "You got some paper and matches?"

"Over there." The woman pointed the flashlight toward the hearth.

Dovey crunched up the paper and put it in the fireplace, then put some light pieces of wood on top of it. She lit the match. The paper caught, then smoldered, then went out. She tried again and the paper lit, then caught the kindling. She put on two larger pieces and stood shivering in front of the fire, rubbing her hands together.

"Don't block the warm, girl."

Dovey stepped to the side. She turned in a circle, trying to dry her dress. The light from the fire danced across the room.

"Stop that turning. You making me dizzy."

"Just trying to dry myself."

Dovey cleared her throat. "You know where they taking the colored? I'm trying to find my husband."

"Don't know nothing. Saw some of your people walking by, going up Franklin, heading for Church Street. Why they heading that way instead of down into town I don't know. Maybe the road's blocked."

The front door slammed and a man burst in. Behind him were two boys and a young woman holding a baby, all of the children crying, and the baby with a bloody hand.

The man stopped short when he saw Dovey. He turned to his wife. "What we got here?"

"She's cold and wet, Henry. What's happening out there?"

"Half the town blowed plumb away. Jessie's roof is gone. Good thing I got there. They going to have to stay with us. You need to get some beds ready and get out the blankets. It's freezing out there. Get the girl to help you." The man pointed at Dovey.

Dovey moved toward the door. "I can't. Got to find my own people."

When she spoke, the little boys stopped crying and looked at her in alarm. The only sound in the room now the baby's wail and the crackling of the fire. Dovey reached the middle of the room, her dress still wet, still clinging to her. She was embarrassed by the dress and covered her breasts. She was so tiny even the boys dwarfed her. As the firelight danced and played, she could see only shadows where faces should have been.

"Well then, get out of here, nigger."

The words came from the shadows, but they were spoken by the young woman who held the baby.

The white-haired woman moved away from the fire. "Don't go talking trash, Jessie."

"She think we running a free nigger boardinghouse here, Mama?"

Sticks and stones, Dovey's mother used to say. Don't pay them no mind. Ain't worth the spit in your mouth. They just words. Dovey had heard it all before, countless times, but here, in this room, it made her feel tired in a new way of being tired. Tired piled upon tired, a-mountain-of-dirty-laundry tired.

Dovey headed straight for the door. She was limping now, the cut in her foot heating up.

She opened the screen door, then turned and looked at the white-haired woman. "Much obliged for the heat."

The woman took the shawl from around her shoulders and brought it to Dovey and put it around her shoulders. "Here."

The shawl was wool. It held the woman's body warmth and settled like a live thing on Dovey's shoulders. She nodded at the woman and tied the shawl across her chest.

Outside, the hail had turned back to rain, colder and steadier than before. The rain now seemed a thing apart from everything else. Her life was this rain, her grave would be a mud hole. Her cut foot burned and throbbed.

Cries for help all around. Louder now. *Oh please! Somebody, please!*

She tripped over something solid, fell on her face, her right hand thrown out automatically to catch her fall. Her wrist gave a little; something sharp on the palm of her hand. A piece of glass?

She reached down to feel the object, which was slick with rain. When she first touched it, it felt like the torso of a baby and she shrank from it. Something dead, or a piece of somebody. Then she touched it again. It was smooth and rounded and cold as ice. What? She put both hands down and picked it up. It rolled heavily toward her belly. Pork! It smelled like pork! She brought it to her nose. Ham. A ham. Had to be one of G. M. Crane's. He had the only white smokehouse in town, down on South Robbins. Her stomach roiled and she dropped the ham. What she and Virgil would have given under normal conditions for one of G. M. Crane's hams! She could have made it last a good solid year, cutting tiny pieces for seasoning her collards and beans and soups. Her mouth watered, then the water turned to bile and she vomited up her supper.

The rain washed her clean and she resumed walking, her foot on fire. Men passed her by, traveling in groups of three or four, checking houses, carrying people out on blankets and doors that had blown into the street. Some walked in front of a truck, clearing the street for it to pass. In the truck bed, hurt people holding other hurt people, everybody crying and moaning and calling out.

A man emerged from the dark. He was carrying a little girl over his shoulder like a gunnysack.

Dovey went up to him. "Mister, do you know where they're taking folks?"

"Down to the Lyric Theatre. Hospital roof caved in. Some folks went to First Methodist but the bad ones they're taking to the Lyric. Got the doctors and nurses there. Popcorn machine sterilizing instruments. It's bad. No anesthetic. The worst ones they're putting on the Frisco. The Accommodation came in right after this thing hit. They're loading it up with wounded. Going to back it up to Memphis. Coming back for more when it unloads those. They're on stretchers, lying in the rain, up at Crosstown, more dead than alive, waiting to get loaded."

"Colored too? They taking colored out on the train?"

The man looked at her blankly. "Don't remember seeing any colored."

Dovey stood in the rain as he walked on. As a girl, she'd loved the Lyric Theatre. On Saturday nights her mother would boil peanuts and take her and Janesy and Uldine and Blue to the vaudeville shows. They would pay their three cents and sit up in the balcony and laugh at white men with black faces sing and dance and roughhouse onstage. It was a job of work to keep her little brother from lobbing the peanut shells on the white folks sitting below; she'd swat at him, twist back his thumb when he misbehaved.

As she stood there wondering what to do next, the man with the girl on his shoulder came back. "Big oak just went over, trunk and all. It's got Green Street blocked. Got to go up to Church Street and go over."

He headed toward Church and Dovey followed, walking a few steps behind. At the corner of Church and Franklin, he turned left toward town. She stopped, the shawl now a wet hairy heaviness on her shoulders. Her knees had begun to buckle. Her bladder had taken on a mind of its own and let go without warning the split second she stepped off the porch of the white lady's house. Now her legs had turned to blocks of ice. To her left, about three long blocks away (and who knew what shape the street was in) was downtown; to her right, two houses up on Church was the McNabb place, the sturdiest house in Tupelo. Even the front porch seemed fortress-like, with its brick and concrete ledges thick enough to walk on, its giant brick columns. Ugly and square and solid as a mountain. Maybe she could rest under the cover of the porch for a while, get out of the rain just a few minutes without anyone being the wiser.

Something else too she wanted to see. Something ugly hopped into her mind. Froze like a jackrabbit in the grass.

*Old storm, you get ahold of that Devil? That why you come to town?*

WHEN DREAMA didn't come straight back from delivering the clean and picking up the dirty that hot, blustery June afternoon more than a year ago, she hadn't worried. She figured her grand-daughter had taken a detour and stopped at Mr. J's down Green Street, the only black-owned food market in Tupelo, where, because of the weather, she might have pilfered a nickel from the laundry money for an ice cream cone—strawberry was her favorite. Maybe she ran into some of her girlfriends. Dovey frowned. Had Dreama left the laundry cart with the McNabb dirty outside in the sun, where anybody could have at its con-tents? The girls might have stood around Mr. J's box fan, their cones melting, yakety-yakking, losing track of the time the way young girls do. Maybe somebody was stealing Mr. McNabb's shirts right that very minute.

By the time it was dark and Virgil got home from the mill, Dovey was pacing around the kitchen table. When he came up to the back door to hand her his mill clothes, he was already half undressed. Dovey poked her head out. "What you think that girl's doing with herself, out past dark? Just sent her by the McNabbs'."

Virgil coughed. He began to unbuckle his overalls.

Dovey knew what that cough meant. That the cotton had been particularly bad that day with the windows closed against the heat. "You reckon she's at Mr. J's eating ice cream?"

Virgil ran his hand through his hair and then scratched his forearms where the cotton had stuck to his skin. "Ain't he closed by now?"

Dovey gave him a little push. "Go find her."

He sat down on the porch stoop, cursing under his breath, reattached his suspenders, and laced his brogans back up. Then he headed down the street to Mr. J's.

By that time, it was full dark. Dovey went out onto the front porch and looked down the street. A half pie of a moon was rising. Did they have another Charlesetta on their hands? Maybe they'd been too easy on the girl. Dovey pondered various punishments for worrying them so, but none seemed to fit. Would she make Dreama stay home next weekend? No picture show, no visiting the girlfriends. That would be fine with Dreama. She loved nothing better than to sit around the house and read her books. Would Dovey give the girl the back of her hand? Neither she nor Virgil had the stomach for it.

Dovey had turned to go back in the house and by habit checked Henry's box on the porch. Henry, Dovey saw, had burrowed down into the sawdust so that only the tip of his nose showed. She touched it, then touched it again. The guinea pig's nose was surprisingly cool for such a hot night. She went back inside and stoked the wood stove to heat her iron. Might as well get a shirt or two done while she was waiting. She washed her hands and covered the bowls on the table with lids from her pots. They should have finished supper by now, she should be washing the dishes and preparing to tackle the ironing, which she'd saved until nightfall when it was cooler. It had been a good supper too, when it was hot. Mashed sweet potatoes, pinto beans with a piece of pickled pork for flavor, corn bread.

Would this night never end? She sighed and tested the iron. Despite the warmth from the stove and the still-blistering heat from outdoors, she shivered, once then twice. She went back to the bedroom and reached up on a nail inside the doorway to get down her sweater. She hoped she wasn't catching a cold.

She had just fastened the top button when she heard something on the porch. A thud. Then, on the heels of the thud, a metallic clanging. She opened the front door and peered out through the dark.

The half-pie moon was coming on strong now. The washtub shone, and below it lay someone half in shadow. This somebody had her laundry stick and was banging away at the tub's legs. This somebody was her granddaughter.

Dovey ran over to Dreama and bent down. She couldn't see the girl well so she tugged on her legs to pull her out from under the tub. When Dovey pulled her into the moonlight, she saw that the girl's face was bloody, her lips blooming, swollen and bruised. There were dark streaks of something—mud?—on the insides of her legs. And where were her shoes? Good shoes. Dovey had planned for them to last at least another year. Now what? How careless!

Then Dovey saw the one ankle, a large, dark knot. Then the streaks turned to blood. Then there was too much to see all at once, and she couldn't, wouldn't, take it all in. She turned away for a moment, looking instead up at her washtub, standing there in the moonlight, solid and clean and not at all broken. But then Dreama whimpered and she had to look again. That's when she saw that the girl's dress was torn down the front.

Dreama began to thrash and pant. She scrabbled at the porch floor like an animal trying to dig a hole.

Still, after seeing all this, Dovey thought Dreama would be all right if she could just get her into the house. She tried to raise her but couldn't. Dreama was, even then, a head taller and twenty pounds heavier than her grandmother. Dovey pulled and tugged but couldn't move her. Through the whole process, Dreama continued to pant, her face turned away. Then she stared up at Dovey with one enormous eye, the other now swollen shut. That one eye was so full of fear that Dovey dropped her down on the porch floor, grabbed the laundry stick from her hand, and hollered out into the dark. "Who's out there? Go way."

When she knelt back down to gather Dreama again, the girl had passed out. By that time the neighbors had been roused. Next door a light flicked on. Dovey hollered again, and they came running, Harmony and Hoover Gates from the shotgun on the right, Melvin and Ollie Hudson from the dogtrot on the left. The men picked up Dreama and brought her inside and laid her on Dovey and Virgil's bed in the back room. Then they went for Dr. Juber. Dovey got out a washcloth and the small tub she used for delicates. She ran some water and heated it in a pot on the stove. She threw another piece of wood in the stove. Each step she took, each action, required every ounce of strength she had.

When she went into the bedroom, the two women, Harmony and Ollie, were standing over Dreama, surveying the damage.

Ollie was humming under her breath, getting louder and louder. Harmony took one of Dreama's hands and rubbed it.

"Shut your mouth," Dovey said to Ollie. Dreama was pumping blood, couldn't they see that? Why were they just standing there? Ollie ran next door for menstrual rags. When Dovey began to wash Dreama's face and Harmony lifted Dreama's legs so the cloths could be placed, the one eye popped open again and snagged Dovey. *You sent me into the lion's den.*

"Aw, no, girl," Dovey said over and over, washing the face, pulling back the hair, matted in blood. "Aw, no."

But the eye kept on saying.


IT WAS that eye of Dreama's, how in that moment it had looked at her and then, somehow, *through* her to the place Dovey had sent her to, *the lion's den*, that made Dovey turn right instead of left on Church Street, north to the McNabbs' on the corner of Walnut and Church instead of south to downtown where her own people, if there were any left, probably would be.

She had to see with her own eyes what had happened to Son McNabb. If there was any justice in the world (which she highly doubted), he'd be dead as one of G. M. Crane's prize hams.

# 4

## 10:17 P.M.

Inside the fireplace, Jo awoke to her mother's screams, which seemed to come, not from upstairs, but from a much more distant place.

*Where was her Tommy? She'd picked him up out of the crib, she swore she had. She could still feel his heft in her arms. She could still smell the rose water and glycerin she'd put in his hair that very morning after his bath. But now he was gone. Where was everybody? Would somebody please come help her?*

Jo tried to call back to her mother, to tell Alice not to worry, they'd find the baby, but Jo's mouth was clogged with something feathery. Was it soot? She couldn't see a thing, that much she knew, and there was something else too, something about Son. Had she seen him, or was she dreaming that part? Was she dreaming now? Son had a way of turning her dreams into nightmares. She'd be dreaming an ordinary dream about everyday comings and goings, school and dresses and parties and piano recitals, dreams any ordinary girl would have, and he would slither out from a crevasse in her mind and strike where least expected, fanged and venomous. She'd wake up in a sweat, her heart at full gallop. The only way she'd be able to get back to sleep would be to take her pillow and blanket and crawl into her closet, shut the door, and sleep on the floor, hidden from sight under the hanging clothes, for the rest of the night.

"Where's the baby? Somebody needs to find the baby." Her mother again. Jo could hear her only faintly, clomping around overhead, banging into things, stumbling through the upstairs bedrooms. Jo opened her eyes to a sea of red-clay mud. Blood? Her arm throbbed. Something was drilling a hole in the front of her head. Where was she? With her right hand she felt around her. The bricks of the fireplace, now loose and crumbling. Then, all of a sudden, the sound of settling: a rumble. Instinctively she jumped aside and something came down. Was it the chimney? There was a scrape, then the sickening thud of collapse. Bricks whizzed by her face, crashing all around her. One grazed her cheek. Was the house falling in? Now she was crawling across the floor, the same floor she had crawled upon as a baby, now covered in bits and chunks of debris. She pushed aside boards and furniture pillows, then a sack of what felt like flour. Where was her father?

Something about Son still nagged at her. Caesar's army popped into her head: the swords, piercing, gouging.

*Serendipitous*: a Word to Keep from her mother. It popped into her head like a cloud above the head of a character in the funny papers.

Everything black as pitch. Her eyes burned. Her broken arm throbbed each time she moved it. There was a stabbing pain in her forehead. Her head felt too heavy for her neck. She rose on her haunches and, squatting, put her hand up to her forehead, touched something hard and smooth and cold. Something the size of a spatula, jagged, sticking out of her forehead. A shard.

Upstairs, still, her mother crashed about from room to room, screaming.

She tried to stand but her knees buckled. When she sank to the floor she reached out with her right hand to catch herself and touched a bare foot, then a leg. She felt her way up the torso, touched the jellied mass between the legs: a man.

She heard footsteps to her left, then her father's voice. "Alice! Jo!"

Why didn't her mother come downstairs?

"Alice!" Her father's footsteps clattering up the stairs, wild horses.

"Mort, oh thank God! I can't find Tommy. He was right here. I had him but now he's gone. He blew away! He blew right out of my arms! Oh God! I think he went through the window."

Now Jo tried to tell them she couldn't see. The words came out muffled. Her mouth still full of soot. She spit once, then twice.

Somebody ran down the stairs and into the living room, then stopped short.

"Daddy?" Jo said, reaching out, feeling for her father, if indeed this was her father.

There was a deep quiet. A complete and utter silence, punctuated only by a clicking—the sound fingernails make on metal—as something—was it hail?—hit the tile on the front porch. A cold wind blew through the living room. Was the door open?

"Dad?"

Then her father's voice, across the room, muffled. "No, no, no, no, no."

"Daddy?"

He was breathing hard now, then the breathing turned to some other sound, so high-pitched she thought for a moment she'd been mistaken and it was her mother.

"Son, oh my sweet boy." More heavy breathing now, labored

and steady. In and out, in and out. *Whoosh, whoosh.* Then her father: "Come on back now, boy, come on back. Don't give up."

More heavy breathing. In and out, in and out. Inhale, exhale.

Jo waited. The drill in her head drilled deeper. Everything was still dark. It was as though someone had thrown a brown paper sack over her head. Was she going to be blind now? Upstairs her mother kept on slamming doors, storming around. Then her mother ran down the steps, screaming. "The baby! We need to look outside, he must have gone right through the window. All the windows up there are broken. There's a hole in the ceiling."

Another long silence. Then her mother screamed once. Then dead silence again. Jo's ears popped once, then twice.

Now the heavy breathing stopped. "He's gone." Her father. He began to sob, great wrenching sobs. She had never heard her father cry.

Jo spit more ashes. "Who? Who's gone?"

Then there was a scramble and she felt her mother's hand on her shoulder. "Oh my God! Mort! What's that in her head?"

Her father's hand felt her forehead, touching the thing. His fingers brushed her eyes. "You see to her and I'll go look for the baby. Keep her still. Don't try to pull it out."

Jo could feel her mother's hands flutter gnat-like around her face, lighting here and there, pushing her hair out of her eyes. A cloth touched first one cheek and then the other, wiping, wiping. Everything was mud. She was drowning in mud. "May-May," she whimpered. "What's in my eyes?"

Her mother gathered Jo up in her arms, exhaling short shallow little breaths that tickled against Jo's face. Alice mumbled something but Jo couldn't catch the words.

"Mother, did you lose Tommy?"

Alice began to rock her. "He's not lost. Your father is finding him. He's probably taking him to the doctor to make sure he's all right. He's probably taking him to Dr. Campbell."

THEY SAT together on the floor, Alice crying quietly and rocking her, stroking the side of her head. Every now and then something in the house crashed, then settled. Something solid but wet had started to blow in and splatter the floor. Jo began to shake with the cold, her wet nightgown sticking to her. Her fingers were icy, her teeth had begun to chatter. Her mother kept on rocking; she'd begun to hum "Lead On, O King Eternal," the song they sang at Aunt Fan's and Aunt Sister's funerals.

It had begun to pour in earnest; a freezing wind blew along the floor. Jo shook harder. "Mother, I'm cold. Shut the door."

"The door's gone, honey." Alice let go of her. "I'll see if I can find you a coat."

Jo heard her mother's footsteps going across the floor, then there was a long silence, then the sound of fumbling, gathering. "Son! Oh my sweet little boy! My baby boy!"

Jo wiped her eyes, but everything was still black. Something nagged at her. "What? What happened to Son?"

Her mother didn't answer, just kept on, her voice growing weaker, as if she were gradually being buried alive.

Jo stood up and began to stumble toward the sound of her mother's voice. Then she heard her mother's footsteps, moving away from her. "May-May. Mother. Where are you?" Jo was shaking so hard now she could hardly put one foot in front of the other; her forehead throbbed, a hammering, interior pain. The cast had grown mushy and heavy, dragging down her arm.

Rain poured into her mouth as she called out, and she strangled on the words. Her own voice could have been mistaken for that of a little child. To her ears, it sounded distant, as though it were coming from the schoolyard playground down the street.

She reached up and felt her hair plastered against her head. Was the roof gone too? Where would they go? What would they do? The cast had turned to putty now; she could feel it slide about on her arm like a heavy coat of wet paste. Rain, sheets of melting ice, rolled down her face. She blinked and tried to focus. Tilted her head up and blinked again. Now the mud in her eyes had turned pink. Now she could see shapes, now her mother, down on her knees, beside—who? And what was that? A spear? A wire? Sticking straight up, out of his chest, impaling whoever it was like a specimen on paper, except that this was no butter-fly, this was her brother Son.

She blinked once, then again. Now that she could see a little through the darkness, she remembered. The coat hanger in her hand, a spear. His eyes when he looked at her, hurt and lost and deeply sad, as if she'd betrayed him in some profound way, as if the tornado that lifted her off her feet (yes, she was actually flying through the air when they collided) had been her own doing. As if she'd planned the whole thing the way an assassin would plan, had honed the coat hanger, held it just so, inserted it precisely in the left lower chest, puncturing his red, beating heart (he had one after all!) so that it exploded into his chest cav-ity, then, she imagined, melted like snow in the sun. And now, it was done: he was dead and dead is forever, and she had been the instrument of that death. She had killed her own brother. Moreover, nobody but she herself knew this, nobody knew she was a murderer.

It seemed impossible that she could have done such a thing, but now her vision cleared and she drew near and touched him. Under her fingertips the evidence: the curved hook of the coat hanger, all around it the dark sticky substance that smelled like pennies, and around that the motionless, fleshy hull of a man's chest.

Was she sorry? Of course she was.

She picked up his hand; it was cold and wet and limp. Utterly powerless now. It felt like it had been blown there from far away, just a piece of debris, somebody else's trash. Would her parents still love her when they found out? Because of course she'd tell; she would have to tell them. What else could she do?

"Thou shalt not kill." It was the first commandment she'd learned, because it was so simple, so easy to remember. Among the shortest and certainly the most easily kept. She'd never in a million years dreamed she'd ever kill somebody, especially her own brother. Not even in self-defense. She was an ordinary girl living an ordinary life in an ordinary town. And of course it was an accident, the way the storm blew her down the hall that way. The fact that she just happened to be clutching that blasted coat hanger. Of course they wouldn't blame her. Of course they would see and understand.

Kneeling there, holding her dead brother's hand, the shard of glass emerging like a unicorn's horn from the place above and between her eyes, she felt like a house with new tenants. Something had been emptied out, something filled again. How remarkable that she had done something so irrevocable, so shocking! She, Jo McNabb, was no longer ordinary, nor would she ever be. Something quite shockingly out of the ordinary had happened. In that moment, too, she suspected something even more surprising: that she'd never been an ordinary girl in the first place, that she'd only pretended to be. The pretending had been like the cotton bales she'd seen being taken off the rail cars down by the mill: huge and heavy and untidy. In that moment, too, two figures popped into her head: that washwoman and her husband, looking up at her father, his napkin still tucked under his chin, on the back step. Something old in that look, something ancient and buried. She dropped her brother's hand; it hit the floor with a sickening slap. She got up. "Mother," she shouted, over the downpour. "I can see now. Now I can see."

She looked around the room. Nothing was where it should be. Even in the dark she could see that the living room and dining room looked like her dollhouse had looked when Son, then eight, had picked it up one day and shaken all the pretty furniture she'd made onto the floor. Every piece broken. The dining room chairs were upended against the living room wall where the sofa used to be. The sofa was completely gone and the windows it sat under broken. Her father's brown velvet easy chair sat on the dining room table, which itself sat in the foyer, in front of the opening where the front door had been. The ice and hail and sleet had begun to clatter louder now. The living room floor was turning white.

She went around the table and stood in the open space where the front door had been. Up and down the street, nothing but black. They needed candles, flashlights, all of which were in the basement. They needed to find a dry spot. Her teeth chattered, her fingertips were now completely numb. Her mother hadn't answered. Where had she gone to?

And her father. Why hadn't he returned?

"Mother!" she called out. "May-May, where are you?"

Over the sound of the rain, she heard doors slamming upstairs. "Up here! Oh my poor little baby! Tommy! Where is he?"

She shouted up at her mother: "May-May, can you bring me a coat? It's in my closet."

"There's no coat."

"It's in the closet."

"There's no closet. It blew away."

*How could a whole closet blow away?*

The blood was still dripping into Jo's eyes. In the doorway she turned her face to the sky, and let the ice hit it, turn the sticky blood to liquid, and wash it away again. Then she turned around to the wrecked sodden living room. In the dark she spotted splotches of white around the room. She went toward one of them and touched it, a piece of something, soaked, a man's shirt. Her father's or Son's. It must have come from the laundry basket piled high with dirty clothes now that Essie came infrequently. Before little Tommy, when Essie came every day, she never let them pile up. Each day she took the dirty from the laundry baskets that Jo and her parents used; Son's she gathered from the floor of his room, where he'd thrown them. All of these Essie put into the sheet she kept on the back porch for that purpose and tied it up for the washwoman. "In case I take sick," she'd said, when Jo's mother suggested she leave the task to one day a week. Could the tornado have untied one of Essie's square knots?

By now the blood had rolled back down. Not seeing was like drowning; she began to pant for air. Her cast had completely dissolved and her broken arm hung loose. She took the shirt and carefully wrapped it around her head in the space between the shard in her forehead, which she was now afraid of touching, and her eyes. Then, using both hands, wincing at a bolt of pain in her left arm, she tied the arms of the shirt at the back of her head. Now, at least for a while until the blood soaked through, she could see what there was to see, which was very little except for the shapes of upended furniture and her brother's body, which oddly seemed to be growing larger each time she looked at it.

She headed for the stairs, guided by the sounds of her mother slamming around upstairs. In the dark she ascended, first feeling for the banister on the left and finding it gone, then moving over toward the wall on the right to guide her. One stair step broke completely through when she put a tentative foot down and she stepped over the opening to the next step, marveling at the fact that her mother and father had avoided falling through to the dark beneath. *Will any of us be alive at day's end?* she wondered. Son dead and little Tommy missing. Her father still gone. What had happened to him?

She reached the first landing and turned to take the next flight up. On the second-floor hall landing she caught sight of a moving shape. "Mother?"

"That's it, he's just gone. I've looked everywhere. I felt all around for him. I felt every inch of the floor and in the closets. He must have blown right out the window. He's out there somewhere, in the cold. *Why* didn't I hold him tighter?"

"Daddy will find him."

"I'm going out there to look for him."

Jo climbed toward her mother's voice. As she ascended, she heard the hail stop and the rain start; then the rain was rolling down her face. She looked above her. There was a broken window over the upper landing; the downpour and a freezing wind almost knocked her off her feet. She could feel shards of glass under her saddle oxfords. She'd always hated those shoes, but now she was grateful for them. Over the downpour other sounds now: screams, sirens, shouting.

"Mother, don't leave me here. Don't leave me in this house by myself. I can barely see a thing. There's a piece of glass in my head."

Her mother was coming down the steps toward her now, breathing hard. "I've got to find my baby boy. One boy dead, the other gone. My fault. Nothing but my fault. Why did I let him slip through my fingers? What kind of mother am I?"

Jo reached up through the darkness and touched her mother's breast, then her hand. Jo clutched at the hand; it slid through her wet freezing fingers. "May-May, come on downstairs with me. I need you to look after me."

"You stay with Son. Maybe he's just in a coma. Maybe he'll come to, people come out of comas every day. Maybe Daddy will be back with the baby. Get a blanket ready."

"Something's stuck in my head, May-May. I'm bleeding. What if I die too?"

"Oh, don't be ridiculous, Jo. You're not going to die. You're just going to have an awful scar once the doctor gets the glass out and stitches you up. You'll just have to wear bangs the rest of your life." Her mother let out a weird chuckle, as if this were all a joke and Son downstairs was going to rise like Lazarus from the dead and little Tommy wasn't in the next county.

Her mother passed her by and headed on down the stairs.

Jo had just opened her mouth to tell her mother about the missing step when she heard a crash. Her mother screamed once; then there was nothing except the sound of the rain. Jo listened, then descended, slowly, slowly, barely touching her foot onto the stair step ahead of her until she came to the missing one.

She leaned down and felt around. There it was: her mother's leg, caught in the opening where the step had been. Jo touched a shard of the wet, jagged bone. Her mother's leg had gone through the broken step, while her body had fallen forward, downward. The leg had snapped at the midpoint of the tibia, between the knee and ankle.

Jo went down a couple of steps to where she thought her mother's head should be. She bent down and felt around for Alice's face, and when she found it, she put her fingers on her mother's nostrils. Alice was still breathing. Jo felt her way back up to her mother's foot. She couldn't see it. A flashlight, a candle. She needed a light.

She got up and went on down the steps. Then she walked around into the hall to the alcove under the steps where the telephone was. The phone rested on the wooden student desk Alice had picked up from Tupelo High School surplus and refinished. It fit the space under the stairs perfectly. Panting now, Jo sat down at the desk and picked up the phone. Of course it was dead. Why had she bothered? What an idiot she was.

Behind the phone and hall closet was the door to the basement, the steep steps leading down, the ones she was always afraid of slipping on, plummeting headlong into the silent gloom of the basement, with its spider webs and old magazines and now-quiet monster of a furnace and the cluster, on a tower of stacked boxes, of candles and matches and flashlights. The pack of batteries.

Again she touched each descending step before trusting it. If she fell, there'd be nobody left, nobody to see about her mother.

It seemed to her that she was descending into an underworld. Once her feet hit the dirt floor of the basement, she walked straight ahead, her good arm outstretched, to the stack of boxes, under the ground-floor window, matted, she knew without seeing, with messy, dense webs, webs with no discernible pattern, the kind black widows make. Her toe touched something and she reached down. There they all were. She gathered the flashlight and batteries first, then a candle, which she put under her arm, and some matchboxes, which she placed carefully in her mouth, between her teeth. She turned on the flashlight. How dry the basement was! How dusty! And so warm. She felt the warmth gather her in. How she wanted to sink down into it, just for a little rest, just a moment's rest. She felt suddenly dizzy, a bit nauseous. She sat down on one of the steps.

It occurred to her that the basement might be leaking so she pointed the flashlight upward. Then she saw it: her mother's foot, hose rolled down to the ankle, sticking through where the upper stair step had been. It was moving, wiggling, very slightly. Something out of place, something alive where nothing should have been. It was as if a snake had appeared over her head.

She rose shakily and grabbed hold of the banister and started back up, watching each step, but moving fast.

When she got to the top she headed around the corner again, and set down the candle and matches on the desk. Then she turned back to the stairs leading up and pointed the flashlight. As she'd first thought, her mother had fallen headfirst, both arms flung out to catch herself as she fell. The leg had snapped like a twig, the way Jo's arm had, except the leg looked like a jagged saw had cut into it after the initial break. She wondered if the leg could be saved. Facedown, Alice was moving a little now, making feeble snuffling noises into the step. She reminded Jo of Snowball's kittens.

Jo climbed to the point in the stairs where her mother's head lay, then farther up to the broken step, where she turned her attention to her foot. "May-May," she said, "I'm going to get your foot loose. It may hurt but be still. Just lie there. Lay your head down." Her mother the grammarian was a stickler for the proper usage of *lie* and *lay*. Jo used them correctly without a moment's thought.

Blood poured from the wound, obscuring the protruding bone. Jo put both hands around her mother's ankle and tugged, once, then twice. Alice screamed once and passed out. The foot didn't budge. Jo grabbed the flashlight with her left hand and took a good look. A splinter of wood had punctured the foot, holding it in place. With her right hand, she pulled on it. The foot gave a little, then a little more. Now she could wiggle it back and forth in the sickening flesh. Jo wondered if she should be further wounding the foot, but what choice did she have? She continued to push at the splinter.

The leg quivered. Jo had gotten her Campfire Girls first-aid badge. She knew Alice was in shock and needed to be dragged off the stairs and covered. The leg needed to be splinted; her mother was in danger of bleeding to death or dying from the shock.

Jo's left arm, taking the weight of the flashlight, had begun to flare. Jolts of pain, coming in waves. She put the flashlight down and kept on wiggling the splinter; finally, when she felt it give and break off, she took the flashlight up again and peered down into the hole. The foot was loose; she lifted it with her good right hand. Her mother's weight shifted and began to slide.

Alice was at the midpoint of the first and longest rise of stairs. With the foot now free, she was in danger of sliding down the steps headfirst, landing on her head, the broken leg bumping along behind her.

Jo sat on her mother's good leg and gently brought the foot up out of the hole. Alice's weight shifted again. Jo lay the mangled foot on the step and grabbed her mother's good leg. Now she was holding back her mother's full weight in her right hand. She straddled her mother and held her in place, first with her good right and then with her bad left. Then she let her mother slide headfirst, face to floor, just a bit at a time, broken leg sliding along behind her, down, step by step, easy does it, step by step. Her mother's head, then the leg, bumped each step with a sickening thump.

When Alice's head reached the bottom, Jo snatched the flashlight and ran back into the living room, barely avoiding tripping over Son, who lay just around the corner. She waved the light around, looking for something to make a tourniquet from. The living room was filled with strange shapes: her brother's body, the coat hanger sticking straight up from his chest, the collapsed chimney, overturned furniture. Was she in one of her nightmares, and her brother, zombie-like, would soon rise from the dead to take his revenge?

She began to tremble, her knees in danger of buckling.

In a far corner of the living room she spotted another piece of white. An apron, one of Essie's, the kind she wore for special occasions, when company came for dinner. Jo snatched it up, wrung out the water, and ran back in to her mother, still lying facedown. She wrapped the tourniquet around her leg, above the break. Then she went to the hall closet, which, unlike her own closet upstairs, was still there, and got out her mother's good wool coat. Clean and dry. She unbuttoned it and slid it under Alice's leg, trying not to look. Then she gently pulled the coat together and standing over her mother, she rolled her over, leg last. She picked up the leg in the coat and turned it too. She shined the flashlight on her mother's face. It was alabaster, her lips white, her eyes rolled back in her head. Jo's first thought was that her mother was dead too, that she had already bled to death, but when Jo picked up Alice's hand and put her forefinger to the wrist she could feel the *thrum, thrum* of her mother's pulse, a sound she knew somewhere deep in her own body, the sound she'd heard long before time began for her. She held Alice's freezing palm to her face to warm it, then ran back to the closet and got out her father's worsted woolen overcoat and put it over her mother, tucking her in.

There was a long moment. Then Alice began to mumble. Jo knelt beside her mother and tried to hear. Something about Tommy. How, when Alice heard the storm coming, she'd picked him up out of the crib. She knew she had. How he was still asleep when she picked him up. How she'd hated to pick him up for fear of waking him.

Jo's teeth chattered. She stroked her mother's forehead, then turned off the flashlight to save the battery. As the dark settled in, she could hear tapping on what was left of the roof over their heads. Hail. The thing wedged in her own forehead seemed to have settled in for the long term. Surely it wasn't as big as it felt! She needed to go out into the street and look for help, and she would, she promised herself she would. She just needed to warm her mother up first. That was the number-one rule with a victim of shock, getting them warm. This much she knew from her

Campfire Girls manual. She lay down beside Alice, whose light breath she could still feel against her fingertips, thank heavens, and put her fiery left arm over her mother. Now that Jo was still, her elbow was hit with a stabbing pain that came in waves, as if someone were driving nails into it.

As she lay on the cold wet floor beside her too-quiet but still breathing mother, she found herself on a ledge overlooking a gorge; she let herself go and fell downward into the dark, into the cold, cold night.

She dreamed a long, complicated dream. It started with little Tommy riding a giant elephant. The elephant wore a silk saddle and its ears, translucent, flapped in the sunshine. Tommy had on a pretty blue turban and a robe made of gold, and everybody everywhere was bowing to him and waving palm branches and calling him messiah, the blessed son. Her mother was smiling and there were parties and dancing and foot washings and sparkling wine. Then a giant cloud descended from the heavens and the sky grew dark. There was a rumble of thunder, and someone from far far away (was it angel or devil?) called out across the sky in a voice that echoed far and wide, across the whole wide world: *No no no no no.*

Then another sound. The mewing of a cat, close by, urgent and intimate. *You, you.* Or was it a baby's cry?

# MONDAY, APRIL 6

# 5

## 3 A.M.

When Dovey turned north on Church Street, the wind and freezing rain slapped at her face the way her aunt used to do when she didn't finish the wash on time. She had to bend almost double, pulling up the white lady's shawl to cover her head and shield her eyes. She walked mostly blind, tiptoeing her way up Church Street, so as not to step on anything sharp, the early wound on the bottom of her foot firing with each step. Above all else, she needed shoes—shoes and a place to get out of the weather.

Every now and then she looked up, hoping for the gray light of dawn, but the sky was still black as pitch, not a trace of moon. How long could one night go on? It felt like a week had passed since she'd seen the sky.

Through the rain—she'd never seen such rain—the big houses on either side of the street loomed dark and broken. Whole sections bashed in. Roofs collapsed and topsy-turvy under the weight of downed trees. Giant water oaks that had once pushed up the sidewalks now sheared off at the tips, bare of their leaves, tilting crazily sideways, or felled. Feeling her way, she monkey-climbed over one that stretched across the whole street. She'd never realized how massive they were, how vast and complicated their networks of limbs and branches.

Up ahead, through the dark, the McNabb house rose out of the rubble, *still there*. So that boy was still drawing breath. Her house nothing but a pile of secondhand lumber, her own family blown to the four winds, and Satan still lived? She'd always suspected there was no justice in this world. Now she was sure of it.

She tripped over a shard of metal and almost fell. She needed to sit down, just for a few minutes, and the big front porch drew her. She passed the long row of crepe myrtle bushes between the curb and sidewalk and hobbled up the six concrete steps from the sidewalk to the McNabbs' front yard and then up the second flight of four red-tiled steps to the front porch. How many times had she dragged her laundry cart up these steps, bounced it back down, filled to the brim with McNabb dirt? The big oak at the curb, which had made huge cracks in the sidewalk on one side and buckled the street underneath it on the other, had been flipped over, its top resting on the house across the street, which had crumbled under its weight, the chimney the only upright structure she could make out in the dark. She hadn't planned on going inside the McNabb place, but the big porch swing she'd hoped to take her rest on had been ripped from its chains and was nowhere in sight. The loose chains still hung from the porch ceiling, jangling and flailing in the ragged wind.

The front door, that door she'd come and gone from hundreds, maybe thousands, of times, picking up the dirty, bringing back the clean, had been blown clear off its hinges. So she walked right in through the door frame, right on into the living room, dark as pitch. She knew this room, every nook and cranny. She'd been in more white folks' living rooms than anyone else up on the Hill, and certainly down in Shake Rag. Despite her aversion to the McNabbs and their dirt, this was her favorite. When she had picked up the McNabb laundry each week, she'd lingered to admire the marble-top tables and dresser, the Oriental rug, the eight-foot dining table, the gold-rimmed china plates with their pretty hand-painted fruits lined up just so in the breakfront. The fire screen in the shape of a peacock's tail in front of the fireplace, Mr. McNabb's brown velvet chair with its lace doilies where that McNabb girl used to sleep curled up like Henry in his box. The lady rocker with the striped silk upholstery.

What a wreck now. In the darkness the shapes all scrambled, chair legs and a legal bookcase she didn't recognize, its shelves separated and propped at weird angles around the room. The pretty living room furniture upended and in pieces, taking on strange, frightening shapes. Rain poured in from above and blew through the opening where the front door had been so that she couldn't tell the difference between outdoors and indoors.

The McNabb place was in pieces. She couldn't say she was sorry.

She tiptoed inside, her feet so numb now she couldn't tell whether she was stepping on anything sharp. What she would give for a pair of shoes.

She felt her way through an open spot, holding on to the upended furniture. She almost tripped over something on the floor. She grabbed the leg of an upturned chair to catch herself. What? She first thought she'd tripped over a pile of laundry. What a joke. But she knew it wasn't that. This was Sunday (or in the early morning hours on Monday, she wasn't sure) and of course she had picked up the McNabb wash Saturday, though it seemed a year ago that she was hanging it on the line. (Where was *it* now? Probably in the next county. Would she be blamed?)

She tried to walk around whatever it was on the floor, but it was large and rubbery and it had what felt like tentacles going every which way, blocking her passage. She sank to her knees and felt around. A leg, an arm, both cold and slick with the rain and sleet that had blown in from the open door. Not something, but somebody. She felt some more, the trousers, the belt, the genitals. A man, cold as ice. She put her hand on his face, felt for breath. *Nobody here.*

She bent over him, trying to see the face. *Could it be?* The end of the coat hanger grazed the bridge of her nose, cut a thin line down the middle. She jerked back. An inch or less and it would have poked her right in the eye. She followed it with her fingers to the entry point, right under the shirt pocket, a pocket she herself had ironed countless times. She peered at the face but couldn't see it clearly.

*Old storm, what you gone and done? You done killed that boy?*

Her heart a jackrabbit zigzagging through the field.

One way to find out. She knew the household's most intimate apparel. The lady's loose silks; the girl's white cotton bloomers, always stained; the Mr.'s patched boxer shorts, thinned in the rear; that boy's nasty briefs. She unbuckled the belt, unbuttoned the fly, reached in. Briefs! It had to be him. Who else in this house? Who else but Satan?

She stood up and something with feathers and talons loosened its grip on the cords of her neck, shook itself, and fluttered. She took a deep breath and the something with feathers flapped its wings. This here—a dead boy, even if he was the Devil—was serious business. Dead is dead. It gave her pause to feel so fine in that moment, so *light.* She thought to ask for forgiveness, but couldn't and didn't.

The rain blew harder through the opening where the door had been and drummed onto the floor around her. If anything, it was raining harder. She needed to get under cover, get herself some warm clothes. She felt her way around that boy's body (*Thank you, old storm!*), made her way into the hall, then froze. Somebody breathing hard, somebody clearing a throat.

A girl's voice, a whisper: "Who's there? Daddy? Daddy? Is that you?"

Dovey peered through the dark. The voice had come from the floor, to the left, at the base of the stairs.

Then again, shrill, afraid: "Who's here? Daddy?"

Dovey wanted to run, but where to? Here in the hall, at least, it was dry. The roof hadn't given way. Not yet anyhow.

"It's me. Dovey."

"Who?"

"Dovey. I do the clothes."

A scramble. Somebody getting up, that McNabb girl, a good two heads taller than Dovey. She'd grown a foot since Dovey saw her last. The girl snatched at her, grasped her shoulder, then her hand. Dovey shrank from her touch. Was the girl going to strike her? Dovey peered at her through the dark. Something sticking out of the girl's head. A horn.

"Oh, thank God you've come! It's my mother. Can you go for help? I don't want to leave her."

At that moment a train whistled once, then again. Time was all scrambled up in her head so Dovey didn't know whether it was the Frisco or the M&O. How could a train get through this mess?

The girl's name was Jo. Dovey had seen it sewn into her underwear when she'd gone off to camp. What a piece of work that had been when that girl came back after two weeks, her clothes musty and stained and smelling like sour milk.

Then, from the shadows, the girl leaned forward, so close that Dovey had to move back to avoid the horn. The girl whispered, "Tell your granddaughter he's dead, my brother's dead. Tell her he can't bother her ever again."

The something with feathers and talons teetered now on the edge of Dovey's shoulder and flapped its wings again. Then a whirring in Dovey's ears, a brush of her hair good-bye, and it was gone, through the dark house and out into the rain and the night. "I will if I can find her. She and the baby gone missing."

"Baby? What baby?"

"The baby that brother of yours give her."

The girl began to sob now. "Oh no! She had a baby?" The girl's left shoulder looked all wrong, poked out crooked. The drumstick swung wide, back and forth. In the dark, her silhouette looked like one of those birds with broken wings Dreama kept bringing home.

Dovey didn't have time for white-girl foolishness. Promise was old news. "You got me some dry clothes and some shoes? Some kind of coat? It's bad out there. I'm near about froze to death."

The girl took one of Dovey's icy hands in her slightly warmer one and led her around the moaning woman on the floor. "You poor thing. Come on. Let's see what's dry."

Then she stopped and squeezed Dovey's hand so hard she almost cried out. "You got to go find us somebody. I got this big old thing stuck in my head and my arm's broken. My mother's leg is all torn up. We need some men and a stretcher. I need somebody who knows how to get this thing out of my head without killing me."

The girl guided Dovey's hand to the shard of glass in her head. Dovey's fingers grazed the cloth underneath keeping the blood out of the girl's eyes. It was saturated, with rain or blood, Dovey wasn't sure.

Dovey touched it. *Lord, mercy.* She felt around. "You wanting me to pull it out?"

"Don't fool with it. Daddy said I could bleed to death." The girl began to sob now, clawing at Dovey's arm. Dovey stepped back. *Crybaby.* "My mother could die, like my brother in there. He's dead as a doornail, and it's on me. I did that. My baby brother got blown away. Now I got my mother to save. You need to get us some help. You got to promise me."

"Give me a minute. I'm so tired. I got to rest." Dovey dropped to her knees. Then the rest of her gave way and she was on the cold wet floor.

She opened her eyes. The horn between the girl's eyes pointed down at her, water dripping off it onto Dovey's face. The girl said, "I'll give you five minutes, then I'm waking you up."

Dovey dropped into sleep like she was falling off a cliff. She began to dream the old dream. The pile of dirty laundry. She tried to carry it, to balance it, but it grew heavier and heavier, knocking her flat on her back, sitting on her chest, furred and reeking. Then it slipped and slid, burying her, suffocating her with white-folks stink.

When she woke up it was still on her chest, heavy and moving around. It leaned forward and tickled her cheek. She reached up to push it off and it had wet fur and dug in its claws, not budging. Then it spoke to her. "*You.*" Then again, "*You.*"

Dovey opened her eyes. The cat was standing on her chest now, its face only inches from hers, its whiskers tickling her nose. "Shoo, now," she said, pushing it back.

"*You,*" it said again, then another time. Then it leapt off her and melted into the dark.

On either side of Dovey, the girl and her mother lay flat on their backs, all three of them laid out like fallen dominoes at the bottom of the stairs. It was the closest Dovey had ever been to white people; she could feel their body heat against her shoulders and upper arms. Both moaned softly.

Now a hand reached out and covered her face, groping about. The girl's mother was waking up, she was screaming. On Dovey's other side, the girl sat up. "Mother, May-May, lie back."

"Where's my little boy?" The mother screamed in Dovey's ear. "Why can't you find him?"

DOVEY SAT up, her ears ringing. Her Promise. Where was he? Out there somewhere in the rain and dark? How could she have fallen asleep? She'd forgotten about the McNabb baby. "What happened to him?" she asked the mother.

"He just flew out the window," the mother whispered. "He just flew right out of my arms like he was riding a magic carpet."

"I flew around like a bird," murmured Dovey. "I got blowed all the way down to Gum Pond. And I landed easy." She patted the mother's hand. "Your little boy, he'll land easy too."

Even as she said the words, she didn't believe them.

"We need to find him!" The mother made a move to rise, let out a high-pitched scream, and collapsed back on the floor.

The girl jumped up. With her good arm she pulled on Dovey. "Come on," she said. "You got to get on up and go for help. You got to help us." Dovey rose to her knees and then stood, her hurt foot leaden and throbbing.

"Can't walk. Got to get a bandage on this foot," she said to the girl. "You need to see if something's in it and then wash it and put on a wrap." Dovey sat back down on the floor, held her foot up.

The girl felt around for her flashlight, then found it and turned it on. Just as she did, they heard the train whistle. *No no no no no.* How could a train travel those tracks after what had happened, wondered Dovey. They must be covered over with rubbish. Outside the flashlight's beam, the hallway seemed to get darker. Had she died and woken up in eternal darkness, eternal damnation? And what for? For wishing a boy dead? For wanting justice in this world?

"Hold that foot still," the girl said. "I've only got one good arm here." The girl reached down and took hold of the hem of Dovey's dress and wiped her eyes with it. "Hurry up, I can't see much and I'm wasting light."

Dovey took hold of the foot and held it to the beam of light.

The girl was quiet for a minute. Then she asked, "Why's your skin so black and the bottoms of your feet so light?"

Dovey lowered her foot to the floor. Something in the girl's tone. "Is there anything in there?"

"Nope," the girl said. "Just a big old ragged cut. Looks like a railroad track. Hold your horses."

She got up and headed into the kitchen, leaving Dovey in the dark. Dovey could hear her slamming drawers, running water. Once she screamed one short but piercing scream and cursed, which caused her mother to startle and moan louder. In a minute she came back.

"Hold it up again," she told Dovey. "Hold it high so I can clean it out."

"That clean water? Don't put no dirty water on it."

"Don't know," the girl said, "but it's better than the mud that's on there now." She poured some water on the foot, setting it on fire. "When you find a doctor, get him to give you a shot or you'll get lockjaw. Hold up now and don't put it down yet." She went off somewhere again. Dovey could hear her rummaging around, bottles falling and breaking.

She came back with something in her hand. "Give me back the foot," she commanded and Dovey held it up. She poured something liquid from a bottle onto the cut and it stung and sizzled and Dovey cried out. "Stop that. Now you hold still," the girl said and she began to wrap the foot in what looked to Dovey like a long scarf, tucking the end inside. "There," the girl said, "now we just need to find you some shoes." Then she was gone again, this time heading for the living room.

She came back carrying a pair of men's shoes the size of shovels. "Put these on," she said, groping around for one of Dovey's legs. "They're my brother's. I stuck some wash rags in the toes. I needed to get some big shoes to fit over the bandage."

"No shoes from the Devil's feet," said Dovey, pulling away.

"Beggars can't be choosers," the girl said, already placing the shoe on Dovey's bandaged foot and tying the laces. "You got to get on into town now. You got to tell them to come to 425 North Church. Or just tell them the McNabb house. Can you remember that? Do that and then get some stitches in that foot and that shot and some more shoes."


WHEN DR. JUBER came to patch up Dreama, he'd said the same thing, that the girl probably needed stitches, definitely a tetanus shot. Dreama had kicked at him when he tried to open her legs to see the damage. The one good eye glared over his shoulder at Dovey. *Don't let him. Nobody looking at me. Nobody touching me.*

Dovey took the doctor back into the kitchen where the neighbors and Virgil were clustered, the women, Harmony and Ollie, sitting at the kitchen table crying, their husbands and Virgil pacing back and forth with clenched fists. The five of them looked at the doctor, who said, "Seen this sort of thing one time too many. Enough to make a man go blind."

"Who?" asked Virgil.

"She ain't saying," Dovey said.

Virgil slammed his fist down on the kitchen counter. "She going to tell me! I'm her Papa." He stormed out of the kitchen and around the corner to the bedroom.

Dovey stepped in front of him. "Don't you go asking her now. We got to get her fixed up."

Virgil didn't even look down at her, just over her head at the small shape curled in a ball on the bed. Dovey sighed and stepped aside, then followed him in.

When they went in, Dreama looked at Virgil and shook her head.

"Baby," Virgil said.

"Not naming names, Papa."

"Baby," Virgil said again.

Dreama shut her eyes. "And have you strung up on the highest tree? Then where'd we be?"

No fool that girl. Just last month over in Itawamba County, an elder at the Mt. Zion A.M.E. named Elijah Smith had been dragged from his bed and taken out in the country and hung by his wrists from a giant cedar tree and burnt alive. All of that for going after a white man who bothered his wife.

"What you thinking now, girl? You thinking I just going to sit back and not do something about this here? What you think I am?"

Behind him, Dovey backed through the doorway and headed for the kitchen. She didn't want Dreama to see her crying. The doctor and other men were drinking something clear out of her jelly jars. The women sat at the table, stone-faced.

She took the glass out of the doctor's hand. "You got work to do in there. This here can wait. Do what you got to do and get it over with."

"Seen too much of this," the doctor said. "Surprised these eyes still open in the morning." He took another gulp, then got the medicine and needle out of his case, and as the rest of them watched, he drew the liquid into a syringe.

When she and the doctor, who held the syringe behind his back, returned to the bedroom, Dreama had turned over in the bed, her back now to the door, her face to the wall. The whiter-than-white sheet under her bloomed like a dark red rose.

The doctor stopped in the doorway. "Have mercy."

Dovey went around him. "Baby, Dr. Juber's going to give you a shot now. Make you feel better."

Dreama didn't budge. For one horrifying moment, Dovey didn't think she was breathing. Then the girl moved her head just a little.

"A tiny stick," said the doctor.

Dovey felt dizzy and breathless when she saw the needle slip into the buttery flesh of Dreama's little arm. "Going to the out-house for some rags," she said.

"No rags," the doctor said. "Clean towels. And get somebody to boil some water."

Dovey put the kettle on, then went out back and vomited.

Once out of the house, she couldn't bear to go back in. She paced between the outhouse and the back stoop, her breath coming ragged and loud. The lightning bugs were flaring across the yard, the frogs down at Gum Pond had revved up. Then she walked around the house to the front. The half-pie moon had made its way from one side of the porch to the other, the light playing on the bare yard that she kept raked. She liked to rake waves into the dust; they looped and curled and, she imagined, crashed onto a long white shelf of sand. She had always wanted to see the real ocean down in Florida, watch those big waves come in. Virgil's daddy had gone once. He told Virgil the sound of the waves took his heart and changed the beat to slow, then slower, until it seemed like it wasn't beating at all.

On the front porch Henry lay curled in his bed. Dovey crouched down beside him. That's when she felt it descend: something heavy and feathered. It got her by the shoulders and settled there, its talons reaching around, curling themselves against the cords of her neck, flexing against them. That night it would go to bed with her, and the next morning and the mornings to follow it would be there still, never once loosening its hold, almost piercing her skin but not quite, kneading her neck silently. She would learn to work with it on her shoulders and neck, she would learn not to turn her head too far one way or the other. Her neck would become stiff and sore and her head heavy as a stone. Some mornings she would feel as though she couldn't lift it from the pillow.

In the moonlight, weak and watery though it was, she saw

something in the dust. Tire tracks from a car with skinny little wheels. She knew then that whoever had done this had dumped her granddaughter like garbage. Used her up and thrown her out.

The heavy, feathered thing flexed its talons. She put her hand to her neck. Then she ran back into the house and called Virgil to bring his flashlight.

He came running, along with everybody else.

"Stand back," Dovey commanded. "Let Virgil see."

Virgil held out the light and looked hard at the tire marks. "Don't nobody walk on them," he said and ran back into the house. A moment later he came back out with a piece of paper and folded it to the width of the tires. He pulled a pencil out of his pocket and marked the tread tracks on the paper. Then he walked on past everybody and headed out into the night.

"Virgil," Dovey shouted after him.

"I'm getting the proof," he shouted back.


NOW, NEXT to Dovey on the cold wet floor, the mother lifted her head again. "Where's the baby? I've got to find him. Jo? Where are you? Where is everybody?"

The girl stepped over Dovey and sat down next to her mother and used her good arm to pull her mother's head into her lap.

The wrap on the mother's leg had shone white against the darkness when Dovey first came in; now the bandage was dark.

Dovey lifted her head and looked through the open doorway. Was the pitch-black turning to gray or was she dreaming? Was it another day?

Dovey rose to her feet. She could barely pick them up in the Devil's shoes. They were twice the size of her feet and kept slipping, even on the wrapped foot. "You got any rags to tie these on? Ain't getting nowhere in these."

*Could you take up somebody's evil by walking in their shoes? Could you spread it all over town? Were these the shoes he wore when he did what he did to my baby?*

The girl put her mother's head down and went back to the hall closet and took out a sheet. She bit into one corner and tore two strips from it with her good hand. She leaned down and wrapped the strips around Son's shoes and tied them onto Dovey's feet. Dovey walked around for a moment, and they stayed on.

She walked in a circle in the hall; then she saw stars and had to sit down again. Her head felt fuzzy and clotted.

"You got anything I can eat before I go?" she asked the girl. "You got any clean water?"

The girl went back to her mother's side, took up her head again. "There's food and water in the icebox. We better eat it anyway before it goes bad. Go see what you can find. Be quick about it. You got to go out there and get us some help. Here. Take the flashlight."

Dovey stepped around the mother and shuffled back to the kitchen. The door to the icebox was partly ajar. When she opened it all the way, something flew out, its wings brushing her face, making a little breeze. It flew around the room, whap-ping into first one wall and then another, faster and faster and more panicked. A bird for sure, but what kind? Then it settled and she heard it scuffling around on the floor. She turned back to the icebox, feeling around, something liquid in a bottle. She pulled it out and drank. Orange juice, blessed orange juice. She recognized it immediately, though she'd never had it out of a bottle. It flowed through her like nectar, making her fingertips tingle. Now she could think straight. She groped around for something to eat and found a stick of butter and ate half of that, then touched another bottle. Milk in a bottle, lukewarm but not yet sour. She drank half the bottle.

She was leaving the kitchen when the bird flew up and landed on the metallic kitchen table. Its feet made a clicking noise on the surface. Then she heard it coo. A dove. *Sister.*

When she was little, her daddy called her by spooning out the sound: *Coo, coo. Got me a baby girl, and where's she at? Got me a baby girl, and where's she at?*

That had been her signal to stop whatever it was she was doing under the house and come inside. She'd liked to play under the house, the coolness and quiet, the bloodworms that sauntered in and out and made brown piles, the spider webs with their struggling flies. It was suppertime or going-to-church time or bath time. He called her that way, making her feel like he knew her in this special way, like he'd been waiting all day to call her back to where she belonged, to the home that awaited.

He was the one who got sick first. It was the middle of August and the cotton was coming in. He came walking through the door from working John Calhoun's field. He told them he'd picked 300 pounds that day at 50 cents per 100 pounds, a full sum of a dollar and a half, and her mama said, *oh honey*, and smiled and held out her hand for the money. He'd just reached into his pocket to pull out the heavy silver coin and the lighter one when a look passed over his face like a shadow and he'd said, "Miss Lou," which is what he called Dovey's mother, "I ain't feeling so good. Maybe I need to go on to bed."

And her mother had said, "And miss Blue's birthday?" It was Dovey's little brother's birthday that day. He'd gotten a whistle their mother had carved late into the nights when everybody was sleeping, a whistle shaped like an angel with wings. He was blowing on it as they were talking. She'd made a cake too. Their mother was the best baker on the Hill. She'd carved it down with Dovey's father's straight razor into the shape of a laying-down lamb with curly hair that she'd fashioned in little waves of white icing.

About then, Dovey's daddy had sagged and headed fast for bed, trailed by her mother and all the children. They all stood watching as he fell headlong onto the corn-shuck mattress in his full work clothes, clutching his belly, without so much as a good night or see you tomorrow or sorry to miss little Blue's birthday party.

Dovey asked her mother, "What's wrong with Papa?"

"He's tired," her mother had answered. "Too tired to spit."

The next day he didn't get out of bed. He tossed and turned and complained of his stomach. Her mother got a bedpan and kept carrying it in and out, with a cloth over it. The house began to stink to high heaven.

He was a strong man. He lived two long weeks. He never got up from that bed, despite visits from the family doctor and then the white doctor sent by Mr. Calhoun to see if his most valuable hand could please God get back into the field, the cotton was high. Dovey's mother spent most of her time inside the bedroom; after the first few days, she told Dovey to take care of her sisters and brother. She would not allow them to come inside the curtain that cordoned the bedroom from the other part of the house where the children slept on one big pad on the floor.

Finally, one morning as the sun was rising and it was already hot as fire, her mother walked out of the bedroom and woke them and told them their father had flown away home. She told them it was time for him to go, it was his time.

Next it was her mother, who lingered just a week, and before she was even gone, little Blue got sick. Dovey put them together on the corn-shuck mattress and then, a few days later, the other two. Each time one of them passed, she went next door and told Ruthie Johnson, called Ruthie the duck lady because she kept ducks in the yard the way some people kept chickens. Ruthie was Etherene Johnson's mother. She didn't let Dovey come inside the house, but she and the other women at St. John the Baptist rolled up their sleeves and made sure Dovey and her brother and sisters didn't go hungry. They brought dishes of food and placed them on the edge of the yard. Each night Dovey went out and collected them. As her family dwindled, the amounts became smaller and smaller, until there was just the one single portion and the aunt was called and Dovey went down to Shake Rag with her and that was that.

Dovey never could figure out why she was spared. There was a shame to it. When she bent over her aunt's washboard, scrubbing the endless clothes, she wondered why she didn't get sick, why God didn't take her. Her aunt said she was left to tell the story, but really, there was no story to tell. After her father's dramatic and precipitous decline, the progression of the others' illnesses and deaths had been messy and tedious and predictable. They were there, then they weren't. No story at all.


NOW, MANEUVERING cautiously in the Devil's oversized shoes, Dovey shuffled her way toward the bird, which was still skittering around on the kitchen table. She wanted to grab hold of it the way Dreama would have done, easy and calm, and take it outside. But when she approached and began to feel around for it, it flapped in a panic and flew around the kitchen again, whapping into the wall over the sink. She could hear it now scrambling around in the sink, agitated and confused.

She turned off the flashlight, thinking it might be scaring the bird, making it lose its sense of direction, and then went for it again because she couldn't stand the ragged sound of its help-lessness. This time she used her white-lady shawl and threw it over the sink. Under the shawl the dove twisted and quivered, but she held on and wrapped it lightly and moved with it from the kitchen out onto the back screen porch where the door to the outside was long gone. Then she unloosed the shawl and let it go, out into the night and the rain and the wind. A wingtip brushed her arm as it took flight.

She stood there in the open space where the screen door had been, following the sound of it, the *whoosh* of its wings, the relieved rattle.

"Good luck," Dovey whispered.

# 6

## 6:37 A.M.

The morning after the storm. Coming up dawn now, gray and still raining. In the first light Jo looked into the washwoman's face. It was like peering through a windowpane into another family's house, watching them sit down to the table for supper, seeing but not seeing their shared life, knowing but not knowing their fears and desires. The ancient eyes, the lines that ran from nose to mouth to chin, the tightness around the mouth. Jo looked greedily, like a Peeping Tom, but the windowpane said no, this is not your story.

The old washwoman was buttoning Alice's raincoat, pulling up the collar, preparing to go. Jo followed the old woman through the living room on her way out the door. She followed her as they both stepped around Jo's brother on the floor, she followed her down the steps to the sidewalk below. She followed her down the sidewalk to the corner. She wanted to follow her to the ends of the earth.

The rain still came down in sheets. There were sounds of people crying out and digging in the rubble. Here and there houses were burning to the ground, even as the rain poured down on them.

"Be careful not to fall in those shoes," she shouted to the old woman. "You could trip and hurt yourself and then you'd never get to town. If you see anybody with a stretcher on the way, bring them back here."

"I got to find my own people," the woman shouted back. She was covered neck to toe in the oversized raincoat and wearing Son's felt fedora, which came down almost over her eyes; she looked like a walking talking pile of laundry. When Jo had pulled the fedora out of the closet shelf and handed it to the woman, she had taken care not to say whose it was and the woman had put it on her head without asking.

Jo wasn't sure she trusted the washwoman. Why would she want to help them? Why wouldn't she hate them for what Son had done to her granddaughter? Jo called out to the woman's receding form, "Promise you'll send us some help. You hear me?"

The horn on Jo's head gleamed in the rain. It had slipped down a bit; if she rolled her eyes upward and cross-eyed, she could see its bright point. It seemed to be growing in length, the tip sharp and dangerous. Was she becoming another sort of creature, strange and fearful? Since yesterday she had felt something changing, a shift. Once her mother had used the verb *transmogrify* over the dinner table. Jo liked the sound of it but didn't know what it meant or whether it was transitive or intransitive. She'd asked and her mother had said it meant shape-shifting but in a deep sort of way so that it wasn't just the shape of a thing that changed but also its very nature, its essence. Jo felt now that she herself was *transmogrifying* or maybe it was being *transmogrified*. She remembered the pictures in her gods and goddesses book. What were the ones with horns and four legs called? Minotaurs?

"All right." At least the old woman threw that bone back at

Jo. It could have meant she promised to send help or could have meant nothing at all.

Jo watched Son's fedora on the washwoman's head bob down Church Street until it melted into the rainy gloom. What a tiny thing under that pile of clothing. Jo thought of all the mountains of dirty clothes they'd handed over to the washwoman, how she'd returned them all, again and again, for years on end, spotless, smelling of sunshine and bleach and starch. How many of their cells had they exchanged with her and her family over the years? Jo must be covered in them, and the old woman in hers. It was like they were related by blood. How much she must know about their most intimate habits. Every day of their lives they wore on their bodies, next to their most private places, the work of her hands, the tiniest hands Jo had ever seen on an adult.

And not to even know her name! There was a shame in it all.

Jo shivered and rubbed her legs, which were bare under her gown and robe. She forced herself to turn back to the lonely square of a house, wanting instead to strike out alongside the old woman and walk away from her mother's pain, to come to the rescue, find someone who would save the day. Clearly her father had failed dismally in his role as protector of the family. Where *was* he? Even if he hadn't found little Tommy, he should have come back to see about Jo and her mother.

Perhaps it was her vision that was cockeyed, but the house looked off-kilter, as if it were a giant ship riding a wave in the ocean. Had it been knocked off its foundation? Part of the roof too, now an off-center peak, which looked like a gable that had been added as an afterthought. Through the sheets of rain she could make out the fallen oak, the perfectly rounded shapes of her mother's crepe myrtles. In midwinter, Alice insisted on heavy pruning of the crepe myrtle bushes. She wanted them to stay small so that all the energy would go back into the blooms, not the branches. The branches, compacted and tangled by years of cutting back, had grown thick as privet hedges. In July, under sweltering heat, the blooms popped from their little balls, then came on like gangbusters, hot pink, breathtaking. When Jo was little, she would pick the balls and squeeze them, popping out the pink fluff. Now, in early April, the bushes had already begun to surge and leaf out.

**JO HEARD** the baby before she saw him. A rattle was all, then a little cough, like an old man clearing his throat; then, as if the baby had just been gathering his wind, an *ahhh*. Then silence, only the sound of the driving rain.

Jo stopped dead and peered through the rain. She didn't fully trust her senses. Her ears had been popping since right before the storm hit. She was at the moment stone deaf in her left ear. She could hear sounds but couldn't tell what direction they were coming from. There was a constant roar in the bad ear, which was on the same side as her broken arm. She felt split in half, one side functional, one not.

Was she dreaming? Was the storm a nightmare she was just awakening from? Was the sound she heard one of little Tommy's bloodcurdling screams, waking her out of a dead sleep, as she had been woken almost every night since he was born?

Suddenly, the rain stopped. It just ceased and then there was a blessed stillness, a deep quiet, and then a wren sang forth, and the sky, glory hallelujah, began to lighten. Unbelievably, the sun was rising, first pink and throbbing with intention, then smearing the horizon in a butter yellow.

With her good right hand, Jo rubbed her eyes. In the light

from the rising sun, she saw the blood on her fingers. The shard of glass above and between her eyes, her horn as she had come to think of it, gave out a deep throb, a warning. She touched it gingerly. Just the light touch of her fingers made it flare and burn. It felt larger than she remembered. Was it possible that it was working its way out? If so, would she bleed to death? Would her father never come? In the growing light she could now look up and see it clearly, see the tip of the thing. It shone pink, reflecting the sun's blessed rays. On the sidewalk a prism of color.

She looked around. The street in front of her house was deserted; she could hear shouts and banging out in the distance. What she'd thought was a baby's cry must have been some effect from the storm in her ears. Or maybe it was just wishful thinking. Jo didn't have high hopes for little Tommy. She remembered the power of the raging wind, how it had lifted her off her feet, blown her through the air from back door to front like she was a leaf or a small branch. To be blown through a second-floor window, heaven knows how far! What chance did a little child have in that storm? She pictured a town littered with dead babies, blown from who knows where. Little Tommy was probably in the next county.

But what a miracle for her poor mother if he were alive! Alice McNabb would be the happiest person in Tupelo, maybe the whole world! There would be no more porch sitting or paregoric sipping or napping the day away. Her mother would be back to her old self, bold and lovely and strong: transmogrified. She'd tie up her hair and get her hoe and weed the flower beds, her face splotched and smiling, that wild hair of hers slipping out of the kerchief every which way; she would drive Mr. Nesbitt the grocer crazy with orders for the good food she would cook;

she'd give Jo a Word to Keep every day of the week so that Jo's
notebook would runneth over. The two of them would head out
together every morning, the way they did before Tommy came,
her mother winding her hair into a bun, prettily flushed, shouting orders: hurry and don't forget this or that and I may be late
this afternoon because of a teachers' meeting, and then the two
of them would scramble for books and papers and their purses
before leaving for the six-block walk to school. On Saturdays
the whole family would all go to the picture show at the Lyric
Theatre again and see John Wayne movies and then out for ice
cream or they would be invited to play games of croquet on green
lawns and drink endless glasses of lemonade at people's houses.

They would take little Tommy everywhere, and he'd just have
to calm down, settle down. And if he didn't, well, who cared?
He was a baby, he couldn't help himself. And nobody stayed a
baby forever; eventually everybody grew up and stopped teething and using diapers and drinking from bottles and screaming
all the time. Poor little Tommy, the life he might have had! She
would have taught him to ride a bike, she would have let him
come visit when she went to college at Belhaven or Millsaps
down in Jackson. He could have been her husband-to-be's best
man in her wedding, and after that a young, boisterous uncle
horsing around with her children, who would have adored him.
(She pushed away the thought that little Tommy, should he be
among the living, was *already an uncle*.)

She should have been a better sister. The last time she held
Tommy he had been crying (as usual) as she struggled to ram a
bottle in his mouth. She had gotten aggravated and pushed it in
too hard, hitting the back of his throat. His face turned a bright
red and he gagged alarmingly. She put him on her shoulder then

and patted him on the back (too hard?) and the gagging turned back to screaming. What an unpleasant baby! Nothing seemed to please him. Her poor mother! No wonder she'd been down and out since he'd been born.

Jo wondered if she had been like that as a baby. If so, she was deeply sorry. A wisp of a thought floated through her mind, made the more terrible when words reached out and captured it. *Would her mother be better off without Tommy? Would they all be?*

The horror, the *shame*, of thinking, not to speak of articulating, such a thought! Here she'd gone and killed off one brother and was wishing for the death of the other, a defenseless baby! What kind of person was she to think such a wicked thing! What kind of sister? She took it all back. If only she could find Tommy, she would make it up to him. She would be a better sister. She would take the best care of him anybody could possibly take.

NOW THE sky was truly light, and miracle of all miracles, the sun was coming on strong. In the first light, she gasped at the damage around her. Before the storm, her town, at least the part she lived in, had been covered over in trees, the giant oaks and magnolias and the smaller gum trees that gave Tupelo its Creek name. Now, stretching out before her, the few trees that still stood were so broken, twisted, and stripped of leaves and bark, they looked as if they might have been dead for years. Jo could see straight across the town. It looked like a scene from a newsreel of Europe in the last war. The fires continued to burn, the smoke making dark clouds against the clearing sky, but she could see even beyond the smoke, into the distance. In that moment she imagined she could see the place at the horizon where the earth began to curve into its ball, where the actual latitudinal turn was. She'd never seen this far in her life and it felt like a tremendous relief to look beyond the town. How vast and beautiful the ruin!

Immediately she felt guilty again, this time for entertaining such thoughts about her whole town, her dear dear town. She could only imagine what sufferings lay beyond her own yard. And here her own mother was, her leg shattered and little Tommy flown away and Son lying there on the living room floor stone-cold dead. (She needed to cover him with something. Isn't that what you do with the dead?) Her broken arm gave out a twinge, as if to remind her that it too was in dire shape, it too needed her attention and sympathy. She resolved to go inside and get one of her father's woolen scarves and wrap the arm to her chest, keep it from swinging loose. She had never felt more alone or full of possibility. Everything, it seemed, was up to her.

When she turned to go up the first flight of steps to the house and back inside, she was so lost in thought she'd actually forgotten that strange little cry she'd thought she heard.

Then something snagged her eye. Something out of place. One of her mother's crepe myrtle bushes, bare now, its new leaves blown into the next county, suddenly quivered as if it had been seized by a palsy. Once, when she was little, she had gotten up one hot summer night for a glass of water and seen something similar: two young raccoons playing in the mimosa tree outside the kitchen window, shaking the branches, sending waves of sweetness from its flowers through the screen and into the house.

One of Snowball's kittens? Then, as she paused and turned to look more closely, whatever it was that was shaking the bush let out a little sigh, not a cry, just a little expulsion of air, as if whatever it was had given up.

Jo walked over toward the bush and bent down to look. The action caused her eyes to cloud over suddenly; a smudge of something dark floated across her line of vision. Was it blood or rain or some combination? She straightened up and wiped her eyes with her sleeve. Blood again, pinker now. Brighter.

The bush had stopped quivering. Maybe it had been a bird, or a flock of those small brown birds, finches that turned nondescript in the fall and bright yellow again by midsummer, that liked to eat the seed balls from the crepe myrtles, landing in raucous groups and feasting enthusiastically, then, in one motion, flying on, to swoop in on the next one in their path. What do birds do in a tornado? She wondered about Snowball and her kittens. Had any of them survived? She wondered about Essie and her daughter Winifred, who lived in half a house perched on the side of a gully up on the Hill, the other half occupied by a family of two adults and four teenage boys named Matthew, Mark, Luke, and John, who kept Essie and Winifred up at night with their raucous goings-on. Some mornings Essie came to work bleary-eyed and complaining. Now there were streaks of gray in her hair and she wore support hose for the ulcers on her legs; her mouth had changed too, the lips thinner and set in a straight line. When she was younger, Jo had thought that Essie loved her the same way her mother loved her; but recently she'd come to understand that Essie's kindness and good nature should not be mistaken for love, that Essie had Winifred, who was now at Howard University in Washington, DC, and who would send for Essie as soon as she could finish college and find a job up North. Jo knew all this because Essie had left a letter from Winifred on the kitchen table. Oddly she had left it propped up against the salt and pepper shakers the way a person would leave a note specifically for another person. The letter said to hold on, that Winifred was coming to get her mother out of that hellhole in another year.

JO BENT over the crepe myrtle bush again, and just as she did, she saw something fleshy. This something opened and closed. It had multiple parts. She was studying human anatomy, and for one sickening moment, she thought it was a piece of intestine. A shred of something from deep inside the body. Something that should never be seen in ordinary life and certainly not in a bush.

She looked closer and then what she was seeing began its long swim along her synapses and neuron connections, and finally, finally, her brain said, *Excuse me. Please pay attention.* It was a tiny hand, she realized after this terrible pause in which anything could have happened, anything at all. The little hand was beckoning her, reaching out to her.

*You.*

She took a deep breath and touched the fingertips. They were icy. They latched on.

She looked closer, peering down into the bush, her mouth partly open, her head feeling the weight of the horn. Again, there was a pause in which the information from the eye had to travel again, faster now, only a split second this time, during which she didn't breathe. Then the information came back, and her brain said: *A baby.* Then the full sentence: *There is a baby in the crepe myrtle bush.* Her brain said: *Pick it up. Be careful.*

The baby was wedged in the bush; she could see its little arms, and below and between them the crown of its head. It seemed to be standing upright in the bush with its arms held straight up, as if it were preparing to do a cartwheel. Jo reached in with both hands and took hold of its little wrists, her own broken arm throbbing with the motion. She began to pull, waves of pain shooting up from her left arm into her left shoulder and across her upper back. The baby proceeded to shriek as if she were hitting it, beating it.

*You? Could it be?*

She let go for a moment and the baby shrieked louder, its little hands flailing and reaching.

"Ok," she said, and her voice quieted it. She reached in again, this time parting the branches carefully and taking hold of the baby at the armpits. She began to tug, her left elbow now a chicken drumstick being pulled apart. The baby took a deep breath and then began again at a higher pitch. It was kicking too. Jo could tell by the movement of the branches below it.

"Push!" she hollered at it, as if it were a mother giving birth to itself. She realized as the word came from her lips that the poor little thing was totally helpless.

In her good ear she heard a branch snap, then another. She pulled harder. Then something shifted and gave way. Then here it came, scraped and bloodied and fighting mad. A boy! Naked as the day he came into the world, his little genitals, shriveled from the cold, retracted between those delicious fat rolls on his thighs.

Squirming and screaming bloody murder, furious and red-faced and utterly alive. There was something biblical about him, something that struck a deep chord: Moses in the bulrushes. With her good right arm, Jo snatched him to her chest like a football and began to run; then her careful brain said, *Slow down, be careful, don't trip, don't drop, don't run. Don't.* She slowed to a fast walk, up the two flights to the tiled front porch, across the porch, through the opening where the front door had been into the gloom of the living room, past her brother's body, larger than she remembered, and to her mother who still lay at the foot of the stairs.

Jo touched her mother's shoulder with her toe. "May-May, wake up, I found Tommy! He's alive!"

Alice's eyelids fluttered, then closed again.

"Mother!" Jo knelt beside Alice. Tommy had stopped kicking and crying now. He was cold, too cold, and still and quiet. One of his arms dangled at her side. His head had collapsed between her breasts, his face covered in blood and scratches. Jo needed her mother, *his* mother, to tell her what to do.

Alice opened her eyes, looked first at Jo, then at the baby in her arms. She rose on one elbow. "Oh! Did you find him? Did you find Tommy? Is he alive?" Her eyes rolled back in her head and she slid back to the floor.

Jo looked around. Behind her, in the dim light, the house revealed the full disaster of the storm. Everything sodden, nothing where it should have been. Through the opening where the front door had been, a thin line of light. Beside it, Son. In the night, something in him had changed. At first she couldn't figure it out; then she saw that his arm had shifted and was now flung outward, the palm up, as if he were gesturing to make a point. Had the incoming rain moved the arm or was this some final fumbling for expression? He was certainly dead as dead could be. His eyes stared, his belly had swelled. There was a peculiar odor in the room now, not totally unpleasant, though

she knew it soon would be, but more like apple cider. The morning light played on his face, his open eyes. She could not look at
him another minute. She laid the baby on the floor at her feet.
He lay there, eyes closed and head turned to one side, his little
mouth sucking mechanically. She spotted a loose napkin on the
floor and placed it over her brother's face.

She came back into the hall and got behind her mother and,
with her good hand, took her under one arm, and tried to raise
her to a sitting position against the wall. Alice didn't budge. Jo
took her good arm and put it under her mother on the other side
and tried again, pain coursing through the elbow up the arm
into the shoulder and on up to Jo's neck. The arm was too weak.
Through her mother's wet clothes, Jo felt Alice's body burning
like a furnace.

On the floor, the baby had begun to shake, his mouth wide
but no sound coming out. Was he having a fit? Was he dying? Jo
eased her mother back to the floor and ran back to the baby. She
sat down beside him and with her good arm pulled him into her
lap, then up against her chest. He turned suddenly toward one
side, began to make a sucking motion with his lips. He brushed
her nipple and tried to take hold through her wet gown. She felt
something tighten, then relax. *This is what it is to be a mother.*

Jo remembered something from her Campfire Girls book
about shock, she needed to warm the baby up. Clutching him to
the side like a football in her one good arm, she scrambled to her
feet and went into the bathroom. She fumbled in the cabinet.
The towels on top were soaked, but underneath there were a
few that were merely damp. She loosened her grip on the baby's
head and reached for one of the least damp ones, being careful
not to strike the cabinet shelf with either her horn, which now
seemed to have settled in and become a permanent part of her

body, or Tommy's head. Then she sat down on the cold wet
bathroom floor with him in her lap and tried to wrap him in the
towel.

It was a trick with one working arm, and in the midst of it he
began to wiggle and cry, a new kind of cry. It was softer, no fits
of rage but steady and sad and resigned. Turning him this way
and that, Jo finally got the towel around him. He cried on.

From the hall her mother called out, "Is he all right? What are
you doing to him? Is he hurt? Bring him back to me. I didn't even
get a good look at him."

Jo got onto her knees and then rose shakily with him in her
right arm. She took him back into the hall and laid him on the
floor. What she needed was clean water and a rag to wash the
cuts and scrapes all over his body. Then she remembered, better
yet, the rubbing alcohol she'd poured on the old washwoman's
feet. She went to get a washcloth.

When she came back with the cloth, the baby had stopped
crying and fallen into an exhausted sleep. A piece of sunlight
played along his curved belly. His hair was wet and plastered to
his head. There was more of it than Jo remembered.

Jo shook her mother. "May-May, listen to me. I need your
hands. You got to hold him while I do this. You got to keep him
from hurting himself. This is going to sting."

Alice's eyes fluttered, then closed again. Jo put the baby on
Alice's stomach and placed her mother's hands on him.

She poked her mother, then patted her hands. "Just hold on to
him." Her mother's hands clamped on. Jo unwrapped the towel
so that the baby's front side was exposed and began to dab on
the alcohol. Tommy's eyes popped open, and he began to scream
and thrash about and kick at Alice's chest. Alice almost lost her
grip on him.

"Hold him, May-May!"

When they finished with the front, Jo turned him over. There was a gash under his arm, but otherwise the scratches were superficial.

"Is he hurt?" asked Alice, over the baby's screams. Her head hung to one side. "I can't see anything. Why can't I see?"

Jo sat down alongside her mother and took him back, rolling him from Alice's stomach to her own lap. He started up again, a quiet dogged whimper, without much hope attached. Jo scrambled to her feet, locking him to her side with her good right arm. He must be hungry, and worse yet, thirsty. In her Campfire Girls first aid manual, dehydration was on the list of top five "Possible Killers in the Wild," alongside heart attack and heat stroke and snakebite.

She took the baby into the kitchen. She turned on the faucet at the sink. Some reddish brown sludge sputtered out, then nothing. Normally Tommy drank a powdered substance mixed in water; her mother made up his bottles six at a time. The icebox door was ajar. Jo cursed the washwoman for leaving it that way. Now the formula would be ruined! But when Jo pulled out a bottle, it was still cool. Normally she would have put it in a pot of water on the stove to warm it, but the stove, splattered in mud and debris, looked untrustworthy.

Standing in front of the icebox, she looked around the kitchen. Cabinet doors were missing and the cabinets were empty. Mud and broken dishes and two overturned chairs. Oddly, Essie's one chair at the kitchen table was in its usual place. She felt suddenly weak-kneed. How easily her own life could have been blown away! What an insignificant pawn she was, the instrument of one brother's death, the means of another's rescue! How

little human will had to do with any of it. She'd been brought up
on the sour doctrine of predestination, which she'd not for a single minute believed, thinking, arrogantly, that she was master
of her own fate, the way the poem said, captain of her own soul.
But now she reconsidered. The storm was the master, and it
had blown her and her little brother through the air without so
much as a thought. And where did that storm come from? Who
thought it up? Who said she lives and he dies? He comes and she
goes? The baker but not the candlestick maker?

She sat down in Essie's chair, situating Tommy on her lap. She
offered the nipple. The baby acted affronted by the offer. He spit
it out, crying hard now, furious at the world. His face bloomed
red, then purple with rage. He screamed louder, his body now
thankfully warmer. Again, he turned to Jo's breast; again that
distracting, pleasant zing from stem to stern.

She touched his lips with the bottle, let a bit of formula drip
on them. He smacked them now and began to suck a little. Then
he began to pull hard at the nipple and settled in, his eyes wide
and watchful. For the first time since finding him, Jo relaxed a
little. He was going to live. Which meant she had managed to
save him. She shuddered to think what would have happened to
him if she hadn't followed the old washwoman out to the street.

She thought of her trudging through the ruined town, wearing Son's shoes and fedora, the one he was so proud of. When
he'd run off with all those hats from Reed's, which Jo thought
at the time was by far the most amusing thing he'd ever done,
he'd neglected to return the gray one. He'd put it on a top shelf
in the downstairs hall closet, at the back, so that no one would
notice. (Jo of course did because she watched him like a hawk,
measured his every move.) After awhile, when the brouhaha

died down, he began to wear it when he went out, the way a grown man would wear a hat to the office or church, except of course there was no office—no work of any kind that Jo could discern—and certainly no churchgoing.

Jo wanted to cry over Son; he was, after all, her brother. She just needed time, was all. Now she was too busy taking care of everybody. She'd found herself rather good at it and wondered briefly what it would be like to be a nurse. A doctor was out of the question, of course, but she would have liked that even better: to have the knowledge to stop suffering in its tracks, to say, *There now, take your medicine and you'll be all better, I guarantee it*, the way Dr. Campbell said a month ago when she was in his office for her tonsils, which were probably going to need to be removed, he told her mother this last time. How remarkable that there were doctors who cut you open and looked at your insides, took this or that offending organ out, then sewed you back up again, like you were a Christmas turkey. Jo would have liked to be that kind of doctor; there was a mystery about the body that intrigued her. Even her mother's protruding bone thrilled her in some strange way, though, of course, she would never put such a thought into words, and shame on her that it had blown through her head. At first, when the bone was still wet, it had looked under the beam of the flashlight like wet rubber and she'd wanted to touch the shards, she'd wanted to fit them back together, to rummage around, touching the networks of blood vessels and tissue that seemed so irretrievable. The wound seemed somehow not connected to her mother at all.

TOMMY HAD come to the end of the bottle and gone to sleep, his mouth slack and twitching. The formula had dripped down his chin, but Jo didn't have an extra hand to wipe his mouth. Toward the end of feeding, Jo felt the towel grow damper and smelled urine. A good sign.

The sunlight had begun to creep across the kitchen floor, across the mud and debris. A crystal bowl from the dining room breakfront lay upside down on the counter, refracting the light, casting, in that moment, the whole kitchen in dappled color. Jo looked down at Tommy. Streaks of yellow and blue and red played across his sleeping face, making him suddenly unrecognizable, as if he were composed of pieces that didn't quite fit.

Was she hallucinating the colors? Such a wave of weariness washed over her that it was all she could do to walk back to the hall to see about her mother. As she rounded the corner, she saw that Alice lay still and quiet, her head turned to the steps as if she were waiting for someone important to descend, her face the color of chalk. There were lines around her mouth; a large maple leaf, still green and fresh, was plastered to her cheek.

She began to mumble, then turned to Jo, her eyes burning. "Look in the buffet," she whispered. "Get out the bottle of sherry in there."

Jo picked her way into the dining room. Outside the dining room windows, now all shattered, the nandina bushes had been stripped of their red berries. When Jo was a girl, she had watched wasps and yellow jackets fight over the little white blossoms while the bumblebees and honeybees crawled among them companionably. In winter her mother had taught her the names of the birds that ate the berries: Old Bully Bluejay, Mr. Robin Redbreast, Miss Rosie the Cardinal, Nutty Nuthatch, Loudmouth Uncle Wren. Alice relished birds; she grew sunflowers for the seeds and put them on trays during the short winters when food was scarce. She'd planted the nandinas for

their berries, not their blossoms. All this, of course, BT: Before
Tommy. Over the past winter, the birds had been on their own,
just as Jo had been.

Jo looked around the dining room for the buffet. It was a massive piece of furniture; the only wall that could accommodate it
was directly under the row of shattered windows. It had pre-
sided over exactly one hundred years of holiday meals, from 1836
when her mother's grandfather, then a boy of four, had traveled
cross-country from Charleston to frontier Mississippi, empty
then of all but a few straggler Indians, mostly Chickasaws in the
northeast, the state having been recently cleared out for settle-
ment. Jo and Son had found arrowheads in the garden out back.
It was a game when they were little, to see who could gather the
most by suppertime. The buffet had a story; it had been brought
across country on a wagon drawn by mules the size of oxen. It
had fallen off when a wheel cracked open and the wagon tipped
and then Alice's people's people had had to fix the wheel and put
the buffet back onto the wagon. When Jo first heard the story,
she didn't understand what her mother meant by *people's people*.
*Servants,* her mother had explained, *they walked all the way, poor
things, and with those heavy chains around their ankles, cut just
long enough to walk,* and then Jo had understood. In recent memory, the open coffin of Jo's grandfather, Mort's father, had been
placed on the buffet for the visitation like a large piece of meat
on a platter and then had sat there overnight until the funeral
the next morning.

Now, unbelievably, the buffet was *not there,* under the windows, the way it had always been. Nor was it anywhere else
in the dining room. It had vanished into thin air. The dining room mirror was there, on its side, slammed up against a

wall. Remains of the eight chairs were scattered about, legs and arms here, there, and everywhere. Even the tea table, Jo's favorite piece of furniture in the house, was there, although it was turned over and one wheel was missing. But the buffet, it was simply gone. Jo rubbed her eyes, forgetting for a moment the thing in her head. A jolt of pain hit her between the eyes. The jaggedly broken windows glared at her like jack-o'-lantern faces.

She turned wearily and headed back into the hall. Alice was pouring sweat and biting her lip. A splash of sunlight caught her nose and made it seem bulbous. "The sherry?" she asked.

"It's gone," said Jo.

Her mother's eyes were still closed. "Just look in the buffet. It's right there. I need some bad, honey."

"It's gone too."

"What's gone?"

"The buffet, it blew away. It's gone."

Alice opened her eyes. "No!"

"Wait," said Jo. "What about some paregoric?"

"In the kitchen, up in the cabinet," her mother whispered.

Jo walked around her and headed back to the kitchen. Surprisingly, some bottles of paregoric, some partly full and some empty, were still on the shelf to the left of the icebox. She brought a bottle to her mother and lifted Alice's head with her good right hand and placed the bottle in her hand. "I can't open the cap."

"Use your teeth."

Jo put her mother's head down and took back the bottle and gripped the top with her teeth. There was leakage around the top and a bitter taste. She twisted with her good hand, and the top came loose. She raised her mother's head a second time.

Alice took the bottle and brought it to her lips and drank down the brown liquid.

"Wasn't that a lot?" Jo asked.

Her mother didn't answer. Her eyelids fluttered and her head jerked once, then again, and then leapt with a life of its own from Jo's right hand. By instinct, Jo leaned over and caught her mother's head in her left hand so it wouldn't slam to the floor. She felt something give way in her elbow. It was a crisp sound, like a twig that had been stepped on. She saw spots.

She felt her knees give and tried to ease herself and the baby down to the floor. In her arm little Tommy flinched, then he stretched first one arm then the other, and, just as her gorge rose from the pain in her arm and saliva flooded her mouth and she leaned to the side to retch, he smiled up at her benevolently and urinated through the towel. Jo didn't remember Tommy having such a fetching smile. She wanted to laugh at the absurdity of that smile and smile back, but the pain pressed down like a vise. In order not to scream and scare the baby, in order not to faint and perhaps collapse on top of the baby, she instead began to hum and her humming quickly got louder and louder until she began to sound like an aggravated hornet, like a whole nest of aggravated hornets.

Was there no one coming to save them? Where was her father? Here he'd gone and left them high and dry with nothing to hope for, except whatever a little colored woman with a bad foot and her own fish to fry could rustle up. If a girl couldn't count on her own father, who could she count on?

*Whom*, her mother would have said had she been in any shape to worry about grammar and dangling prepositions: *On whom can you count?*

# 7

# 8 A.M.

Dovey walked in a dream. Her head throbbed and her foot throbbed. After a while, they throbbed together, at the same time.

From under the big fedora, which smelled like Brylcreem and cheese, she heard drums. She touched her ear and came away with blood on her fingers.

The drums drummed on. Before Virgil there'd been a Shake Rag man who played a pair of bongos. Played them hard and fast, with his palms, and one time, when he really got into it, his elbows, deep into the wet-hot summer nights, down at Freddie's juke joint on East Main. She would sneak down there, waiting until her aunt was asleep then tiptoeing on bare feet out the back, careful not to rattle the kettle on the woodstove as she clicked shut the door. She would feel those drumbeats in her chest even before getting within earshot of Freddie's. She was just a girl then, but they rocked her and she'd get up before God and everybody and dance, hopping up and down in her bare feet on the splintery wood dance floor, not a thought in her head. No why and why and why. No Mama or Daddy. No Janesy or Uldine or little Blue, sweet boy Blue. The Shake Rag man said she looked like a little jackrabbit out there, hopping high in the air, like she was getting ready to take to the sky. "You got a cottontail?" he asked with a wink.

What was it she listened for when she listened to the Shake Rag man play? Was it the sound of the drums or something lodged deep inside the belly of the sound, under the heart?

When the Shake Rag man left Shake Rag, he left alone, in the dead of early morning, leaving even his drums behind, scared off by who knows what. Something about a woman, somebody's wife, maybe white, maybe not. Chasing tail all right, but somebody else's.

It was said he had a wife and some children over in Itawamba County. By day, he'd worked as a yard man all over town so who knows what some white lady might have decided she wanted when she looked out the window and saw him bent over her irises, shiny with sweat. Or maybe it was just the Itawamba wife getting crazy from all that sitting at home nights. Maybe she'd sharpened her knife.

THANKFULLY, THE walk into town was downhill. Dovey put her good foot down and slid the other one to follow, the huge shoe getting smaller and smaller as the cut foot swelled. No hopping or dancing now, maybe never again. She skirted huge water-filled holes on the ground where the root balls of giant trees had come up. One of them had a man in it. He was floating facedown on top of the water. A blessing she hadn't wandered down this way in the dead of night and driving rain. A blessing the white girl had given her the shoes. No telling what kind of trouble might have found her.

Now she walked through a desert where there were no trees,

just pieces of leftover trunks from the storm, bare-limbed against the sky. Piles of ruined, broken things two stories high, not just the trees but houses and cars and wagons and doll babies and toy trains and diapers and broken china and dead birds and squirrels.

There was something about the walking that seemed old. Her grandmother from Alabama had come to northeast Mississippi in a wagon train, having been sold to the young couple from South Carolina. It was three years after the stars fell. She skipped her way to the new territory, out ahead of her mother and daddy and older brother, who walked clip-clop alongside the wagons.

Why clip-clop? Dovey had asked.

Her grandmother had shaken her head, pressed her lips in one long line.


**NOW DOVEY** came upon strange things, things that made her stop dead in her tracks.

A cock crowed, then sauntered in front of her, its waddle quaking angrily. Not a single feather left on it. Looking like it just emerged from the egg.

She came upon a nanny goat tied to a small tree whose top and branches had been sheared off. What was left of the tree was covered in clothes. Pajamas and nightgowns and girdles and a wedding dress turned gray as a tombstone. A sealskin coat plastered on the stub of a branch like a large dead animal. Dovey spotted a scarf and pulled it down and wrapped it around her neck, then thought the better of taking white folks' clothes without permission. Who knew what some Miss Lady might accuse her of? She untied the scarf and let it drop to the ground.

The goat bleated miserably, pulling at the rope. It picked up the scarf and started chewing on it. Dovey recognized the goat as a family pet, but the house it belonged to, the house she'd come to and gone from, picking up the dirty, bringing back the clean for the past two decades, a fancy house with huge columns inhab- ited by some people named High, had crumbled into a pile of timber set in place for a giant bonfire. The Highs, now brought low, were nowhere in sight. She stopped and untied the animal. At least it might find some grass left in this world to graze on, if the storm had left a blade or two. At least it wouldn't starve to death. It ran away, what remained of the scarf dangling from its mouth like a grotesque tongue. Then Dovey looked up at the pile of timber and gasped when she saw the arm and leg sticking out from one end of a fallen column; a sodden napkin covered the upturned face at the other end, plastered down by rain like a mask.

*Old sun, new day, things are going to go my way.* It was the song her mother used to sing to wake all of them for school in the morning. It popped into her head and took up residence there, next to the drums. They played well together. As she walked along, the shoes had become an aggravation. They were soaked through now, heavy as shovels on her feet, *toting ugly, toting sin,* so heavy she considered taking them off, an idea she rejected the minute it posed itself in her mind.

Unbelievably, old sun was climbing now, just like it did any ordinary day. How dare the world go on! She shut her eyes and saw little Promise hurtling through the air, Virgil's crushed bed. Now where'd that old man of hers gotten himself off to? She'd never had to ask that question. Virgil was true-blue, solid as a rock, a man who was always right where he said he'd be, not one of them run-around, juke-jointing kind. Never been slippery a day in his life.

She stopped for a moment and tried to think above the drums in her head. She was heading south on Church, toward Main Street. Should she turn around and head back north, back up to the Hill? If Dreama and them were alive, is that where they'd return to? Doubtful. Food and shelter would be downtown where the white folks were. If Dreama and them hadn't had the sense knocked out of them by the storm, they'd head into town, especially with the baby. You had to feed and water a baby else you could lose it. The three of them had maybe caught up with each other and would be looking for Dovey now. Maybe Virgil was busy dragging Gum Pond for her that very minute.

And wouldn't that be just like him? Since Charlesetta died, Virgil had turned into a bit of a pessimist. Truth be told, his down-and-old moods followed Dovey's spells of coldness as predictably as the moon following the sun. She'd tried to forgive him for Charlesetta, truly she had, but those spells of hers had a mind of their own, rising like yeast on this day or that, and then all she could see when she looked at her husband was that pine box of a coffin being lifted indifferently from the freight car by the M&O conductor and station manager and laid on the gravel platform beside the track. When she gave him that look, the one with the coffin in it, he would know. His cough would get worse and he wouldn't work on the house or help people fix what needed fixing. He wouldn't come up behind her and pick her up and talk about how scrawny she was, how she needed some skin on those bones. He would develop a look about the mouth that was almost, but thankfully not quite, a sneer. After work (he always went to work no matter how bad he felt) he sat himself down on the front porch and stared into space. People would stay away. *Virgil got the fantods again*, they'd say. Her fault, though only she and Virgil knew that. Neither of them spoke of it, to each other or anyone else.

She almost turned around and headed home, wanting more than anything in the world to find him sitting on the log pile that had been their front porch.

She decided to take her chances with downtown.

One step with the good foot, then drag the other. One step, then drag. The drums drummed on.

Up ahead, as she crossed Jefferson and neared Main, people milled about in a cluster, jabbering and crying and calling out names. She tried to get the attention of a white woman who looked uninjured, but the woman shoved her to the side. "Out of my way, nigger," she said when Dovey didn't yield what was left of the sidewalk. Dovey stumbled and almost fell but caught herself. When she looked down to get her footing, the drums became one long beat that bore down for one unbearable moment, as if the fedora had become a vise.

A small crowd had gathered around what was left of a huge tree, now stripped of bark and leaves and twisted into a cross. Between the two crisscrossed branches at the top, something large.

Dovey looked up but the sun spliced her line of vision, blinding her. She drew closer (step, drag; step, drag), then looked up again. A woman in a nightgown lay drooped across the fork in the branches, a white woman, young and pretty, though getting less so by the minute. One leg hung down, a bedroom slipper dangled from the foot. Everyone milled about, the men debating how to get her down. A man knelt and prayed in a booming voice at the base of the tree, his face turned to the trunk. *Deliver us.*

Some women stood around him, wailing and carrying on. "That's little Myrtle Crisp, the new teacher from Oxford," one said to the other. "The one that took Alice McNabb's job when Alice had her nervous breakdown back in the fall. What a crying shame."

When Dovey was a girl, she'd tagged along with her father in the late fall when he went out to Savery Woods to hunt squirrel and possum. It was November, and she remembered enjoying the way the dead leaves crunched under her bare feet. Her father had just turned to tell her to walk like an Indian when a shadow fell and she looked up and saw the man up in the tree, his arms tied above his head, his trunk burned black as coal, the flesh on his legs welded together by the flames so that he looked like a merman with one large flipper hanging up there. All her hungry eyes could do was look and look, unsure of what they were seeing but curious, oh so curious.

Even before he turned to look up too, her father had known. He turned only his head, the rest of his body staying completely still, his hand squeezing her shoulder hard, indicating that she should stay still too. He took only a sideways glance upward; then, without even seeming to move a muscle, he felt for her and got her around her waist and picked her up and carried her away from the clearing and back into the woods, forcing her face-down and away. Lickety-split, lickety-split, his feet making all the racket in the world, kicking the leaves right up into her face so that she began to cough and sneeze.

When he got her away from the clearing and back deep into the woods, he put her down, took her hand, and half-pulled, half-dragged her until they reached the M&O tracks on the woods side of Gum Pond. There he let go of her hand. Shaken by his uncharacteristically rough treatment of her, she felt her legs buckle. He touched her on the shoulder and took her arm again, this time more gently, and pulled her along.

"Daddy?" she began, as they threaded their way across the tracks.

"You didn't see nothing," he said. He spoke in a tone she'd never heard, like he was spitting gravel. He didn't turn his head to look at her.

She never told a soul, and they never spoke of it. But through the years, the merman in the tree never left her side. He hung there, above the clearing with its stomped-down grass, just to the left of her left eye. She never looked at him head-on, but he was always there, casting his long, bulky shadow like a big, slit-open fish.

She looked up again at the very moment the slipper hanging from one of the woman's feet fell softly and landed on the back of the praying man, who snatched it up and held it to his cheek. The woman's neck had been twisted into an unnatural angle, sideways and peeled back, white and tender as a radish, not forward and down and burnt black, the way the merman's had been. The woman looked like somebody in a picture show, a lady who'd gone to sleep up there in the tree and would soon awaken and burst into song. A flock of blackbirds circled, cawed, and then landed all around the lady in the tree, their heads bobbing up and down, as though urging her to wake on up, rise and shine.

*Old sun, new day.* Dovey walked on. Around her, houses still smoldered. In the distance she saw a blaze, heard sirens. She saw some white ladies and white boys in uniforms up ahead. She stopped one of the boys. "Where they taking the colored?" she asked.

He eyed her soberly. "Ma'am, you're bleeding down the side of your face. Looks gruesome. Is it coming out of your ear? Did you hit your head?"

*Ma'am?* The drums paused. He hadn't called her auntie or looked over her head when he spoke to her. The drums said he wasn't from around there. His uniform said CCC. The CCC boys were President Roosevelt's Civilian Conservation Corps; they'd been living in barracks out in the county for a year now, planting trees, building earthen dams and playgrounds and schools. They were poor and quiet and glad for the work, glad to have the $25 a month to send back home, plus five to keep for themselves. By some quirk, most of the ones around Tupelo were from Chicago, plain Midwestern boys with large round faces, soft-spoken and shy, invariably polite.

Dovey again reached under the fedora and touched the ear and came away with blood on her fingers. Where was it coming from? "Where they got the colored?" she asked again.

"They got morgues set up in the old Hardin's Bakery building and in the basement of the courthouse too. Got them piled up like cordwood, colored on one side of the room, white on the other. There's some colored laid out in the alleyway off Broadway too."

Dovey wasn't studying morgues. "I'm talking about live people. What about them what got hurt? What they done with them?"

The boy brightened. "They put some on the Frisco and took them north, up to Holly Springs and Memphis. Frisco's been coming and going all night once we got the tracks cleared. They loaded up the Accommodation with the wounded and backed the train up all the way to Memphis, then came on back for another load. Greyhound too, taking folks to Meridian and Columbus. They going all over the place."

"Colored too? They taking the colored up to Memphis?"

The boy looked down at his feet. "They're putting the Negroes in the boxcars. They took some of them down to the Lyric. They're using the stage to operate and the popcorn machine to clean the instruments. Chopping off arms and legs like they're chopping a load of wood, then propping folks up in a seat just like they're getting ready to run a picture show for them. Whole bunch of them arms and legs just piled up in a corner. Tried to make me gather them up and take them away, and I say no siree bobtail, I ain't gathering no arms and legs like a load of brush. Last I heard they ran out of ether and was using whiskey. People rowed up in there like sardines in a can, black and white together, waiting their turn at the table, screaming and hollering like the world coming to an end."

The boy's nose, Dovey noticed, was peeling. His face was ruddy and covered with freckles, his hair red and curly. "I'm looking for some folks of mine. You see a colored girl about sixteen? Light-skinned and pretty?"

"I don't think I seen nobody like that, but things is crazy in town. Everybody's running around trying to save the ones they can save, bury the ones they can't. Never seen so many undertakers in one place. Some mill folks named Burroughs down on South Thomas lost everybody in the family, thirteen in all, including a little baby."

Dovey shivered. A mule team clattered by, loaded with pine coffins.

"See what I told you?" the boy said.

Dovey touched her ear again. The drums under the fedora

had grown so loud she could barely hear the boy. "My folks ain't dead. I just need to find them. Anybody around who know who got took where?"

"Doubt it. No time for that. Lot of people hurt bad. Hospital roof fell in on some. Me, I'm going around saving people. Heading up to Gum Pond now. They're draining the pond."

What was wrong with her? As he headed in the opposite direction, she thought how much she could have told him, *should* have told him. How there was nobody left to save in Gum Pond. How he would have done better to head up to the corner of Church and Walnut. She should have told him about the white lady's leg, about the girl's piece of glass big as a steer horn. She laid it to the drums. They were too loud. Her thoughts a load of wash on the line, whipping in the wind.

"Wait up," she called out to the CCC boy. "Hold up." She hobbled toward him. "There's folks that need help up on Church Street. A girl and her mama. The mama's hurt bad, she's got a broke leg. You're going to need another fellow and a stretcher. Corner of Church and Walnut."

The boy ran back. "Yes, ma'am! Let me go get some of my buddies."

SHE WALKED on, slide-drag, slide-drag. At the corner of Church and Jefferson, she stumbled over a tire and fell. She broke her fall with her right hand, but the forward motion shot sparks through the bad foot and her right wrist began to keep rhythm with the head and foot.

She fell because she was looking up at the roof of the First Baptist Church, rather than down at her feet where she should have been looking. The church was on her weekly route because the First Baptists ducked each other in a swimming pool behind the altar and if you ducked you needed clean towels. Plus the First Baptists liked to eat after church so there were the white tablecloths. Each Monday morning she gathered the tablecloths and, if there'd been a baptism, the towels. In the middle of July, during revival week when there were duckings galore, she went twice. What got her attention on what was left of the roof were buzzards lined up on the raggedy edge gazing down at her. She studied their attitude and didn't care for it. *Get on, old buzzards,* she said to them loud and clear. She clapped her hands over her head. They ruffled their feathers and eyed her with interest.

The fall made her afraid in a new way, her head barely missing a shard of concrete where the sidewalk had cracked and upended. She began to tremble and couldn't stop. She felt suddenly unable to get back on her feet. The drums drummed on, faster now. She put her hands over her ears. Lying there, she saw feet go by. Bare feet, and then feet covered in everything imaginable—boots and high heels and wingtips and bedroom shoes and rags, sometimes in odd combinations. She sank back down. The sidewalk scraped her cheek but she didn't care. She couldn't go another step. She lay there and shut her eyes.

She slept for a while. Now somebody had taken her arm and tugged. She squinted upward. Old sun now directly overhead.

"Come on now, auntie, you don't want to get trampled on. Get on up from there." She looked up. A man. He was standing directly over her. The sun peered over his shoulder, blinding her. Who? She recognized the voice, but couldn't place it. The man's face was dark, though by the voice she could tell the man was white.

Now he leaned down and pulled at her arms and shoulders. She made an effort to rise, but her legs were rubbery. He shoved one arm under her shoulders, another under her legs, gathering her up like a little child. She opened her mouth to protest, but his arms felt solid and warm. There was something dreamlike about the way he held her, as if her own daddy had come back and was taking her to bed the way he used to when she was little, clucking softly under his breath, except that this man wasn't clucking, he was breathing hard under her weight. He smelled like starch and man sweat.

"Dovey?" the man said suddenly. "Dovey? Is that you?"

At the sound of the white man's voice, so close to her ear that it tickled, *saying her name, not once but twice,* Dovey began to struggle to get down. *Who?*

"Dovey, is that you?"

Dovey opened her eyes, and there he was. There he was up close and personal, the Judge, the Devil's daddy, the *dead* Devil's daddy. Wide awake now, she scrambled down from his arms, standing before him dizzy and fearful, still possessed by the sound of drums in her head.

"Dovey, is that you?" he asked a third time, bending over and peering at her as if she were out there in the distance somewhere, a distant star instead of nose to nose. His breath was sour, his sweat rank.

She looked up at him. She hadn't realized how large he was. It was not so much that he was tall, she knew that, but she was struck by the breadth of his chest and shoulders. He was shaped like a bull, and blackened by the sun's light, he looked like one. Instinctively, she shrank from him and started walking backward onto the lawn between the sidewalk and the church.

He followed her onto the grass. "Dovey, where's your grand-daughter and the baby? What happened to the baby?"

He sounded fretful, like a child himself, fussing and whining over some small matter: a toy or bedtime or some such.

"Don't rightly know," Dovey murmured, still moving away. "I'm looking all over for them. Virgil too."

"Trying to find my baby boy too," he said. "He flew right out the window. Can't go home till I find him. Alice'll have my hide." He looked over his shoulder as if worried that his wife would be standing behind him.

Flying babies. Last night the sky must have been full of them. She could see them as they must have been, hurtling through the night like dying stars. They didn't seem unhappy or afraid but rather full of themselves, cooing and laughing and reaching for the sun. Where were they now?

The drums drummed on, but just in her head now; her foot had gone dead. "You need to get on back home, baby or no baby," Dovey said. "You need to get on back. The girl and her ma'am in bad shape. They need tending to."

"Can't go back without my boy."

"The family you got left is the one you need to take care of. Go on home now. Your wife fell down the steps and broke her leg bad," said Dovey. She made a shooing motion with her hands. She didn't have time for white folk foolishness and the possibil-ity that flying babies could land without a scratch. She began walking, the dead foot treacherous and heavy, dead weight.

He turned to go and then stopped and turned back to her, his hand raised, as if to say something, to give her some instruction.

Dovey shooed him again. "Get on. No time to lose," she said sternly, as if she weren't talking to a white man, as if she were talking to a child.

He turned. There was a deep line between his eyes; he looked hawk-like. "There's no going back," he said. "There's never any going back from something like this."

She looked at him full in the face. "You can go anywhere on God's green earth if you got a mind to."

He looked at her like he knew it wasn't true, especially for her in that time and that place and she knew it wasn't true either, but she said it anyway, feeling the urgent necessity of making that particular declaration on that particular sidewalk next to the barely upright First Baptist Church, lily white and proud of it but now burdened with buzzards. Because, she figured, what else was there left to do now but declare her intention to make her way through this world, drums or no drums, foot or no foot, buzzards or no buzzards? So much of her life she had spent looking out a kitchen window at the blue blue world, watching the geese dust the sky on their way somewhere else, places she'd never get to, watching the clothes on the line and wondering when they would finally be dry, helpless before their natural progression.

Now she was in charge, taking action, putting out the one good foot, sliding the other dead-as-a-doornail one along behind. This was what her whole life had led her to, this sliding walk, this strange dance.

So she turned and left the Judge standing there, trying to decide whether to come or go, continue to search for his lost baby son or rescue his wife and daughter, and who would want to be faced with a decision like his? At least Dovey's mission was straightforward, find whoever was left. She turned down Jefferson to cut over to the Lyric Theatre. She would go there first and then, if necessary, to the morgues, and then, if none of that bore fruit, she would turn back toward the Hill in hopes that Virgil and Dreama and Promise had gone back home, or what was left of it.

She headed east on Jefferson, toward the courthouse and the Lyric. The closer she got to downtown the better things looked. The storm had spared most of the buildings, and there was little debris in the street except for broken glass and an occasional piece of furniture. She heard an agitated cackling above her and when she looked up, there was a coop of chickens directly overhead in a big oak. The chickens were clustered helplessly in one downward corner of the coop two and three birds deep. They pecked at one another, squawking and shitting and beating their wings against the sides of the coop. It was a low-lying branch. She reached up and unlatched the coop and they came tumbling out, wings flapping wildly.

She'd overshot the Lyric on Broadway but decided as she moved along to go first to the morgues, get that out of the way. Then she would allow herself to hold out hope. Before she reached the courthouse she heard a loudspeaker coming from the lawn. Someone was calling out names and announcements. As she drew near, she saw a crowd standing below, listening. They stood under the sheltering wings of the Temperance Lady, the massive statue erected by the Ladies' Temperance Society that normally shaded a group of old white men with seedy eyes who slouched about the town square sipping paregoric out of the little brown paper sacks they kept in their jacket pockets. At one side of the square, colored folks milled about, waiting for news, but no colored names were being called out, no announcements to or about anybody from up on the Hill or down in Shake Rag.

As Dovey approached the square, an open-bed truck clattered up, piled high with rough pine coffins. There were two men in the truck cab and two more hanging off the sides of the back. A Red Cross lady stood in the doorway to the courthouse. She went over to the driver of the truck and gestured toward the basement. Then she stepped back into the doorway and picked up a large black notebook and began to write and the men began to unload the boxes. They were all sizes, tiny ones and medium-sized ones and large ones.

The man on the loudspeaker called out a name Dovey didn't hear and a woman on the edge of the square collapsed onto the ground, the small group of people around her bending over her. Then he called out another name: "Burroughs baby." Women in the crowd began to wail. One said to another, "That's the last of them. Thirteen in one family, all gone, right down to the little one."

Old sun was in the west now, and the afternoon light played on the piney wood of the coffins. After the men had carried them all into the courthouse, there was a long pause. Then they began to bring them back down, this time struggling under their weight, sometimes two men at either end. There were names written on the sides of each box, a last name and a first initial. When the small ones started coming, the crowd burst into a collective moan. Then, as suddenly as it had begun, the moan shattered into a thousand shrill cries: bedlam.

Under the fedora, the Shake Rag man drummed on.

Dovey picked her way through the crowd. People were strid-ing back and forth now, an agitated mass of bodies. A woman stood alone, trembling violently and tearing at her hair. One man was beating his chest with the palm of his hand. A little boy pulled on an older boy's sleeve and pointed upward. "Is Mama up there in the clouds, then?" he asked. The older boy nodded, biting his lip.

In the doorway to the courthouse the Red Cross lady bent over and read the sides of the boxes and checked off each name in her notebook.

"Please, ma'am," Dovey began. "You know where they took the colored?"

"Not now," the Red Cross lady said without looking up.

"Please, miss."

The Red Cross lady looked up quickly, sweat pouring out from under her little hat, which was crooked, having become loose from its pin on one side. "No Negro dead at the courthouse," she said. "They're in the alleyway over by the old Hardin's Bakery. Check with Porter's. They've already picked some up." Then she took a second look at Dovey and frowned. "There's blood on your face. Where's it coming from?"

"My ear."

"Let me see it. Take off that hat."

Dovey took off the fedora and turned her head. The Red Cross lady leaned and peered at the ear. "That blood's coming from inside your head, honey. You need to get over to the Lyric and let a doctor look at that. You may have some serious damage, a concussion at the least. Do you have a headache?"

Dovey nodded.

"Get over there right now, you hear me? You hear me now?" Another small coffin arrived at the door and she turned back to her task.

Dovey turned and began to walk the way she'd come, toward the theater. She needed to relieve herself. There was a house on the corner of Jefferson and South Green that looked unoccupied.

She went around to the backyard, behind a row of boxwoods that still had most of their leaves. Just as she was squatting, an old man stuck his head out the back door.

"What you doing out there?" he called. "Get out of my yard. You think you can sneak up on me and take my money? I ain't having niggers walking through my yard like it's Grand Central Station. I'll show you!" He disappeared back into the house.

Dovey realized he took her for a man, with the hat and long coat, but it was too late for her to stop herself. She remained squatting, hoping she could finish before he came back. Just as she was finishing, he reappeared, a shotgun in his hand. He pointed it in her general direction and fired, missing her but not by much. She scrambled to her feet, pulled up her underwear, and took off as best she could, pulling the bad foot along.

He fired a second shot. She felt it whizz by her head. The first shot hadn't had much to say except get the hell out of Dodge, but this second one sang in her left ear, over the drumbeat in her head, over the sound of the train whistle now signaling the arrival of another Frisco, over all the shouting and crying out in the streets. It sang to her like an opera singer. It sang to her like a blues singer. It sang all the nastiness of white folk, all the ugliness of the world. It sang the dirty linen, the spots that won't come out, the tears in the fabric.

She hurried along as best she could, a snail's pace, though in her mind she zigzagged through the street like a rabbit in the field. When she finally turned the corner onto Broadway where the Lyric was, she came to a halt. A straggly line of ragtag people stretched down the block like they were in line for a Saturday matinee. Some were crying, some silent as death. Some bled from open wounds. At the end of the line a large man stood on one foot and leaned heavily on his wife's shoulders. She was a small woman, and when she turned to look at Dovey, her face was gray with the strain of his weight. In front of them a little girl stood alone, crying quietly, a bloody rag wrapped around her hand. Dovey had never stood in this particular line but rather in the one for Negroes around the corner, next to the outside open-rail steps leading up to the balcony. Briefly she wondered whether the colored were supposed to stand in the line around the corner, but then she saw several Negroes up ahead. A Red Cross lady pushed a cart with a large water jug and some paper cups, offering drinks. A nurse moved down the line giving tetanus shots, causing a stir among the children, not taking no for an answer. Some people the nurse pulled out of line and escorted into the theater. A CCC boy brought up the rear with sandwiches wrapped in waxed paper.

Dovey took her shot, then a sandwich, cheese and liverwurst and butter. It was heavy with grease, the last thing she wanted to eat. In fact she didn't want to eat at all. She accepted the offering because the boy's eyes had filled with tears as he talked to the little girl and by the time he reached Dovey they had plowed trenches down his cheeks.

"That little one lost everybody," he said, gesturing toward the girl. "Her mama had a chimney come down on her and her dad and little brother got burnt up when the house caught fire." Then he turned to her with his wet cheeks and glistening eyes and asked, "Sandwich?" and there was no refusing him. Now, as she held the sandwich, saliva filled up her mouth, whether from the need to eat or to upchuck she wasn't sure. Thankfully, the lady with the water arrived and offered her a full cup and she was able to drink and ask for another, please, and then she knew she needed the sandwich no matter how much she hated the smell of liverwurst.

She peeled back the waxed paper and began to eat, the white bread sticking to the roof of her mouth. Dovey and Virgil and Dreama didn't eat store-bought bread. For one thing, they couldn't afford it; for another, they didn't much like it. Dovey made corn bread and salt-rising bread and Dreama's favorite, biscuits, which rose fluffy as clouds in the baking pan. Dreama liked sorghum on hers, Virgil preferred the apple butter Dovey put up in the fall. Little Promise had just begun eating his mashed up in milk. Once, a hundred years ago, they had all sat down for supper together, Virgil in his old comfortable house clothes, having shed his cotton-covered overalls; Dreama with Promise bouncing in her lap, waving those fat little hands of his, whapping the table so the plates rattled. Dreama, her head bent over the child, a bowl of porridge before her, the spoon in one hand, a rag to wipe his face in the other. How he fought that washrag, kicked and squirmed and fussed to be let down on his pallet. "He done," Virgil would pronounce, "past done." But Dreama was a good mother, she wouldn't let well enough alone, insisted on that last bite, even if half of it dribbled down the side of his chin.

All that work for nothing! Baby blown to kingdom come. Little mother too. Virgil, well Virgil, no telling about him. No telling about any of them.

The line moved forward. Dovey took a few steps. The bad foot had come back to life. Now it was a tinny little marching drum, *ratta tat tat, ratta tat tat.* Syncopated and irregular, playing backup to the heavy throbbing beat in her head. Faster and faster now while the drum in her head got slower and slower.

Then, just as she swallowed the last bite of the sandwich, the drum in her head stopped in mid-beat like a radio turned off in the middle of a song and her knees sighed one long exhausted sigh and gave way, and then, to her surprise and deepest embarrassment, she felt someone grab on to her (*who?*) and holler, "Need help here, got one down back here."

And then, with no warning at all, old sun gave up the light and the bright, the too-bright afternoon went dark as pitch and the night came rolling rolling in to claim the sky.

# TUE/DAY, APRIL 7

# 8

## 12:30 A.M.

Jo was asleep when they came. They came like rising water, silent and deadly. She didn't hear them until one of them tripped over Son and whispered *crap*. Then a cigarette lighter flicked and there was a long pause and a different one said, "Goddamn, ain't that Son on the floor?" Then a scramble and more cursing. After that they all went quiet again, too quiet. She could hear them in there moving around, and there was a stealth to it that frightened her.

It was dark as pitch again. Where had the day gone? When was the last time she'd fed the baby? Late afternoon? It had been all she could do to get on her feet and get to the kitchen and pull the bottle from the icebox. Only one left now. She wasn't thinking straight. Why hadn't she taken little Tommy and headed out to get help? It was her mother, lying there so helpless, so vulnerable, that stopped her initially and after that, she'd stopped thinking in terms of going or staying. She just wanted to sit there, propped up against the wall, little Tommy in her lap, neither of them moving a muscle.

In the distance she could hear a hound bay, long and mournful. She put her hand to her forehead and touched her horn, which now didn't seem foreign at all. It felt like it had been there

since the beginning of time; it felt as though she'd been born
with it. But it was heavier now; her neck ached from it, her head
a drooping sunflower, stranger than any dream.

Was she alive?

Her lap felt suddenly, warmly wet. She welcomed it because
it meant life, the baby was alive and so was she. He had begun
to stir.

She reached over to touch her mother. Alice moaned once,
then lay still again.

She could hear them moving around the front of the house,
living room and dining room, picking up things and putting
them down. She'd propped herself up against the wall that led
from the circular hall to the living room, around the corner and
out of sight. She thought maybe she ought to call out to them,
ask them to help her with her mother or go for help, but just then
one of them said something about the good silver, where was it
kept, and she shrank back against the wall. She recognized their
voices. Son's friends. They wore shiny black lace-ups and oil-
stained T-shirts with packs of Lucky Strikes rolled up in their
sleeves. They kept their hair greased, parted down the middle.
She hadn't seen them in over a year, since the day her father
kicked them out of the house.

They'd been looking at her. When they came in that afternoon, she'd been sneak-reading a Nancy Drew book. Her mother
disapproved of Nancy Drew. Nancy Drew was below Jo's reading comprehension and there were most certainly more edifying
and challenging books to read: *Les Misérables*, *The Hunchback
of Notre Dame*, *David Copperfield*, serious books about serious
topics like war and poverty and deformity, books that would
teach Jo what the world was like, how people ought to live.

The house was empty. Alice had had to stay for a meeting after school that afternoon, and Jo had taken advantage of her mother's absence to pull the Nancy Drew out of her secret stash under the sweaters in her cedar chest. She'd gotten into her favorite reading position, draped over her father's velvet armchair. It was spring and her legs were bare and white; they dangled over one arm of the chair and she rested her head on the other. She rubbed the worn velvet as she read, an old child-hood habit. Touch and touch again. Nancy Drew was deep into the kind of trouble only she could get into, something about an old clock, a pendulum. Vaguely Jo knew Son and his friends had come in the back door, through the screen porch, but she hadn't worried. It was 5:30; her father was due home any minute. Absorbed in the book, she hadn't seen the three of them loung-ing in the doorway from the hall to the living room, waiting for her brother to come downstairs. When her father came in through the back door and walked up behind them and started hollering, she about jumped out of her skin. When she looked up, she saw them and could tell they'd been eyeing her, were still eyeing her, actually. He told them to get the hell out of his house and never come back. He told them he had a gun, which Jo knew for a fact he did not—he didn't like guns, said they caused more trouble than they were worth unless you needed to go to the woods for your food. The fact that he threatened them with a gun got her attention. She scrambled out of the chair, blushing, her skirt hiked up in the back from the lounging, which got their attention even more as they were leaving, smirking at her and walking out the front door so as to avoid her father.

When they paused in the front doorway, her father shoved them forward. They allowed themselves to be pushed along, even as they looked back at her lazily, even as she looked over her shoulder at them. When she got into the kitchen and felt her skirt hiked up in back, she blushed even more, imagining them seeing, almost but not really seeing, her underwear, oh please don't let them have seen her underwear! The thought of their eyes on her body made her feel feverish and shaky.

After they left, her father went up to Son's room and shut the door and begin to shout. Son had had every advantage. He could have gone to Ole Miss, could *still* go to Ole Miss, he could be anything he wanted to be. He was a freeloader, a ne'er-do-well who had ruined the good family name. Now he was bringing trash into the house, polluting his own little sister. What Son said back, Jo didn't know, but the friends had never entered the McNabb house again.

Until now.

The baby stirred again. Soon, Jo knew, he would begin to whimper and then rev up to scream bloody murder. She pulled him to her with her good arm, held him against her breast. He began to flail about, twisting his head this way and that to get his breath. She loosened her grip and stuck her forefinger in his mouth. He sucked hard for a few seconds, then, outraged at the lack of nourishment, gathered himself into a tight ball to scream.

"What the hell's that?" one of them whispered.

There was a pause and then she could hear them coming, tip-toeing across the living room floor. One stepped on something that clattered.

They were in the hall now, and the lighter flicked again.

"Holy shit," one said.

She tightened her grip on the baby. The light hurt her eyes. The three of them were in a semicircle. They peered down at her.

She saw herself reflected in their pupils. A mother rabbit with her young, frozen in the tall grass, except there was no grass.

"Look what we got here," one said. "If it ain't the little sis and the baby brother."

Alice stirred and moaned then and the men shifted the light. One found the flashlight on the floor beside Jo and pointed it at Alice, moving up and down until it found the leg.

"Look like you folks in a mess here all by your lonesome," another one said, bending closer to Jo. "What's that thing sticking out of your head, girl. You look like a billy goat, little sis."

Jo patted little Tommy, trying to calm him. He screamed louder, his legs and arms thrust out, trembling with rage.

One of them snickered. "If it ain't the little mama."

Jo felt hot, then cold. In his fury, Tommy was about to leap out of her one good arm. "We need help here," she stammered. *Why* couldn't she sound firmer? Now her face was wet, wetter than her lap. She wanted to slap her own face. She struggled to sit straighter without dropping the baby. "My mother's leg is broken bad, and I've got my arm and this thing in my head . . ." She trailed off, uncertainly. Now there were two of them in the front, looking down at her, one in the shadows behind them. She looked back and forth at the three of them in the dim glow of the flashlight. Their mouths were what shocked her, the half-smile they shared.

"Where's the big-man daddy now?" one said.

"Maybe out catting around up in nigger town?" another one said.

The smiles became grins. They moved closer, their faces serious now, intent.

They were taller than she remembered. She gathered the

baby around the middle, pushed down with her bad arm and scrambled to her feet. The pain made her gasp, but she righted herself and backed up into the living room, holding the baby on her hip, his back against her rib cage, his arms and legs circling air. She backed up some more, feeling her way to the front doorway. The night was clear and the moon and stars cast a light. Back, back. She stumbled over something, then realized it was Son's outflung arm. Were it not for the hand, she would have thought she was looking at a tree limb. Was the old Son back, blocking her way, tricking her?

She could feel Tommy's shallow little breaths under her arm, next to her own lung. She panted along with him, willing him to become part of her own body, an outcropping of her rib cage, Eve to her Adam. She would lay down her life for him. No one would harm a hair on his head.

In the moonlight she saw her shadow, the bulk of the baby at her side, her dangling, useless arm extended but drooping and curled under like a spider's leg, her wild hair and horned head. She looked monstrous, dangerous.

"You bother me, and my daddy will shoot you with his gun. He's coming back any minute now. He just went next door." Her own voice echoed in her one good ear as if it were coming from far away.

From the hall her mother groaned and cried out for water, somebody please get her some water, she was dying of thirst.

One of them came toward Jo, panting a little.

At that moment a streak of white shot out from under the debris in the dining room and skittered across the living room floor in front of the one who was coming. The one coming toward her tripped and fell then, cursing the cat, who'd run behind the upturned sofa, waking the kittens she'd moved there, then swatting at them when they pounced on her to nurse. The other two laughed. One said, "You a clumsy fool, lover boy."

Jo saw her chance then and turned to run, but the one on the floor reached up and caught her on the ankle.

"It's all right," he said. "We ain't going to hurt you none. You just put the baby down in the corner and lay down for us and then we'll leave you be. Won't bother you for nothing else."

He spoke softly, and with her bad ear she wasn't sure she heard him right. Was he telling her to rest herself, not to worry? But then he reached up and touched the inside of her thigh. She kicked out at him, making contact. He laughed and jumped to his feet like a monkey. She thought to pull the coat hanger from Son's chest, but she had to hold on to the baby with her one good hand.

He rubbed his shin. "Now that weren't nice. That weren't nice one little bitty bit. And here I was saying we'd be nice and friendly. What you being such a fool about it for? Think you're better than us like your stuck-up daddy?"

They had managed to back her into the corner of the dining room where the buffet had once stood. How had she let that happen? Jo wondered what Nancy Drew would do. Nancy had never been bothered. Bad men wanted to lock her up or choke her or push her down the stairs, but nobody had tried to bother her. Plus Nancy had a father and a brother, unlike Jo, whose big brother was not only dead but also wouldn't have been of help anyway, and whose father was on the lam.

Tommy gathered himself and began to shriek, his head bobbing up and down like a turtle's. He kicked at Jo's side. She tightened her grip on him, causing him to scream louder.

Then from the hall, Alice McNabb started singing tonelessly. The song was a hymn Jo couldn't place, dirge-like and slow and otherworldly. The baby stopped crying and it was just Alice singing.

The hymn, Jo realized, contained snatches of several hymns. The tune seemed Alice's own. Something about Shadrach, Meshach, and Abednego and a fiery furnace, Christian soldiers, guilty stains. Plunging behind the flood.

There was a horrible scraping from the hall and Alice rounded the corner in a sitting position, pushing herself along the floor, her raw leg stretched out before her in the moonlight, impossibly twisted. She pointed one trembling finger, casting a stick-like shadow against the wall: "You. Leave my daughter alone. Leave her alone. Get out of here."

The three of them froze in their tracks; the one that had Jo loosened his grip.

The one back in the shadows stepped around the other two. He was shorter than they were and lankier. Jo thought he was coming for her and edged along the wall toward the doorway. She wanted to make a run for it but was afraid she'd trip in the dark and drop the baby on his head. And her mother. How could she abandon her mother?

Then the shorter one turned to the other two and said, "Nothing here. Not a damn thing here. Move on and leave Son here in peace. Son, old man, you starting to stink like a dead fish." He walked around Jo to the doorway and motioned to the other two.

Jo shrank against the wall as they passed and then walked out into the night, their white undershirts bobbing against the dark like clothes on the line.

She put the baby on the floor and ran to see about her mother. "Get your notebook," Alice said. She had ended up in the doorway from the hall to the living room and now she slid back to the floor.

Jo went over to her mother and touched her cheek. Hot, blazing hot.

"*Predation*," her mother whispered. "Write it down."

Jo opened her mouth to tell her mother there was no getting to her notebook of Words to Keep; there was a solid wall of furniture between her and it, if indeed it too hadn't blown away. At that moment, little Tommy began to cry from the far corner of the living room.

Jo groped her way back toward the baby. The men had taken the flashlight and the house was black as pitch. The rain had started up again. Jo could feel it on her face.

"You can't leave a baby on the cold floor," Alice said. "He needs his bottle. Go get his bottle."

"It's the last one," Jo said.

"Well, he's got to eat. Bring it to me. Smell it first. Make sure it's not spoiled."

Jo tried to push her mother into a sitting position but couldn't. She laid Tommy in the crook of her mother's arm and went back into the kitchen and got out the last bottle. When she brought it back, her mother had pushed herself up and had the baby on her shoulder. He sobbed on and she patted his back.

"He's wet," her mother said. "Bring me something to put on him. He's messed his diaper too. He needs changing. No wonder he's crying. I wish I could see him. It's so dark, I can't make out a thing."

Jo groped her way back into the kitchen and got a clean cup

and towel and brought it to her mother, who put the baby on her lap and began to change him. "Bring me a wet cloth," her mother said. "I need to clean him. He smells to high heaven. How'd he get so filthy?"

Jo laughed and the horn in her head said, *Hello, I'm still here.*

Alice finished changing the baby, who was screaming bloody murder, and handed Jo the towel. "Throw it outside," she said. "Get it out of here. What's that other smell?"

Jo didn't answer.

Her mother's eyes gleamed out of the dark. "How'd that coat hanger get into him?"

"I don't know," Jo said, and strictly speaking, that was the truth; she had no earthly idea how she'd gotten blown from one end of the house to the other, why she'd held on to the coat hanger. Her hand had simply frozen around it; it could just as easily have plunged into her, both ends equally lethal.

Alice turned up the bottle and Tommy began to gulp. Then she started in: Why had no one come to see about them? Why hadn't Jo's father returned home? Where *was* he?

After awhile Alice stopped talking and there was only the sound of the baby gulping at the bottle. Then, out of the dark, she said, "Jo, honey, you've got to go out on the street. There's nobody but you. You've got to find us some help." She coughed once, then again. There was a whistle to her breath, a sour smell when she exhaled. Then she moved a little and moaned under her breath. "Just go straight on down the street. Go on till you get to Jefferson, then walk on over to the square. Now you listen to me: You need to be smart about it. If you see those men, run in the other direction, no matter what." Alice reached over and touched her daughter's chin, felt around her face and tucked her hair behind her ears. "And get somebody to pull that thing out of your head."

Jo felt leaden, unable to move. She was almost asleep. Why wouldn't her mother be quiet? Let her alone? She opened one eye.

Alice's head had slipped down the wall. "Here, put him down beside me. He'll be all right for a while, but you need to go. Hurry, we don't have much time. He's all right now, but he'll be awake in a few hours."

**JO PICKED** her way across the front porch, down the steps, and headed for what she calculated was the street. When she looked to the north, she saw a bonfire lighting up the colored side of town, up on the Hill near Gum Pond, and there was the smell of flesh burning. Her first thought was that they were burning people, but then she realized it must be animals. It would have been barbaric to burn people, no matter how many had died. She had a picture in her mind of rows and rows of coffins lined up, the single line disappearing across the horizon like a train track.

Something needed to be done about Son.

It was quiet now, deep shadows, no one in sight. Down the way, though, she could see lights. The electricity must be back on downtown. She pushed her way through the dark. A few slivers of moonlight bobbed up against tree trunks and the deep ponds of water where the enormous tree roots had come up. Debris everywhere, lurking in the shadows like strangely shaped predators. It was impossible to tell where the street was. Had the old washwoman made it into town? At least she'd gone in daylight. Jo tried to move quickly and carefully, giv-

ing wide berth to large indiscernible objects and the pools of
water. She put each foot down lightly at first until she was sure
of her footing.

She came to where she thought the aunts' house should have
been. A strange hulking shape in the front yard, no sign of the
pretty white house where the two old ladies had sipped tea and
gossiped and played gin rummy and told stories of the days when
they were young and pretty and had handsome beaux lined up
and down Church Street begging for their hands in matrimony.
Then the moon emerged from behind the clouds and Jo saw that
the shape was an overturned magnolia, the aunts' house now
obscured from view by the massive root ball.

The aunts and blind Miss Edwina were gone now, but whenever Jo let herself go back to that time, she mixed up the old
ladies, innocent as they were, with the trick. Old Major too,
crippled and half blind himself, though he was the only one who
had had any inkling of what had happened to her; he was the
only one who was troubled even in the slightest way, pacing and
whining behind the fence when the boys had her down on the
ground. Why couldn't he have jumped that fence and charged
like lightning, teeth bared, torn those boys apart, made them
pay? And the aunts, didn't they wonder why a lively girl would
stop every single afternoon and visit for hours on her way home
from school? Did it cross their minds that it was not their company but their protection she craved?

Jo had just turned onto Jefferson when a small lone figure
approached out of the shadows. A girl. Smaller than Jo but about
her age. The girl was shaking and crying. Jo stopped several feet
from her. Jo didn't recognize the girl, which was odd since Jo
knew most of the students in her school. There was something

about her that was strangely familiar, yet at the same time foreign. Almond eyes set wide and a full mouth that looked bruised;
her hair stood out around her face, dark and wavy and wild in
the moonlight. The shirtsleeve on her right arm had been ripped
away. There was long gash down the side of the arm and a scrape
on her chin.

The girl was crying. "Have you seen a little baby anywhere
around? You heard a little baby crying? Or an old woman and old
man? I'm looking for my boy. He's lost." She wrung her hands.
"I was right there on top of him in the street, and the wind just
blew him right out from under me. I've been looking high and
low for him. And my granny and papa too. I've been to town and
now I'm going back home."

So that was it. Jo could tell by her soft vowels the girl was
colored, though she didn't look it. Jo didn't know any colored
girls, though she'd seen them walking to school and around
town, cutting her looks and then giggling among themselves.
She often wondered what they talked about. Did they play Chi-
nese checkers and ride horses and go to parties? Did they read
Nancy Drew?

There was still something about the girl that reminded Jo of
someone she knew, the smallness, the set of even white teeth,
the delicate forearms.

Then it hit her. "Is your grandmother the washwoman?" Jo
asked. "She does our wash."

The girl's eyes flashed. "My granny is a *laundress*. Her name
is Mrs. Dovey Grand'homme and my papa is named Mr. Virgil
Grand'homme, and my baby, he's named Promise. I came down
here to find them, but they aren't here." She came closer. "What's
that you got sticking out of your head, girl?"

Now Jo knew who the girl was. How tiny she was! A child herself. How could her brother have done what he did? She was glad she'd killed him, he didn't deserve to live. "What's your name?" she asked the girl.

"Dreama."

"Then I have news for you."

"What? You found my people?"

"Your grandmother was at my house yesterday. She came up to our house to get some help and I gave her some shoes and a raincoat and something to eat and then she headed out for downtown to find the rest of you."

Dreama's eyes filled. "Oh thank goodness! I thought I'd lost them all. I'd about given up. Did she say anything about the baby?"

"She was looking for him too, looking for all of you. Last I saw she was heading into town, the way I'm headed now. I walked out to the street with her. She was supposed to get help. Right after she left, I found my little brother in a crepe myrtle bush outside my house."

"In a bush? Was he dead?"

"He's scratched up but all right."

"Maybe my Promise will be too. What house? Where do you live?"

Jo hesitated. If the girl knew who she was, Son's sister, she would hate her.

"Tell me where you live so I can go up there and look around."

"Babies don't go flying all the way across town. You ought to go look in bushes around your own house, not mine."

Dreama shook her head. "No bushes left up there on the Hill. Nothing left but piles of stuff and dead folks and people walking around like they don't have a brain in their head. If you find my granny, tell her I'm alive and looking for Promise." She turned to go.

"Wait," Jo said. "I have something to tell you."

The girl turned, her face carved ivory in the moonlight.

That was the moment Jo should have said it, that she'd killed her brother Son, that he was gone forever, that he'd never bother Dreama again. Dreama's face, hopeful, desperate, stopped her. In it was that story older than either of them, the story Alice used to tell Jo but then one day stopped telling. That long trip a century ago of Jo's mother's family, the wealthy Longs and Langstroms of South Carolina united in a pair of newlyweds, she the daughter of a wealthy planter, he the nephew of Michael Langstrom, who owned land up and down the eastern sea-board, Alice's great-grandparents, striking out with wedding presents, hand-carved walnut and marble chests, beds and silver, the missing buffet. They stopped in Alabama and stayed for one growing season but the soil was poor so they loaded the wagons again and bought more slaves to replace the ones who'd died on the journey and headed west. Their people's people had little ones by then, and their mothers wrapped them in swaths of cloth they tied in complicated knots around their waists and shoulders. The young couple, frayed by the bad year, looked at the babies and calculated their worth.

Alice had stopped telling the story of her family because, she said, it didn't fit their lives now. Tupelo was a forward-looking city. There were telephones and electricity and air shows and the fishery and mill and now the new garment factory. Bustle, progress, everything cotton could buy and more. No need to focus on the past when the present shone so bright.

But the shadow of the past had lingered. When Jo was little and Alice still told the story of Ellen Long and James Langstrom, Jo imagined the two of them, Ellen in her long dress, James in his waistcoat and boots, walking hand in hand among the fallen acorns from the giant oaks and the tumble of wild iris in swamp-land and muscadine vines that climbed the trunks of ancient trees. In the early days, Alice said, there had been wolves and panthers and Carolina parakeets, now extinct from the farm-ers' guns; strange red-headed creatures called scorpions, which barked like dogs and jumped from tree to tree like squirrels; vast virgin forests with sage grasses as high as a man's head. Bloodshed too, men fighting over land and railroads, and cotton, always the eternal cotton and the fields with the bent figures planting and picking and hauling despite the hilly red-clay ground.

She and this girl mother were in it now, the long arc of his-tory; they were playing their part, larger and more daring than either of them would ever have imagined, and what they did now would shape what came after and what stories might be told and listened to. The storm, it had changed everything, it had made their lives large and momentous.

Looking into the girl's face, Jo thought, *This storm is the most important thing that will ever happen to me*, not thinking of Dreama at all but of her own self, for really nothing of any conse-quence had happened to her up until the storm, at least nothing she wished to remember. She walked along the ledge of history now. She, Jo McNabb, had been blown through the air with that coat hanger outstretched and where it went and what it did were miracles like an angel is a miracle, like the way a bone resetting itself is a miracle. One day she would say to someone somewhere that she had lived through the Tupelo tornado of 1936 and she

had met this colored girl on the way into town and they had spoken about how babies could fly through the sky and arrive safe
and sound with barely a scratch to show for it. And why not?
She'd seen a baby who'd flown through the air and landed in a
bush; she herself had been lifted off her feet. This would be her
story when she was old and sitting by the fire and sipping her
tea, for as long as she drew breath: this would be who she was.
And the part of the story that could only be whispered, that this
girl was in more than one way her sister, would she tell that too?
Or would that part of the story slip into the night like a cat, leaving no trace of its secret, hungry life?

Dreama turned to go. Jo followed her a few paces and touched
her arm. "Just be careful. There's some mean boys roaming
around."

"White boys?"

"Yes."

"I've had my fill of white boys."

"Me too," Jo said. "Take care. There are three of them. They
have on white undershirts. You ought to be able to spot them in
the dark."

Dreama reached out as if she were going to take Jo's hand but
then didn't. "Did they bother you?"

Jo shook her head. "No, but they almost did." Just then Jo
saw some men coming up the street. She pulled Dreama into the
shadows of a ruined house. They crouched together in the rubble, clutching each other. Dreama's hair tickled Jo's face like a
spider web, sticky and wet.

There were four of them. Two carried what looked like laundry, one carried some picks and shovels, another something that
appeared to be a first-aid kit.

"They look all right," Dreama whispered.

"You stay here," said Jo. "Then if they get after me, you run for help." It was the least she could do for the girl. She found a loose board on the side of the house and pried it off, glad to see that a nail was still imbedded in the end.

When she stepped out, the men stopped what they were doing and flashed their lights at her. She brandished her board.

"You need help, miss?" one said, and the way he said it made her know he was all right, they were all of them all right. Then she saw their uniforms. CCC boys. Now, at long last, she could give the things that burdened her over to them: her horn (heavier and heavier it had grown over the course of the night) and her mother's leg and her famished little brother and her treacherous big brother, too long dead, and they would take them all off her hands and she could rest. She could have herself a good sleep. She began to cry then and it was loud and embarrassing for an ordinary girl like herself to cry that way, especially with the girl, who could have cried a bucket of tears over all she'd lost, watching.

Jo told the boys where to go and that there was a baby to take care of, not to forget the baby, and they said they were heading to the corner of Church and Walnut anyhow, an old Negro woman had sent them yesterday, but they'd gotten sidetracked fighting fires. Then one of them took her by the arm, her good arm—so careful he was with her. She looked back for Dreama—where had she gone?—and the CCC boy told her not to worry, the other three would go straight to her mother and little brother. See? They were already on their way. And yes, not to worry, they had milk too; they knew about the babies, how they had to eat or they would die. Jo should see the babies they'd rescued, lined up like glads in a funeral spray down at the Lyric. And yes, they would send someone for her deader-than-dead brother after they got the living sorted away. Now, though, it was her turn and she needed to go with him, the CCC boy. She needed to get that thing out of her head and her arm back in a cast. His face had a dappled look in the moonlight, like the skin of a trout wet from the stream.

Jo began to laugh then and talk to him about the ants. How they'd probably return to plague her once she got her cast back on. How she'd missed them!

She looked back again. She was going to tell that girl to come on, come on back to town with her and the nice CCC boy and they'd find her grandmother, who was surely there somewhere. But the girl, Dreama, her face a petal floating on the moonlight, shook her head no and shouted to Jo something about the baby she was bound and determined to find. Then she melted into the night.

# 9

## 10:02 A.M.

Dovey woke to the smell of popcorn. How she'd loved that smell when she was a girl and scrounged up the nickel it took to get into the picture show, inhaled the odor of rancid, smoky oil from below, leaning over the balcony to see the little paper sacks the white children held, her mouth watering for a piece, just one piece. She'd wanted it so much she could actually taste it on her tongue, crunch it between her teeth. She'd have done anything, almost anything for a handful. The slimy peanuts her mother had boiled and put in a brown paper bag didn't alleviate her craving. Later on, when she went with Virgil, he said he didn't care they wouldn't sell to colored, he didn't care for popcorn, reminded him of cotton.

The spot where they'd laid her was dusty and still, a corner at the back. She'd been put on a pallet on the floor and someone had covered her with a blanket and her arms were folded over her chest as if she'd died in the night. What a joke. Had to have been white folks who'd arranged her body like a corpse. White folks been trying to kill her and hers since the beginning of time. If not the merman in the tree, then working her and Virgil and everybody else she knew to death for peanuts. And if all that weren't trouble enough, weren't a big-enough mess, then what that boy had went and done to Dreama was sure enough the icing on the cake.

She looked down and saw she was in different clothes, something large and rough, a gown of some sort that smelled of bleach. It swallowed her. She reached for the ear that bled and found it bandaged over. The thought of white hands touching her in such an intimate way was a tickle in her throat.

Her foot was bandaged and on a pile of towels. That much she appreciated.

The room plunged as if a wave had broken over it. It was only when the seats began to float in the waves that it came to her: where she was. The Lyric, whose downstairs she'd never entered. She'd thought it was finer than this, finer and cleaner. (Why had they laid her on this nasty floor?) Now that she'd seen it, she preferred the balcony.

Something skittered across the floor. Peering through the dark, she could see wads of gum on the undersides of the up-turned theater seats. Then here it came again, among scattered popcorn kernels and candy wrappers. A roach? Roaches plagued her. She hated the sickening crunch they made when Virgil stomped them, the way they dodged and pitched and hissed and squeezed themselves into cracks in the floor, only to return when least expected. Once, after her family was gone and the aunt took her in, she woke in the middle of the night to find one preening itself on her bare arm, not far from her open mouth, bathing its nasty self in the trickle of spit that had gathered in the elbow crevasse of her outstretched arm. When the tickle aroused her and she opened her eyes, it had stared at her like it was boss of the world. She'd screamed and jumped up to shake it off her arm. Her aunt came running and swatted at it and it stood on its back haunches in a corner of the room and boxed the air until she mashed it with one of Dovey's slippers. Then she whapped Dovey up side the head for waking her up in the middle of the night for a *roach.*

Dovey lifted her head. There was the stage and the heavy red velvet curtains that hung to either side of it. When she was a girl, she always came early to the picture show so she'd get to listen to the piano man play and watch those curtains go up and the lights go down.

Now there was a commotion on stage. Somebody screamed a piercing scream, then hollered *no.* A line of screens hid the people on the stage from view but the lights were bright and Dovey could see a table of some sort and clusters of people in white around it. A scramble and then someone raised something that look like a giant sausage in his hand and dropped it to the floor with a thud. Then someone else came and picked it up in a towel and hurried off with it.

On a theater seat one row up, a man bent double and moaned. Then a baby from over the way started up. Through Dovey's bandaged ear, the sounds gurgled and waned as if coming from underwater.

Now something, a monster with sharp teeth and long finger-nails and hair all over its body, climbed onto her chest. Then it kicked open the door and memory flooded in.

*The storm. Virgil. Dreama and the baby.* She sat bolt upright.

A Red Cross lady saw her and brought over a cup of juice and asked her how she was feeling. She said she couldn't rightly tell, her words echoing back to her.

The Red Cross lady leaned down and pushed her back onto her pallet on the floor. "You need to lie back. You've got a concussion. The more you rest, the sooner you'll feel better." The lady's eyes were shiny, like she was proud of herself.

Dovey popped back up. "My people." She spoke louder than she meant to and the lady put her finger to her lips. "I got to find my people," Dovey whispered to the finger. "I got people."

The lady whipped a notebook out of her breast pocket. "A husband? Any children?"

*Charlesetta.* The world was filled with lost children on the other side. But it was this side she needed to tell. She tried to sit back up but couldn't. "Dreama Grand'homme, sixteen years. Promise Grand'homme, three months."

"How do you spell that? Are they boys or girls?"

"Dreama's the girl, Promise the boy."

The lady looked up from her notebook. "Her baby?" Of course that's what she'd be thinking. Dovey would have loved to sit her shiny-eyed self down and tell her the whole story, rub her nose in it. Dreama had been a *good* girl.

The notebook the lady wrote in reminded Dovey of the notebooks she used for laundry, the spiral at the top like a stenographer's pad, the lines across and the one red line down the middle. Dovey was good at numbers, Charlesetta had taken after her in that way. Dovey kept a running tally of her laundry in the books, always counting everything before she left white ladies' houses. She had her own form of shorthand: capital S for sheets, lowercase for shirts, SK for socks, T for tablecloths, N for napkins. If something looked off, one sock instead of two or an odd number of napkins, she'd ask about it. No point in getting blamed for losing something she didn't lose. She inspected things too. If a sheet had the beginnings of a tear, she'd be sure to point it out and ask whether the lady of the house wanted her to mend it before it got worse and she got accused of doing the damage. Then she'd charge extra for the mending. The books she had kept her tallies in, all of them, she saved in a corner of the bedroom. There were piles of them now, or had been before the storm took them, halfway up to the ceiling. Virgil grumbled about them. They didn't have room to be stacking useless things in corners. But Dovey kept them. One day, when she was old, she was going to take them down and count all the loads of laundry she'd taken in over the course of her grown-up life. Now that would be a pretty number! Then she'd figure on how much money each load had brought in over the last fifty years. She'd raised her rates four times, at the beginning of each new decade, as a gift to herself for the special new year, the zero at the end of the number. When she did her final tally, she'd have to remember to add that in.

"Where do you live?" the lady asked and Dovey said she lived up on the Hill, or used to.

The lady frowned, then touched Dovey's hand. "Do you want me to check the funeral home up there for you, honey?"

Dovey hated her then, talking about funeral homes, not minding her own business.

"Porter's, right?"

"My folks ain't dead, they just missing."

The lady looked at her and the shiny eyes got shinier.

So there was nothing left to say. The lady went off and Dovey fell back, first resting, then gauging her strength, flexing her legs. All in working order. The years at the washtub had made her strong. She moved her arms, then mustered her courage to try to sit up again. The dizziness had returned, crashing and surging back like the tide. Dovey knew the comings and goings of tides. A year ago, she'd ridden the M&O down to New Orleans with Virgil to see his people. She hadn't wanted to go. What had happened to Dreama was still fresh and fresher yet the knowledge that she was carrying a child. But Virgil's father had died portering. He'd been hoisting some luggage onto the train and collapsed right there on the landing, just as he was throwing a heavy trunk into the underside of the M&O passenger car for two girls going from Tupelo to New Orleans for a debutante party. An ambulance was called. By the time it got there, the train was on the way, Virgil's father was dead, and the young ladies were seen by one of Virgil's father's porter friends giggling among themselves while they pulled dinners of fried chicken and potato salad out of a large hamper. Virgil was determined to take his father home to New Orleans and just as determined to take Dovey along. He asked Etherene Johnson to let Dreama stay with her. Etherene jumped at the chance to drill Dreama on her grammar so everything was settled before Dovey knew it.

The family gathered in the little shotgun on Galvez after the funeral and burial, which involved sliding Virgil's father into a concrete vault aboveground, one that housed other members of the family. How did they all fit? She didn't ask, knew it would be wrong to. Later Virgil would explain how each coffin took its time. Then when the tomb was needed again, a crew came out and opened the oldest one and dumped what was left, not much, into the back corner. Virgil had a cousin who did that kind of work, which he said was like a treasure hunt. There were rings and brooches and pocket watches. You'd be surprised what people take with them, he'd told Virgil. Bone picking. She'd shivered when Virgil had told her and was glad she took in laundry.

It was the first time she'd met any of Virgil's New Orleans family and they'd taken her in like one of their own. There were pots simmering on the stove, collards and pickled pork, a gumbo with shards of crab shell floating on top, some oyster dressing in the oven. It was crab season so there was a pit fire and a big boil. She'd never tasted such food, had never eaten any fish but the catfish and trout that Virgil and his friends caught in the Tallahatchie River. She ate what Virgil's people fixed with no discrimination, some of it more than one helping. Virgil's sister Hattie said that for such a scrawny little thing Dovey sure knew how to pack it in, and everybody laughed. When she finished, she sat down on the couch with everybody talking around her and fell asleep sitting up. She was dead tired. They'd sat up on the train overnight and she hadn't slept. She'd never set foot on a train, much less riding almost 350 miles in one trip. The seats in the colored car were lacquered pine, hard and splintery, and the clatter of the wheels kept her awake. She sat next to a window and over the early morning hours she watched the strong jaw of her own serious face float like a ghost over the dim first light of the piney woods of southern Mississippi and later the still, green swamps of Louisiana; she'd never seen water that still. White birds with long necks waded in the swamps on gold needle legs and portly blue herons stood on the edges, staring down. Gulls swooped and screamed and she shivered thinking of the snakes that must surely live their secret lives under the water, busy with the cycle of killing and birthing, slashing the water. The swamps must be teeming with them, the smoky cottonmouths with their blunted heads and little necks, the harmless green water snakes that scooted here and there.

Cushioned so nicely on the couch between the plump thighs

of Virgil's sister and Virgil himself, her head against an afghan somebody had kindly placed behind her, she'd drifted off, dreaming an elaborate dream about a bloodstain on a nice white dress that wouldn't come out, scrubbing and bleaching the spot over and over until it shrunk to the size of a grain of pepper, which only she could see but which bothered her nonetheless. Bloodstains were the easiest—cold water, every woman knew that. Why wouldn't this one disappear?

So, in the middle of everything, in front of this family she'd never met, she'd embarrassed Virgil by sleeping hard, her head thrown back and her mouth open. Finally, he shook her and told her to get up, they were going to see the ocean. His tone stern.

They walked under the live oaks up Esplanade into the Marigny, and boarded the Pontchartrain Express to Milneburg, ten cents for a round trip. At the end of the line, they got off and he pointed the way and they walked the remaining blocks to the water.

It wasn't what she expected. Swampy and rank with garbage from the ramshackle fish camps up and down the piers. No beach and the water a dingy brown rather than the clear green she'd imagined. There was a long pier where a vessel the size of a mountain was docked and men were unloading pineapples. Up and down, men in enormous straw hats were fishing. But there were waves, little ones but regular and steady as a heartbeat, and they came in and swished up on the wood pilings, making a nice sound. See, Virgil said with a sweep of his hand and she could tell he was proud of that brown water and the fact that he could take her to it and she said yes she did see and they were right pretty, those waves, she was pleased to make their acquaintance.

**NOW THE** waves that made everything slip and slide before her eyes had calmed. The one baby's cry had turned into a chorus and not far from her. They must have put them all together, all the lost babies.

She pushed herself up on the pallet and got to her knees. If she could just get up into a seat, she could see around the theater. She walked on her knees over to a seat at the end of the closest row and took hold of the chair arm and pulled herself up. When her foot took on weight, it felt like somebody had stuck a knitting needle in it. She gasped and fumbled with the upturned seat and sat down hard, before it was all the way down. She sat with tears streaming down her cheeks, gritting her teeth against the needle, scanning the theater for the babies. In the middle aisle, some ladies were bending down and coming up with writhing blankets. She rose again, this time not putting weight on the foot, steadying herself on the back of the seat in front of her, and hopped her way over to the middle aisle. She dropped into the last seat. There was a cluster of bassinets in the aisle and some children were sitting in seats next to them. A Red Cross lady, not hers, stood talking to some of the older children and writing things into a notebook.

*Got to get back up. Got to see.* Clutching the backs of seats, she hopped up the aisle until she came to where the babies were. One of the ladies holding a baby asked her what she needed, and she told her about Promise. *These here are the white babies,* the lady said, holding the one in her arms toward Dovey to make her point. The baby was splotched bright red. It gasped for breath between screams. Some folks don't know how to fix a baby. When she was little, her mother always handed the youngest to her. First Janesy, who whimpered like a puppy; then Uldine with her colic; and finally little Blue, who took the cake with his hollering. But even him she could calm. Her grandmother had taught her. It was all in the grip, a firm hand on the seat of the britches; that, and holding the screamer next to your liver. The liver is full of blood and blood calls out to blood, her grand-mother had said.

Dovey didn't know what to say back to the woman who held the baby. That Promise was, by hook or crook, almost all white and sure enough looked it? Would the woman then say, a drop is a drop? And what then? Should Dovey say a drop may be a drop but this baby's drop don't show, she wished it showed more? Life would be less complicated. Should she tell the woman to get out of her way and run the risk of the woman slapping her? None of it seemed right or wise. Instead she ignored the woman and hopped by her and peered down at the little ones in their bassinets, examining each face to make sure. Oddly, Promise's face had clotted in her mind. Was his mouth full or straight? His hair, she seemed to remember, was chestnut, but his fingers, long and slender or thick? All she could remember, really see in her mind's eye, were those copper eyes. These babies here were most definitely not her great-grandbaby. Promise had some-thing special about him, a little added extra thing. Virgil called it salt, that baby's got salt, he'd say. She thought it was more like sugar, a sweetness that lifted them all up and made them wonder how in the world it had happened, given the ugliness he'd come out of. She'd always wanted to see her Charlesetta in him, some little something, the shape of the cheek or Charlesetta's bow of a hairline, just a whisper to remember her by, but she never had, just like she'd never seen Charlesetta in Dreama.

The thought occurred to her that maybe there was something about Promise that white folks could see that she couldn't, maybe they could see blood where she couldn't.

"Where the colored babies at?" she asked the woman.

The woman shook her head. "I don't know. Maybe ask the Red Cross people?"

The waves crashed in now, splattered the pier. Everything went under: the seats, the stage, the lined-up lost babies. Dovey collapsed into a seat.

The woman leaned over her. "You all right, auntie?"

Dovey tried to nod but her chin had stationed itself on her chest and wouldn't move. *Old chin.* Then there was the underwater gurgle of the woman's voice calling for help. Some hands took her arms and then she was flat on her back again and they carried her somewhere, and then there was nothing but time.

WHEN SHE awoke again she was back on her pallet in the corner. Things had quietened down. Moans but no screams, no babies hollering. The lights had been dimmed, and there was the hum of a motor. It was true dark in her corner now but she could see the shapes of people lying around her. Some talked quietly among themselves. All colored people. Their voices rose and fell, rose and fell, and lulled her back to sleep.

The second time she woke up the lights were back on and shone in her eyes. A girl she didn't know stood over her.

"What are we going to do, Granny? You hear anything about Papa?" The girl bent over her, took her hands and held them up to her face. *Who?* Rain from the girl's eyes splattered Dovey's face. "I searched high and low for him, Granny, and he's nowhere. I can't find him. I had him under me in the road. How'd he get out from under me? I looked and looked. He's not anywhere."

Dovey could smell the rain on the girl's face, it smelled like swamp, salty and coming from a dark and mysterious place. It splattered Dovey's face, pooled between the chords of her neck. It tickled her good ear and soaked into her hair. "Everybody's somewhere," she said to the girl.

"But I've been looking two days and two nights."

Two days? Where was Virgil? "Maybe three's the charm."

The girl drew closer. "They say your foot's bad and you've got a loose brain. They say they've got to keep you. You got to tell me what to do, Granny."

Sweet, Dovey thought. She could just lie here now and somebody else would do the laundry and she could rest. She flexed the foot and the needle found its mark. No point in fighting it. Who was this girl with her thicket of words? Her outrageous demands? It occurred to Dovey that she herself might be dead and this girl someone she'd known from a long time ago, maybe a girl from the one-room schoolhouse where Dovey had learned to read and make her numbers. Most of Dovey's classmates, the ones she'd kept up with, had passed; maybe this girl was one of the early ones who'd succumbed to whooping cough or typhoid or polio or TB or just a chest cold.

But now this girl, this irritating girl, poked her on the shoulder, once, then again, and the rain on Dovey's face turned into a downpour.

"Granny, you got to wake up. The nurse says I got to wake you up every two hours." Now the girl patted Dovey's cheek, gently at first, then harder. "Open your eyes, Granny."

Her eyes *were* open, was the girl blind? As to that old dog Virgil, well, he'd just have to find *her*. She'd looked for him long enough, she was flat worn out with looking for him, sick to death of him running off and leaving her like that. How come him to go and do that? Was he catting around with some woman? After all those loads of laundry and all the corn bread and biscuits and pulling some flavor out of the beans and staying awake in bed for him to do his business on nights when she was dead on her feet? What had he done for her?

The girl was pure aggravation. A pesky mosquito, jawing at her, keeping her from taking her rest.

Another Red Cross lady came up. "You two want some sandwiches?"

The girl reached out and took two, then poked Dovey again. "Wake up, Granny."

"Let me be." As if she hadn't worked hard all her life. As if she didn't deserve a little rest. The girl vexed her. Who did she think she was?

The girl put a cool hand to Dovey's forehead. "You're hot. Let me look at that foot." The girl pulled the covers off of Dovey's leg. Then Dovey felt air as the girl unraveled some of the bandages. There was a long silence, then the girl put the covers back so lightly Dovey could hardly feel them. "I'm getting somebody to look at this leg."

When the girl got up to leave, Dovey opened her eyes, missing this aggravating girl already. The girl walked with a firm step toward a cluster of women in white. She spoke to the women and pointed back to where Dovey lay and the women looked. One broke away from the group and followed the girl back. The woman pulled a thermometer out of her pocket and put it in Dovey's mouth and took Dovey's wrist and looked at a watch on her arm.

"She's got a fever," the girl said to the woman. "And the foot, it's swelled up all the way to her knee. Don't you have any medicine you can give her?"

The Red Cross lady brought out a stethoscope. When the cold instrument touched her chest, Dovey's heart kicked back. The woman listened for what seemed like a long time, then turned back to the girl. "Who are you? Are you kin to her?"

"My name is Dreama Grand'homme. She's my grandmother. She has a husband, but we can't find him."

*Dreama.* It was a pretty name, Dovey thought, a pretty name for a pretty little girl. How old was she? Eleven, twelve, maybe younger?

The nurse pulled back the covers. She poked at Dovey's leg and the bottom of her foot.

"Do you feel that?" she asked Dovey.

Dovey shook her head. The foot felt like a piece of meat attached to her leg. An improvement over the knitting needle.

"I'm going to get somebody to take a look. It may have to come off." Then the nurse was gone and Dovey was glad because that meant she had the aggravating girl to herself again.

The girl hovered over her, clucking over Dovey and raining on her face again. Dovey licked her lips, coming up with salt.

"You got the nurse," she said to the girl.

"Probably would never have come over here if somebody hadn't. Probably wouldn't have given you a second thought."

"But you got her."

The girl's almond eyes hardened. "I did. I got her and I'll go get her again if she doesn't get back here and see about you."

"What she say about my foot?"

"She said it looked bad."

"What they going to do with it?"

"I don't know, Granny."

"Don't let them . . ." Dovey fell back into a doze, forgetting what she didn't want them to do, and here came the storm again and took her up in its long, cold arms and flew her all over town, except that the town was bare as a bone and there were no children anywhere, only old folks, white and black, skin and bone and naked as jaybirds, rummaging around in what was left, which was nothing but garbage, piles and piles of it. An upside-down cow sailed by, barely missing her. The cow had no hair and it looked surprised, not fearful but just surprised. "Morning," she said to the cow. "Morning," it said back to her before it was swept away. Then she looked down and saw a little child, a baby, naked too, in a bush, bawling its eyes out. "Morning," she said to it too, but it screamed on, shaking its little fists at her. She reached out to take it but the storm was jealous and swooped her up and her mouth opened to tell the wind to stop but the words fell like stones onto the doomed landscape below, into deep pools of water and twisted, sheared tree trunks and piles and piles of ruined houses and cars and stores and churches and all the other things that people build or buy to make themselves feel at home in the world.

The girl pushed at her again. "Don't be going back to sleep. You hear me? I told you about that. What am I going to do with you, Granny?"

Now it all came back to her.

*Dreama. Oh.*

Dreama bent over her. "You remember me? I was afraid you didn't know who I was. I was afraid you'd gone mental."

They both laughed a little, and Dreama put her hand on Dovey's head. When the doctor came, he squatted down and lifted the covers and took off all the bandages and looked at the foot, turning it this way and that. He was a plump man. There were beads of sweat on his brow.

"Why don't you take her up there on the stage so you can see what you're doing?" Dreama asked him.

"Crowded up there," he murmured. "No need for that."

Dreama's eyes narrowed. "Looks to me like there's room for an elephant up there on that stage."

"Don't you sass me, girl." He didn't look up at Dreama when he said it, and Dovey barely caught the words.

"You just going to let my granny die back here on the floor in this corner? You can't see a thing. Floor's filthy. Dirt and roaches and probably rats. No place for somebody who's sick as she is." Dreama's voice rose and people started to look.

Girl got her sass from her mama, Dovey thought.

Another Red Cross lady, this one a Yankee by the sound of her, came over and asked if she could help.

Dreama turned to her. "My grandmother needs to be up off this dirty floor and in the light where somebody can see about her. She's about to lose this foot if somebody doesn't do something."

"Don't let them," Dovey murmured.

"Is this woman in sepsis?" the Yankee Red Cross lady asked the doctor.

"Her foot's pretty bad."

"No," Dovey said. She'd come into the world with that foot. It was small like her and slender and high-arched. Once she'd been vain about her feet, the way the toes lined up from big toe to little, as regular as stair steps. Promise had her toes.

"Well then, I think the girl has a point, don't you? Now why don't I get someone to take this *lady* up onto the stage so you can keep a better eye on her? Looks like you have plenty of room up there."

"Down here we don't mix," the doctor said under his breath. He still hadn't looked up.

"Oh dear, that's not emergency protocol," the Yankee Red Cross lady said. She said it as pleasantly as if she were talking about what to have for supper or inquiring about the weather. Her mouth smiled, but her eyes were fiery. "We treat everyone by the severity of the injury. Now let's get this poor unfortunate woman up into the light. Honey, have you had a tetanus?"

Protocol? The unfamiliar word frightened Dovey in some deep way, conjuring endless lines of people waiting and waiting, bloodied and ragged, the lines in their faces train tracks on a map. The lines turned a corner and went into a building of some sort and folks were being told to take off their clothes and go inside. Then there were rows instead of lines, endless rows of them, naked as jailbirds, skin and bone, like crackers in a box. She'd never seen such a thing, though she'd heard about whole villages in Europe wiped out in the Great War, the dead lined up in open trenches they themselves had been forced to dig. The evil in this world, how it dipped and swooped! Her grandmother who saw the stars fall in Alabama used to talk about pattyrollers. If you walked out at night, there might be no coming back, or at least no coming back without damage. They patrolled the countryside and took you by surprise, and if you were a girl it was your lookout. On hot summer nights Dovey and her sisters and brother used to play pattyroller, one of them on the lam, scuttling from tree to tree, the rest tearing around on imaginary horses beating whips made from forsythia branches, and hollering about what they were going to do when they caught the one who ran.

Dreama leaned down and touched Dovey's shoulder. "There's babies everywhere, Granny. The place is running over with them. I'm going to see if I can find Promise. I'll be back."

Dovey opened her mouth to tell her there was no point, she'd already looked at the babies, not to worry, though—there was a baby to match everybody who was looking for one, you just had to find the right fit—but then some men came with a stretcher and slid her over onto it and lifted her up and the needle in her foot pitched and plunged. She cried out, couldn't help it, and one of them put his hand on her belly to hold her steady. The bare underside of his arm, white with freckles and little brown hairs everywhere, blocked her view. The hand was heavier than it ought to have been and it pressed down. Her bladder was full and the pressure unbearable. She pushed the hand away but it came back. "Got to hold you steady," the man murmured. She stopped fighting then and let her bladder empty, turning her face away from the man.

When the men began to ascend the stairs to the stage, the stretcher lurched and she slid down on it, sliding into the pool of her own urine, which had gone from warm to cold. For a sickening moment she thought she was going to fall off, but the hand steadied her. One of the men brushed the foot and the needle twisted and she cried out again.

The hand patted her belly and the man on the end of it said they were there now, somebody was going to take a look at that leg. They put her in a corner of the stage behind a screen. She opened her mouth to ask for her doctor, Dr. Juber, but then the storm took her up again and blew her backward, back to yesterday and then the whole blessed day before when there was no weather and it was Palm Sunday and Dreama and Promise were on their way home from church and Virgil was dead to the world in his bed and the children were dancing in the street and the worst thing that had happened was the McNabb wash about to get rained on.

"Granny, you wake up. Don't you go dying on me. Don't you dare go dying on me."

Dreama stood over her again, her eyes wide and full and now running over. Lord, that girl could rain tears.

"What you know good, girl."

Dreama made a sound like a puppy. "Nothing. Don't know nothing good. Can't find my baby."

"I gone and wet the bed."

"Oh Granny." Dreama patted her shoulder. "You wait right here. I'll be back."

Dovey pushed herself up on her elbow. "Don't want no white folks changing me. Get a colored nurse."

"I been changing a lot of diapers lately. I can sure change one more."

When Dreama came back, she had sheets and towels and a nurse who smiled at Dovey and said she was there to make her more comfortable. She pulled another screen around the stretcher and set about her task. Dreama helped roll Dovey over and pull the wet sheet out from under her. She didn't look at her grandmother, just at the nurse, waiting for her next instructions. Then she helped roll her back onto the clean sheet. Dovey smelled bleach and smiled and went back to sleep.

SOMEBODY WAS ironing her foot. How come you to iron my foot? It was burning burning—would somebody please take that iron away? She shivered and shook. Now she was on a burning plain, lights in her eyes, stars falling like stones.

Dreama stood talking to a colored man in a blood-splattered gown. The nurse who'd changed Dovey came up behind him and untied it in back, then replaced it with a clean one. Then the nurse came forward with something in a glass that looked like maple syrup and told Dovey to drink it down. The liquid scalded her throat and she gagged. She tried to hand back the glass but the nurse frowned and put it back up to her lips.

Somebody rolled in a tray with small shiny knives on it and something that looked like the tongs she used to pull her clothes from the hot water. The doctor came toward her then, his shadow looming over her, and when she saw what was in his hand, she began to scream. The nurse came and held her leg and then the men who had carried her stretcher came around her. There was a slowness to their coming, as if they were ashamed. They surrounded her and took hold of her. Two on her arms, two on her legs, which were pulled apart.

Dreama leaned down and kissed her on the forehead and wet her face, that girl was going to drown her in tears before this was over. Then Dreama, that cat, was gone, and someone poured something liquid and strong smelling over her foot and ankle. For a moment she wondered if it were gas and they were going to burn the foot off. She floated somewhere above herself, looking down at her limbs splayed like Crosstown, where the Frisco and the M&O crossed in a perfect X. She thought for another moment that these serious-looking young men were holding her down for the man in the clean apron and after he'd taken his turn they'd each have theirs.

*This is how Dreama must have felt, like Crosstown.*

Then the man in the clean apron, who was colored but who she didn't know from Adam—though maybe she did, maybe he was Dr. Juber after all—said to Dreama he was sorry that they'd run out of anesthesia but he had to do something about this foot. Dovey opened her mouth to tell him to take off the iron, but nothing came out. A piece of her covering had crept over one side of her face, and all the laundry of the past fifty years, all the laundry in her tally books once so neatly stacked and now cast to the four corners of the earth, came tumbling down on her, heavy and slick and gray with white folks' dirt. There was more and more of it and it smothered her and she tried to fight it but her arms were gone and so were her legs.

So she didn't notice when the knife made its first cut into her tree-trunk ankle. Only later would she remember that the touch of the blade was cold as ice, a blessed relief.

# 10

## 4 P.M.

The new cast was cool, smooth to the touch, not rough and ragtag and itchy like the old one. Jo's head felt lighter too, and when
she touched it, the horn was gone and in its place a massive bandage that covered all the way from the top of her eyebrows up
into her scalp and from one side of her forehead to the other. She
missed the horn, the heft of it. Without it, she was just a girl.

When she opened her eyes, the glare of the overhead lights
blinded her and she quickly closed them. She yawned, and when
she did, her bad ear popped once and then opened up and the
hubbub around her rushed in. Something metallic fell to the
floor, clattering and banging. There were cries for help and piti-
ful moans, the sound of heels hitting the floor; and underneath
it all an insistent scurrying, as if large noisy rodents had been
loosed. The low, intense murmur of voices. *Here, there, give me
this, take that, go, stay, no I mean go and go right now this minute.*

The bedlam jolted her, and her eyes flew open again. She was
lying on a cot of some sort, narrow and hard and dipped in the
middle so that she rested in a trough. Now, thank heavens, the
brouhaha faded gradually, as if she were cantering a horse into
the distance, into a thicket of silence.

She dreamed about her cat. She saw Snowball glide through

the house, where she had never been allowed, a long smooth strand of unraveling silk, darting and dashing, saving Jo from Son's friends again and again. The cat took a leap and landed in Jo's own bed, the three kittens the color of dirty snow right behind her. *You, you, you,* they said to her. Jo had worried about them finding food after the storm. Before she left the house, she'd opened a bag of dried food on the back porch. Now, in Jo's dream, she saw the cat eating something under the bedcovers, something with fur that struggled. When Jo drew closer, she realized that the cat was killing one of her own kittens and eating it. She lurched toward the cat, intending to pull the kitten from her jaws, but before she could reach them the kitten disappeared into its mother's mouth and that was that. Snowball began to purr and clean herself, as if nothing had happened.

When Jo awoke the second time, her hair clotted with sweat, there was a baby crying next to her, screaming to high heaven. She turned her head, slowly, carefully, still aware of the horn's absent presence. How bad would the scar be?

The baby continued to scream. Jo opened her eyes and looked for the source of the sound. Red-faced and furious, the baby flailed about on his back in a bassinet rolled up next to her cot. *Little Tommy?* She pushed herself up with her good arm and leaned over and took a look. *Yes.* He still had the scratches from the bush running like train tracks across his face. She touched his cheek. He reached up and snatched at her finger and stuck it in his mouth and began to suck frantically. Bless his heart, he was hungry. How could these people—doctors and nurses from the looks of things—let a little baby go hungry? What a simple thing, warming a bottle. Why hadn't someone thought of it? Where was her mother? The thought of Alice and Alice's leg made her sit bolt upright. She'd done a report in history class earlier in the year about the Great War, how the soldiers' shattered limbs could sometimes never be made whole: how, in cases of severe injury, the pieces could not, even with the best of intentions and expertise, be reassembled; how "drastic action" was required. She had interviewed Mr. Lewis, who had been a lieutenant colonel in the army. He taught French at Tupelo High School and had lost his arm from a piece of shrapnel. He spent his spare time on the front porch of his rented duplex, sitting in a rocking chair holding a book in one hand. He had to put it down in his lap each time he turned a page. That was the worst thing, he told Jo, having to put that book down every time he turned the page. What an infernal aggravation! Imagine it! She couldn't, and especially now when it was her mother and a leg not an arm. How would Alice get up and down the stairs? How would she water her garden? Take care of little Tommy?

Jo wasn't sure how long it had been since the night of the storm—two days? three?—but she suspected that too much time had elapsed for her mother's leg, that "drastic action" would be required. How much of her poor wounded mother would be left?

What she couldn't bear to think about was sepsis. She'd read about the creeping poisons that killed, how limbs were packed in ice to slow their progression, how they continued to infuse the body after death, causing red streaks in the affected body part so that, oddly, the part that had been killed appeared the most alive. Back at the house, she'd thought of sepsis, of course she had, no one could say she'd hadn't, but there'd been no ice. All she could have done—pouring alcohol over the wound, making the splint and wrap—she had done and done well. Nobody could say she hadn't done the best she could—the best anyone could have done—under the circumstances.

The baby paused in his sucking and cried out, one foreshortened pathetic little cry, then resumed with her finger. Jo looked around for someone who might bring a bottle. She squinted against the glare of the lights, which made things worse since squinting caused her bandage to ride down over her eyes. From what she could tell, there was a sea of white, some of it splattered in red, and lumps of people covered in bandages. Doctors and nurses and other people who wore uniforms and seemed to know what they were doing, moved among the cots and the wounded lying on them as if they were a smorgasbord, spread out before them. They were all on a stage of some sort. From her cot Jo could reach over and touch a crumbling velvet curtain. She could smell the old dust in it. She sneezed and wiped her nose on the sleeve of what appeared to be a man's dress shirt that someone had put on her. The other sleeve had been cut off to make room for the cast. She blushed to think she'd been undressed (and bathed?) top to bottom and then repositioned inside the strange garment, which smelled of bleach. Even her underpants were gone. On the bottom she was wearing only a man's pajama pants of scratchy white cotton.

The baby spit out her finger again, his face purple with rage. He took a shaky breath and opened his mouth to scream. Jo kicked off her sheet and threw her legs over the side of the cot. She leaned over his bassinet and gathered him up just as the scream burst forth, using the cast to nudge him into her good arm and then hold him in place.

"Oh Tommy," she said. "It's going to be all right. You're going to be all right." She jounced him in her good arm the way she'd seen her mother do.

The baby stopped in mid-scream and regarded her, his head bobbling on his neck as he fought the glare of the overhead lights, his eyes strangely iridescent, the color of pennies, momentarily mysterious and foreign. She'd heard somebody say that all babies were born with blue eyes and that they changed color, if they were going to change, later on. Little Tommy's eyes must have changed in the midst of all this. How remarkable the way the body goes on when everything else comes to a screeching halt, how resolutely it makes its way through time. She'd read somewhere that hair and nails grew after death and the horror of Son with Dracula fingernails flashed unbidden in her mind.

To dispel the image, she kissed the baby on his nose. Then she rose with him in her arms, her knees wobbly and sore. The soles of her feet burned when she put her weight on them. Once, when she was little, Son had dared her to climb barefooted onto a pile of gravel. The two of them were in the back alley of the Leake & Goodlett lumberyard while their father was inside getting some boards to put up shelves in the garage. She had fought hard to go along with the two of them, her father having asked Son, but not her, to come on the errand. It was July and early afternoon, the sun blazing, the gravel dark and hot. Of course she'd taken Son's dare and run right up to the top of the pile, burning and scratching the soles of her feet. After that, her feet had turned sensitive and easily aggravated. She never went barefoot again, and when it came time to wear stockings and high heels, they became her tormentors. Over the years, the burn would rise to the surface from time to time to plague her. It had come back after Son and his friends had played the trick that day, and then again after she fell off the horse. Once, too, when she made a C in algebra, which she got because her teacher, the high school football coach, was stupid. Now here they were again, raising their ugly heads, her sad mad feet, burning and throbbing, just because she didn't have enough on her plate right now, just because she didn't have more than enough to contend with.

Some CCC boys carrying a stretcher passed by; on it was a small form the size and shape of a Thanksgiving turkey, covered with a blue-and-white-checked dish towel. An arm or leg? A baby? What had the CCC boys done with Son? There was a family plot in Glenwood Cemetery at the end of North Church Street. The aunts were there, under a stinky gingko tree that flared a brilliant yellow in the fall and dropped its rank fruit—a mucky cross between shit and vomit, Son used to say—that adhered to the soles of your shoes.

Aunt Fan had gone first. She had a nagging cough, Aunt Sister said, and in the middle of the night, she turned on the light and got a peppermint to soothe her throat. The aunts shared a bedroom in the old house. It was a large room and they had two double beds with a table between, where they placed their nighttime glasses of water and peppermints and whatever books they were reading at the time. The door to the room they kept locked at night because they worried about bands of Negro men breaking in and preying on innocent ladies like themselves. To Jo's knowledge they knew only one, Joshua Moses, who brought them eggs from his farm out in the country. Once he'd fixed a loose shingle on their roof and pulled down the ivy on the side of the house. He was nice as nice could be. But they'd heard stories. They needed to protect themselves.

After her coughing spell passed, Aunt Fan turned the light back off and unwrapped the peppermint and sucked on it for a minute or two; Aunt Sister could hear her. But then, just as Aunt Sister was drifting back to sleep, Fan bolted out of the bed and poked her hard on the shoulder. Aunt Sister sat up and turned on the light to find Fan standing over her, her face turned a horrible shade of plum; she was slapping her own chest frantically. *Frantically*, Aunt Sister said, over and over she slapped herself and looked at her, Sister, with eyes like plates. Sister didn't know what to do, but she got up and went over and patted Fan on the back, timidly at first, then harder, all the while fussing at her for waking her up from a dead sleep. Fan knew she had insomnia. How was she expected to get her rest?

Then Fan collapsed on the threadbare Oriental rug and stopped breathing or moving or doing anything but staring that awful stare.

That was October. The gingko was in flames and the fruit had dropped and stunk to high heaven. The men from Pegues Funeral Home placed the chairs in a semicircle on the opposite side of the tree, but the smell made Jo gag. Her mother handed her a lavender-scented handkerchief to put over her nose, and thankfully the graveside service consisted of "The Lord Is My Shepherd" and a hasty prayer, though by the time it was over Jo had upchucked into the handkerchief.

Two weeks later Alice sent Jo down the street with a plate of fried chicken and mashed potatoes for Aunt Sister. The front door was locked so Jo picked up the pot of mums on the front porch and retrieved the key from its hiding place. The flowers changed with the season, but the key had been under the pot since the beginning of time, always warm to the touch.

The living room was cold and dark and quiet, the drapes closed as if Aunt Sister had gone on a trip. There were dead flowers in vases of brown water everywhere, on the floor and dining room table and buffet. The aunts' two rocking chairs sat

dreaming in their place by the window, the crystal bowl of peppermints on the scalloped marble-top table between them.

Jo stopped midway through the living room and called out,
"Aunt Sister? Are you home?"

The silence of the house reached out and patted her cheek the
way Aunt Sister used to when she was little. What a beautiful
child, Aunt Sister would say, her touch papery and smelling of
talcum and ginger. It was the only time Jo had ever been called
beautiful.

Once, after the trick and when she'd started coming by every
afternoon after school, Aunt Sister had patted her cheek again
and said, *Don't you worry about a thing.*

The house pushed Jo backward. After what seemed like an
eternity, she touched the doorknob behind her and then turned
her back on the house and dead flowers and Aunt Sister's silence
and streaked across the porch and then the yard and then up
Church Street to get her mother.


NOW, SHE thought, there might well be more of her family
underground in Glenwood than aboveground in the house on
Church Street. Also buried under the gingko were her father's
parents and another baby brother named Henry, after Henry
Wadsworth Longfellow, her mother's favorite poet, born blue
when Jo was two years old. Over the years Jo had come to think
of him as Baby Blue. She pictured him floating up beyond the
clouds, translucent and motionless, like a jellyfish.

After Baby Blue, Jo's mother had borrowed Imogene Gillespie's
Charley and wouldn't give him back. Aunt Fan was a firsthand
witness and told the story to Jo one dark winter afternoon. Imo-

gene had taken little Charley with her to Lil's Beauty Parlor and parked him in his carriage by the sunny window up front next to Lil's overgrown philodendron. Unfortunately, Alice was there getting her first wash and set after losing her little Henry. You could tell, Aunt Fan said, that Lil was kicking herself for booking the two of them back to back; it was a terrible mistake and Lil's face turned white as a sheet when Imogene came sashaying in with that perky little baby boy of hers and all the ladies in the shop except Alice ran over and began to ooh and ahh over little Charley, who, Aunt Fan said, was a particularly well-formed child.

Alice got out from under the dryer for her comb-out, her cheeks flame red. She glared straight into the mirror while Lil took out her rollers and combed her out. She handed Lil two quarters, no tip. Then, as she headed out the door, she took the handle of the carriage like it and what it contained were hers, and twirled it around and opened the front door and had the baby out on the sidewalk before anyone could ask her what she had in mind. Just as the door closed, she said, "A bit of air." Just that, Aunt Fan said. A bit of air. Even the words sounded airy.

Meanwhile, little Charley's mother, Imogene, who had both sets of fingers immersed in soapy water, nodded sleepily, and the manicurist smiled and nodded too.

Aunt Fan had a bad feeling but she was in the middle of her Silver Satin treatment, which was tricky; she didn't want to end up purple like poor Minnie McFadden. When she was finished, Alice had not returned with little Charley. It was sprinkling outside, most definitely not baby-walking weather. Aunt Fan threw a scarf over her head and headed up North Church to find out what had happened. The baby carriage was on the McNabb

front porch. Aunt Fan marched into the house and called for
Alice, then when she didn't get a response, headed up the stairs.
She went from room to room and finally found little Charley
sleeping peacefully in what was to have been little Henry's cradle and Alice standing over him singing snatches of "When at
night I go to sleep, fourteen angels watch do keep." Alice had a
pretty voice, Fan said, but the song was eerie, especially when
Alice got to the part about the two angels whose job it was to
guide the baby's feet to heaven.

Aunt Fan said she didn't mince words. "That's Imogene Gillespie's baby, Alice. You need to give him back."

Alice cut her a look to kill. "Don't you go telling me what I
have to do, Fan McNabb, you're not the boss of me."

About that time Imogene burst through the front door downstairs hollering.

Alice glared at Aunt Fan and snatched little Charley from
the bassinet, whereupon he began to cry. Imogene came galloping up the stairs and burst into the room. She hurled herself
at Alice, screaming, "What are you doing to my baby? Are you
hurting him?"

Then Aunt Fan got into it. She went up to Alice. "Let me
change him, dear. Let me have him a minute."

As if things couldn't get any worse, Aunt Fan said, little Son
burst into the room and stopped short when he saw the baby in
his mother's arms. His face brightened, poor little thing, Aunt
Fan said.

"I thought we didn't get my brother," he said, clapping his
hands. "I thought God flew him away."

By now Imogene had fire in her eyes. She pulled her Charley
from Alice's arms, in the process knocking Son down.

"Don't you steal our baby!" he screamed, leaping up and lunging at Imogene's legs. Imogene pushed out her knee to dislodge him, knocking him to the floor again. He got up and ran to his mother crying, Aunt Fan said, like his heart was broken.

"Where was I?" Jo had asked Aunt Fan.

"Oh my, child, you were right there, tagging along behind your brother like always. You hated to let him out of your sight. And after he'd gotten up off the floor, he snatched you up and grabbed your hand and dragged you over to Imogene and said, "Here, take her and give me back my brother.""

Imogene, meanwhile, quieted her Charley. Then she looked at Alice. "This is *my* boy," she said. Aunt Fan said she didn't say it in a mean way, but as if Alice were a little child with a lesson to learn that she hadn't quite gotten yet. Then Imogene pointed to Son. "This is *your* boy, Alice. And soon you'll have another. But this one is mine."

Then Imogene gathered Charley's things and Aunt Fan followed her down the stairs to the porch and told her how mortified she was and how sorry Alice would be when she returned to her right mind.

And that was the end of it, except when Aunt Fan came back upstairs, Son was nowhere in sight and Alice was staring out the front window watching Imogene wheel her boy home in the drizzle.

NOW GLENWOOD would have another resident McNabb. Two days and two nights had passed since the storm. Son would be in a sorry state. But how could they just take him up there and plant him in the ground like an old dog without any family to

stand at the grave and sing how, in the sweet by-and-by, everyone would meet on that beautiful shore? (Which Jo sincerely
hoped would not be the case.)

Tommy's diaper was wet and he stank. She took a few steps
toward a nurse, who was bent over a cot several yards away. As
Jo approached, the nurse looked up and frowned. "You're going
to drop that baby," she called out. "You shouldn't be holding him
like that with your arm in a cast. Give him here."

Jo tightened her grip. "He's my brother."

*Brother.* Until now, the word had never entered her mind
without bared teeth. Now, though, with Son dead as a doornail,
dead as anybody could possibly be, the peckish creature called
*brother* that gnawed at her from time to time had disappeared
into thin air. She had come to the conclusion that Son's death
had nothing to do with her; the storm had done it, which meant
it was God's own doing, she was merely His instrument. Moreover, why trouble her parents, if by some miracle they were
ever returned to her, with the peculiar circumstances of Son's
death when none of it mattered, not one whit? When, as her
father was fond of saying, it was a moot point? Jo smiled a little
at her own cleverness, then stopped herself. Here she was, making wordplay out of her own brother's death; some might call it
something else if they didn't know about that strange gust from
the tornado that blew her forward into his shocked arms, almost
as if they were long-lost lovers. She looked down at the baby.
At least there was little Tommy, whom she herself had saved,
literally singlehandedly. Now the word *brother* had returned to
her mouth tasting like cinnamon, reminding her of the toast the
aunts sometimes made for her when she came in from school.

The nurse's name, Jo saw on her lapel, was Sue.

"Brother or not," Nurse Sue said. "You've got only one good arm." She reached for the baby. "Let me have him now, please do." She smiled at Jo.

Jo found the smile insincere, something about Nurse Sue's eyes, which were red with fatigue. Nurse Sue wasn't from around Tupelo either, Jo could tell by the crispness of her consonants. Jo backed up and shifted her grip, startling the baby, who exploded into a blood-curdling scream that caused heads to turn. "I've got hold of him just fine. I found him half dead in a bush and I've been taking care of him ever since and if I hadn't found him he would have died in that bush. The reason he's crying now is that nobody around here has seen fit to give him a bottle. So, if you want to be so all-fired helpful, go get me a bottle. *Somebody* needs to feed this baby." She had never spoken to an adult in that tone. If her father could have heard her, he'd have had a fit. But her father, of course, was missing in action, and her mother lost to her, so there was no one at present to say you go or you stay or you wear your hat just so and behave.

Then, to Jo's surprise, Nurse Sue's eyes filled and a tear rolled down her nose and hung on the tip. Then she wiped it off and smiled a real smile. "Whoa, hon. I'll get him a bottle. You're quite the gal, now aren't you, for taking such good care of him. Now let's you sit with him." She put one hand under the baby and the other on Jo's good shoulder, guiding her, then pushing her back down. "It's going to be all right now. You're going to be all right, sweetheart."

"My mother. Can you find out what happened to her?"

As Jo spoke, the baby slipped a little in her grip and then began to slide down her thigh. Quick as lightning, Nurse Sue snatched him up and Jo let her because something inside had broken open when she spoke of her mother, and she worried that what the nurse had said was true, that it was quite possible she might yet make a terrible mistake, she might just drop her baby brother no matter how careful she tried to be (and nobody could say she hadn't been extra careful) and therefore manage to kill not one but two brothers in the space of less than three days. Then there'd be nobody left but her, not the father she'd counted on her whole life without a shadow of a worry because she knew, come hell or high water, he would have come back to save them if he'd been able, which meant that something terrible had happened. Probably he'd fallen into one of those bottomless water holes made by the root balls from the giant oaks pushed over by the storm, or maybe he had run into a burning house to save a girl like herself and had perished in the attempt. He would have a beautiful monument at Glenwood detailing his valor. *Hero, Father: He Did the Best He Could.* She enjoyed thinking of her father as a hero; before the storm she'd considered him rather dull.

Nurse Sue took the baby and started to walk away. Jo got up to follow her.

"You take a little rest, honey," the nurse said. "And don't you worry. I'm going to feed him and change him and bring him right back here to you." She stood beside the cot and waited until Jo lay back. Then she reached down and stroked her hair, which Jo knew was a terrible mess. Still, she inclined her head toward the nurse's touch. She couldn't help herself. The McNabbs were not ones to display affection, and the nurse's touch felt like something Jo had been waiting for her whole life. Nurse Sue had blond hair held up in a twist under her cap; her uniform was starched and tidy. Maybe Jo would become a nurse. She fell asleep, her mouth half open, with the nurse's hand on her hair.

Now, though, Snowball was flying around town like a huge bird of prey, Jo's sweet little cat grown monstrous, swooping down on small birds and chipmunks and squirrels lying helpless on the ground and carrying them off in her claws, then landing on the branch of a tree, now bare from the tornado, to eat them. *Snowball, stop,* Jo called up to her. *You don't have to do that.* But the cat just stared at her, wide-eyed as an owl.

*You, you, you.*

When she woke up the third time, the place had quieted down and the lights had dimmed. She wondered if it was the middle of the night. There was no way of knowing since there were no windows in the theater. She looked out over the theater and saw colored people lying on pallets on the floor, sandwiched in between the rows of seats.

She peered over into the bassinet. The baby was sleeping on his stomach, his rear end pointing to the ceiling. A little tadpole of a boy. Where was their father? What if she were the only one left to take care of little Tommy? What would happen to them? They would be orphans. Their closest relative, her mother's only brother, Johnny Trotter, lived out on a piece of land near Pontotoc. Uncle Johnny was a confirmed bachelor and kept rough company. They had visited him once, but the cabin he lived in was filled with spider webs littered with dead flies and wasps, the kitchen counter covered in greasy dishes. There were not enough chairs for all of them to sit down at the same time so she had spent most of her time on the back stoop watching chickens peck the dirt around her feet. What she found odd was how they seemed to enjoy eating gravel. They ate it with relish, as if it were feed.

Now, there would be nothing to do but for Jo to take care of Tommy. She would be Joan of Arc, burned at the stake of necessity. They would rattle around the big four-square house, just the two of them, checking doors and windows at night, sleeping together in a locked room. Everyone would feel bad for her. The colored who worked for her family were good people. Surely they wouldn't abandon her in her hour of need. Bless her heart, dear dear Essie would surely work for free, cooking and cleaning and watching the baby while Jo was at school and for special occasions like the cotillion dance in the spring, and that little washwoman with the name of a bird would do the laundry every Saturday like before, just out of the goodness of her heart. There was a handsome new preacher at First Presbyterian, and he would be compelled to counsel and advise her. Her teachers would arrange special tutoring sessions to help her with her studies since so much of her time would be taken up with little Tommy. Her friends wouldn't abandon her either. They would come by in the afternoons after school. She would find their petty little spats and adventures ridiculously puerile (a Word to Keep). She would want to laugh at them and tell them they knew nothing whatsoever of the cold, cruel world. But she wouldn't because by then she would have become kind and mature and brave and immensely patient. She would have *transmogrified.* Then one day a special man (a man, not a boy, possibly the preacher himself, who was a bachelor and pretty as a girl) would present himself and there would be a kiss and after that a wedding and little Tommy would then have a new father and Jo and this man, yes, most likely the preacher (who would have overlooked the hideous scar on her forehead), and little Tommy would live happily ever after and she would no longer be alone and afraid.

The baby lifted his head and looked at her sideways. He

seemed momentarily puzzled by her, as if he'd opened a door and she was not the one he'd expected to find on the other side. Then his eyelids fluttered and he went back to sleep, his mouth in a half-smile, twitching a little. What a precious angel he was! How could she have thought any different? She chastised herself for not being more charitable about his bouts with colic, his furious rages that drove them all to distraction but that now the storm had seemed to blow away.

*Oh, let her never doubt how lucky she was to have him!*

Though, if she didn't, her life would be much easier. He was, after all, something of an encumbrance. Were it only herself orphaned, she would be asked, she felt sure, to join the family of one of her friends, Lois or the Wesson twins, preferably Lois because Lois was an only child and lived in a huge house with gables and window seats. Jo would acquire not only a ready-made sister but also her own room.

She gazed around her, looking out again over the dark sea of the theater, where some people sat and slept, and between which some others lay unconscious or sleeping she couldn't tell which. She assumed they weren't dead by the fact that the CCC boys hadn't come and thrown a sheet over them and carried them off.

There was a woman in the bed next to her who kept moaning. Jo didn't like the sounds she made; as a matter of fact they were downright irritating, and if she thought for a minute that the woman was, well, *aware* enough to know just how aggravating she was being to everyone around her, Jo would have been quite angry. But, of course, the woman—the *poor* woman, who looked at least fifty, half a century, think of it, and looking older, old as the hills, surely one of those millworkers since she'd obviously not taken care of her complexion—had no idea what a horrendous sound she was making. Of course she didn't, and so Jo felt sorry for her and if she'd been a nurse, which she intended to be soon, she would have done something, offered the unfortunate woman a sip of paregoric perhaps, to shut her up.

Now the woman, horrors, sat up in bed and stared at Jo like she was a ghost.

There was a desperation to her stare, as if the poor thing were stranded on an iceberg and searching the horizon for the boat that would rescue her.

"What?" said Jo, because she didn't know what else to say.

"Jenny?" said the woman. "Jenny, dear?"

"No. I'm not Jenny." Jo said it more firmly than she meant to. The poor woman was obviously in distress.

"Jenny? You're not my Jenny?" the woman said again. Then her head fell back on her pillow and her neck lay at a perplexing angle as if the two, the head and the neck, weren't even connected, and then, Jo didn't know how she knew this but she knew it beyond a shadow of a doubt, the woman was alive one minute and dead the next, and sure enough, when Jo cried out for someone to come, a doctor came over and took the woman's pulse and then pulled her sheet up over her face.

Jo fingered her own sheet. If she died like that, suddenly and quietly, her own neck at that odd angle, would someone come and pull this very sheet over *her* face and then take her off, like the CCC boys in white were doing that very minute to the poor mill woman, maybe even to Jo's poor mother?

There was death all around her in this place. How could she not have seen it? She could kick herself. Why, when the poor woman had called out for her Jenny, whoever she was, hadn't she, Jo McNabb, answered, *Here I am, my dear, your Jenny. I am right here. Here is my hand on yours, darling?*

A DOOR at the back of the theater opened now and a figure strode in, looking from right to left and back again, as if he, and Jo thought surely it was a he by the fact that she saw pants, were searching for someone. The person, and yes she could tell now it was most definitely a man, came up the middle aisle, stopping at each row, peering at the people slouched in the seats and those on the floor in various stages of unconsciousness. There was an impatience in the man's movements, an urgency, as if he were going to punish the person he was looking for when he found him or her, as if he were going to give that sought-after person a good talking-to.

He had a familiar gait and the way he put his hand up to his eyebrows to shield his vision from the bright overhead lights made her think of her father when he fished. Mort McNabb liked to fly-fish, and once he'd taken her up to the river and they'd floated along with their knees up to their chins in a very small rowboat for one long hot day because dawn and dusk are the best times to fly-fish. He showed her how to cast and set the line, then slowly skip it through the water in the most alluring way possible. She didn't catch anything but she had the most seductive nibbles. Her father insisted that she not jerk the line and set the bait, they were probably turtles; she obeyed him, but reluctantly, envisioning a five-pound trout on the end of her line. She knew that if only she'd had another chance, a second day, the fish were bound to hit and hit hard. They were just getting to know her, they just liked to tease. Her father had worn an old hat made of burlap grown loose and soggy with age and moisture; he had stuck his lures into the fabric and their weight had folded the hat over his ears. She had loved him in that hat.

Now, as the man came closer, she saw that indeed it was Mort McNabb. Where, pray tell, had he been all this time? Why had he not come back for her, and also for her mother and little brother, both of whom, no thanks to anyone but her, had been rescued from the pit of death? (Well, she'd give the old wash-woman some credit for sending the CCC boys her way.) Now, when it didn't matter, here came her on-the-lam father to the rescue, looking resolute and worried and responsible; he looked like the man she'd thought he had been before the storm had proved otherwise.

She watched him come, but she didn't call out to him. Maybe it was a proprietariness about little Tommy. He was safe and sound because *she* had saved him and she was prepared to take care of him all by herself if her mother didn't turn up, or even if she did. If she could ever find a working stove, she would warm his bottle properly and dribble it on her wrist to make sure it wasn't too hot. She had come to know what his various cries meant and what would comfort him and make him stop crying. She had come to know him like the back of her own hand because he was her own dear brother and she his sister-mother-father all rolled into one. It was as if she had hooked him with an invisible line and drawn him in. She'd caught him so that he might live, not die. She alone had pulled him from that bush. She alone had kept him warm and clean and nourished. She'd made the nostrils flare on his little smushed-in nose and his cheeks turn rosy and his eyes flicker and shine, all in the short time it took for blue eyes to change to copper. Her father had had nothing to do with any of it. Mort McNabb was now, what was the Word to Keep her mother had given her? *Redundant.*

But still here he came and there was no wishing him away, and after a few minutes he turned his attention to the stage where she lay and it was a matter of moments before he would spot her. So she raised her hand, hesitantly, as if she were in school and answering a particularly difficult question the teacher had posed, as if she weren't sure of the answer.

And then she called out "Daddy," thinking, suddenly, with a rush of relief, that this man was her very own father, and surely there was some good reason he had not come to save them when they needed saving, some very good reason that he would soon divulge, and she, Jo, his one and only daughter, would understand.

Now that he'd come under the lights, Jo got a good look. Mort needed a shave. There was a bandage on the side of his neck and a cleft the size of an earthworm between his eyebrows that hadn't been there before. His cheeks hung in pouches and his eyes were rimmed in red.

"Jo, thank God," he called out and came toward her, winding between the maze of cots that separated them. When he reached her, he tried to gather her up into his arms, cast and all, knocking into the bassinet, jostling the baby, who whimpered, then began to kick and fuss. Her father didn't look down at the baby, her brother, his son. "Where's your mother?"

"I don't know. Nobody will tell me, but look, I found little Tommy and he's just fine."

"Where? Where was he? I looked everywhere." Mort McNabb snatched up the baby, who began to scream.

"You're scaring him," Jo said.

Her father ignored her. He held the baby high in the air and kissed his stomach. Tommy used to like it when their father came home from work and held him aloft and kissed his little belly. He would kick and giggle; now he just screamed louder, his face red, his little fists clinched as if to protect himself from the evil giant who dangled him in midair.

*Fe, fi, fo, fum,* Jo thought.

Mort handed her the baby. "I'm going to find your mother," he said.

He moved from cot to cot, working his way from one side of the room to the other. He stopped and spoke briefly to a few people who lay under the sheets, but he didn't pause long at any one bed. Jo watched as he went about his search methodically, finally ending in a corner of the stage. Then, as Jo watched, he approached a nurse, who beckoned him to follow. They both disappeared behind a curtain into a side exit and it was as if he'd been swallowed whole, or worse yet, had never been there at all, as if Jo had conjured him up. She looked down at the baby, who had, mercifully, stopped crying and now looked up at her impassively, a slight and strangely unrecognizable smile playing at his lips.

She wondered suddenly whether she even wanted her father to return. He was bossy and sometimes even rude. He slurped his coffee and lectured her ad nauseam on the merits of objective justice. He'd flat-out refused to let her go see Herb Bassett's world-renowned air show. Herb had worn goggles and had a lazy smile and a curly lock of dark hair that hung over his eyes. She'd told her parents she was going to Lois's and the two of them had sneaked off and gone anyway and she was eternally glad they had. The plane had done twirlies and curlicues and had made her heart stop when it landed on one wheel. A year later, when it came down in a blaze of glory in Biloxi, she grew to believe she'd seen that too, though she had only read about it in the newspaper and cried herself dry for Herb Bassett.

Then too there was the fact that, until Son turned bad, Mort had always favored him because he was the boy, he was the *son*. In truth, she was generally sick and tired of her father's ways, and especially his discourses on justice, how there was a right way and a wrong way for everything under the sun, how the path toward justice was always brightly lit and abundantly clear to him, how justice was clean as a whistle, blind as a bat to love and pity and selfishness, those ragtag beggars. (And such a paragon of virtue her father was, with his hidden stash of moonshine and that unspeakable book, the latter so disgustingly obscene Jo couldn't bear to think about it: men with body parts the size of elephant tusks, women twisted in impossible positions, with *smiles* on their faces. No wonder her poor mother was beside herself!) To Jo, justice seemed more like a dark and foggy day, the kind Tupelo got in November, near her birthday, when the hills and the sky seemed indistinguishable. Oh, and good grief, here he came back again, striding up the aisle, followed by a man in a white coat, both of them climbing the steps to the stage and heading for her and Tommy, who'd just now drifted back off to sleep, thankfully. She hoped her father wouldn't wake him a second time. She was tired of all the screaming, no matter how much she loved her baby brother.

"Jo!" Mort's voice rang out, causing several bandaged heads to rise off their cots.

Jo put a finger to her lips. She had learned over the past few days how to be quiet.

"Jo, they've got your mother over there." He gestured toward the far back of the stage. "They took her straight into surgery."

Jo looked back and forth between her father and the man in white. She prepared herself to ask about the word *surgery*, what it meant, but then her father's face crumbled and the man in white put his hand on her father's shoulder and she knew without asking.

She put her hands over her face and began to cry, and as if on cue, so did the baby. "Pick him up," she commanded her father, but he was already gone, following the man in white, both of them making their way across the sea of white, leaving her with little Tommy to deal with, yet again.

So she got up and reached for him. Damn her father's hide, she would take care of her baby brother if no one else would. She would save him for her mother, and her mother would have to live because he would be there needing her every minute of every day, leg or no leg. Now he was wet again and there was a pile of clean diapers at the foot of the bassinet, so she opened each diaper pin one-handed, with the utmost care, then pulled out the wet and pushed in the dry. She drove each pin through the cloth with the utmost concentration, first the bottom piece of cloth, then the top, petrified that she might stick him, and after that, her bandaged brow furrowed with the effort, she managed to secure the left pin with her good right hand, then the right. All this despite the fact that Tommy was kicking the air and hollering like it was the end of the world. It was an accomplishment. When it was over, he stopped the brouhaha and smiled up at her and patted the bandage on her head where the horn had been. She smiled back because what else was there to do?

He was still on his back, sucking hard at his bottom lip, his eyes glazed over.

How odd that every time she looked closely at him, he seemed strangely altered from the time before. She could almost see his cells divide, his features shift and settle. His ears appeared larger than they had this morning, the lobes longer and more pointed, his almond eyes now tilted upward in a way they hadn't before, a little Chinaman. She took his dimpled arm in her hand. He was nothing short of a miracle. Tomorrow she would bring him in to see their mother. Would Alice even know her own baby boy? If not, Jo would explain that this was the way of babies, and what a lark it would be for her poor maimed mother to wake up each morning and look into this dear little face and find that one mutation, that minute alteration.

*Obligation*: it was the last word Alice had given Jo before Tommy was born. In Alice's mouth, it had had a leaden ring.

But Jo did not think of obligation as what bound her to the child before her. Because this was the one true thing: how she, Jo, could see *through* her brother's own flesh and blood and bone in the most intimate way possible and watch time at work, as if he had come from her own body, her own cells. As if time were not something they shared but the clay they were made of. This above all else, not the third pew in the First Presbyterian Church, not the sweet by-and-by, not the Thou shalts and the Thou shalt nots. This was the storm, the tearing down and the building up, the coil and recoil of it all: this was the inscrutable. How she wanted to pierce it!

He was asleep now. She pulled the covers over him and went back to her cot and shut her eyes and waited for morning, her breath slow and steady as a purr.

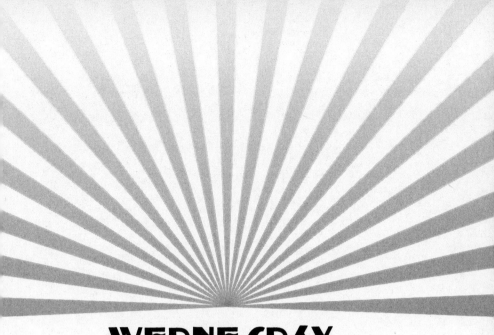

# WEDNESDAY,
# APRIL 8

# 11

## 7:32 A.M.

Dovey woke with a start, in the middle of a dream about the Devil's shoes. They seemed to be nailed down and her feet glued inside. She couldn't get her feet out and she couldn't pick them up to walk. Now they'd begun to sink into mud. Then the mud became quicksand, sucking her under.

She was up to her knees when she awoke. She lay on her left side, her hands curled under her chin, fingers tucked. At first she thought she was home, in her own bed, and it was morning. She tried to remember the day of the week, whose wash needed to be returned and whose needed picking up, whether she had ironing waiting on the board.

What woke her was Promise and his big mouth. He was squalling and hollering to raise the dead. She knew his cry like she knew the tops of her own two hands, now staring her in the face, veiny, the knuckles covered in callused knots from the scrub board. He was mad as a hornet, hungry and wet and probably worse. Why didn't Dreama get her backside out of that bed and see about her own child before he woke up everybody in the house? People needed their rest, especially Virgil, who faced a ten-hour day at the mill.

She reached for Virgil and touched air. Then she opened her

eyes and saw nothing but white all around her. It was as if she'd been swallowed whole by white folks' laundry, her nightmare come true. The belly of the beast. What had she done to deserve this?

She sat up and began waving her arms wildly in the air, pushing back at the sheeted enclosure that surrounded her. It hung there whitely indifferent.

The baby hollered louder, a ragged cry, unraveling at the edges like rope, scarcely a breath between whoops of fury and something else: fear?

*Where was that girl?*

Dovey struggled to get her feet out from under the sheet that covered them. She liked her top sheet loose at the bottom. How had it gotten tucked so tight?

Then the bad foot said, *Whoa, horse, remember me?* And, instantly, she knew.

The foot felt lighter now. And the drum in her head was gone too. What a surprise to wake up so unburdened.

Then she remembered the chill of the knife and her heart turned to ice. She looked down, expecting to see what she couldn't bear to see, which was nothing where there had been something.

What she saw was an enormous bandage made from strips of sheet. *Elephant foot, you hiding in there? You playing pattyroller? Say yes. Say old sun, new day. Say you playing with me, old foot. Say you back, sassy and pretty like you used to be.*

She'd had the prettiest little feet, high-arched and size four and a half, the bottoms hard as hooves from her barefoot habit, but soft as a baby's cheek on top. Even now, when she'd let him, Virgil liked to cup both of her feet in his one hand just to look at them. Back in the day he'd put them to his cheek and say *poor little feet* and play little piggy with them. Then he'd kiss them, one toe at a time. *This little piggy went to market, this little piggy stayed home.*

At the thought of Virgil, she began to cry, remembering the crushed house and under it the empty bed, or what used to be the bed where they'd slept for umpteen years. And no sign. Him gone, without a trace, like he'd never drawn breath.

She deserved whatever she got, she'd been cold, she'd laid blame. She'd never forgiven him for Charlesetta. She'd made him carry that pine box for sixteen years. A heavy load.

But he was alive. She knew it. If he'd been gone for good, she would have known, she would have felt him pass, he would be with her now, touching her here and there with ghost fingers, toes to nose, playing fast and loose, not wanting to go, asking for her forgiveness. And he wouldn't go, she wouldn't let him. She would tuck him into the pocket of her old sweater, next to her rib cage. She would keep him warm with her own heat, and he would stay.

But she didn't feel a thing, no sense of him at all, which meant he was still somewhere out there in the world, still flesh and blood and bone. He'd be looking for her. She needed to be watchful.

Promise cried on.

She wiped her eyes and tried to wiggle what she thought were her toes. The motion set off the needles. *Good.* She bent over and assessed the bandage. Was there a foot under there, or just a stub? She knew from old Leroy Moore across the street, whose leg had been taken by the sugar sickness, that a lost foot can become a ghost, make itself felt, make demands. Old thing keeps telling me it hurts, needs rubbing with Dr. Tichenor's, Leroy Moore would tell anybody who would listen. Sometimes I want to beat it with a stick, make it behave, but I look down and ain't nothing left down there to beat.

She willed the bandage to give her a sign. *Move.*

Nothing. She wiggled the imaginary toes again, this time harder.

Was she seeing things or did the tip end of the bandage, right where the toes should have been, sure enough move? Was there a foot under that monster bandage, hiding out from the patty-rollers? Did she, *please Lord,* still have two feet and they could make a party?

*Hello, foot. Is that you?*

*I'm here, old woman.*

She felt like planning a party, hopping up from her cot and dancing the way she used to when she was a girl and the Shake Rag man beat on his drums.

A little yip and the baby stopped crying, as if someone had stuffed a rag in his mouth.

About time somebody paid him some mind. She lowered her good foot to the floor. She would claim him. She wanted him safe in her arms more than she'd ever wanted anything.

First she had to find him. She followed the good foot with the bandaged one. It hit the floor and here came the needles again, pricking and slicing, worse than before. They took her breath away, made her heart race. She lay back down, hoisting the bad leg back onto the cot. She lay back and waited for someone to come and see about her. She needed a set of crutches.

She cried out and a nurse came through the sheets. "You looking good, Miss Dovey."

"It's an improvement." She recognized the woman as one of Dr. Juber's nurses. She was a young married woman, pretty, with no children yet, one of the Heroines of Jericho at Saint John's. She played canasta on Wednesday nights after prayer meeting. Dovey wanted to call her by name but couldn't remember it.

Dovey lifted the foot. "How come I still got this thing?"

"You living right, Miss Dovey. The doctor drained off the infection, and that elephant foot of yours started going down like a balloon out of gas. Now you get your pretty little foot back. The white doctors, they were going to chop it off like a hunk of meat, but Dr. Juber he say, now everybody just hold your horses, she's been my patient for forty years. Let me see about this, and when he say that, they say, fine, kill her then, no skin off our nose."

"What he say back?"

"He say I don't aim to kill her."

"He cut it."

"Opened it up like he was filleting a catfish. You going to need that bandage for a while. Going to have some scars. Long white threads, like runs in your hose. Cheap price to pay."

Dovey smiled a little. She'd never worn hose a day in her life. She always meant to buy a pair but then once she'd tried on Charlesetta's. The garters had felt like bits of ice against her legs and thighs, and the stockings themselves were clammy and unsettling. Under her long skirts, she wrapped her legs in rags when it was cold. Most of the year, she went bare-legged.

Promise again, hollering his head off. She needed to see about him.

"That's my great-grandbaby doing that hollering," she said to the nurse, whose name she suddenly remembered was Glendola Harris, married to Raymo Harris from over in Iuka. "Can you bring him over here so I can watch him until Dreama comes back from wherever she's off to?" She said it all in a rush. She wanted to be the one who said to Dreama, *He's found, he's alive, look.* She wanted the words to spill from her lips like a pretty little waterfall.

"Miss Dovey, honey, that baby's not yours," said Glendola. "That's some white baby cross the way. Him and his big sister. The mother's bad off, doctor cut off her whole leg."

Dovey pushed herself up on her elbow. "You don't think I know my own grandchild's cry?"

"You been through a lot, Miss Dovey."

The McNabb lady. She remembered the lady's broken leg and she remembered the girl's bad arm. The girl must have found theirs, the boy she was looking for.

A piece of granite settled on Dovey's chest. *Promise.*

"Your granddaughter's all right, though," Glendola said quickly. "Been in and out, seeing about you, then running back out again to try to find her baby and Mr. Virgil. We're hoping they're in the hospital up in Memphis or Holly Springs. That's what we're hoping. Nobody made a list of the colored they put on the trains."

"You sure that one over there ain't ours?"

"I'm sure."

"Any word of ours?" A little baby. No telling.

"Afraid not." Glendola cleared her throat. "The paper's running lists of the deceased, but only the white folks. Ain't bothered to count our people."

The baby across the way cried on, louder than ever.

"Wish somebody'd shut that child up," said Dovey.

"You and me both." Glendola fussed with the sheets that hung around Dovey and gathered some towels and took a basin of water off the floor. "Now it's time for your bath."

Dovey shut her eyes. When she was a young woman, just married, the aunt had woken up one morning unable to move. Dovey had to bathe her every other day, the aunt staring at her with one bulging eye, the other closed, guttural sounds erupting from her slashed mouth, whether of pleasure or rebuke Dovey never knew as she washed and powdered her. The aunt lived for two years, and when she died, Dovey felt such a surge of relief that she couldn't suppress the smile that played at her lips during the funeral and gravesite services. She'd never felt such pure joy, not even when she and Virgil made their home together, not even, later on, when her very own baby was born.

Now here she was, getting bathed herself. She'd rather stay dirty.

Glendola said then, "Take that frown off your face, Miss Dovey. You going to be out of here before you know it. We're going to get you up and walking in no time."

"Folks a lot worse off, I expect."

"Believe it. Did you hear about that family down in Milltown? Twelve of them, plus a little baby, every last one of them dead. Twelve caskets going into the ground at the same time. They put the twins in together. Raise your arm for me."

"How many folks from up on the Hill?"

"No telling. Scarcest thing in town right now is pine boxes. Mr. Porter and them called in three undertakers from Holly Springs to help out. Three days now after the storm and there's a burial every ten minutes up at Springhill and in the Porter cemetery too. Nobody knows who, though, nobody's counting the colored."

"How come?"

"Just a bunch of dead Negroes to them."

"How we going to know whether one of ours is under ground or above it?"

"Turn over on your side. J. W. Porter knows just about everybody from up on the Hill, and a whole lot from Shake Rag too. He's keeping the records. They're being careful about where they plant folks."

Dovey let Glendola's good hands do their work. "I got to talk to Dreama and get her to go up there."

"Don't you think she thought of that? That girl's been up there every morning, checking the lists. There was a baby boy nobody claimed, looked to have been walking already, but she looked at it just to make sure. You got a smart girl there, Miss Dovey. If that child's to be found, she's going to find him."

Glendola washed Dovey's good foot, then ran the cloth between her legs, a scrubbing and then a rinse, not remarking on the invasion of privacy, just doing what was necessary.

After Glendola put her in a clean gown, Dovey fell back on the cot. Why was she so tired? She hadn't done a lick of work since the storm, just lolling about like the queen of Sheba. "I flew," she murmured.

Glendola gathered the wet towel and basin. "You what?"

"I *flew*," Dovey said again. Then, as if this had been a burdensome message she had needed to carry for a long distance and could now lay to rest, she entered the welcome dark.

She dreamed about Henry the guinea pig. He was fat and sassy, living in a hole underground like a mole. She could see only his twitchy little nose and those beady eyes peeking out at her. When she reached into the hole to take him up in her hand, he took her forefinger in his mouth and bit it off. It fell to the ground in a pile of leaves.

She woke up sucking the finger. Dreama was leaning over her, her hair gone wild and tangled, her eyes burnt coals.

"Searched high and low, Granny," Dreama whispered. "He ain't nowhere."

"He bit me," Dovey replied. "He bit my finger off."

"What's the matter with you, Granny? What you talking about?"

Dreama's face floated above her, her wild hair a storm cloud against the white ceiling.

Dovey pushed her back and sat up in bed. This girl didn't sound like Dreama. The girl who talked like Etherene Johnson had taught her to talk. *Ain't*, Dreama used to tell Dovey, isn't a word. Well, if it ain't a word, what is it then? Dovey used to answer. Dreama didn't smell right either, old sweat and something underneath, sour as buttermilk.

Why did she always have to be the one taking care of everybody? "Go find Glendola Harris and get yourself cleaned up, girl."

"But Granny, didn't you hear me? I can't find him. And Miss Etherene, she drowned."

"Drowned?"

"She was wandering around in the dark and fell into one those big old holes. One of those holes where the tree root came up out of the ground. That big old tree up at the top of the Hill where the water tower used to be before it blew away too. Remember that tree with the big pointy leaves?"

Dovey struggled to sit up. "Sweet Jesus. I saw her right after the storm. She told me about you and the baby getting caught on the way home from church. She drowned?"

"She drowned. They found her floating facedown, bald as an egg. She was laid out up at Porter's. Nobody claimed her, so they buried her yesterday." Dreama began to sob and pull at Dovey's arm.

Dovey pushed herself up on the cot. "Which just means somebody's got that baby of ours somewhere. Nobody's making a list except the undertakers, and that's not a list you want him on. Maybe somebody put him on the train to Memphis."

"They didn't keep a list of the Negroes they put on the train, just the whites."

Dovey raised her eyebrows.

"You think I didn't think of that? Not a single baby boy without a name on the white list. Two no-name girls but no boy."

Dovey considered the muck of Gum Pond, the tree roots and lumber and trash under the water. The hollows in trees where a baby could easily lodge and bramble bushes and holes in the ground and secret places under cars and wagons and wrecked houses. Nooks and crannies, high and low. The world was large and dangerous and surprising.

"Quit that. We got a long way to go. We ain't done yet." She reached over and wrestled Dreama's hands from her arm.

Dreama began to wail.

Glendola Harris pulled back the hanging sheets enclosing Dovey's cot and stuck in her head. "Still can't find him?" she asked Dreama.

"I searched high and low. Nobody's keeping records. Negroes wandering the streets looking for their people. Can't find any-body."

"Burns me up," said Glendola.

Dovey pulled her feet out of the covers and dangled them over the side of the cot. "I got to get out of here. I need me some crutches."

Glendola came and stood over her, her hands on her hips. "You need to stay right there in that bed, Miss Dovey. No way you going anywhere."

"Watch me," Dovey said, and she rose. The needles did their business but this time she was ready for them. "I'm going to walk out of here with crutches or without. I got business to take care of."

"If you so bound and determined, hold your horses and I'll get you some crutches. Sit back down. Might be nice to have some clothes on your back too before you go hitting the streets. You planning on heading out in that nightgown?"

"All right then," Dovey said. "Bring me some clothes and a pair of crutches and I'll be out of your hair."

"Only if you promise to come back tonight and let me change that bandage. And don't let that foot touch ground. I'm going to keep your cot here for you to sleep on. Nobody needs to know you're gone. I want you to come back tonight and sleep, you hear me, Miss Dovey? You too, girl. I'll get some blankets for you to put on the floor."

Dovey and Dreama nodded.

"Hold your horses. I'll be back." Glendola sniffed once, then again. "Girl, you look like you been crawling around in a pig-pen. Smell like it too. I'll be back with a washtub and some more clothes for you too. And, Lord, a comb. Where you been sleeping?"

"Here and there."

"You sleeping right here with your granny tonight. Dangerous for a young girl to be wandering around by herself. People talking about a band of no-count white boys roaming around."

Dreama shuddered, then collapsed in the chair next to Dovey's cot and laid her head down on Dovey's hip bone, her hair splayed across Dovey's lap. Dovey gathered a piece of it and began to braid it, which was pointless since there was no thread or ribbon to tie it off. But the hair play soothed the girl, and by the time Glendola returned with the basin and towel and clothes, Dreama was dead to the world.

"Let her be," Dovey said.

"Water be cold shortly," said Glendola.

"Look at her."

Glendola sighed. "All she's been through and then to lose that baby."

"He ain't lost," said Dovey. "He's just missing, like that husband of mine."

"I forgot about him."

"I haven't."

The baby across the way started up again, but then stopped abruptly.

"There go that child again."

"He's over there with that McNabb girl."

"Up here on the stage too?"

"Yes."

"She must have found him after I left."

"What you doing up at the McNabb place?"

"I was there with the mother and the girl. That Devil too, laying up on the living room floor getting deader by the minute. Ought to be ripe by now."

"Tornado did some good then. Where was the daddy?"

"I ran into him walking around looking for the baby."

Glendola snapped her eyes at Dovey. "Probably looking for Etherene too."

"Say what?"

"You don't know about them two? The Judge been visiting Etherene every Thursday night for the past eight years."

"Visiting? Our Etherene?"

"Yes ma'am. That boy of his just a chip off the old block except he took what he wanted instead of asking for it."

"How come nobody told me?"

"I don't know, Miss Dovey. You all the time busy with the laundry, not the talking sort."

"You mean not the gossiping sort."

"I don't mean nothing I ain't said, Miss Dovey. But here's a fact: Etherene Johnson and Mort McNabb. That Plymouth of his parked up in front of her house every Thursday night of the world, come hell or high water."

"Not now."

"No, not now."

"Maybe when I saw him he was looking for Etherene, instead of his child."

"Maybe he was looking for both."

"Maybe."

"And there she was, telling Dreama she needed to talk right. What she meant was talk white."

"Nothing wrong with an education, Miss Dovey. Wish I'd gotten myself more. I'd liked to have made a teacher like Etherene."

"Why didn't you?"

"Oh, the usual reasons. I was lucky to get to be a nurse. Only way I did was my Ray. He worked sanitation to pay the bills while I got my schooling up in Memphis. I cleaned houses weekends and nights. About killed us both but we made it through two years."

Dreama stirred in Dovey's lap, then lifted her head and looked around, bleary eyed.

"Time for a bath," said Glendola and thrust a bar of soap and a washcloth at Dreama. "I'll be back with some clothes. Red Cross has a pile of them out back. Going to bring you a rag for that head of hair too."

When Glendola left, Dreama drew the hanging sheets together and took off her shoes. The shoes were twice the size of her foot and covered in muck.

"Where'd you get them things?"

"Off a dead man in a ditch. Storm took mine."

Dreama pulled off a jacket that Dovey didn't recognize. Under it, two dark spots on the front of her Sunday dress. She pulled her dress over her head and started on her slip. "Turn your head."

Dovey turned but she couldn't stop looking. The girl was beautiful. Her motherhood showed. Small high breasts, now sagging a little, with tracks of stretch marks running from the outside to the nipples, the sweet loose spot in the stomach, the firm backbone and dappled buttocks. Girl mother.

Dreama washed her face first and the washcloth came away brown. Then she worked her way down from underarms and breasts to between her legs and finally her feet. By the time she wrapped herself in the towel and came to sit in the chair beside the cot, the water in the basin was muddy.

"Need some fresh water if you going to do anything about that hair," said Dovey.

"The hair can wait."

"You hungry?" asked Dovey, who couldn't remember the last time she herself had eaten.

"I got some soup at the food kitchen. When I saw Miss Etherene, it came up."

"When I saw her the night of the storm, she tried to get me to go along with her. Good thing I didn't."

"Of all people, why her?"

"No telling."

Dreama shivered in the towel. "Ain't no justice in the world. Where're them clothes?"

Dovey frowned. "You know what Etherene Johnson would say to that? She'd say talk right, Dreama Grand'homme, you got a future." She hoped Dreama would never hear about Etherene and Mort McNabb. The girl needed somebody to look up to.

The sheet parted and Glendola came in with the clothes and three pairs of shoes, one for Dovey to try for her one good foot and two for Dreama to choose from; then she bustled out to get Dovey something to eat.

Dreama dressed herself, then her grandmother. She was buttoning up Dovey's sweater when the baby began to cry.

Dreama froze, head cocked, in an attitude of listening. She put her hand on her left breast.

Then the baby stopped.

"That's that McNabb child," said Dovey quickly.

Dreama didn't answer, her head still cocked.

"I know what you're thinking. I'm telling you that's that McNabb baby."

"Say who?"

"Say Glendola Harris. She seen him."

Dreama stepped away from her grandmother. "I'm going over there and see with my own eyes." Her bottom lip trembled and she glared at Dovey.

"Whoa, horse. I'm coming too." Dovey took up the crutches.

Just as she hit the floor, Glendola came back with the tray. "Got you some tomato soup and saltines and a glass of milk, Miss Dovey. It's not much, but it's all I could rustle up until supper. Got you some good news too. They're setting up a few boxcars for Negroes down on Spring Street on the M&O line. I gave the Red Cross lady your name and she's saving you and Dreama half of one. They're bringing bedding and a table and chairs in now, so you can sleep there tonight if you go on down and claim it. Don't mistake it for the one on up the tracks. That's for whites."

Glendola stopped and looked at them both. "You two look like bird dogs on the scent."

"That baby crying across the way," said Dovey.

Glendola turned to Dreama. "I told your grandmother, that's the McNabb baby. The sister is taking care of him."

"He sounds like Promise," Dreama said.

"He do," said Dovey. She didn't mention the outrageous fact that the McNabb baby might be expected to sound like Promise because he was kin to Promise, was, in fact, Promise's uncle.

"I can see y'all ain't going to be satisfied until you take a look," Glendola said.

"You see right," said Dovey, gathering her crutches again.

Glendola put her hand on Dovey's shoulder. "Eat first. I about had to wrestle somebody to the ground to get that cup of soup."

The soup was lukewarm, so she brought the cup to her lips and drank it down, then turned up the glass of milk and put the crackers in her sweater pocket. None of it tasted good to her, but the surge of heat in her midsection was welcome.

"All right," she said to Dreama. "Let's us go see. Settle this once and for all."

Glendola had been stacking the dishes on the tray. She put the tray down. "I'm going to take you two over to where that child is, but watch yourselves. No trouble."

The crutches were too tall for Dovey. On the first swing, she sailed through the air.

"Watch out, Granny," Dreama said. "You're swinging up too high."

Dovey liked the feeling. It was a bit like flying.

"You going to kill yourself on those things, Miss Dovey. You stay right here." Glendola disappeared again. This time she came back fast with a pair of child's crutches. Then she lifted a piece of the hanging sheet and the three of them emerged onto the stage.

Dovey blinked. More white. Cots lined up with only narrow passages between. White nurses and doctors in white uniforms going about their work, bending over the cots, moving quickly from one to the next.

Sick to death of white. She wanted color. Red poppies and yellow forsythia, the blue of hydrangeas, orange maple leaves and purple plums, the airy blue of the sky and the smoky blue of the jaybird. She considered how many shades of green you could see in spring, from the yellow-green sprigs of first grass to the waxy dark of the camellia bushes to the lively emerald moss that covered the dead up at Springhill.

"Come on now," said Glendola over her shoulder. "Make it

quick. They're over here." She threaded her way through a main passage, then cut toward the back corner, near the piano.

Then she stopped in her tracks. "Right here, they were right here."

Dreama peered out over the cots. "Was the baby in a crib?"

"He was right here in a little bassinet, next to the curtain. That girl right here beside him on a cot. The baby came in with the mother. Her eyes rolling back in her head, half alive. Had him in a death grip with her on the stretcher and he was mad as a hornet, filthy and hungry and scared. The daddy still on the lam. No telling where he was, chasing down . . ." Dovey cut her eyes at Glendola and they both looked at Dreama. Glendola took a breath. "Then they took off the mother's leg and the daddy he finally shows up, and they're all here now, except for the dead one."

"Satan," Dovey said.

"You *think* they're all here now," said Dreama.

"The mother's sure not going anywhere. Maybe they let the other two go. The baby and father were fine except for a few scratches. The girl just had a broken arm and a big piece of glass in her head."

"Where'd they put the mother?" asked Dreama.

"At the back of the stage, with the critical."

Dreama began to thread her way toward the back of the stage. A white nurse came up to them. "What you girls doing, traipsing around over here?"

Glendola pushed Dreama forward. "We're looking for the McNabb family. They want to pay their respects."

"They're all gone except the mother and she's still critical. Hasn't even woken up yet."

"Did they take the baby too?"

"This is no place for a healthy baby. They just now headed for Crosstown, for the boxcars."

"Doesn't seem like a boxcar is much of a place either," said Glendola, her voice steady. "These ladies knew the baby too."

"Said they'd all be back tomorrow to see the mother."

Dreama had begun to pull at her hair. Glendola took her by the arm and turned her around.

They proceeded back through the cots, this time Dovey first, Dreama in the middle, and Glendola nipping at Dreama's heels. Dreama's crying had become a high-pitched whine. A moan broke from Dovey's throat. White faces stared up curiously, some bandaged, some creased in pain. One man had stitches running from the outside corner of his eye down to his chin. A woman lay weeping, asking for a drink of water.

As they made their procession, Dovey put down her crutches carefully, trying not to hit any of the cots. Dreama's whine and Dovey's moan had congealed into a kind of harmony. Then Glendola chimed in, humming tunelessly. Dovey turned to look. Glendola's lips had disappeared.

Dovey remained dry-eyed, intent on each hobbling step, each strike of the crutch, trying not to fall, trying to make it back to the colored side of the stage, behind the curtain.

Then, just as they drew near, she tripped on a full bedpan. Dreama reached to grab her but was too late. The tip of the crutch slipped in the urine and Dovey fell sideways, sprawling on top of a man who lay asleep on a cot. He flailed about and sat up, knocking her to the floor, the blanket on his bed covering her so that when she opened her eyes all she could see was white.

She thought she was dead until she heard Glendola call out, "Stretcher!"

Some CCC boys came running down the aisle. Dovey's ear was to the floor and, when she heard them galloping up the stairs, she thought they were horses coming to trample her. And good riddance too. She was plumb worn out with this world.

# 12

## 4:17 P.M.

Jo trudged along behind her father. He carried little Tommy and a satchel of clothes for him. She carried her brother's bottles and diapers, actually makeshift diapers made from cut towels; they were scratchy with bleach and had already turned his bottom an angry red. She carried the bottles and diapers in a knapsack on her good shoulder, the bandage over her forehead shading her eyes from the late afternoon sun.

They'd been given directions to the boxcars by the Red Cross lady. They headed that way now, passing the houses on Broadway, only minimally damaged, turning west on Main, heading for Crosstown. They passed other families walking, and everyone walked in the same direction. Some Jo's father knew and spoke to briefly; no one slowed to talk, fearful that one's assigned boxcar would be given away. They walked by what was left of the hospital with its collapsed roof and blown-out windows. Jo's father didn't comment on the ruin. From the back, Mort looked a bit like a stork, his shoulders stooped, his head thrust forward. He looked around with an air of preoccupation, as if he were still searching for Tommy, as if he needed to be somewhere else.

There, in front of the hospital, at the corner of Main and

Church, he stopped short and struck his forehead with his palm. "The aunts' house," he said. "Why didn't I think of it?"

He had tried to sell the aunts' house after Aunt Sister died, but nobody wanted a ramshackle old place with its wandering, pocked screen porch, an old bathroom beyond repair, and the kitchen not much better. Scores of people came through, but nobody made an offer, even after he lowered the price to the ridiculous figure of $3,999. Then they'd received word that the First Baptist Church across the street was raising money for a Sunday school classroom building, so Mort took the place off the market and waited. Then, of course, came the Crash: the banks collapsed and Nash Cunningham, father of seven and grandfather of many more, one fine fall morning climbed up to his study on the second floor of the house next door and blew his brains out, the bullet lodging in the side of the aunts' house, right above a window outside their upstairs bedroom. The bullet remained beyond anyone's reach, and nobody was buying anything anyway, not even First Baptist. So the house had sat, for six years now, growing more resolute in its decay, the once-white paint splotched with mildew, the bullet long ago covered over by ivy. Wild cats skittered about, tearing their way onto the screen porch, lolling about in the swing and rockers where the two sisters had once sat and watched the world go by.

Jo wrinkled her nose. "It's going to be a mess."

"Better than a boxcar." Her father tossed the words over his shoulder, grimly. There were tears on his cheeks again. He hadn't asked about Son, how the coat hanger, which Mort had last seen in his daughter's hand, had come to be implanted in his son's chest.

Mort turned and they headed north, up Church Street, skirting a black car flipped on its side like a monstrous dead roach. On her father's shoulder, little Tommy raised his head, stared bleary-eyed at Jo, then put his head back down into the crook of Mort's neck.

*Brother.* The word roiled in Jo's throat. She wanted, suddenly, to shout it to the twisted tree trunks, the smashed houses, the whole lost town. In the late day sun, the world seemed flung open and shiny, like foil. There was pleasure in it now, and promise. A path through the ruin. She trudged along behind her father. Before the storm, she'd never thought about whether she knew him; now, afterward, she realized she didn't know him at all. Was it possible to love someone you didn't know? Well, she most certainly did, she loved her father, and she loved her little brother above all. She loved him fiercely, more than she loved anyone in this whole wide world. Under the knapsack and the cast, she felt as light and insubstantial as a speck of dust, as if their weight alone held her to the earth, as if without them she might lift off and drift up into the sky and disappear.

Only the top half of the aunts' house was visible from where they stood. They picked their way around the downed magnolia in the front yard and stepped up onto the front stoop. The place was smaller than Jo remembered: insubstantial, as if its weathered boards were made of paper.

The pot sat undisturbed and dreaming in the exact spot it had always sat, though now bare of the spring pansies the aunts would have planted had they been there. When her fingers touched the key, still in its hiding place under the pot, she felt a rush of relief so strong it flooded her eyes. It was the same feeling she had had years ago when she came to the aunts' house after school, hiding out from Son, filled with the anticipation of being met by two cooing old ladies inviting her into their nest for a while, offering tea and peppermints, sometimes a short-bread or toast. "Sister," Aunt Fan would say, folding and unfolding her handkerchief, "I expect our guest would enjoy some cinnamon toast with those good fig preserves." And Jo would nod and breathe in the clouds of camphor and rosewater and glycerin that hovered around the two of them.

She turned the key and pushed down the lever, but the door was stuck. Mort kicked it once, then again, disturbing little Tommy, who thrust his head up and out like a turtle.

Just then two CCC boys passed by and asked if they could help. They put their shoulders to it (what muscles they had, those beautiful boys!) and finally it popped and they almost fell into the house.

When Jo followed her father through the door and into the living room, the house sighed as if it were relieved, as if it too had been waiting for rescue.

The house was deeply sad. Jo felt it the moment she entered the living room. It had been lonely, it complained, it had been blue. What a relief it was to see her! Why had she waited so long?

A piece of the mantel over the fireplace had loosened and sagged, giving the living room wall a downturned mouth. She brushed a cobweb from her cheek but it clung and tickled. She put the knapsack onto the couch, raising a puff of dust, and looked over at her father. The baby's head was bobbing and he had begun to fuss. Her father wasn't holding Tommy properly, not supporting his upper back and neck.

She pushed the dusty cushion from Aunt Sister's rocking chair and sat down. "Give him here, Daddy. Prop him here in my lap and hand me one of those bottles."

The CCC boys stood in the middle of the room, looking around.

What a sight she must be! Her filthy hair plastered to her head, the bandage a drooping sail covering the top half of her face. She peered out from under her bandage. "Do y'all have time to help us get this house in order?"

"Sure," one of them said. "We're all yours." The other one grinned at her. He had freckles and the reddest head of hair she'd ever seen.

Her father handed Jo the baby. "He's wet."

"Well, get me one of those towels then." Jo said it more sharply than she intended. Had her father never changed a diaper? "I've only got one hand."

She looked at the boys. "There's brooms and dishcloths in the hall closet. Can you get us some beds ready upstairs? And wipe down the kitchen and bathroom?"

"Yes, ma'am." The cocky one saluted. "We've got some candles for you too."

Was this how the queen of England felt? Ordering everybody around, making everyone bow and scrape? She pushed the sagging bandage (her crown!) out of her eyes.

THAT NIGHT after the boys had left and her father had gone out for a very long time, returning with a plate of congealed meat and potato salad for her and a jug of water, she settled herself and the baby in Aunt Fan and Aunt Sister's room. She lit one of the candles the CCC boys had placed on the dresser and laid Tommy on Aunt Fan's bed because it was the one next to the wall. She took a towel from the stack used for the baby's diapers and moistened it from the jug of water they'd also left. When she turned to the baby, he was watching her, his golden eyes reflecting the candle glow, lively and interested.

"Ok, dirty boy," she said, sitting down beside him. She pulled the gown over his head and began to wipe his face, gently patting the scratches. He kicked her in the stomach and began to fuss. She put more water on the towel and went for the creases in his neck, which were filthy with dirt and grime. When she reached his trunk he stopped fussing and began to coo. She pulled up his left arm and wiped the dirt from under his arm. When she pulled up his right arm, there was a complicated gash that took her breath away. How had the doctors and nurses missed it? It looked red and infected; it was caked in blood. She dabbed at it, fearful of starting up the bleeding. Tomorrow she'd have a doctor look at it.

He'd begun to fuss again. There was a discoloration under the gash. *A bruise*, she thought, *the poor thing has a bruise*. How lucky he was to be alive, sucked out of their mother's arms and blown about like a stick of furniture! She dried him from the waist up, pulled a fresh gown from her bag, and put it on so he wouldn't get cold. Then she pulled off his diaper and washed his bottom, wishing she had some salve for the angry diaper rash. She ended with his toes, pulling the rag between them. The cloth was filthy. She threw it to the floor and put a fresh diaper on.

"Now," she said, smiling down, "you're all clean." He cooed at her again then and shut his eyes. "Good boy," she said. She covered him and put pillows around him.

Standing in front of the mirror over the dresser, she moistened one of his clean towels with a bit of water and dabbed it over the lower half of her face, then scrubbed her teeth with it. She found a nightgown in a dresser drawer and, with her good right hand, pulled off the unfamiliar dress she'd been given at the theater, tearing the sleeve to get it out of the cast. She washed herself, standing before the mirror with nothing on her top, her wet breasts gleaming. She touched the right one, wondering, if push had come to shove, might she herself have produced some milk for the baby? Might her body have responded to such a desperate need? She considered waking Tommy and putting her breast in his mouth just to see, but then a wave of shame came over her for even thinking such an odd thing and, with her teeth, she quickly tore a sleeve of the gown and drew it over her head. She looked at herself again and saw something about her mouth that reminded her of her mother, a resolute look, something close to stubbornness.

She crawled into Aunt Sister's bed. (Had she ever in her life been so tired?) She lay first on her good side, then on her back, then on her good side again. Her bad arm ached. The biting ants rummaged, taking a nip here and there. The ghostly aunts tiptoed in, offering toast and tea. They whispered to each other, not of the past but of the future. Something brewing on the horizon. Another storm? Around her the house complained. It had been lonely, it had been sad.

The cats outside on the porch hissed and screamed. Where was her Snowball? Snowball's kittens? Were they roaming in and out of her own house wondering where she'd gone? Were they wandering the streets starving? Thinking of them, so cast adrift, she began to cry.

At dawn a wren lit in the ivy outside the bedroom window and sang its heart out. A woodpecker pecked at the side of the house where Nash Cunningham's bullet had lodged. Something skittered in the attic, directly above her head.

She got up and pulled away the pillows and crawled into Aunt Fan's bed with the baby, wondering why he hadn't woken for his early morning feeding. He slept on and she rested her cast on his little chest and closed her eyes and waited for him to stir. As she lay there, she planned the day. She would feed Tommy and then wake her father. They would go out to get some breakfast. The Red Cross lady had told them the Kinney Hotel on Main was serving whites. The Palace and Penn's Café were actually closer, but they were for the colored. She and her father would eat and then they would head to the Lyric to see how her mother was doing and show her the baby, how well he was doing. Her mother would be thrilled beyond anything, despite Son, despite the lost leg. Her eyes would light up in the old way, when she used to go on about poetry: Whitman's impossibly long lines, Longfellow's melodies. She would rise up on her cot and give Jo a new Word to Keep. Jo would take care of her mother along with the baby. She, Jo, would take care of everyone. She was certain now that she would become a nurse; this was her calling, this would be her life. She would go out into fields of battle, a brave dot of white against a brutal landscape, dodging bullets, moving among the bruised and broken and torn asunder.

She dozed finally, dreaming of bending over a half-dead soldier, wiping his brow, telling him to hang on.

Little Tommy woke up coughing, alarming her. It was all she could do to take care of a well baby, much less a sick one. She changed him and quickly used the chamber pot the aunts kept in the corner. It was chilly so she wrapped him up in a towel, which he struggled against, then picked him up and started down the stairs to give him his bottle.

The nightgown she wore dragged the floor. She descended

the dark stairwell step by slow step, terrified that she would trip and fall. Tommy flailed away in her arm, fretting and straining and coughing.

The milk she'd been given for him was powdered; the Red Cross lady said it wouldn't spoil if she mixed it with clean water. She wiped off the kitchen table, laid the baby at the back next to the wall where he couldn't roll off (he was so strong for a little baby, much larger and more unwieldy than she remembered). She poured the fresh water from the jug into a clean bottle, spilling about half of it, and shook up the mixture. She sat down on a kitchen chair and pulled him onto her lap and gave him the bottle. He sucked frantically for a moment, then spit out the nipple and began to scream. She realized then that his nose was stopped up, that he couldn't breathe when he took the bottle.

"Oh sweetheart," she said aloud, and the aunts leaned in. *Dear, dear,* they whispered. "Daddy?" she called out, and there was silence. She called louder but there was no response. *Gone again. Where?*

Maybe he'd gone for food. She was hungry, beyond hungry. What would she give right now for a piece of the aunts' cinnamon toast? A cup of tea?

Tommy took another plunge at the bottle but then turned beet red and began to scream bloody murder. She snatched him up, a bit impatiently she realized, and headed for the bathroom and began rummaging in the medicine cabinet. There was Milk of Magnesia, castor oil, foot powder. And, glory be, a small bottle of paregoric. That, at least, she knew was safe. Hadn't her mother used it all the time to quiet the baby? But how much? A capful wouldn't hurt. Juggling him, she managed to use the hand on her bad left side (which hurt like the devil, but what choice did she have?) to unscrew the cap and pour. She sat down on the commode, put him back on her knee, and poured it down his throat. He choked and his eyes popped open. She set him upright and hit the cast against his back, whereupon he screamed louder, kicking now, throwing his head back and sideways. She stood up with him, walking back and forth, trying to calm him.

He screamed on and then fell into an exhausted sleep. She took him upstairs and put him back in the bed. *Pillows, remember the pillows.* Anything she did wrong, any little thing she forgot to do correctly, something like the pillows to keep him in place, and then, too bad so sad, she would have gone and killed him too, he would be dead like Son. Just like that. She pictured his limp body facedown on the dusty floor, his roly-poly neck twisted at an impossible angle.

She opened the aunts' closet and chose a dress, a serviceable gray. She tore the sleeve, starting it with her teeth as though she were about to make a meal of it, and put it on, found a belt to draw it higher around her waist so she wouldn't trip. She didn't look in the mirror when she was dressed, afraid, not so much that she would see the aunts hovering behind her, but that she herself would have become one of them. She repacked the knapsack.

Then she went over to the bed, wiped the baby's runny nose and picked him up and descended the stairs and walked out the front door, not bothering to shut it. Maybe her father would be back, maybe not. She'd come to think of him as an island apart, appearing and disappearing with the tide, as insubstantial as the dead aunts and even less helpful. Not to be relied on.

She set out, heading back down Jefferson, back to the Lyric. There at least was shelter, people who could, if called upon, dia-per a baby. Maybe her mother would be awake and know what to do. In the crook of her arm, the baby's head lolled about like a cantaloupe. The laziness of his barely discernible neck wor-ried her. Had she given him too much paregoric? His nose was running, his breath ragged. She touched his face to her cheek. It was hot.

She walked as fast as she could, the dress slipping out of the belt in back and growing longer so that she looked like a bride trailing a dingy train. She felt slightly dizzy; she wasn't one to go without breakfast. She was a girl who ate three regular meals a day and sometimes had corn bread and molasses before going to sleep. She wasn't fat, but she was tall for her age and she had her father's shoulders and arms, which were muscular for a girl and useful in the situation she found herself in. She hoped she would grow into them.

To her left, the bell tower of First Presbyterian had been blown through the roof of the sanctuary, leaving a ragged hole. Next to the church, the parsonage, a stone structure like the church, had simply disappeared, and on its foundation lay the massive double doors of the church, frame and all.

Her good arm ached from the baby's weight. A breeze blew across her face, smelling like dust and mildew and rotten meat. As she walked along, she grew homesick for her town, the easy come and go of the residential streets, the bustle of downtown on a Saturday morning, all the country folk in their wagons or on foot, buying groceries at Nesbitt's and nails from Tupelo Hardware and, if there were anything left over, splitting a choc-olate malt at the TKE lunch counter.

She missed the shade of the great towering oaks, some left over from Indian times. It had been exactly a century (was the storm a reminder?) since the Chickasaw had been removed. They left in dispirited clumps, saying good-bye forever, some to their plantation-style home places and some to smaller dwellings and all to the original paths up and down the Natchez Trace where for centuries they had hunted and traded and farmed and lived out their lives. A whole layer of life lay hidden under this town a hundred years later; and now that much of Tupelo and the country around it was stripped clean, the tornado having done in a few seconds what had taken the early settlers a century to accomplish, another layer would emerge. Time isn't a river, Jo thought; time is ground and dirt and the roots of ancient trees and the bones of past things. Time is underfoot.

As she walked along, strangers came and went in the rubbish, skirting corkscrew tree trunks and debris. Young men, the white giving the black orders, cleared the street and stood precariously on ladders, restringing the precious electric line. Lil, who did Alice McNabb's hair, sat in the middle of the street, staring into space and muttering to herself. Her dress was torn and filthy, and the peroxided hair on the left half of her head completely gone. Had it not been for little Tommy, Jo would have stopped and tried to help her. Instead she averted her eyes and pushed on through the debris.

As Jo turned the corner at Jefferson Street toward the Lyric on North Broadway, she almost collided with her father. Surprisingly, he was coming from the opposite direction of the theater, hurrying along, his eyes as neon red as the Lyric's marquee, his face streaked where tears had plowed downward furrows through the dirt and grime.

He stopped short when he saw her. "What are you doing here? Why aren't you back at the aunts'?"

Jo glared at him. "You mean the house you left us in without food or water or anybody to help me with this sick baby?"

"People died," he said without preamble, as if that explained everything. "Good people died." He looked at her then and there was a veil over his eyes. *Something lost there.*

He had come from the direction of the Hill where the colored people lived. Why had he gone up there when there was her mother to see about? Why had he gone wandering (again) when he should have been getting something for them to eat?

Then it dawned on her that he must have gone up to Glen-wood Cemetery, at the base of the Hill, to see about Son, to see whether he'd had a proper burial. But was Son good people? Quite the opposite, and the opposite of good was Evil with a capital *E*. How do you tell a father his son was not *good people*, was anything but? And didn't somewhere, in his heart of hearts, Mort McNabb know this already? He'd have to be deaf, dumb, and blind not to.

*How smoothly the coat hanger had gone in, how slight the resistance, as if she were piercing butter.*

Now here her father was with his filthy face (even she, a girl on her own, had been able to keep herself and Tommy decent) and his torn clothes and that wild hair *crying*, a man bawling his eyes out like a baby when he should have been taking care of the living, being a father. Had he lost his marbles? When this was over she would have to talk to her mother about sending him down to Whitfield for a rest cure. Well, maybe not Whitfield where the truly crazy people went, maybe a nice private place out in the country where he could pull himself together.

"You love people and then they die," he said.

"Yes," she said. "I know *some* good people have died. And more could die too, *this baby could die right now this very minute.*" She gestured at little Tommy with her chin, her bandage now loose and slipping down farther over her eyes, aggravating her, infuriating her. She tilted her head downward and reached up with the hand on her bad side and ripped it off. She was immediately blinded by the sun, a cruel sun now that there were no more trees, no more blessed shade.

Standing between her and the morning sun, her father had become a dark shape. She could not see his face, only the motion of his gesture when he reached out. "Give him to me," he ordered.

In her arm Tommy's head seemed to have grown heavier and even less attached to his neck than it had been before. Jo squinted at the dark shape that was her father. How she wanted to let go of this heavy heavy child, turn him over, give him to somebody responsible, somebody with two good arms.

But there was something about her father's reach that put her off; it seemed halfhearted, insubstantial. The little hot cantaloupe head now resting on her arm, her aching arm, demanded more. She backed away from her father and turned and began to walk fast toward the Lyric. Over her shoulder she said to him, "The baby's asleep. I just want to get him to a doctor."

She hurried along, afraid her father would catch up with her and take the baby. She had never defied her own father so completely. Her feet, her strong able feet in her father's wingtips, took on a life of their own.

Behind her, she could hear his footsteps; but as she walked along, as fast as she could, almost running in fact (now she was the engine, she was the Frisco carrying precious cargo), she could hear him falling behind. She didn't turn to look. After a few minutes, the footsteps faded into silence.

When she reached the double doors of the Lyric, she turned to look. He had slowed down and was strolling along the sidewalk, his hands in his pockets, as though he had all the time in the world. Then he crossed the street and sat down on a bench in the little park across from the theater and leaned down and retied first one shoe and then the other. He still had on his Sunday shoes, now caked in mud.

Then he buried his face in his hands and his shoulders began to heave.

When Jo turned to pull open the door to the theater (she didn't remember it being this heavy), she caught sight of two small figures walking away, in the opposite direction of her father, south toward Main. She saw their skirts, so she assumed they were girls together, surely no older than twelve or thirteen, one dark-skinned, one light, the first on crutches, the other carrying a large sack in one hand, holding the first girl's arm with the other. Both thin as rails.

Colored girls alone! Where were they off to? Where were their parents? Jo wished she had a house to offer them; she wished she had the biggest mansion money could buy and she could say to everyone in poor wrecked Tupelo (everyone except those terrible friends of Son's), *Come in, stay as long as you like, we are all going to be all right.* And then, glory, the word would get out and every poor homeless soul would come. Everybody in creation, white and Negro, rich and poor, smart and feebleminded, everybody in Lee County would sit down together and be safe and warm and comfortable and good-hearted and grateful, and there would be dogs and cats and cows and birds and goats eating and drinking too, and nobody would say *you come and you go, or you go first and you go last.* The last would be first, the way Jesus said, and it would be as if God had planned the storm all along to bring them together.

Pausing at the door, Jo watched the two figures grow smaller in the distance. There was something about them that looked familiar, but she couldn't quite put her finger on it. In that moment, just as she was turning away and going through the door, the one on crutches stumbled and almost fell. Jo caught her breath, but the other one, the light-skinned girl (white or Negro, Jo was actually not sure), caught the one on crutches before she could fall.

Then the one on crutches pointed to an object on the ground, and the other one picked it up and handed it to her. It was, Jo saw, a tattered umbrella. Just then the one on crutches dropped them on the ground. They landed in a heap. She pointed the tip of the umbrella down and began walking again, using the umbrella as a cane, and the other one kicked aside the crutches and followed.

THE FIRST thing Jo did when she entered the theater was to look for someone in white and the first person she saw was a colored nurse (if she was a real nurse; was there such a thing as a colored nurse?). The woman looked like a nurse; she had on a little name pin that said GLENDOLA HARRIS, RN, and she was carrying a pail of dirty diapers to the exit where a woman from the Red Cross sanitation staff awaited them. Behind her, four white babies lay sleeping in bassinets. Briefly Jo wondered how the colored nurse had managed to get four babies to sleep at one time. She would have to ask Glendola Harris how she did it. Before the tornado, Jo had entertained the idea of someday having quintuplets like the Dionne babies up in Canada. Rowed up in their pretty lace dresses, the baby girls looked completely manageable, like dolls. Now she knew better; she could barely manage one baby, much less five.

Glendola Harris. Jo rolled the name off her tongue. She was determined to remember it. She'd already forgotten the name of the washwoman, something to do with a bird, and that girl, her granddaughter, was her name Dream?

JO THRUST Tommy at Glendola Harris. "Please," she said, "he's sick."

Glendola dropped her pail and picked up a bottle of clear liquid and poured it over her hands. The smell of alcohol knocked Jo back on her heels.

Glendola touched the baby's cheek. "Fever," she said and took him from Jo's arm. "When did this come on?"

"This morning. He was fine yesterday."

The nurse gave the baby a little shake and patted his cheek. Tommy didn't move. His dark curls were damp, the back of his head soaked. She took him to an empty bassinet and picked up a jug of water on the floor and a towel from one of the seats and thrust them at Jo. Then she pulled off the baby's gown and laid him on his back and turned to Jo. "Bathe him. Cool him down. He ought to wake up."

"He might not. I gave him paregoric," said Jo.

Glendola Harris frowned. "Paregoric? What on earth for? Was he upchucking? Does he have diarrhea?"

"He had a cough and his nose is runny. He wouldn't take his bottle."

"You don't give a baby paregoric for that. You don't give a baby paregoric period. How much you give him?"

Who'd this nurse think she was? Jo had never had a Negro talk to her this way, pepper her with questions. It set her teeth on edge. "Just a little," she snapped. "A capful."

The nurse went back to Tommy. She looked at him from several different angles. His head had flopped to one side. She pulled open his eyelids, tapped his cheek, turned his head this way and that. "I'm going for the doctor. Do like I say now. Wet him down. And watch the other little ones while I'm gone. You hear me?"

Jo nodded. *Responsibility*: her mother had given her that one when she entered first grade. Before the storm, Jo had associated it with picking up her dirty clothes and making As.

Speaking of responsibility, where had her father gotten off to? He should have come in by now, no matter how much shoe-tying and boohooing he had to do. She wet the towel and began to blot little Tommy. She got him soaking wet on his front, and turned him to wet his back. He was still limp as a dish-rag but had started shivering. Then, to her horror, it was as if some rough hand seized him by the shoulders and shook him violently. She screamed for help, waking all four babies in their bassinets. On the stage, the white people sat up in their cots. On the floor, the colored popped their heads up between rows to look in her direction.

Glendola Harris, up on the stage, waiting for one white doctor to stop talking to another, was drawn by the commotion and looked across the theater at her. Jo saw something in her face, a tightening of the lips, a whisper under her breath, that mirrored all of Jo's fears. Then the nurse tapped the doctor on the shoulder, interrupting his conversation, causing him to look up at her impatiently. Jo knew that look. It said: How dare you? It said: This better be good. She screamed louder and waved with her good hand. *Please come.*

Then she could tell the doctor was listening hard, not to her, but to Glendola, who now pointed at Jo. This time he paid attention and strode across the stage, not running but almost, jumping easily from the stage and coming down the aisle toward Jo. By now Tommy had conked out, the fit over. He oozed sweat, his skin as shiny with it as if he'd been oiled; it collected over his closed eyelids, in the rolls of his neck, in the indentation between his nipples. His hair was soaked and stuck to his head, his eyes were glassy. He coughed weakly and then was quiet.

The doctor pulled open the lid on one of Tommy's eyes and then put a stethoscope to his chest. "Shut those other ones up," he snapped at the nurse. "Can't hear myself think."

Glendola cut her eyes at Jo. "They were all sleeping when I left."

The doctor removed Tommy's diaper and turned to Glendola. "Find me a thermometer in this mess. Sterilize it in alcohol."

"I always do," said Glendola under her breath. She whipped a thermometer from her pocket, shook it down, and dipped it in the bottle of alcohol.

The doctor turned Tommy on his stomach and inserted the thermometer. He looked up at Jo, his eyes full of trouble. "How much? How much paregoric did you give him?"

Jo could barely utter the words. "Just a little." The truth was everything since the storm seemed like a dream. Maybe she'd poured the whole bottle down Tommy's throat. Maybe she had killed him. Maybe she had made him feebleminded. What an idiot she was!

"Less than a teaspoon?"

"I think so."

"Do not *ever* give this baby paregoric."

Jo wanted to say her mother had done it. Done it more than once. She never would have done it without her mother doing it first. But that seemed disloyal somehow.

The doctor pulled out the thermometer and read it. "Not too bad," he said to the nurse. "I think he's sweating it off. And no pneumonia. He's going to be all right, just needs some nursing. He needs to eat, so let's get that nose unplugged."

A wave of relief washed Jo under and she staggered sideways, up against the outside seat of the row.

Just then she felt a heaviness at her side: her father.

"Are you the father?" asked the doctor. Jo heard the question but not the answer. Instead she saw a white light in the midst of darkness; then someone blew out the light.

SHE WOKE flat on her back with the nurse (What was her name?) leaning over her, patting her cheek, and behind the nurse's dark face, her father's streaked one. The babies were still crying. Beside her the doctor, on his knees, held the wrist of her good arm and looked at his watch, his lips counting. Then, as Jo still lay on the floor, gazing up at the three of them, the nurse turned and looked at Mort McNabb head-on. Her jawline hardened, and there was such an expression of disgust on her face that Jo flinched and closed her eyes.

"Your *wife* is awake, Mr. McNabb," said the nurse, "been awake all morning, asking after you."

Lying there, underneath the two of them, Jo looked up and saw the word *wife* fly from the woman's mouth. It struck her father on his left cheek and its fangs struck and struck again. Mort's mangled face dipped and plunged, his neon eyes flashed and flickered.

"Please," said Jo. "Does anybody have a cracker or bread or just *something* I can eat?" Her own voice sang high and wide in her own ears. It blended with the chorus of the four babies (not her Tommy, who was still limp as a dishrag, but not dead, hopefully not dead) and echoed again and again until she could not tell where her voice ended and theirs began.

"Get this girl something to eat," the doctor said to the nurse, that awful woman, and the snake (It was the color of dead leaves in autumn. A copperhead?) let go of Mort McNabb's face and dropped to the floor. There it recoiled itself and remained motionless, staring at her, flicking its tongue as if deciding whether to bite her too. Then, oh glory!, it slithered away.

# THURSDAY, APRIL 9

# 13

## 11:13 A.M.

The boxcars for the colored were rowed up at attention, the two doors of each one facing the back of the car next to it, blocking the light of its neighbor. Portable steps of splintery pine had been placed in front of each set of doors, a cookstove and an oil can for trash outside every car to the right of the steps. Two privies squatted like twin guard dogs at either end of the rows. Stretching out in the midday sun, the ground between rows was the color of dried blood and hard-packed in gravel, as if everything were resting on a large piece of raw meat sprinkled in salt.

The boxcars were only five blocks from the Lyric, on a set of side tracks, but Dovey was panting by the time they approached them. The umbrella had tended to stick in the mud, making it more trouble than it was worth. Dreama had had to support her for the last half block, fussing at her every inch of the way for throwing away the crutches.

They'd gotten a late start on the day. After Dovey's fall the afternoon before (tripping over that bedpan like an old fool), she'd crawled gratefully back onto her cot and collapsed, not waking until midmorning. Now, as they stood before their box-car, Number 4, Dreama was chomping at the bit. "I'm going to get you settled, then go look for Promise and Papa," she told Dovey.

"How am I supposed to get up them steps?" Dovey asked.

Dreama shook her head wearily. She brought her hand up as if to make some bold gesture then dropped it to her side.

Dovey saw despair in the girl's twig of an arm. How come everything bad seemed bound and determined to happen to one little girl? That monkey had jumped on Dreama's back the second she poked her head out into the cold world and saw a dead-as-a-doornail mama, and it hadn't let up on her since, coming in the form of that McNabb Devil, then the pregnancy. She'd borne it all, right down to the boy the color of mayonnaise. She'd given the monkey a kick, the baby boy her heart.

Now the monkey was back. It rankled Dovey like nothing else. "Don't worry, I can do it. I can get up them steps," she quickly told her granddaughter (miracle of all miracles that the girl was there by her side instead of dead in a ditch!).

Dovey sat down on the next-to-bottom step of the boxcar and began to push her way up with her arms and one good foot, first one step, then another. She muttered, "Hope they got something I can lay down on in them boxcars."

Dreama stepped around Dovey and started up the steps. "Let me see what they've got in there. No point in you climbing all the way up if there's no place to sit down."

Dovey stopped on the step and waited. Other families had arrived, weary and tattered and bandaged. She didn't recognize any of them and thought they might have come from Shake Rag, not from up on the Hill where she knew almost everyone. Or maybe they'd dragged themselves into town from out in the county. They smelled like fish and looked disheveled and less than respectable, though Dovey suspected she looked the same. They whispered among themselves, jostling one another to peer inside the boxcars, trying to figure out which one had been assigned to which family. One little boy ran up the makeshift steps to the third car down from Dovey and stuck his head back out the door, hollering that there was some sure-enough store-bought white bread sitting on a table inside. His mother, right behind him, carried inside a yellowed pillowcase a baby whose wizened face stopped Dovey's heart (thankfully Dreama was still inside the boxcar). "Don't you go getting into that bread," the mother said. "That bread got to go round."

The boy stuck his head out. "Daddy ain't here no more," he said. "I'll eat his."

His mother was on him then. She slapped his face once and then twice, the second time backhanded. "Your daddy not cold in the ground and here you go talking about eating his bread." The baby in her arms began to scream and the little boy too. Then the mother folded up like a fan on the steps to the boxcar and began to cry.

The little boy went up to her. "I sorry, Mama," he said. "Don't be mad."

Dovey sighed. She would have gone over to the mother and taken the baby and quietened it down, turning away to give the woman's grief its privacy. She would have, but her foot throbbed and, between the crutches and the umbrella-turned-cane, her shoulder, the bad one from years turning the wringer at the laundry tub, was talking back.

So she sat still and put her head on her knees, waiting for Dreama. The mother cried on, and so did the baby and little boy, the three of them an out-of-key chorus.

At least Virgil weren't dead. But where in this far-flung world had he wandered off to? What ailed him so bad he couldn't track down his own wife who'd heated the water for his bath and scrubbed his back twice a week on Wednesdays and Saturdays since the beginning of time? Old fox better be flat on his back somewhere far away, Memphis or Holly Springs at least. She pictured him on a hospital bed wrapped in white, broken bones from head to toe, looking the way he looked when he came home from the gin covered in cotton, sneezing and coughing and carrying on about scrawny, pasty-faced children climbing up to change the bobbins, raveling and unraveling the thread, cutting their bare feet on the machinery.

"Them white children getting higher wages than you, old man," she would counter.

He'd frown at her then. "Girl, what they doing to them babies a crime. At least none of ours climbing around on machines like monkeys. I see those little children's feet. They got to wrap them up to keep the blood from getting on the thread."

*Virgil. How she missed his good heart!*

The man loved children, wanted a houseful. When Dovey had woken up in the colored ward at the hospital with Charlesetta by her side but without her vital woman parts (she never got a full explanation of why they'd been taken), Virgil had said it was all right, they had their baby girl now. But it wasn't all right, something had been taken from him just as something had been given. After Dovey, Charlesetta was his sun, moon, and stars all rolled into one. Dovey's too. Maybe that's why Charlesetta needed to put so many miles between her and home, to get some breathing room from all that love. When she left, she took a chunk of her daddy's heart with her.

He'd gone after her, Dovey would give him that. Early the Saturday morning after Charlesetta had disappeared on Friday night, Virgil had gone down to Crosstown to ask after her. The Saturday Curb Market was in high season, and there were the usual colored families from out in the county who had come into town the afternoon before, hauling in rickety wagons their field peas, sweet corn, cantaloupe, and oozing peaches covered in yellow jackets. On Friday nights they parked their wagons in a cluster in the dirt lot behind the train depot and sat around on fruit crates, the men smoking pipes and the women shelling peas. Then, a few sips of bootleg liquor and they rolled out their pallets and hit the dirt so as to be ready for the early morning market the next day. Virgil had talked to them that Saturday morning as they sat beside the wagons displaying their produce. He came home with the news that Charlesetta or her dead-ringer had boarded the M&O around ten the night before, heading for New Orleans.

That's when they knew they'd lost her, though at the time Dovey thought it was temporary.

If Dreama had to lose Promise, better to lose him at three months than eighteen years. The longer you have children the more they crawl up under your skin. They are heart-hungry and they won't stop until they nibble their way into the heart's innermost secret chambers, until, before you know it, they are coursing through you, head to toe. They are the hair of your head, the nail on your little finger.

It was the first time Dovey had seen Virgil cry. It wasn't a pretty sound, or even sad. A bit of a wail, high-pitched and nasal: a foghorn, resembling a snore.

"Lord," she said to him. "You'd think she gone and died."

"That girl ain't never coming back," he said. "Not in this life. Mark my word, woman."

She didn't like it. What kind of man carried on so? Back then, she'd expected a letter in the coming week. It would say Charlesetta had gotten a steady job waiting tables, not at a juke joint but in a fancy restaurant where she wore a nice uniform (well starched, Dovey hoped) and took orders for gumbo and oysters and barbecued shrimp. She'd write back and tell Charlesetta where Virgil's people lived so she could drop by. Dovey pictured Charlesetta's return visit, a few years later, with a neatly dressed Creole man and two or three bright children in Sunday outfits. Dovey would worry about how to fit them all under one roof for the visit. She would have to borrow some cots from the neighbors. She would cook for days on end, pickling beets and peaches, frying okra (she hoped they would come in midsummer when her garden had come in), and stewing a hen in brown gravy the way Charlesetta liked it. Charlesetta would draw her mother aside and say she was sorry she'd run off the way she had; her eyes would tear up when she said it. She would invite Virgil and Dovey to come down and visit her little family. They would have a picnic on the levee by the river and watch the steamboats go by, they would eat whole crabs, hot and peppered, on a table covered in newspaper. They would visit Virgil's family.

But Virgil had been right. And when Charlesetta came back in that M&O boxcar, that was the second time she saw him cry.

That's when Dovey's heart had turned into a block of ice. What right had he to cry? If he hadn't shoved their one and only daughter, fueling the fire that burned in Charlesetta, none of this would have happened. Charlesetta would have been alive and kicking, herself a mother several times over more than likely. She would have found a nice man, maybe lived right down Green Street and Dovey's grandbabies would be popping in and out of the house, making mischief, playing their games in the dirt yard.

But Charlesetta wasn't made for Tupelo, she would have left no matter who did what, Dovey knew now; and her own block-of-ice heart had been the curse her good man had had to shoulder along with everything else. It had covered him like the cotton from the mill, her coldness. The storm had melted it. Where was he now that she could explain herself? She needed to tell him she'd been wrong to fault him, she needed to make some nice flat biscuits the way he liked them and sit him down and tell him she was sorry as sorry could be. Was she wrong about him being alive? Was she wrong about that too?

The thought that Virgil could be gone like Charlesetta stopped her breath. She put her head in her hands, blocking the early afternoon sun, which had suddenly gotten hotter.

She sat like that for a good long time. She didn't cry but she sweated through her head rag and now the sweat rolled down into her eyes, burning and stinging. She could hear people walking past, talking softly, but she didn't raise her head.

She felt a bump on her calf, then quickly another bump. Then *you, you, you.* She looked up and saw the cat. It had climbed the one step and was butting as hard as it could against Dovey's leg. She reached out and touched its head. The fur, a dirty white, was splotched and oily. It pushed harder on her leg, crying now. *Hungry.*

She let the cat come onto her lap. A little mama from the loose feel of her underside. The cat settled, purring and kneading Dovey's little pouch of a stomach with her needle claws. The claws pierced Dovey's skin, but the hurt, it came as a blessed relief. The pain of the foot and her head had taken all her attention, as though she were nothing but a pair of feet and a floating head, a great chasm of emptiness in between. She stroked the cat, encouraging it.

She called for Dreama to come see, but there was no answer. She called again. What was that girl doing in there?

She began to push herself up the rest of the steps with her good foot, the cat riding her lap, hanging on to Dovey's dress with her claws. When Dovey got to the top, she turned herself to see inside the boxcar, but there was a curtain made of sewn-together burlap sacks blocking her view. She saw a rail on the side of the door and grabbed hold of the cat and took the rail and pulled herself up. She pushed aside the curtain and peered inside, trying to adjust her eyes to the dark.

She heard Dreama before she saw her. She was crying, a soft mewling sound not unlike the mewling of the cat, and she had the hiccups. She sat in the dark on one of two cots in the corner.

When Dreama saw her grandmother, she got up and came over and took Dovey's hand. "What you doing with that dirty old thing, Granny? Put it down. You're going to fall and break something."

Dovey looked at her. "No."

"What you mean, no?"

"No, I ain't letting go this cat."

"Well, sit down then. What are we going to do with a mangy old cat?"

"Feed her," said Dovey.

The boxcar was divided down the middle by a makeshift wall from the same rough pine as the steps. The nails were uneven

and the wall didn't quite reach the ceiling, but the scent of pine
was refreshing. "We only get half," Dreama said. "There'll be
another family on the other side."

Dovey breathed a sigh of relief to be somewhere private. In
the center of their side was a small table piled with canned goods;
sacks of cornmeal, beans, coffee, and some sugar; a glass jar of
congealed bacon fat; some powdered milk and a jug of water;
and a loaf of store-bought white bread. There was a fat candle in
the center of the table. In one corner, on a crate, lay a skillet, a
large cooking pot with a big spoon in it, and a percolator. In the
opposite corner a chamber pot and a stack of newspapers beside
it. Directly inside the door were a stack of wood, some newspaper, and a large box of matches.

Dovey hobbled over to the table and found two plates and
two spoons and a can opener. Two folding chairs had been
pushed neatly under the table, the two cots covered with one
blanket and one pillow each.

It was the twoness of everything that broke her concentration. No third cot.

No bassinet either. She sat down at the table, rocking back
and forth, moaning more than crying. The sound she made
shocked and embarrassed her. Worse than Virgil's caterwaul-
ing. The cat jumped down and ran into the dark back corner of
the boxcar, crouching there warily, a splash of white against the
creosoted wood.

Dreama walked around behind Dovey and held down her
shaking shoulders as if Dovey were going to fly away. She put
her chin on Dovey's head.

The two of them stayed that way a good while. The only light
in the boxcar filtered weakly through the burlap curtain at the

opening. Then the cat leapt up on the table and started pawing at the bread, tearing open the paper it was wrapped in.

Dreama shooed the cat away from the bread. The cat retreated to the corner of the table. "How we supposed to wash these dishes?" she asked angrily. "How we supposed to keep clean?"

Dovey raised her head. Cleaning interested her. "Expect we take them outside and pour water over them. Don't know about us getting clean though." Despite their sponge baths, both she and Dreama stank. They'd sweated through their clothes on the walk to the boxcars, she because she could walk only with a struggle and Dreama because she was walking for two. She could smell Dreama's young-girl vinegary stink as she stood over her, and she was dead sure Dreama was picking up the odor of her old woman's flesh, the odor of school: chalk and dust and schoolteacher talcum-powdered sweat; under it all, a hint of mold.

The cat had returned to the bread. Dreama swatted her off the table. She opened the bread and took out a piece and stuffed half of it in her mouth. "Tastes like air. Nothing to it." She pulled out a chair and went to get the bowls and spoon. "I've got to go, Granny. I've got to keep looking. You going to be all right in here? You want some water?"

A sliver of light caught her as she stood before Dovey. The girl was a mess. It wasn't just the hair. Her face was as puckered and drawn as Dovey's. She'd swallowed her lips and her eyes were so bloodshot they looked like they were bleeding. She looked three times her age and mental to boot.

"Wait up a minute." Dovey hobbled over to the table and looked over the cans and settled for potted meat. She fumbled around for the can opener. "Before you go, eat some of this."

Dreama backed away. "Granny, I got to go."

"Not getting far eating air." Dovey opened the can, took the spoon, and smeared the potted meat on a piece of bread. The cat jumped back on the table. "Here," she said, handing the bread off to Dreama, "sit down a minute."

Such a relief it was to cajole the girl to eat, such a dear return to everyday life. From the word go, she had been always after Dreama to eat. When the girl was a baby, cow's milk made her sick, so Dovey had had to borrow a neighbor's goat until she got the child weaned. Then, the moment her two feet hit ground, Dreama never could find the time to eat. She was too busy, she would announce, downing a few bites and running out the door to play with her girlfriends, who circled the house like earth-bound buzzards waiting for her to come back out. In those days, Dreama was full of plans and schemes, making a party wherever she went.

Then she discovered books, and it was studying or reading stories, they were her bread and butter. When that Devil went and did what he did, after he dumped her like garbage in the dirt in the front of the house, after they brought her inside, the first thing she did was look at the food Dovey had set out on the supper table earlier that night and vomit. After that, they couldn't get her to eat. The Heroines of Jericho brought everything from a ham with pineapples and cloves in a pretty star pattern on top (the prettiest ham Dovey ever saw) to jars of bread-and-butter sweet pickles and pickled peaches and raspberry sherbet from Nesbitt's Grocery, the latter dripping so by the time they got there with it that, when Dreama turned up her nose at it, Dovey and the Heroines had to sit down and eat the whole carton in the space of a few minutes. The girl barely drank tea, the only thing keeping her alive the sugar in it. Dovey shoveled it in, making a dark sludge.

Dovey tried everything. All the old favorites, then all the foods the three of them ate when they were sick: chicken-neck soup and mashed sweet potatoes, applesauce that Dovey had put up in the fall. But no, nothing would do. Dreama wouldn't lift her head from the pillow unless she went outside to use the bathroom. When Dovey would approach the bed with something new, even the plate of fudge Etherene Johnson brought over, Dreama would take one look and turn her stony face to the wall.

Seven days passed, a whole week, and still the girl hadn't touched a bite of solid food. Her hair looked burnt. The Choctaw in her face had risen to the surface, the chiseled cheekbones, the hollowed eyes. She and Charlesetta had Virgil's Choctaw bones. They came from his grandfather, whose mother been the daughter of a runaway slave who'd been sheltered by a remnant of the tribe down on the coast and had taken up with a Choctaw man and borne him three children, or so the story went.

On the night of the seventh day, Virgil had descended into a serious silence and borrowed a rifle from Joshua Walker down the road. When Dovey found the gun, loaded, propped up out in the shed behind the house, she stormed back into the house and woke Virgil from a dead sleep to ask if he could tolerate being strung up on a tree for shooting the Devil, if he thought that might improve Dreama's mood. Virgil considered both ifs and returned the gun.

The next morning Dovey remembered the dessert she'd put together by accident one rainy Sunday afternoon when Dreama had the mumps, sick as a dog and burning with fever, her cheeks puffed out like a chipmunk's full of nuts. She could barely swallow. She'd named it Angel Dreama: a concoction of homemade angel food cake covered over with boiled custard and, in a flare of Dovey's imagination, meringue on top. Over the course of two days, the girl ate the whole thing, the cake by then soppy from the custard, grateful tears running down her face.

On that eighth day of Dreama's hunger strike, Dovey gathered the eggs and spent one long afternoon making the dish, first the cake, then the custard, which required two solid hours of stirring, and finally the meringue. Each of the three components had its pitfalls: the angel food cake, with its dozen egg whites, could fall flat as a pancake; the boiled custard, with all the egg yellows, treacherous for scorching if she turned her back on it for one measly minute, or, if provoked by weather or outright orneriness, refusing to thicken the least bit; the meringue, in wet weather, could end up a gummy mess. As if aware of the urgency of the situation, the whole thing turned out perfectly. She set it on the table to cool and allow time for the custard to soften the cake, and did the dishes.

Instead of taking a small bowl of it to Dreama, she carried in the whole casserole dish, along with two spoons. She'd taken off her apron and tucked her hair into its pins. She'd gone to the bathroom and splashed water on her face. It was midnight on the dot. Dreama was officially into day nine of her plan to starve herself.

Dovey bore the dish as if she were approaching a testy queen, not pausing at the bed as she'd come to do and touching Dreama's shoulder to let her know she'd entered the room. She walked right in and pulled up a chair. Dreama opened one eye, then the other. Dovey slid the dish onto the bed beside the girl, letting her smell the nutmeg that had taken Dovey three days of laundry to buy. Dreama lifted her stick arm from the cover and tried to push the dish away. But Dovey held it in place with one hand and pulled up her chair with the other. She took up a spoon and dipped it in, making sure to get some cake. She brought the spoon up to Dreama's lips and let a dab of custard and meringue linger. Then she pulled the spoon back and out came, glory, a tip of tongue. When she brought it up a second time, the lips twitched and then parted for the first bite.

NOW, DOVEY dipped the spoon back into the potted meat and tore another slice of bread and smeared it again and put it on the floor. The cat jumped down and began to devour the bread.

Dreama, meanwhile, had eaten her bread and meat and licked her fingers. "Can I have another one?"

"Sure you can, honey, sure you can. And when you get back tonight, I'll have some good corn bread for us."

"I'll have my baby back by then," said Dreama, straightening her shoulders.

Dovey hobbled over behind Dreama and began to smooth down her hair. Pieces stood out from the sides of her head. Dovey took some pins from her own hair and pinned them down. "Course you will, honey. And you look for Papa too. Go over to Crosstown and ask around if anybody put him on the train."

"I already did that."

"Do it again. Maybe they have a list by now."

"Granny. They're not counting us. You know that."

Then Dreama was gone, brushing aside the curtain and disappearing into the brightness outside, gone to find Promise.

Had the girl stashed away a piece of herself, because that's what mothers must do—hold something back just in case—but of course the answer was no, of course she hadn't because, and Dovey knew this for a fact, it's not possible to hold anything back with a baby; everything has already been opened up, everything yawns toward hunger and need, everything says, *Take me, use me, this is my body and my blood and no one else's will do.* Dreama was just a piece of water going to the sea.

She didn't for one minute expect Dreama to return with that baby.

Over the years Dovey had tried not to let herself linger on Charlesetta, that cowlick on the left temple, the mole on the top of her head that grew big as a dime one summer and had to be cut away, the surprisingly large flat feet that wouldn't stop growing the year she turned fifteen. Dovey tried not to let herself knock on that door, knowing that if it opened, a tiger would leap out and take her by the throat. She sniffed at the door like a wary dog from time to time; behind it the white coffin with cornflowers around the edge, that good potato salad—not too much onion— that Etherene Johnson had brought over, the headstone she and Virgil had bought on time that read "Charlesetta Grand'homme. *Daughter. Mother.*" But that was as far as she let herself go, and honestly, even it was too close to the mark.

Behind that door too was Virgil's sadness. And her own block-of-ice heart that had turned his sadness into something else, something beyond sad, something that howled in the night.

THE CAT had settled back in her lap and gone to sleep. She carried it over to one of the cots, hobbling only a little now. Her foot

was better, the needles had been replaced by a general tender-
ness. She lay down, not pulling up the blanket though she was
chilly. She didn't want to get too comfortable. She just needed to
rest her head for a minute, just a minute. Then she'd make that
corn bread for Dreama. The cat crawled onto her chest, turned
once, then twice, then settled.

When she woke up, a thin shaft of late day sun had come in
under the burlap and sliced across the wall of the boxcar. Bright,
too bright. It made her squint, and when she turned away, she
saw spots. She pulled up the blanket and lay still until it faded
and a sunset red took its place.

SHE OPENED her eyes to pitch-black. Dreama wasn't back and
the cat was gone from her chest. She got up and used the chamber pot and went over to the table. She felt around for the box of
matches and lit the candle. She smelled food cooking outside. It
made her mouth water, but it was too late to mix up corn bread
now. There was a can of pintos on the table. It would have to do.

She sat and waited. Then she peeked out the door. Twilight
now. Lightning bugs flared here and there, strangely early this
spring, against the rusted gray of the boxcar across from hers.
The stench of muck and decay, a rottenness, lay heavy on the
night air.

The little boy down the way was jumping around aimlessly
outside his boxcar. Then he started singing. "You put your right
foot in, you put your right foot out, you put your right foot in
and you turn yourself about. You do the hokey pokey and turn
yourself around, that's what it's all about."

The song took her back. Charlesetta and her little friends had danced to it endlessly, as if in a trance. Bent over her washtub, she had grown sick to death of the dreary repetitiveness of it, sometimes hollering at them to go play something else, jump some rope, play Holy Ghost, which was louder but not so monotonous. When they got to screeching and chasing each other and screaming that this one or that one was the Holy Ghost and the Holy Ghost was going to put a fix on the others, Dovey had to laugh, though generally she frowned on folks talking about fixing somebody. You never could tell when that kind of talk was going to circle back around. How the children thought up the Holy Ghost game Dovey didn't know, but she preferred it to pattyroller. She had encouraged it by providing the child who had the good fortune to play the Holy Ghost instead of being chased by Him a torn piece of sheet to wear in the role, despite her misgivings about encouraging the wearing of a sheet. Enough of that already.

The game died with Charlesetta, and by the time Dreama came along, the Holy Ghost had become the Boogey Man, which of course he was all along.

The boy played alone. No sign of his mother, no one had lit that family's stove either.

"You hungry, boy?" she called out to him. "You want some beans?" She wondered how Promise might have looked at that age. Would he have been a beanpole like this one?

The boy stopped in his tracks.

"Come on then," she said.

He hesitated. "Not going to bite you," she said, moving back into the boxcar. Either he'd come or he wouldn't. Either way she had to eat. She opened the can of beans.

He appeared at the door. "Well, I'm hungry," she announced

and began to eat out of the can. No point in dirtying up dishes with water so hard to come by. The jug they'd been given would scarcely make it through the night.

He came closer. "Here," she said, offering him a spoon and the can. "Dig in."

He took the spoon and the can and began to wolf down the beans.

"Save some for me," Dovey said, taking back the can.

The boy grinned suddenly, then ducked his head.

"What's your name?" she asked.

"Ray Jackson," he said, "same name's my daddy." His face changed and he put the spoon down on the table, his eyes filling.

"What happened to your daddy?"

"He stuck up in a tree."

What popped into Dovey's head was the merman. "How'd he get there?"

"The storm took him, the storm got him."

"Same thing happened to me. I flew."

"But you here, you drawing breath."

"I didn't get blowed up a tree, I got blowed into Gum Pond."

"How come you didn't drown?"

"Beats me," said Dovey. "Luck." She reached across the table and took his two hands between hers. "It's a shame about your daddy."

The boy ducked his head again. "He hung upside down all night long. All by hisself, in the rain. My mama sat under the tree all night long."

No words for that. No wonder the poor woman wasn't fixing supper. Dovey shook her head and looked down at his hands. They were baby-round, brown on top, pink underneath. In the candlelight he looked like he was wearing mittens. The boy had started to cry. She pulled out the handkerchief Glendola Harris had tucked in her pocket. "Blow your nose."

He blew and they passed the can of beans back and forth until it was empty. They didn't see or hear the white woman until she poked her head around the curtain covering the door.

"Yoohoo," she said. "Would y'all like some bananas?" She took a few steps into the boxcar carrying a bunch under each arm. "The Dole folks sent a whole boxcar-full up from Gulfport. They just came into the station. Take as many as you like. Watch out for spiders."

Bananas. Of all things. Dovey loved bananas. A dozen for twelve cents, seven for a penny each. Once, for Virgil's birthday, she had splurged and made a banana pudding. When was the last time she'd made a special dish for him?

"Much obliged," she said to the woman, taking one bunch. Then she added, "This boy has a family of his own next door." She hoped the woman would give him the other bunch.

"Don't worry, I'll drop these off over there," said the woman. Her eyes were moist, resting on the two of them, full of something Dovey didn't much care for. She didn't like anybody, much less white folks, looking at her like she'd grown a tail, like she was some kind of stray dog.

When she left, Dovey peeled a banana and gave it to the boy. Then she took one for herself. It was bruised and overripe, the way she liked them, and tasted like melted sugar.

When he finished, she told him to go on back to his mother. "You the little man," she said. "You got to take care of your mama. Help her with the baby. Behave. You hear me?"

He toyed with the banana peel. "She didn't hold on to my daddy. She ought to held on to him."

*Oh Virgil, what a heavy load.*

Dovey took the boy's hand. "Baby, the wind was too strong."

He didn't want to go, that much she could tell, but now the block of ice in her chest had suddenly melted and it flooded her eyes. "Get on now. Get home to your mama."

When he was gone, she took the banana peels and empty cans and walked to the door and tossed them in the oil can outside.

She pulled the burlap curtain back from the doorway to get some air. Then she settled herself at the kitchen table to wait for Dreama. This was the time of evening when she and Virgil would sit down and listen to their shows on WREC: *Luci and Abner, Amos and Andy,* and, if she could stay awake, *The Voice of Firestone.* Tonight nothing to listen to but a mix of bullfrogs and crickets and even they sounded muted. Virgil was out there, resting on the long cold arms of the world, but where? Tomorrow, foot willing, she would begin to look. She put her head in her arms on the table.

When she woke, she knew it was dawn by the gray tone of the sky coming through the curtain, which remained pulled back over the doorway. The candle was out and she was stone-cold, despite a blanket that had been draped around her shoulders. Her shoulders ached and there was a crick in her neck from sleeping at the table. In the half-light she turned and saw Dreama asleep on one of the cots, a patch of white tucked into her side. The girl looked worse than she had when she'd left, her face swollen and filthy, her hands and forearms scratched and bleeding. The cat opened its eyes once, then closed them.

Dovey went and lay down on the second cot, dragging her blanket behind. As soon as she put her head on the pillow, the cat leapt silently from Dreama's cot to hers and curled up in her arms.

She woke for the second time to someone calling her name. Bellowing was more like it. The bellow had authority. It ricocheted off the boxcars outside, growing louder as it approached.

She felt around for the cat, but it was gone. When she heard her name being called in that commanding voice, the voice of a man or a man-angel, she figured she'd passed in her sleep. St. Peter was calling her home. She wasn't happy about this. She'd always seen St. Peter as an ancient white man in a white robe loosely tied with a gold cord like the gold cords on the shoulders of the Carver High School band uniforms that shimmered and shook. She liked the shoulder cords on the band uniforms, but in St. Peter's case, it seemed rude to have a single, loosely tied cord the only thing hanging between a man (especially a white man!) being covered and being uncovered. It was careless. Nor did she cotton to the idea of a white man in sandals and no underwear tallying up her sins in a big book, meddling in her own personal business, which was, in her view, between her and God, and while she was on that subject, she couldn't think of a whole lot of things she'd done that she'd count as actionable *sins*. There was the Shake Rag man, but she was young then, and it was well before Virgil. It was true she'd looked at Jim Salter, who delivered ice for Bryant Ice House, but what married lady with eyes in her head, colored or white, hadn't? Those undershirts of his, wet from sweat, smelling of Clorox and man salt, those little curls of hair poking out from under his arms. Those arms! What harm in looking, even if there was a child in your belly, even if, later on, that child was wrapped around your legs? You'd tell that child to go play and offer Jim Salter a cool glass of tea, make him sit for a spell, take a load off, watch those lips talk, not caring what they said, not caring if they were saying kiss my foot. Maybe it was a little sin, she'd give St. Peter that, but not of the variety that should get you kicked out of heaven and no need to stick his nose into it.

The big sin, the sin that might send her to hell, was that block-of-ice heart of hers. But it was Virgil she'd sinned against and Virgil who'd have to do the forgiving.


"DOVEY GRAND'HOMME." Her name again. So loud she could see it writ against the sky.

"If you so bound and determined to kill me," she whispered to God, "why didn't you just drown me in the pond? Why didn't you just hang me in a tree?"

"Dovey!"

Dreama hadn't stirred, which only confirmed Dovey's sense that it was she alone who heard her name being called. She sat up on the cot. When Old Pete came, she'd meet him nose to nose. She slipped on the one shoe and patted her hair, her hands shaking. She wished she had her hairpins back from Dreama, she wished she could have taken a real tub bath. She was flooded with embarrassment at the thought of J. W. Porter (she hoped it would be J.W., not one of those out-of-town undertakers they'd called in to help) having to turn his face away when he prepared her, though surely he'd seen worse in the past few days and who could blame her for being unable to take a real tub bath when her whole house had been blown away?

Would J.W. wash her poor foot or leave it bandaged? Would he attend to her private place, now hairless as a baby's?

That bellow again, right there outside the burlap curtain, which now trembled. Someone was climbing the steps to the boxcar.

But it wasn't a white man's voice, and in that moment just before the curtain opened, she thought she recognized it, which is when the man—trailed by someone small, huffing and puffing, a Red Cross lady, judging from the jaunty angle of her hat—groped his way through the burlap curtain.

He burst into the boxcar then stopped short, peering through the dark. The light was behind him, and it was too dark to see his face, but that silhouette Dovey would have known anywhere. Those arms, longer than an ordinary man's, reaching almost to his knees. The neck long too and straight, the face narrow with those Choctaw cheekbones up around the outer corners of the eyes. The lips she knew though she couldn't see them, thin and straight as a ruler.

Dreama, on the cot beside her, sat up suddenly.

In that moment Dovey and Dreama rose in one motion and looked at the man and he looked at them, the only sound in the boxcar the Red Cross lady's wheeze.

The Red Cross lady coughed once, then twice. Then she walked to the center of the car.

"Well?" she said, looking up at the man.

He opened his long arms, and the two of them came, Dreama flowing like water, Dovey pitching and stumbling like a drunkard.

"All right then," said the Red Cross lady, clearing her throat. "I'll have to order another cot."

"Another chair too," Dovey murmured into Virgil's chest.

They stood there locked together after she left. Then the burlap curtain flapped open, making the slightest ripple in the silence.

Only Dovey heard it. She opened her eyes and looked out from under Virgil's arm. The cat was back. She padded toward them, carrying in her mouth a little struggling sack of bones and

fur. She dropped the kitten in the place between their feet, causing them to pull apart and look down in astonishment.

"Well now," said Virgil, bending down, his long, patient, ever-
lasting fingers grazing the pocked floor of the boxcar. "What
we got here?"

# FRIDAY, APRIL 10

# 14

## 6:32 P.M.

Jo awoke in a front-row seat. She'd never sat up this close at the Lyric, not liking to be so near the screen. She eyed the back corner of the stage where a makeshift curtain of sheets, held in place with thumbtacks, stretched from the back wall to the side wall, forming a triangle. The curtained area, she surmised from the moans and occasional screams coming from that direction, was where the seriously wounded were being kept.

Glendola Harris stood over her. "About time you woke up," she said. "Look what I got here." She pointed at the bassinet in the space between the front row and the stage, right in front of Jo's feet.

"What day is it?" Jo's neck had a crick. She felt like she'd slept for a hundred years.

"Friday. Good Friday," said Glendola. "You flat slept right through Thursday, honey. Sitting straight up the whole time. You almost missed Friday too. It's nighttime."

*Her mother.* Jo stood up suddenly. The theater swooped down on her like a bird of prey, caught her, and shook her. She collapsed back in her seat.

"You need to eat." Glendola put a ham sandwich in her lap. "And here's a glass of water."

She ate and tried to decide how she was going to tell her mother all that had happened, how to form the words into one glorious sentence that Alice McNabb the English teacher would properly appreciate and maybe even applaud when all was said and done.

*Mother,* she would say, *I was the one who got you help and I found Tommy in a bush and took good care of him (despite the fact that Daddy left us high and dry, not once but twice, and my arm was in the cast and Tommy got a terrible cold and couldn't eat), but (drum roll) he is alive and kicking (hard!), and here he is: I saved him for you.*

This version was self-serving and undiagrammable, mostly one long parenthesis, but she liked it for all of those reasons. What it lacked in sophistication and nuance (both Words to Keep), it captured in ebb and flow. It was a story in itself, lapping at the outer edges of factuality to be sure, but all of it there, stated, once and for all, roundly and soundly. Moreover, in the past few days, she'd found herself inhabiting the space of what seemed to be one long parenthesis, as if she had plunged into the middle of a sentence from which there was no escape, everything being contingent on everything else.

Of course, the second part of the sentence wasn't precisely true. She'd saved Tommy for herself, not for her mother; she'd saved him because he was hers. Each time she laid eyes on him he looked new. Even now she could hardly keep her eyes off him as he lay asleep in the crib beside her, his face flushed, his lips twitching slightly. She itched to pick him up and smell him. The top of his head carried the odor of fresh bread.

Just as she'd finished the sandwich (and was wishing for another), her father wandered in and sat down in the seat next to hers and patted her hand as if *she* were the one who needed taking care of (what a joke!). Mort McNabb stank. His hair was shiny with grease. More shocking, there was hair on his face, wild and curly and surprisingly white, hair she'd never seen in her entire life. She didn't like it. Her father was nothing if not fastidious. He bathed every night and shaved in the mornings. On nights when he went out, which was usually every night of the week but Saturday, he shaved a second time and put on a fresh shirt. On Thursday nights, he took a long second bath before leaving, humming in the tub. Now he just sat beside her like a bump on a log, oblivious to the fact that he smelled like a cross between salt fish and garbage. He was hunched over like an old man. He rubbed his eyes, which were still that startling shade of neon red.

"We need to take Tommy in to see your mother." He mumbled the words, his head down as if he were talking to his lap.

Jo leaned over. "What?"

Now he looked at her, his eyes vacant and unfocused, as if he'd been struck blind. "We need to take the baby to your mother. He'll cheer her up."

*Yes, it was time.* Oddly, though, Jo hesitated. For one thing, she was coming around to the belief that her mother had not taken particularly good care of Tommy *before* the storm. Witness how little he had cried when he was with Jo. As if by magic, he'd become the perfect baby. Either the storm had blown all the badness out of him, which Jo believed highly unlikely, or her care of him, under the most intolerable of circumstances, had been far superior to Alice's when there had been a roof over their heads and one day had followed the next, as predictable and dull and ordinary as peach cobbler on Sunday.

Was her mother ill-suited to motherhood? Were some women just not natural mothers?

Jo's first memory was of peering through the bars of her crib and seeing her mother's face; she couldn't remember her mother's expression as she looked back, if she indeed did look back, only the red red bow of Alice's mouth, which, when Jo reached through the bars for it, had already receded into the distance until it was only a red fleck at the end of her wobbly line of vision. Something that had once been there and then was gone. When she grew older and noticed how her mother seemed to look through her as if she were a window to something else, she came to know instinctively that her mother saw in her, not a daughter, not Josephine Alice McNabb (the middle name her mother's own so that her mother somehow squatted inside and between the *Jo McNabb* that she saw as her own dwelling place), but a different life, another life, waiting out there far ahead of her, a horizon she could never quite catch up to, a life that could only be watched from afar the way you'd watch a sunset or heat lightning. Absent was that ripple in her mother's eyes, that telltale bubble from something submerged but deeply present, something that moved under the surface.

Her mother, she'd been told, came alive in the classroom. She'd heard the students laugh (but not in a mean way) at how Mrs. McNabb wept when she read Shakespeare and Keats, how she paced out Lord Tennyson's lines *half a league, half a league, half a league onward*, marching like a soldier around and around the classroom, flinging over her shoulder a maelstrom of martial words at her students until they felt dizzy and giddy and ready to go out and do battle with any foe imaginable; how once, toward the end of the term, she'd sneaked in a story from

*The Forum* magazine by some crazy writer from over in Oxford, Bill Somebody, about an old woman killing her boyfriend and then sleeping, *sleeping in the bed*, with his icky, stinky, putrefied corpse *for a good long time*. Alice, moreover, had read the story *out loud*, the latter getting her in deep you-know-what with not only the principal but also the school board. In the classroom, at least, Alice McNabb was never dull.

But Jo's quiet, matter-of-fact, and, most recently, wretchedly sad mother was as different as daylight from dark from the fiery, passionate Mrs. McNabb of Tupelo High School. Now that Jo thought about it, there was something about her mother that simply wasn't, well, particularly *motherly*. Not that Jo had ever felt deprived of anything important, not that she didn't believe her mother harbored the best of intentions toward her children. Naturally her mother loved her one and only daughter. Of course she did. But there wasn't an easiness between the two of them that Jo saw between some of her girlfriends and their mothers. Alice and Jo's autumn trips to Reed's or Black's or Pryor's for school clothing didn't result in giggles at how hilarious one of them looked in an outrageously feathered hat or a badly fitted dress. No shenanigans with the sample sprays at the Reed's perfume counter, no chitchat with the other mothers and daughters on similar missions.

When Jo got old enough to handle money, she preferred to go shopping alone or to tag along with her girlfriends, Taffy Spicer and Lois Clayburn and the adorable Wesson twins, and their normal mothers. These other mothers went to bridge parties where aspic with eyeball olives and tea sandwiches of cream cheese and cucumber and towering slices of Mrs. Polk's caramel pie were served on card tables covered in linen cloths, which were later removed when the cards came out. These other mothers volunteered at the hospital, delivering coloring books to sick children, bouquets of hand-cut jonquils from their own flower beds to old ladies. They baked hams for the poor at Christmas and made flower arrangements for funerals and weddings. On special occasions they took their daughters to Memphis, where they stayed at the Peabody Hotel and drank gin fizzes and watched the ducks come and go from the pond inside the lobby.

Jo wondered how Taffy and Lois and the twins, Sally and Stella, had fared in the storm. She had caught glimpses of lists from the *Tupelo Journal* posted in the lobby of the Lyric. The papers printed the names of the displaced and where they were staying and with whom, along with lists of the dead and injured, but she hadn't had time to pore over them.

She wondered too what had happened to the washwoman with the bird name (Oh please! *Why* couldn't she remember it, and after the dear woman had sent help to her mother and little Tommy? How things blew in and out of her head!) and, for that matter, the washwoman's granddaughter (Dream? No, that wasn't quite it). Had the girl ever found her baby? How terrible to think of one's own child, a little baby, hurt and alone.

And if she thought hard about that little baby, she must not forget it was her own niece or nephew. A colored baby! (If, by some miracle, it was found, should she send it toys and worry about its welfare, the way she'd worry about a regular nephew or niece, a child who would come with his mother at Christmas and Easter and maybe be a little ring bearer at her wedding, alongside her darling Tommy? A colored child in her wedding? She couldn't picture it.) Into her head the child crawled like a nocturnal animal: she saw herself all grown up and beautiful with her own family, her mother's round oak table extended to

an oval, the washwoman at one end, Jo and her (handsome) husband at the other, the children dark and light in between, dressed
nicely of course, clean and fresh. It would be a private gathering.
No one need know. She didn't think she'd mind that so much,
she rather relished the idea in fact; but what would people say?
What would Taffy, Lois, and the twins think? They'd think it
was as wrong as two left shoes, that's what they'd think. They'd
say she'd gone mental.

But she couldn't help but wonder about the two of them, the
washwoman and her granddaughter, sister wanderers of a ruined
landscape, cast out from home and loved ones, searching for that
little child. Both of them as small-boned and fragile as birds. Jo
towered over them. The papers, she noticed, hadn't published
the whereabouts of the colored and there were no death and
injury lists for them either. It was as if the people who had made
the households and yards and barnyards hum all over town had
vanished from the face of the earth without a trace. How could
anyone who lived up on the Hill in one of those flimsy houses
have survived that wind? Most of those folks were probably still
stuck headfirst in the muck of Gum Pond (she pictured rows of
brown legs turned skyward) or blown clear across the railroad
tracks to the east, strung up in trees like Christmas ornaments
up and down the county and maybe even beyond. And the
dogtrots and shotguns (one family of six lived in an abandoned
school bus!) up on the Hill, they were palaces compared to those
shanties down in Shake Rag. The washwoman and her granddaughter must have been among the few who survived.

JO'S FATHER stood up and ran his hands through his hair,
which made it stand on end in whipped peaks of grease and filth.

"I'm going to go see about your mother." He spoke in a vague murmur, still speaking so low she could barely make out his words. She leaned in to hear him, his newly sprouted whiskers almost grazing her cheek. Then she nodded, relieved he wasn't demanding that she wake up Tommy quite yet.

Mort rose to go, but instead of climbing the steps to the stage, he headed up the aisle to the front of the theater and assumedly right out the front door to wherever it was he kept disappearing to. Jo wasn't surprised. As she watched him go, she thought he looked shorter than she remembered. He sagged, he bagged. Was it the angle from which she viewed him? But no, it couldn't be; the front of the theater was lower than the back, of course, silly her. He should appear taller, larger than life, not smaller. People did shrink as they got older, she'd heard, and certainly this had been true in the aunts' cases; the two of them had even cheerfully remarked on it. But this shrinkage of her father's, it seemed sudden and acute. Had this happened over time and Jo just hadn't noticed? Her father was forty-six and while that seemed terribly old to her, she knew it wasn't really *old* old. Not old like the little wizened washwoman, not old like the aunts had been.

Little Tommy slept on. She leaned down and touched his hand. When his fingers closed like a clam shell on her index finger (as she knew they would), her chest clenched and then unclenched in a motion that was so violent it caused tears to spring to her eyes, tears of fear and surprise. How hurtful love was, how terrifying.

And to think she could have lost him forever, to think he might still be hanging in that bush like a strange blossom, still and cold.

She took a shaky breath and looked behind her. The theater had cleared out a bit since the first day she and Tommy and Alice had been brought here, the walking wounded having gone their way, heaven knows where, people being so flung about. How many days since the storm? Had she really slept over twenty-four hours? How many days and nights in their house with most of the roof gone, the rain pouring in and Son taking on the shape of a seal on the living room floor and her mother's raw bone gleaming wetly in the night? Time had gotten so jostled about in her head.

After Son's friends came and went, cloaked in pure evil, she had sunk into a swamp she might not have crawled out of had it not been for the baby. And how many days and nights in the theater before her father showed up? Then that awful night in the aunts' noisy house. It seemed like a hundred years had passed since the storm. For all she knew, she might be as old as the aunts now. She felt it.

The baby's eyelids began to twitch. She pulled her finger from his sticky grasp and checked the towel between his legs. Wet. And he would be hungry. She needed to find the nurse, but she didn't want to leave him alone. She stood up and scanned the theater for a white uniform. At that moment Tommy began to fret and cough a little. She saw a nurse moving between cots up on the stage. She raised her good arm as if summoning a waiter, but the woman didn't look up.

Now Tommy let out an alarming sound, something between a scream and a strangle. Quickly, she put her hand under his neck and brought him upright. He coughed a phlegmy cough. She leaned down and gathered him in her good arm, pushing him into place with the cast on the other, and rose with him writhing and fretting in her grasp. Out of the corner of her eye she saw the white of the nurse's uniform and climbed the steps up to the stage slowly and presented him to the woman, who, when she turned toward Jo, revealed a face like a turnip, pinkish gray, pinched and tucked at the edges.

"He needs changing and feeding," Jo said.

"Ah, and here's the little one with the cold. They told me to watch out for you," said the nurse. "Let's see about you, little tidbit." The pinches and tucks deepened, and a dimple appeared on the nurse's cheek. "I know somebody who wants to see you." She gestured with her head toward the curtained area at the back corner of the stage. "Your own dear mother."

"Is she awake?" Jo asked as she handed the baby over. Tommy seemed unwilling to be taken, his face tightening with alarm, his bottom lip downturned and trembling.

"She was a few minutes ago. She's still groggy, but I told her we'd bring the baby back to her when he woke up. I'll take him when I finish cleaning him up. She'll want to feed him."

"No!" Jo didn't appreciate being rushed by some busybody nurse. She'd bring Tommy to her mother in her own good time. "We'll wait for my father to come back," she said in what she hoped was a firm voice.

"Your poor mama is all by her lonesome in there. Where's that daddy of yours anyway? We haven't seen much of him."

"I think he went to see about our house," Jo lied. She wished it were true; their house needed a new roof, maybe a new everything, and the sooner the better. She didn't relish the idea of going back to the aunts' old dust-clotted place, noisy with ghosts. She was sorry her father had suggested it, for Tommy's sake and her own; at least the boxcars had been swept out (surely!).

She looked at Tommy in the nurse's arms. He was thrashing and kicking. He was getting stronger. Now, suddenly, he looked like Son, something about the cheekbones, the position of the eyes, wide-set and amber, darker than Son's, the color of a worn penny. When Jo was little, she'd loved Son's eyes. They'd sparkled with fun. Son didn't seem to mind her then. He'd insisted on teaching her to walk. She remembered his arms reaching out at the end of a long unsteady stagger down the hall. He held her up when she got to him, and his arms were sturdy and true. That memory was why she had trusted him, why she came around to the back of the garage when he called to her that day.

What had happened to that boy at the end of the hall? She needed to know because now she needed to make sure it didn't happen to Tommy. She needed to be vigilant.

Because sometimes evil didn't show its ugly self; it could put on the clothes of an ordinary boy. The boy could sit across the table from you, a stray lock of hair hanging in his eyes. He could be doing all the regular things boys do, shoveling in the mashed potatoes, pushing the peas around on his plate, preferring peach cobbler over rhubarb in the late summer while the wasps batted the window screen and the fan on the sideboard rotated.

Once, Jo's father had received a box of pears at Christmas from a distant relative in California. When Jo unpeeled the foil, the pear she'd chosen looked and smelled like heaven. Then, when she cut into it, there was a monstrous green worm with horns curled up inside, and the core was hollow.

So she knew to be watchful. She would read Tommy stories about good boys doing good deeds; she would make sure an ugly thought never entered his sweet head and, if it did, she would swat it like a fly. She would read him the Bible, Genesis through Revelation and back to Genesis again. Every night she would get down on her knees with him to say his prayers. They would pray for the afflicted and feebleminded, the mean and the ugly, people with terrible deformities, sinners everywhere. They would pray to be good, and they would be, they would be nothing but good.

But now here Tommy came in the nurse's arms, wailing forlornly, sniffling and squirming, pushing against the nurse with his legs.

"Here," Jo said. "I'll take him now. I'll feed him."

"Well, sit down somewhere," the nurse said. "You can't feed him standing up with only one good arm."

Jo sat down on an empty cot and patted her lap. "Here. Put him here."

When the nurse gave him to her, Tommy stopped in midscream and looked up at Jo expectantly. The nurse handed her the bottle and he followed its path with his eyes as it moved from one hand to the other above his head.

"He sure knows where his food comes from," said the nurse.

"He does," murmured Jo, pulling his legs down farther toward her middle, rocking him back and forth a little. "He sure does."

He began to suck before the nipple touched his lips, a glazed look coming over his eyes. She gave him the bottle and they settled in.

When he finished, a bubble of milk erupted from his mouth and he grinned at her. She settled him back on her lap, and he looked at her and began to gurgle and pat his hands together.

The thought popped into her head that this would be a good time to take him to see their mother. She tried to dismiss it, but her conscience nagged at her. How could she not? And her poor mother must be lonely. Was she afraid? Did she know where she was? Was she wondering where her family had gone?

All right then. She took a deep breath and touched her hair. She could feel the tangles and tried to get her fingers through them. Her scalp felt oily and crusted over, with what she wasn't sure; she hoped it wasn't blood. She pulled a strand of hair to her nose; it smelled rank. She wished she had a comb. She wished she had a mirror.

Well, maybe not a mirror. She touched the row of stitches on her forehead. There would be a scar. She wasn't a pretty girl to begin with. Her nose (how she despised it!) was larger than normal with a hint of a hump; her eyes were a nice green but a little bulging (well, maybe not bulging, but certainly prominent) and too far apart, giving her, she thought privately, the appearance of a praying mantis. Once she had passed a schoolhouse window after school where some older boys were watching girls go by on their way home and commenting back and forth among themselves. *What about that one?* Jo heard one say. *Oh, about average,* another answered, *nothing special.*

Nothing special was how she'd thought of herself ever since, and now when she walked to school and sometimes past those same boys, she'd tilt her head forward so her hair covered her face, making sure they couldn't get a good look at her. The Wesson twins said she would grow into the nose and eyes; they said she had cheekbones like an Indian, high and broad. Her mother said Jo's face had *character*, that when she grew up, she would find someone who thought she was the most beautiful woman in the world.

Now, as Tommy looked up at her, she felt she'd already found that someone. He wanted her nose. He was reaching for it now.

She gathered him and rose. He gurgled at her, a river of drool cascading down the side of his mouth to his chin. She carried him up the steps to the stage and across to the curtain in the corner, skirting the cots. When she reached the curtain, she walked around to an opening where one sheet stopped and another began and elbowed her way through.

On the other side of the curtain, a large man with a stethoscope around his neck loomed in her path. "What are you doing in here?" he demanded. "No visitors." His eyes, Jo noticed, were kinder than his voice.

"My mother," Jo said. "I want to see my mother. Alice McNabb. The nurse sent me. How is she? Are you her doctor?"

The man nodded wearily. "The leg, it's set her back. We had to remove it all the way up to the thigh. She's pretty low. We're having trouble getting her to eat."

The word *remove* (such an innocuous, first-grade sort of word) knocked the breath out of her. For a moment, she felt woozy and took a deep breath. She absolutely could not faint with Tommy in her arms.

The doctor took her elbow. "Are you all right? Where's your father?"

"I don't know. He was here, but then he left."

"Well, let's see if a visit from you and the little one won't cheer her up. This is her baby?"

"He's all of ours." Jo looked down at Tommy. He'd fallen asleep again, his breathing still a wheeze.

"He sounds croupy," said the doctor. He pointed to a long table and took his stethoscope from his neck. "Let me give a listen."

Jo looked down at the table. It looked like their kitchen table at home but large, some form of metal with a speckled white top. It didn't look clean.

"I'll just hold him. He gets to crying when I put him down."

The doctor came closer and pulled up Tommy's nightshirt. When the stethoscope touched the baby's chest, he startled and began to whimper.

"He doesn't like anything cold," Jo said. Tommy's face contorted, his bottom lip trembling. Now that blasted doctor had gone and done it.

The doctor pressed the stethoscope here and there on Tommy's chest, listening. He lifted Tommy a little and put the stethoscope around his side, under his right arm, where the gash was. Tommy let out a whoop of surprise and began to kick and squirm.

"That's quite a cut he has under the arm," said the doctor, pulling back. "Someone should have stitched that up. It's going to take awhile to heal. I'm going to bandage it up."

"Is he all right?" Jo whispered. How could she have forgotten the wound under Tommy's arm? What a terrible nurse she was!

"He's going to be fine if you take good care of him. He's got bronchitis, but that should clear up. You just don't want this going into pneumonia. Now, put him on the table so I can bandage him up."

Jo eyed a stack of towels on a smaller table. "He needs something under him. He hates the cold."

The doctor took a towel and spread it on the examining table. He turned to her, expectantly.

"I'll wait until you're all ready," Jo said. "He's going to cry."

The doctor reached for some gauze and tape and a bottle of iodine. He turned back to her.

"Aren't you going to wash your hands?" It was not a question a girl should ask of a doctor but she didn't care; she had read about wounds getting infected.

"Quite the little mother, aren't you?" He went over to a basin and took a jug of water and passed it over his hands and turned back to her. "Now put him down."

Jo took Tommy over to the table and laid him down carefully. "You'll have to pull off the shirt," she told the doctor.

He pulled it over the baby's head, and Tommy began to flail about and shriek.

"Hold him steady," said the doctor. "Hold that arm up."

Tommy was like a rubber band now, stretching every which way. Jo hadn't realized how long his limbs were. Had they grown since the storm? He was strong, stronger than she'd ever imagined him to be. One day, he'd be stronger than she herself was; one day, he'd be a man. How remarkable!

"What's this?" asked the doctor. "Is this part of a birthmark under here?"

"It's a bruise." What was wrong with this doctor?

"Whatever it is, the scar will grow over it," the doctor said. "It's overtaking it already."

He swabbed iodine on the wound until Tommy's right side looked drenched in blood and wrapped a bandage around the baby's chest, taping it in place. "Let's leave this on at least a week. It'll keep that gash clean and dry." He put Tommy's nightshirt back on. "Just give him sponge baths."

Jo nodded. She was more concerned about Tommy's state of mind. He was screaming bloody murder. As she gathered him up again, she debated whether she should take him to see their mother. Did her mother really need a bellowing, writhing baby right now?

As if in answer to her question, Tommy drew two shaky breaths and fell into an exhausted sleep, turning his head so that he could rest his cheek on her breast.

"He's going to be fine," said the doctor a second time. "A lot of stories haven't ended this well. This town has had a lot of flying babies. There're children still missing."

A deep weariness crept over her. Once, when she'd gone with her family to visit her uncle in his ramshackle place out near Pontotoc, she had witnessed a terrible sight: an ox under yoke pulling a plow in the field next to her uncle's land. A man beating and beating the ox, which moved slower and slower down the row, its head down. Then, in one unbelievably slow motion, the animal's front legs folded and it went down, then flipped on its side, its eyes rolling back in its head, showing its teeth, exhaustion overpowering fear and pain. She felt suddenly as beaten up and bone-weary as that ox, her arms and legs leaden. If only she could crawl up on that hard cold metal table and sleep. Just half an hour. That's all she would ask.

But now the doctor was speaking to her. He was telling her where to find her mother. The back corner. She would be able to spot her easily; the bandage on her abbreviated leg, the leg elevated.

She shuddered at the mention of the leg, then began to make her way through the beds, not cots here, but actual hospital beds, brought in, she assumed, from the hospital. Some of the people in them were deep in sleep, some in something deeper than sleep.

As she passed through the maze of beds, an old man, just skin and bones, poor thing, smiled a toothless smile at her, then reached out and grasped her wrist and held on. "Hold my hand, girlie, I'm getting ready to die," he croaked, his breath smelling of cider.

She tried to pull away. "I have the baby."

"You, girlie. Take hold of me. Hold me down. I'm about to fly away."

She remembered the woman who had cried out for Jenny. "All right," she said. She stopped next to his bed, and he tightened his grip. She leaned against the bed for a moment. Just when she was preparing to pull away, his eyes closed and the hand slipped from her arm, grazing her hip, and fell to the side of his bed.

**SHE FOUND** her mother in the corner, the stump of a leg suspended by a pulley and cords, the rest of Alice swathed in white. She was staring at the ceiling. She had a dreamy look, as if she were looking at something through and above the ceiling. The blue sky, birds and trees and clouds. Alice had always had a high, wide brow, and now, with her hair pulled back in some sort of barrette, the brow seemed to take up most of her face, lending it a blankness, the sense of an unwritten-upon page.

"May-May?" Jo whispered. Her voice quavered.

Alice continue to stare upward. "Oh," she said.

Jo came closer. "Mother, we're here. Tommy and I are here to see you."

Alice blinked once and then twice. "Oh," she said again. It seemed to be the only word she could manage. She seemed to be trying to summon herself, the way you'd summon a child from play as the twilight fell, the child reluctant to come back into the lighted, busy house.

Then slowly, slowly, she turned her head toward them. There

was something reptilian in the way her head moved, a deliberateness.

Jo tried to smile. "May-May, how are you feeling? Are you in pain?"

"Not anymore," her mother said. That was all she said.

"That's good," said Jo. "I'm so sorry about your . . ." Something in her mother's face, a slight frown, stopped her.

Then Alice turned back to her contemplation of the ceiling.

Jo decided on a more authoritative tone: "Mother, we are here to see you. Tommy and I. We are here to visit you and help you." She moved closer to her mother's head. She wanted to stroke that broad high forehead but she didn't have an extra hand.

Alice closed her eyes, the slight frown reappearing, two parentheses between her eyebrows.

With her hip Jo pushed on the bar of the bed, jostling it. "Mother! Wake up! I want to talk to you."

The two parentheses deepened. Alice turned her head, eyes still closed. "Please," she said. "I want to sleep now."

"But I've got little Tommy right here safe and sound." She wanted to say the sentence she'd memorized, but then her mother opened her eyes and what Jo saw there stopped her.

Just then the nurse with the turnip face came over. "Oh look, Mrs. McNabb, isn't this wonderful? Your daughter and your little boy, here they are all safe and sound." She turned to Jo. "Your mother came in asking about you." She turned back to Alice: "Oh honey, here are your sweet *children*. Blessings from God!"

Suddenly, in an odd scramble, Alice bolted upright in the bed and turned as if to strike the woman, her eyes flashing, her mouth slightly open, incisors bared. "Don't talk to me about

God. I lost my firstborn son," she snarled. "Now I've lost *this*." She gestured at the stump.

Jo jumped back, almost stumbling. The baby was getting heavier by the second, her arms had long ago gone numb. Now her legs had begun to tremble.

Oddly, Alice didn't look at Jo and Tommy, or even at the nurse anymore. Instead she scanned the room as if searching for an escape route, as if she were planning on leaping from her bed and crawling away from them all like a wounded animal. Poor thing, Jo thought, now she'll never be able to escape us; she'll never be able to go back to who she was. Once, when Snow-ball was little, Jo couldn't find her for days; then one Saturday morning, when she and her mother were getting in the car to go shopping, she had heard a feeble *you, you, you* at the back of the garage. It came from a cabinet where paint was kept. When she opened the cabinet door, she saw two eyes staring out from the dark, searching for a way to get out, afraid of her, afraid of getting closed up again. (Son, Jo had thought at the time.) That look spoke of betrayal, the way her mother's did now.

Alice remained rigidly upright, her eyes on Jo. Then, Alice sighed and sagged and shook her head as if to clear it. Jo took a step toward her then, lowering the cast so Alice could get a good look at Tommy. The baby opened his eyes at the movement, drawing closer to Jo, still wheezing a little. "Isn't he a sight for sore eyes?" Jo asked her mother. Jo drew her breath to begin her lovely, perfectly memorized sentence.

"Your boy is sure enough the pretty one," interrupted the nurse, hovering at Jo's elbow. "Look at that head of hair."

"Sweet too," said Jo to her mother. "He's been good as gold."

Jo took a deep breath, preparing now, finally, to launch into her story, but, then, as if her words had summoned them, the ants were back and busy. They pounced, vicious and full of heat, preoccupying her for the moment, so that she didn't see her mother lean over and peer at the baby in her arms.

When she looked again, her mother was glaring up at her, her brow looming large as a plate, a drop of spittle on her upper lip. "That's not my Tommy," Alice hissed. "How many times do I have to tell you? That baby is not mine. You, Jo. Go get your notebook. Write it down. That is not my baby. *Charlatan.*"

Jo flinched and tightened her grip on the baby, who, without warning, gave a sudden and surprisingly powerful lurch backward, as if he too were reacting to Alice's (his own mother's!) words. Jo's shoulders, by their own volition, folded around the baby like wings, as if to ward off a blow. She took one final look at her mother, who had undoubtedly gone and lost her mind. The sight chilled her. Alice, her mother, had thrown herself back on her pillow and now glared up at Jo, her eyes darkly accusatory, as if her daughter were somehow to blame for all of this, as if Jo had summoned the tornado that had done them all in, as if she had snatched some strange baby out of the sky to trick and torment her poor mother with.

"Oh dear," said the nurse. "Why don't you give me the baby? I'll take him back in after awhile. We'll sort this out."

Jo shrank from her too and pushed back against the curtain surrounding her mother's bed and then let it fall in front of her, leaving a dingy opaque whiteness in place of her mother's face.

Why would any mother deny her own child?

Why?

Jo turned and carried Tommy back by the old man's bed. His mouth was open and he seemed to be sleeping, not dead, but one never knew, did one? She pictured piles of dead people, stacks of severed limbs, common as the limbs of trees, littering the land-scape, the piles reaching to the sky. (What had they done with her mother's lost leg? She suspected they tossed it aside like gar-bage, which didn't seem right.) She pictured little babies flying in lazy circles like buzzards, then settling on top of the piles, sucking and pecking and burrowing down.

The turnip-faced nurse followed her. "You. Bring that baby back here. A baby needs its mother."

Jo clutched Tommy and hurried down the aisle of the theater; then, outside, she headed up Broadway. When she turned the cor-ner onto Jefferson and looked back and the nurse was nowhere in sight, she stopped to get her breath. She looked down at Tommy, who, oddly, didn't seem bothered by the jostling. It was the nose that worried Jo, that and the hair. She tried to take a closer look but now the ants had set up shop in her left eye, burning and stinging. Her eye stuttered, and then began to speak, haltingly telling her things she didn't want to hear. If her mental mother said Tommy wasn't theirs and her equally mental father believed Alice (and there was no reason to think he would not because, really, her father didn't give a flying flip about Tommy or Jo or any of them), then Tommy would be taken, *taken*, from her, Jo McNabb, his loving sister. And that would never do. She (her eye told her) could not, would not, countenance the idea of losing him, not if she had to take him and run away and live forever in exile from Tupelo and her mother and father and Taffy Spicer and Lois Clayburn and the Wesson twins and everyone else in the whole wide world she knew. She must take Tommy and run for her life, and his. She must leave now, before her father returned and the trap shut. She had never felt more certain of anything in her life.

She looked down at her father's wingtips, scuffed and filthy. How far would they take her? To the ends of the earth, if necessary, to the moon. She squared her shoulders, shifted the baby from her good but exhausted arm to her broken one, just for a quick respite. But that hurt too much, so much she almost dropped him, so she shifted him back to her right side, jutting out her hip to take more of his weight. How heavy he'd become!

Her eye ran in circles, nipping at her heels. She would need formula and bottles and diapers. She would need time to plan their getaway. She would need someone to take her in and shelter them both. She would need someone to take care of Tommy while she went out into the world and scavenged for all the things a baby needs.

As she made her way up Jefferson, she thought suddenly of the little colored washwoman, whose name still eluded Jo but who, after all, hadn't forgotten Jo and her mother and little Tommy. Who had sent help when help was needed.

# 15

## 8 P.M.

Raining cats and dogs outside when those shoes sashayed in. Dovey would have known them anywhere. The Judge's wingtips. Big as life and twice as ugly, scuffed and dusty and shit-colored, in the wet pool of moonlight at the bottom of the door to the boxcar. The bile rose in her throat and she felt the urge to hawk and spit.

They'd been shiny as glass the day after that Devil had bothered Dreama, she could see her face in them. She'd wanted to spit that day too, dirty those shoes. Her and Virgil standing there in the blazing noonday sun, Virgil thirsty for blood, the Judge presiding over the two of them like some old plantation master talking down to the field hands at the back door, a white napkin hanging from his collar, a crumb of something flaky (corn bread? a biscuit?) on his lip. Those wingtips of his had faced straight out, at the level of her belly, like bird dogs on the point. Shoot to kill. And what difference would it have made if somebody had shot her through the heart, her already half dead with what had happened to Dreama? By then the hawk already had her by the cords of her neck; soon it would settle in, clawing through flesh and gristle.

He hadn't even invited them to come up onto the porch, out of the sun. After what his own son had done, he hadn't even offered them that courtesy. The sun overhead had pecked at her scalp. Briny sweat inched down her forehead, breaching her eyebrows, stinging her eyes, bringing on the tears she'd been set on not shedding.

NOW, THOUGH, the shoes were just shoes, filthy and beat-up. Her eyes followed them upward and ran into bare ankles, and then not the pants she'd expected but a dress, torn and dusty too, a too-long dress, and then, Lord, what? Something alive, wrapped in a shawl against the soft rain outside, and that white girl with hair that hung in filthy clumps around her shoulders. The girl's left arm wrapped in white, a cast, white against the girl's dress. That McNabb girl and something in the shawl.

When the girl came in, Dovey had been in the middle of a knot of a worry so tangled and vexing it taxed even her. Dreama and Virgil had set out at dawn, Dreama proclaiming that she wasn't coming back till she found her boy, Virgil intent on checking to see how the mill had made out in the storm, saying the last thing they needed was for him to lose his job now that they hardly had a pot to piss in. After that, he planned to head out to look for Promise too. Him and Dreama had planned it out. He'd go looking around Milltown, she'd head back up to the Hill, combing Glenwood Cemetery on the way. Now here it was dark again and growing darker still. Had one or both of them fallen into one of those treacherous water holes? Had they run into trouble with white folks? She'd heard about gangs of white boys running wild. She pictured Dreama cornered, splayed, and bloodied, left for dead. She pictured Virgil trying to fight off those white boys, now hanging from a tree for his trouble. She saw it all in her head, clear as day, and when the McNabb girl came through the door and stood there in the moonlight wearing those wingtips of her daddy's, Dovey was sitting at the little table in the boxcar quaking like a leaf.

There was something else too, a commotion in her chest that hadn't been there. It felt like a baby bird learning to fly, reminding her of the first time she'd felt Charlesetta move in her belly. Now it left her chest and fluttered down into her arms and fingers, making them twitch and shudder. That morning the flutter had taken up residence in her upper thigh; she had watched the skin jump with it. Was she *becoming* a bird? Since the storm, she flew through her dreams. She flew without fear, with a steady heedless curiosity; nothing could hold her down, not the sweet dear earth, not the people who had held her life in place. She wondered if she were getting ready to die.

THE GIRL stood there not moving, just panting a little. She seemed proud of herself. "I asked the Salvation Army people and they said to look here. I went up and down the row, asking." She took one step in Dovey's direction, moving into the candlelight. There were smudges on her cheeks, the place where the horn had been now a train track of stitches running above and between her brows. She loomed: a big girl, tall and broad-shouldered. She'd make two of Dreama. She took another step, toward the chair on the other side of the table from Dovey and slid into it without asking. She seemed relieved, moving toward Dovey with confidence, as though she were a long-lost friend, as though Dovey would be happy to see her.

The girl leaned across the table. "Thank you for sending help. We're much obliged."

Was Dovey never going to be free of these infernal McNabbs? Would they insist on plaguing her to the end of the earth, trailing their secret filth, their never-ending mountain of wash? The thought of the Judge with Etherene made her sick, him with a wife and three children. All those years them two carrying on like dogs in heat. Small wonder that son of his went and did what he did. The apple doesn't fall far.

The bundle in the girl's arms began to cough a syrupy cough. So she'd found her little brother. No justice in the world.

And poor Dreama still out there. Full dark now. How long would she keep looking? How long before you call calf rope and quit? A month or six? A year? Two? Already there were stories moving up and down the row of boxcars. A little colored girl, eight years old, blown down from the Hill over into Whitetown, through an attic window of V. H. McCoy's house, not a scratch on her. A nine-month-old baby found alive and kicking down on the M&O track. Another of the town's laundresses, name of Marcella, who, Dovey thought privately, was a bit much, carrying her laundry on her head like some African with a bone in her nose, spun in circles ten feet up in the air like a flying Jenny (or so she claimed), then put down on Jamie Settle's roof, not a scratch on her either. Mrs. Fred Price, holed up with her daughter in the icebox with their pet canary, coming out to find their whole house blown to kingdom come around them.

Dovey didn't like these stories. They illustrated the fickleness of Luck with a capital L. The flip side of the coin: the man stuck to the bottom of Gum Pond, Etherene's mistaken step in the dark. For every baby found, there were, she expected, a dozen lost.

**THE KITTEN** they'd found dead that morning on the washcloth they'd laid down for it in the corner of the boxcar. The mother cat had vanished.

**EVEN IN** good times, even as a girl, Dovey had been a worrier. She saw fate and circumstance as ruthless predators ready to pounce when least expected. Who could have imagined her whole family gone in the space of two weeks, felled by the typhoid, leaving her with the sour-faced aunt? Who could have thought up this devil of a storm? (There was talk that the tornado was God's punishment of Tupelo for getting too big for its breeches, seduced by the sin of pride. First TVA City, cheap electricity for all and not even a city, just a dusty little town that had had the good fortune of having the Frisco and M&O make a big bull's-eye in its center.) Even before the tornado, Dovey had stewed about the weather, whether the jigsaw of rusty tin that served as the roof of their house would keep the water out when it rained, whether the clothes on the line would be dry enough to iron. She read the newspaper and therefore worried about that little man with the mustache across the ocean who said things that didn't seem good or right. She worried about the miles-long lines of his uniformed men who held up their right arms and hollered those two foreign words, one of which sounded like *Hell*. They reminded her of peckerwoods in sheets, whom she also worried about, along with the way Dreama held Promise up in the air over her head, him screaming (with delight? with fear? she could never tell), his neck gone slack. She worried about Virgil's cough, how he had trouble catching his breath when he slept on his back, gasping off and on all night, his nails digging into her arm like talons. She worried about stains in the laundry, whether they would come out, whether she'd get paid if they didn't.

All of these worries mere grains of sand beside the boulder that was Promise. Was she being greedy, asking for too much good luck with Virgil and Dreama safe? She'd been holding her breath all day for news. The Salvation Army lady had taken down their names and the number of their boxcar, which was the number they should be as a family, and Dovey had waited all day in the dark in case somebody found Promise and brought him back.

None of them had slept the previous night, the boxcar an oven. Nothing stirred. Inches apart, the three of them lay there in the dark breathing softly but there was no ease to their breath. Dreama tossed and turned, her stomach growling from lack of food. After the CCC boys brought the extra cot for Virgil, Dovey pushed her cot up to his. During the night she reached out and touched his chest and he gripped her hand until it grew sticky with sweat. When Dreama rose the next morning, her face was the color of old ashes.

Dovey had dozed off and on the whole day, exhausted but also sick to death of staring at the same four creosoted walls, no food to prepare, no laundry to wash and hang out and iron, no house to clean. Nothing to do but wait.

AND NOW this McNabb girl. Plopping herself down like she owned the place.

The girl put the baby on her shoulder (how she maneuvered him with just one good arm Dovey didn't know but admired) and began to pat him on the back with her cast, which was no way to take care of a baby with the croup. Any fool knew to make a mustard plaster to put on the child's chest and then to put a hot wet cloth on top of the plaster to make it penetrate. Promise had been a croupy baby. Sometimes, if he couldn't breathe, she would put some of the mustard plaster on his upper lip. You had to take care to rub the chest with lard first, so the plaster didn't burn, especially with babies.

The hair on the back of the baby's head was soaked. Did he have a fever?

Of course, there was no mustard powder to be had, and the girl looked like she was in no condition to attend to what she had in her arms. Her eyes had a strange milky cast to them. There was a hangdog look about her. Dovey chastised herself for being uncharitable. The girl was doing the best she could. Where were her mama and daddy? What was she doing wandering around like a lost dog toting a sick pup?

Dovey held up a can of potted meat. "You hungry?"

The girl leaned over to look at the can. She licked her lips. "I hate to eat up your food."

"There's more where that come from." Dovey picked up the can opener.

"I wouldn't mind if you can spare it," said the girl. Something—not a smile but close to it—splashed across her face, the flick of a fish tail. She settled in the chair, put the baby back down on her lap. Dovey leaned over to look, but he was in a deep shadow. He'd settled down, making little scuffles of sound. Every now and again a little fist emerged, opened and closed.

The little fist rocked her. Until now Dovey hadn't allowed herself to think about Promise's whereabouts, where he might now be lying, dead or alive. Secretly, she thought he was dead. But, seeing that little fist, she had a sudden vision of him, cold and wet and trembling in the wind, waiting in George Walton's cornfield south of town, half buried by mud, two little fists and two little bare feet pushing up toward the sky in those odd jerky motions babies make. Waiting and waiting. Waiting for someone to come along and look down and say *oh*. The corn not more than knee high, a tender translucent green, rustling in the breeze.

Sometimes, and she'd never told a soul this, not even Virgil, for fear of being thought dotty, Dovey saw things. These sightings, if you could call them that, happened just once in a long while. Years would go by when she'd forget about them, but then one would tiptoe in, strange but strangely accurate, not a dream but dreamlike: quicksilver. The first time was when she was a girl and she had a vision of Erlene Phillips from across the street being bitten by a snake. The next day the copperhead sunning itself on Mrs. P's back stoop found her ankle. Another time, she saw Lyle Smith, a boy she knew, choke on a chicken bone, and choke he did the following Sunday night at a church supper, requiring Dr. Juber, who luckily happened to be sitting nearby, to cut a hole in his throat with the very knife he'd just used to cut the piece of rump roast on his plate.

Was it possible their baby was buried in mud, half dead in George Walton's cornfield? Possible that he was still alive?

She dropped the can of potted meat back onto the table, forgetting she'd offered it to the girl, forgetting the girl was even there, and held on to the table's edge. Should she hightail it over to George Walton's field and see for herself? Problem was it was black as pitch outside, and still raining. Not to speak of how she'd manage to get there.

THE GIRL eyed the can, dog-like. She'd settled herself into the chair and the baby, now asleep, onto her lap, his head on her knees, half under the table.

Dovey wanted to ask how long she intended on staying. Instead she asked, "You got a bottle for that baby when he wake up?"

"I've got some powdered formula and a bottle and nipple in that sack there. You got some water?"

Food was one thing, water another. There was precious little, and Virgil and Dreama would be coming in thirsty. But this was a baby. Dovey got up and went over to the corner of the room and got the jug the Red Cross lady had brought that morning. "Don't spill it. It's all we got." A week ago, she would never have dreamed of speaking to a white girl in that tone.

The girl didn't seem to take offense. She rooted around in her knapsack and handed Dovey the baby's bottle. "It's just for him. I don't need any."

Dovey took the jug to the table and poured the water into the bottle until it was three-quarters full. She pulled up a corner of her dress to cover her fingers, then squeezed the nipple shut and shook the bottle. She handed it back to the girl. The baby slept on, his breathing raspy but regular.

"I'm going to wait until he wakes up," the girl murmured, setting the bottle back on the table. "I'm sorry to have to use your water." She looked at the jug, now half empty.

Dovey poured her a small glass and she gulped it down. "Thank you. That's all I'll be needing," she said apologetically.

"Where'd you end up finding him?" asked Dovey.

"You'll never believe it," said the girl and then proceeded to tell her about pulling him out of the crepe myrtle bush like Moses in the bulrushes and taking care of him through thick and thin and their mother losing not only her leg but her good sense and denying her own child and the daddy taking off at the blink of an eye (probably looking for Etherene, Dovey inserted), leaving the girl, whose name was Jo, to take care of her baby brother, whose name, Jo informed her, was Tommy. A silly name.

Almost as an afterthought, the girl added, "And now I'm on the lam because I'm scared they're going to take him." Her eyes returned to the can of potted meat on the table.

Dovey reached for the can opener and opened the can. She gave it to the girl, along with a spoon, and the girl began to eat, holding the can with the hand on her bad arm, eating with the hand on the good, the baby balanced on her knees. She finished within seconds, scraping the sides of the can, then handed it back. "Much obliged."

Dovey took it outside to the oil can. Then she stood on the top step of the stairs leading to the boxcar and peered out into the dark. Up and down the row of boxcars, slivers of candlelight filtered through the sackcloth that covered the doors. Where were Dreama and Virgil? Tomorrow she would insist on going out with them, tomorrow she wasn't going to be stuck in a gloomy old boxcar all day. She needed to use the outhouse, but didn't cotton to the idea of Virgil and Dreama stumbling in dead tired to find the white girl sitting there, taking up the whole place with her big old self. She especially didn't like the thought of Dreama being confronted with that baby. The girl was sad enough. That morning she'd refused to eat before heading out. Dovey had quickly stashed a few pieces of that useless bread in the pocket of her dress.

But Dovey had to go. She wasn't about to squat over the

chamber pot with a white girl watching, and the older she got the less wise it was to wait. She sat and scooted down the steps, then moved through the dark, down the row between the cars favoring her good foot only slightly now. She should have taken the lantern, but then she'd have to go back inside and explain to the girl that she had to do her private business. Better to do it quickly and get back before Virgil and Dreama came in.

When she returned, the girl was dead to the world, her head lolling to the side, her mouth a big O, as if she'd been surprised by sleep, the way a murdered man's mouth will betray his dying grimace. Lord, she could catch her some flies in that mouth. It, like everything else on the girl, was overlarge. She seemed to take up the whole room. One hand was on the child in her lap. The shadow of the table enfolded him like a caul. Her good hand clutched the top of his diaper. She was careful with the child, Dovey would give her that, careful as any mother.

The girl opened her eyes, felt around on the baby, who was still quiet.

"He's still there," said Dovey. "What you planning?"

The girl rubbed her face. "I was hoping maybe you could keep him for me so I can make some plans. That's why I came here. You sent us help. I know you're a good person. I'll pay you when I get settled."

"Whoa, horse. We got our own baby to find. If this one ain't yours, then there's folks out there looking for it. We can't be stashing somebody's child." She wanted to say *white* child.

The girl snapped her eyes at Dovey. "I told you. He's ours. He's mine. Nobody's coming looking for him."

"You think your mama don't know her own child?"

"My mother's headed straight for Whitfield once that stump

of hers heals up. Maybe my daddy too. I don't have anybody I can count on. I don't have anybody but my Tommy."

"Losing a leg. That take some getting used to. Give her time."

"I don't have time. I can't let them take him away."

At that moment, the white cat flicked the curtain at the door and appeared. She stood in the doorway, then ran and leapt onto the girl's lap, on top of the baby. There was a scramble. Dovey snatched up the cat, Jo took hold of the baby, who began to scream.

"Snowball!" The girl grinned, flashing pretty teeth, large like the rest of her and white. The cat rubbed the chair leg where the girl sat. "This is my cat!" she shouted, drowning out the baby's screams. "How'd you find me? And where are your kittens, Snowball? Your poor little kittens."

Dovey opened her mouth to tell about the kitten.

BUT JUST then the girl reached down and made a gathering motion, and then, in one endless moment, she raised the baby's head. He stopped crying and began to coo. The candlelight flickered over his face, giving it the appearance of being underwater. "Look ahere, Tommy," she said, "here's our Snowball."

Dovey's mouth snapped shut. She blinked, then blinked again. She'd expected to see a white child, somebody else's child, a child she'd never laid eyes on, whose diapers, whose little clothes she'd picked up every Saturday since he'd been born. And washed and hung out to dry and returned neatly folded, the diapers doubled so they could be slid right on, no refolding. Diapers and baby clothes were her specialties; she used glycerin soap, no bleach, and prided herself on their softness.

The moment was a long hall with many doors. She opened the one marked *eyes* and there, before her, were her own Charlesetta's (Why had she never seen her own daughter in this child?) and her own dear mother's, the color of pennies, with flecks of olive, upturned at the outer corners. She opened a second door marked *mouth* (oh, that precious mouth), the cleft a deep pinch, Virgil's and Dreama's dimpled chins.

The baby looked at her and broke into a grin. One early tooth on the bottom. The grin Charlesetta's too, gummy and wide as the sky.

She could have picked Promise out of a hundred, a thousand, a million babies.

What was this crazy white girl thinking?

SOMETHING DEEP within her, the something that had protected her all her life (she thought of it as a gnome-like figure, an old woman, her head wrapped in a white rag like Dovey's own, veiny hands, callused, bony fingers), tapped her on the shoulder and said, *Take care now.*

Dovey remembered then what she'd chosen to forget: the fact of the blood tie.

Was she the crazy one? Seeing black where this girl was seeing white? She wished it was daylight and she could take him out in the sun.

"Isn't he a beauty?" the girl said, holding his head higher.

Dovey didn't trust herself to speak. She nodded.

His eyes shone. He reached for her.

What is flesh but a vessel? She could see through to the bone.

Another tap on the shoulder. Harder than the first and more urgent. *Take care. White folks.*

The girl put the nipple to the baby's mouth and he began to suck, still gazing at Dovey.

Dovey reached out and touched his head. "Got him a head of hair."

"More than he did at first," said the girl. She bent over, smiling at him as he watched Dovey.

*Use your brain.*

Dovey leaned forward in one long wary motion as if she were about to capture a standoffish dog. "You say you wanting me to watch him for you?"

"I thought you said . . ."

"Maybe I could. For a while. Just till you yourself settled. Tonight, if you want to find some place to stay." Dovey left it unspoken that the girl couldn't stay there, sleeping in the same room with them, eating at the same table. "Tonight. Then we could see. You bring enough of that powder and nappies to get us through the night?" She took care with her words, each one a polished river stone, cold and pure. Her voice pitched and quaked.

The girl began to cry then, her tears coming hard, wetting the baby's face. "Don't think I'm making you do it." Her eyes searched Dovey's. "Don't think that."

"You ain't making me do nothing." Dovey bit her bottom lip, tasted blood.

The baby spit out the nipple, having had only half the bottle. He blinked, his eyes heavy, his eyelashes long and curly like Virgil's.

"Here now," whispered Dovey. "Let me have him. You get on along now before it gets too late."

When the girl rose to hand him over, he jerked in alarm. He clutched onto the girl, his eyes wide and questioning when Dovey took him.

"All right now," she said, rocking him back and forth. The warm weight of him in her arms heaven.

The girl hovered over them. "He likes to have his back rubbed. If he fusses, turn him over. He's teething, so rub his gums if he gets to crying. My mother rubbed them with paregoric but I don't have any and the doctor said not to anyway. I feed him whenever he acts hungry. There's towels for diapers in the knapsack. Raise his head if he starts to cough. I'm scared he's going to strangle."

Dovey nodded, eager, too eager. "You ought to get on now."

The girl still hovered, casting a massive shadow in the candlelight. "I hate to leave him."

Promise gave a lurch. Dovey held on to him. "You got your business to do. I'll take care of him. Don't you worry none."

Would the girl never leave?

She turned to go and was almost out of the door. Then, she looked back, her eyes full, like Lot's wife looking back to her home, and, in that moment of looking, something happened: a shadow passed over the girl's face and her eyes narrowed.

She looked from Dovey's face to Promise's and back to Dovey's. She strode back over to the table.

"I've changed my mind. Here, I'll take him back. I'll take him with me." The girl's voice was every bit as careful and measured as Dovey's had been a moment before; Dovey recognized that voice as her own. The girl took another step toward Dovey, her arms outstretched.

Dovey backed up and held on. "What you going to do toting around a little baby? Better he stays here."

"No. Give him back." The girl took another step, showing teeth now, looming large.

Dovey backed up. "You got your business to do. You got to make some plans. I'll take good care of him. You can come get him once you get settled."

"No. Let me have him." The girl moved toward Dovey. Something had hardened in the girl's face.

The girl was between Dovey and the door.

Again the tap on the shoulder. *Take care now.*

She put on her best talking-to-white-folks voice. "Now missy, how come you don't want old Dovey to take care this here child? I took care of three generations of my own. I know how to take care of a baby."

The girl reached out now, her eyes narrowed. "I know you do, but I want my brother back now. He's mine to take care of and I want him back. He needs his sister."

*Take care now.*

No care to be took.

Dovey drew a breath. "Truth is, he ain't yours."

The baby had begun to kick and fuss. Dovey shifted him to her hip, she'd need one arm to defend herself and him. She would never let go of him. Not in this life.

The girl stopped in her tracks, her face suddenly red and splotched and astonished. "What are you talking about? You know good and well that's my Tommy. What are you trying to do, *nigger*, steal my baby brother?"

The word hit Dovey like a billy club. She staggered, then righted herself.

The girl's mouth fell open, as if it were dismayed by its own utterance. The baby shrieked once, then began to cough. "Now look what you've gone and done. You're *hurting* him! Let go!"

The girl was upon her, prying the baby with the hand on her good side, pushing at Dovey's turtle-shell chest with the cast. Dovey held on, but the baby, now screaming at the top of his lungs, was slipping from her arms.

"You *hurting* the child," Dovey said. "I'll give him to you if you sit down."

The girl walked over to the chair and sat, not taking her eyes off Dovey. She held out her arms.

Dovey eyed the girl, then the door. No outrunning them legs. The girl was a cross between an elephant and a giraffe.

She brought the child to the girl, who snatched him up, grabbed her knapsack, and rose. "I don't know what you're up to, old woman, but you better move out of the way and let me go."

"Where you going?"

"If I knew, I wouldn't tell you."

"Hear me out, girl. This here's *my* grandbaby. His name is Promise. He's my Dreama's boy. He looks like your brother because y'all are related."

The girl shook her head vigorously.

*Use your brain.*

Dovey tried to muster a smile. "He's *ours*. Part yours, part mine."

The tap on the shoulder again. *Take care.*

Dovey ignored it. "This why your mama didn't claim him."

"Don't you think I know my own brother?"

Dovey looked at her, not answering. The girl was a mess. Snotty and wet-faced. Hair stringing down, nose splotched and swollen and red.

Dovey spoke gently. "You saved our Promise."

The girl glared at her. "I saved *my* Tommy."

The baby had quieted down. He coughed quietly, then shut his eyes.

The girl put her knapsack on her shoulder. She towered over Dovey.

"Don't go."

The girl was shaking now, shaking and crying again. "I thought you were my friend."

"Friend?" Dovey raised an eyebrow. "Your nigger friend?"

Tap, tap. *Take care now.*

"I didn't mean to say that." The girl hung her head, her hair falling in clumps over her plate-like cheeks.

"You said it."

The girl sighed, opened the curtain, and stepped out into the night. Dovey waited a moment and followed.

With the baby on her hip and the knapsack on her back, the girl looked like a hunchback making her way down the row of boxcars. Behind her, Dovey slid into the shadows, but the girl saw her.

"Go away. Leave us alone," the girl shouted over her shoulder.

People started sticking their heads out of the boxcar doors, looking first at the white girl passing, then back at Dovey following.

"Where you heading, sister?" said a man Dovey didn't recognize. "You gone plumb crazy chasing white folks?"

Dovey didn't pause. The girl was almost running now. Her legs, like the rest of her, made two of Dovey's.

Dovey started to run, her foot firing, but the bird in her chest became a trapped wasp, her chest a closed window it flailed against. "Wait up," she hollered, panting for breath.

The girl didn't look back. She turned a corner, heading for Crosstown. For a moment Dovey lost her.

YEARS AFTER, Dovey would try to explain what happened next, but people would laugh and say she dreamed it. She dreamed this crazy dream because of what happened to her in the storm. But what actually happened, and what Dovey would swear to until her dying day, was that, when she lost sight of that girl, her arms started flapping and reaching, and she went up and up, swooshing through the trees, cutting through the sky in great looping circles.

It was not like being blown by the storm. It was not like the sluggish breaststroke of her flying dreams before the storm. It was something altogether different, a lift and a flutter and a glide, a power honed and harnessed and utterly hers. She could feel it in her arms, which were nothing more or less than wings.

She almost forgot about Promise it was so surprising, so thrilling.

Having collected laundry from west to east, north to south, she knew Whitetown like the back of her hand, all the shortcuts and alleyways. She sped up Gloster Street, cut through the Spicers' yard on Rankin to Mound Street, then doubled back down the alleyway behind the Curb Market. She cut the girl off just as they approached Crosstown, the girl (the crazy girl) galumphing toward the depot, Dovey cutting her off from the east.

The nine o'clock Frisco Accommodation sat on the tracks. People were getting off, some of them with casts and bandages, some hobbling on crutches. People were hugging and kissing loved ones. Others, bandaged and bruised, were boarding. Some were being transported on stretchers, some being helped onto the train.

The girl went over to a porter and lifted the baby up in her arms, talking and gesturing and pointing to the train.

Dovey landed hard next to the tracks, kicking up gravel. She tripped and fell, then picked herself up and made her way toward the girl, her arms now heavy as two pieces of lead pipe. As she approached, the girl turned and faced her.

Dovey tried to stretch out her leaden arms, but they wouldn't move from her sides. "Don't take him. He ain't yours for the taking."

The girl didn't answer, her face ugly now, mean as a warthog's.

Dovey came on, her feet leaden too. How tiring flying was. It took the starch out of a body.

The girl had the baby around the middle. He was wailing a thin frail cry.

There was the toll of a distant bell. All Saints Episcopal on West Jefferson, still standing.

The girl had taken the first step onto the Frisco, the baby, now shrieking, under her good arm. She turned to meet Dovey. When Dovey tried to mount the step too, the girl raised the cast on her monstrous, wounded arm, the smell from her underarm spicy and sour.

Dovey flinched, took a step back into nothing but air, and fell sprawling onto the rocks next to the train tracks.

In the split second of falling (she would remember that moment for the rest of her long, long life), Dovey recalled the birthmark shaped like a cloud under Promise's left arm: dark and irregular and sweet. Dreama called it his little thunder cloud. When she kissed it, Promise would giggle.

"Birthmark," Dovey called out to the girl and then opened her mouth to say it again. But now the baby bird that had brought her to this place was pecking right through her turtle-shell chest, cracking her open like an egg.

Then she was blown back by a wind that swept everything clean, that roared through the ruined trees. A second storm.

# 16

## 9:03 P.M.

At least she hadn't actually hit the crazy old colored woman. The fact that the woman lay sprawled on the rocks next to the tracks wasn't Jo's fault. She had simply tried to ward her off, make her leave them alone. Yes, she had called her a bad name, and yes, she felt bad about that and about her falling (Who wouldn't feel bad? How long was the poor old thing going to have to lie there before somebody came to see about her?), but at least Jo didn't have to add hitting an old woman to her list of Sins Committed Since the Storm, of which there were many, including kidnapping, some might say; not to speak of the fact she'd lied to the porter, telling him that Tommy had pneumonia (which might not be a lie after all; he'd just that minute had a coughing fit that shook his little body so hard he almost slid from Jo's good arm).

How the old washwoman caught up with them Jo will never figure out. She was too old to run. Old as the hills. (How *could* she, Jo McNabb, raised to be decent and kind to the colored, have called that poor old woman, that poor old *crazy-as-a-Betsy-bug* woman, what she called her, a word Jo had never once uttered in her entire life, a word she'd never even formed on her tongue. A sin too, the worst of them all, and it stretched out before her like an endless row of corn, tall and sassy.)

Although.

It *was* a good thing that the old colored woman fell instead of climbing onto the train and causing all sorts of trouble, raising a ruckus about Tommy, claiming him for her own, upsetting him even more.

And upset he was. He was whooping like a banshee, thrashing about furiously. How strong he was getting! She took her seat next to the door and put him on her lap and took the half-full bottle from her knapsack and tried to poke it into the cavern of his wide-open mouth. Which just enraged him more. He gagged, flailed from side to side, screaming louder and louder, attracting the consternation of some of the older passenger/patients, who sat slumped in their seats, one man holding his arm as if he were afraid it would fall off. Another who looked like a sheik with a bandage wrapped around his head like a turban scowled at Jo. "Can't you shut the kid up, for Christ's sake?"

Jo put the baby on her shoulder and rubbed his back the way he liked, to no avail. He kicked her in the ribs, whammed the side of her temple with his arm, causing the wound on her forehead to fire. He felt like a sack of unruly potatoes, jumping this way and that.

Below her, beside the tracks, a CCC boy had spotted Dovey lying under Jo's window. He lifted her and shouted for a stretcher. Her head lolled to the side and her eyes rolled back in her head. Then her whole body seized up, and the CCC boy had to bring her back to the ground a few yards from the train, in front of the little box of a station. Jo pressed her nose to the window. The old woman writhed and thrashed on the ground, the CCC boy holding her head in place. It was as if the old woman and Tommy were connected by some invisible thread, each fighting for something only their own thrashing bodies could recognize. Then, as another CCC boy arrived with the stretcher, the old washwoman seemed to fall into a deep sleep.

*Would this child never stop crying? What the devil was wrong with him?*

Now the CCC boys lifted the old woman onto the stretcher (how deliberate they were, how careful; what good, beautiful boys they were). The first boy went up to the porter, talking and gesturing toward the stretcher. The porter nodded and pointed down the line on the train. The four of them lifted her and (oh!) carried her down the line to the last car.

Jo stood and stuck her head out the open top window of the train and watched them lift the old woman onto the last car. Jo's heart stopped. Which was not an overstatement—she swore she felt it pause and drop like a stone from the top of her chest to the pit of her stomach when they put the old woman on the train, on *her* train.

Would she never be free of the old colored woman?

Much as Jo wanted her to be all right, to recover fully from her unfortunate accident (yes, it *was* an accident, Jo told herself firmly), she didn't like the idea of the woman riding caboose, ready to lurch into consciousness at any moment and start talking nonsense about whose baby was whose.

*Birthmark.* The word an icicle dropped from a tree, hard and fast and unexpected. It drilled into her scalp. The figment of a crazy old colored woman's imagination.

Tommy had cried himself out. She sat down and pulled out the half-full bottle again. She didn't like the idea of carrying around lukewarm formula, but she couldn't bring herself to throw it away. She had only another day's supply of the powder. He took a few draws on the nipple and then fell into an exhausted sleep.

The train lurched and clattered, gathering itself.

Now something plucked at her sleeve; something said, unaccountably, *Get off this train, get off now.*

The door beside her had not yet closed. All she had to do was get down the steps to the door.

She gathered the baby and the knapsack and rose to her feet.

She took the three steps down. They were steep; she had to be careful not to let the weight of the child tip her over headfirst.

The train shuddered.

She hesitated. Why get off now? What was the sense in that?

Then, down the aisle, the door to the next car swung open and a nurse came down the aisle, reassuring the wounded, a beatific smile on her face. It was the turnip-faced nurse from the Lyric Theatre, the nurse who had tried to take Tommy.

The train lurched.

*No no no,* she thought, and she clutched Tommy's head and took the one long step to the gravel below, barely landing upright, fighting for her balance on the uneven ground.

*Now,* she thought, *we're free.*


SHE STOOD there as the train began to move, slowly at first then gathering speed. What a clumsy, rattletrap thing a train was when it began to roll. It reminded her of a blue heron she'd seen up at Gum Pond, gathering itself to fly, the way it galumphed along the shore, gawky and awkward.

Tommy flinched in her arms at the train's racket and began to shriek again. The cars slid by, faster and faster now. The moon was rising and it flashed on her face at each gap between cars, momentarily blinding her. Now the train was singing *Cadillac, Cadillac, Cadillac*. She stood mesmerized, watching it pull out of the station, gathering speed.

When the caboose slid by and she turned to go, she saw a motion in the weeds on the other side of the tracks. A small draped figure limped into the dark, then disappeared into the night.

LATER THAT night, back at the aunts', which was the only place Jo knew to go, Tommy's cough grew worse. There was dust in the house, old dust; she could smell it. Dr. Campbell used to say old dust was the worst dust. It had little bugs in it, spider-like mites that couldn't be seen with the naked eye. They made their nasty little way up the nose and into the sinuses and bronchial tubes, wreaking havoc. She used some of the water from the jug she'd left there to make more formula and fed the baby on the sagging screen porch, then pulled out a drawer from the aunts' china cabinet, dusted it out, and put a few towels from her knapsack in it. She laid him in the drawer and placed the drawer on the porch swing and sat down beside him, pushing the swing back and forth. It was warm and there was a single bullfrog revving up.

When he fell asleep, she went upstairs to the aunts' bedroom at the back of the house, lit a candle, and began to clean. She threw open the windows and pulled away bedding and curtains and dumped them in the extra bedroom. The aunts' room she swept and dusted. Under the beds were dozens of dead roaches, and two mouse skeletons. She beat the two mattresses with a broom, and threw the pillows and spread and sheets out the back window.

She worked through the night and when dawn came up, it surprised her. She collapsed onto one of the bare mattresses and fell into an exhausted sleep. At that exact moment, the baby began to cry downstairs. Her eyes, bloodshot and rheumy from the ancient dust, popped open and she began to cry herself, filthy and tired to the bone.

*Was this a nightmare she would ever wake from?*

She staggered downstairs and picked up the baby. The sun had come up. A beautiful day, actually. The ravaged landscape seemed less strange and stark and inescapable. The ruin had become to seem natural. There was even a breath of possibility in it.

And now, there was one clean room.

She laid a towel on the bare bed next to the wall and put the baby on it and fell down beside him. Then, miracles of all miracles, he went back to sleep, without a change of pants, without a bottle. His hands and feet were white with cold and the tape holding the bandage under his arm had come loose. She fastened the tape back and chastised herself for not covering him better against the early morning chill. She warmed his hands and feet by turning him toward her and putting her casted arm over his torso. They slept then, face to face, exchanging breath.

He woke her up by patting her face and cooing. The sun was straight up in the sky and there was a light breeze coming through the open windows. Jo opened her eyes and looked directly into the baby's. They were open wide, all pupil and darker than she remembered, dark as golden plums. She tickled his cheek and he gave her a one-sided grin, then kicked her in the stomach.

"Ouch. Cut it out." She laughed and rose on one elbow.

He broke into a full smile, reaching for her. He smelled awful.

"Let's get you cleaned up." She sat up and put her feet on the floor, every muscle in her body crying foul, her stomach grinding acid. She thought of the potted meat the colored woman had given her, a kindness. She hoped the old woman would recover, really she did.

Why had she gotten off that train? She could be in Memphis by now, safely anonymous, lost in the city bustle. But what then? Would she have stood on a street corner begging like a bum? Or worse. She'd heard of girls who lived in places with gold brocade curtains and Duncan Phyfe sofas and sold themselves to men. She shuddered. Would she have gone into the lobby of the Peabody Hotel, the only landmark she'd heard of, and found an easy chair and slept until someone came along and told her to move on? Was there an orphanage in Memphis where she could have gone? It was too frightening to think about. At least in the aunts' house she had shelter; at least she knew her own town, its inhabitants. At least she had girlfriends here who might be persuaded to offer food and money, if she could find them without herself being found—a big if.

She was terribly thirsty. She got a jug from the hallway, the last of the water her father had brought. She turned it up and drank. Then she wet a towel and cleaned Tommy. The bandage under his arm flapped loose and she pulled it away. The gash was healing nicely. She dabbed it with the wet rag, and he giggled at her.

There was what appeared to be a dark patch of blood right under his arm. She dabbed at it, then began to scrub in earnest. The dark patch did not come off. He'd started to fuss.

That doctor, he'd said something about a birthmark next to the wound.

She looked at it again. A cloud passed over the sun. The breeze was gone and the room grew still and dark.

Her eyes drifted up to the ceiling. It had once been painted white. Jo remembered the summer the aunts had had the house painted. A colored man did the work, arriving each morning at seven in his paint-splattered shirt and pants, eyes downcast. Each morning the aunts had met him at the back door and told him to be careful, not to break anything. Now the ceiling was gray with spider webs. Bare of curtains and bed linen, the place looked like a barracks.

The ants had migrated back to her left eye. She blinked once, then twice. She looked down at Tommy, who was gathering himself for an eruption.

Her eye burned and watered, blurring her vision. She rubbed it, then dabbed it with her sleeve.

She rinsed out the bottle, got another nipple from her knapsack, and held the bottle steady with the hand on her bad arm while she measured out the formula and then poured the water to mix, the baby watching her every move. She was getting good at this.

She sat down on the bed and gave him the bottle as he lay there, not wanting to dirty him by holding him on her filthy lap. She could smell herself, and the feeling of engorgement (a Word to Keep) she experienced right before her period was upon her: another complication, another need to fill.

How unimportant words were when the body asserted itself.

When the baby went back to sleep (he was such a good baby, or maybe he was just tired like she was), she cleaned herself as best she could and put on another of the aunts' dresses and some underwear so dusty it felt as if she had put talcum powder in the crotch the way her mother used to do on hot summer days.

Outside, the clouds darkened further and there was a gust of cool air. Then the rain came. It came all at once, in a deluge, sheets of it. She struggled to close the windows, soaking the front of her dress in the process, the shape of her body, her belly, which had once been nicely rounded, now concave, her breasts somehow smaller and more singular.

The baby made a snuffling sound. He slept turned toward the wall, the bottoms of his feet facing her, whiter than the rest of him. He seemed very small on the bed, very alone. *Little tadpole.*

She touched her hair, how filthy it was! It was sticking to her head, oily and crusted over with dirt and mud and old dust. Her scalp itched. What she would give for a nice shampoo and set at Lil's. Then it occurred to her that the rain—all that blessed water pouring down like Niagara—might supply a decent washing, and she snatched up an ancient bar of soap from the bathroom and took the now almost-empty jug of water and ran down the steps. She grabbed an old raincoat that hung on the back door to keep the cast dry. She slipped out of her father's wingtips and left them just inside the back door.

The backyard was a tangle of honeysuckle and hedge. She stood still, the green wildness encircling her, letting the rain flatten her hair. Then she took the soap and began to scrub at her scalp, loosening crusty debris and dandruff and oil. It was heavenly. The downpour continued and she managed to scrub and rinse once, twice, three times. Then, under the raincoat, she unbuttoned the dress and let it drop to the ground and after that the underwear. She opened the raincoat and took the soap to herself, top to bottom, bottom to top.

She'd never felt so deliciously clean.

It was a warm rain, and she thought of Tommy. He had a diaper rash and cradle cap. He needed a good wash as much as she did. Still naked under the raincoat, she ran back up the stairs and snatched him up, pulling off the diaper and gown he wore, and brought him down into the yard. She knelt in the overgrown grass and put him between her bare legs and scrubbed his hair, making him cry from the soap that stung his eyes, and then the rest of him. Just as she finished, the rain stopped and the sun came out.

By the time she got him upstairs he was rigid with cold, his fingers a peculiar shade of yellowish gray. She held him to her chest to warm him and he stopped in mid-cry. Then, fast as lightning, before she could do a thing about it, he turned his head and nuzzled her bare breast and latched on.

*Just like a little goat,* she thought.

He sucked hard. She froze, feeling suddenly quite warm, as if she were melting, as if she were turning into a puddle on the muddy ground. It was a strange sensation, not altogether unpleasant, his nub of a tooth sending a signal to her thighs, no, not her thighs, between her legs.

*What is this?*

Now (all too soon) he spit out the nipple, her very own nipple, and began to cry furiously, pounding at her breast with his fist. *Nothing here.*

She dried him off and wrapped him in the towel, which he immediately kicked off. Quickly, she let the raincoat fall to the floor, toweled herself, found another dress in the closet, shook it, and slipped it on. She felt too clean for the dusty underpants, so she went without. She ran back downstairs and found the jug, now filled with water from the rain, and brought it back and filled it for another bottle.

The tears dried on Tommy's cheeks while he drank, and after he finished, he lay in her arms looking up at her with that steady gaze. There was an odd veneer to his eyes, a kind of film. His nose seemed to have grown wider, his hair was curlier than ever, fluffed from its washing, resembling a halo. The one tiny tooth a pearl.

She sat on the side of the bed, holding him.

He was still naked. She raised his arm again to look at the dark spot. He gazed up at her, a half-smile playing at his lips, as if there were something he was waiting for, something more she could provide.

She didn't like birthmarks. Son had had one on his belly. He'd been self-conscious about it and had always worn a shirt, even at the lake.

She had seen it only once, looking up, his shirt lurching open above her, the day of the trick.

There was something in her eye again, this time the right one. Another stray ant, burning and biting, making her eye run. She rubbed it, but it didn't stop. She shook her head and the baby eyed her seriously, as if she had spoken to him.

She felt woozy. Here it was afternoon and she hadn't had so much as a saltine cracker. What she would give for a piece of cracker, a crumb, even a tiny one the size of those pieces in the communion plate at church. She would let it melt on her tongue (she was always famished at church and picked the largest one) and then drink the sweet sweet grape juice and she would sing glory hallelujah at the top of her lungs.

THERE ARE unexpected moments when the eye breaks free, packs its bag, tips its hat to the tedious brain, and goes on the lam.

*What was wrong with her eye?* It watered and burned, causing her to blink and squint, and when she squinted, little Tommy looked like . . . well . . . in all honesty, he looked like a little colored boy.

A ridiculous thought. Put into her head by the old woman.

*But.*

She tried to conjure up an image of Tommy before the storm. He'd looked like an old man, she used to say, with his bald head and unfocused hazel eyes. Hazel? What color was hazel? She remembered asking her mother the question. *Light*, her mother had said. Anything between blue and green and yellow.

Then, Tommy's eyes had been his best feature, a cross between green and blue. The color of her mother's garden in late afternoon.

He'd had a tidbit of a nose, almost no nose at all. When she'd play with him, which had been rare, she'd pretend to snatch it up between her knuckles.

But babies' eyes did change, also their hair and skin. She knew for a fact that her own had been a watery blue when she was newborn and then changed to the run-of-the-mill brown they were at present, and she had pictures to prove it, or did before the storm. And of course, noses just got bigger and bigger, like her own, which was entirely too big.

*But what about the birthmark?* her on-the-lam eye asked.

She didn't remember Tommy having one, but that was nothing to remark at. And heavens, surely it was possible for two babies, especially if they were related, to have birthmarks. Her mother was the one who would know, of course her mother would know.

But she couldn't ask her mother because Alice had gone mental and would tell Jo to give Tommy back.

LET'S JUST let the eye play and say this wasn't Tommy. Let's just, for the sake of argument, say this was the colored girl's boy. Would Jo give him back?

She looked down at him. His eyes were drooping, his eyelashes black and thick as a brush. Tommy's eyelashes had been blond and sparse.

No. Jo most definitely would not give him back. She had saved him and loved him and cared for him, and he was hers. Observe how he adored her, how he trusted her.

She was, at the very least, his aunt, and was being one's aunt really that different from being one's sister?

Or mother?

Well, *mother.*

But, wasn't he better off with Jo than with that little colored girl? Was her name Dreama? *What names colored people had!*

Jo had promised to keep him safe.

A promise was a promise. Once, her mother had promised to take her to Memphis to the Peabody Hotel. They would go in style. They would ride the Frisco Accommodation, the very train Jo just hopped off of. They would spend the night in a fancy room. They would watch the ducks waddle down to the pond in the lobby, single file, in the morning, and then waddle back up to their coops on the roof when the sun went down. Her mother had whispered this promise to Jo in her darkened room, shades pulled and secured, when she'd had the red measles and couldn't read or look into the light for two weeks. She'd been tossing and turning, feverish and deeply alone in her predicament. In her fevered brain, the promise had taken the shape of a beautiful girl, the girl she wanted to be. The beautiful girl had kept her company, through the whole measles ordeal, clucking over her, reminding her of the upcoming trip.

An unkept promise is a festering sore. When Jo recovered, Alice was terribly busy with school and tired on the weekends. They would wait until summer, but when summer came, her mother was pregnant again and sick to her stomach. Then there was Tommy, and that was the end of that.

HER UNRULY eye, that mischief-maker, whispered a Word to Keep in her ear. *Dehiscence. A splitting open, a rupture.*

Her mother had given her that word on her thirteenth birthday. It had come with a warning, a double meaning. First, rupture. A sutured but infected wound could rupture, sowing destruction throughout the body, killing the patient. Or, happily, her mother said, *dehiscence* could mean the breaking open of a seed pod, scattering seeds to grow and flourish. *You're almost a woman now. You get to choose,* her mother had said. *Write down both meanings.*

She hadn't understood her mother at the time, but had heard the warning in her voice.

THE TORNADO had split something open; something had fractured, like the bone in her arm. Now all she needed was food and diapers and water. She needed to go out into the town and find those things she and this child, *her* child, needed to sustain themselves.

She would have to leave him for a little while. Otherwise, she would be found out.

But now he was bucking and crowing in her arms, wide-eyed and rambunctious. Delighted with himself and her.

She'd never been so hungry. She felt as hollowed out as an empty bowl.

The room lurched and pitched. One of the aunts walked by the door to the bedroom, her dark skirt swishing.

*Tell me what to do,* Jo begged, but the aunt was gone.


**SHE AWOKE** when he hit the floor.

A thud, followed by a sharp intake of breath. Then he began to scream. It was a different kind of scream, higher pitched, a spiral of sound.

There he lay, unbelievably, on the hard floor, the wood floor, under her feet, sprawled on his back, arms and legs gyrating. There was a baffled look on his face.

She fell to her knees. "Oh good lord Jesus," she breathed, trying to gather him up, but succeeding only in shoving him across the floor with her one good arm. "Oh baby, oh no."

At that moment, inside and over the baby's shrieks, she heard footsteps on the stairs. Then Aunt Fan and Aunt Sister were there, taking up the whole doorway. They wore long night-gowns, yellow for Aunt Fan and a faded blue for Sister. Their hair was wrapped in paper curlers.

They frowned and shook their heads at her.

*Merciful heavens, Jo, what are you thinking?*

Aunt Fan swept in and bent down and helped her pick Tommy up from the floor. Aunt Sister told her to put that poor child down on the bed. *Support the head*, they instructed in unison. *Look him over, head to toe.*

They hovered, their freckled fingers touching the baby here and there like a sprinkling of pepper. *Broken neck, make sure, careful now.*

On the bed Tommy screamed on.

Jo patted his face and belly. The head was the worry, the back of the head. She was afraid to look.

*Lift it, touch it.*

A bloody pulp. That was her fear. But it didn't even feel dented, and when she brought her hand out, there was no blood on her fingers. Not a drop, she turned to tell the aunts.

They just looked at her, their heads cocked. There was a question forming on their lips.

Jo put her fingers in her ears.

Go away, she told them, you're dead. This is none of your business.

They ignored her, whispering back and forth to each other.

Tommy stopped screaming abruptly. His bottom lip quivered, his eyes closed.

*Doctor. Head injury.* Which one of them said it she didn't know.

THE MINUTE she walked through the door of the theater, she burst into tears. A colored nurse she hadn't seen before came running and took the baby from her arms.

"Calm down," the nurse said. "What's the matter?"

Jo stopped short. The nurse's tone was stern and her clipped speech seemed foreign.

"He took a fall. He fell off the bed. He hit his head."

The nurse put Tommy on a spare cot and started poking on him. "He looks all right. I'll go fetch the doctor. You stay with him."

The nurse turned then. "This baby's your maid's?"

"What?"

"This child's a Negro."

"No, he's not. He's my brother."

The nurse looked at Tommy again and pursed her lips, then took off down the aisle toward the stage.

The doctor wasn't one Jo had seen before. He had a boyish look, too young for a doctor.

He examined the baby from head to toe, waking him to peer into his pupils. "Whose child is this?" he asked Jo.

"He's mine. He's my brother."

How many times would she have to lay claim to her own flesh and blood?

The nurse pulled the doctor (if he was that) aside and whispered in his ear.

The doctor turned back to Jo. He put his hand on her shoulder. "Now I know you've been through a terrible ordeal already, but this child may be a case of mistaken identity. We need to look into this baby's identity. Where are your parents?"

A pesky gnat of a question. She brushed it aside.

Tommy had begun to fret. "Let me hold him," Jo said. "He needs me."

The colored nurse made a move toward the baby. Jo stepped in front of her. "Let me settle him down."

The doctor and nurse exchanged glances. The doctor made a motion to the nurse, and she stepped back.

"He's hungry," Jo said to the nurse.

The nurse looked at the doctor and he nodded and she hurried off.

Jo picked up Tommy and quieted him.

There was a scream from one of the cots up on the stage. The doctor turned and ran toward the commotion.

Jo looked down at Tommy. He smiled, waved his arms at her.

She wondered whether her mother was better, back in her right mind. She wanted to ask her something. She walked up the steps to the stage and back to the corner where her mother had been. She parted the curtain.

Her mother lay there asleep, her mouth slack, one hand, mottled with scratches hanging over the side of the bed. What was left of her leg had been taken down from the sling and was hidden under the sheet.

"Mother," Jo said.

Her mother opened her eyes. They were red and swollen. "Dear Jo," she said. "You're really alive. I thought I dreamed it."

Jo walked toward her, smiling back. She came to her mother's side and sat down on the edge of the bed, turning Tommy toward her.

"Where's Daddy?"

Her mother sat up in the bed and took her hand. "I have something to tell you, honey. They found our Tommy. They found him in George Walton's cornfield. He was already gone." She began to sob. "My baby boy. Your daddy's gone to bury him."

There was a chill now. It started at the top of Jo's head and began to descend. It glided down, icing her ears, then her lips and neck, then moving into the good right arm, then freezing the ants in the bad left arm, then settling in the pit of her stomach and after that slithering down into her thighs, and after what seemed like hours, into the soles of her feet until she was nothing but a block of ice.

Then her mother looked at the baby in Jo's arms. "Whose baby is that?"

SHE FLEW, she scurried. She knew the way. Right on Main, the long blocks up Main toward Crosstown, then over the tracks, to the left and down the highway toward Verona.

The colored boxcars sat, dark and streaked with rain. She went to Number 4.

The old colored woman sat at the table, her head in her hands, the cat sprawled under her chair. A candle flickered on the table.

Her name, Jo remembered suddenly, was Dovey.

"What are you doing here?" Jo asked Dovey.

The cat stretched and yawned.

Dovey raised her head. There was a knot on her temple the size of an egg. Her eyes gathered time and split it open.

"Waiting for you." She pushed her chair back from the table and stood up and held out her arms.

Jo held Promise close. His breath tickled her cheek. She closed her eyes, knowing, suddenly, that one day he might turn and look at her with hatred and despair in his eyes, accusing her of crimes she had yet to commit. Even then she would put her flawed arms around him, even then she would hold him close.

*What a beautiful name, Promise.*

Dovey leaned toward the baby. "My Charlesetta come back to me."

"You have a daughter?"

"Had."

"I'm sorry."

"This her grandbaby."

"He's mine too. I have a claim."

"You sure do. You saved him."

"He saved me."

Dovey looked at her. "You his aunt. Claiming your own and standing by your own two different things. I got my own business to take care of in that department."

"So do I," said Jo, remembering her mother, how she looked like a tree struck by lightning, everything burned away.

Dovey moved closer, touching her now, reaching for the child in her arms. In the candlelight, Dovey's face was smooth and radiant, revealing the girl she'd once been.

Jo opened her mouth to speak, to say something about love. But not just love; love was easy. Something about *affiliation*, a Word to Keep if there ever was one. Definition: standing by.


NOW, THOUGH, there was no more talk but a flurry at the door. Now there was that other girl, the mother, Dreama, her face full of light, her hair a halo in the flicker of the candle. Beside her an old colored man (Would Jo never brush this caul of color from her eyes?). His face a row of furrows, the long haul of seasons. His eyes watchful.

Promise had begun to squirm and kick. He'd become heavier and heavier. Now, in that eternal split second, he gathered himself and pushed off Jo's protruding hip bone (oh, she was hungry, she'd never been so hungry in her life) and leapt like a slippery fish.

A flash in the water, a ripple in the stream of a long life.

There he goes, here he comes.

Years later, Jo will look at him, a man now, and remember his sheer beauty in that moment.

And when he leapt from her one good exhausted arm, it was Dovey who caught him.

# AFTERMATH

"This is Tupelo! From the wreck and ruin we must rise again." So began an editorial in the Tupelo Daily News published a week after the F5 tornado carved its fifteen-mile-long path through town, destroying most of what was in its wake.

And Tupelo did rise from the rubble, at least part of Tupelo did. The All-American city's recovery from the tornado of 1936 was swift, thanks in large part to a remarkably effective coalition of local, regional, and national government agencies; businesses; individuals; and news agencies. Within hours of the storm, the American Red Cross had assembled personnel to establish a disaster headquarters that would provide food, tetanus shots and other medicine, clothing, and housing. The American Legion quickly mobilized more than 500 trucks of 1,400 men to remove debris and provide food, clothing, and medical supplies. By 2:30 A.M. on April 6, only a few hours after the tornado, a special relief train carrying doctors, nurses, and medical personnel left Memphis for Tupelo. Later that day, caskets were rushed in and at least sixty embalmers converged from surrounding towns to assist in the grim task of preparing bodies for burial; and by April 7, the work of burying the bodies had begun, with graves being dug by the Civilian

Conservation Corps (CCC), one of President Franklin Roosevelt's New Deal agencies. There were no funeral services; the hasty burials took place about every ten minutes. The many animals that died were piled on the banks overlooking Gum Pond and cremated.

Another of Roosevelt's New Deal agencies, the Works Progress Administration (WPA), developed a clothing distribution center, and the Junior Red Cross provided schoolbooks for students. Reed's Department Store opened its doors to those in need of clothing. Most of the schools had been destroyed, but, once debris was cleared and housing needs were taken care of, students returned to schools in alternate locations.

In the week after the tornado, property owners signed authorizations for the removal of debris by government agencies, Tupelo Hospital was repaired and reopened, and the Resettlement Administration began clearing a thirty-two-acre plot for the construction of housing for homeless storm victims. The Frisco Railroad turned over all the boxcars needed for housing the homeless. Two "Boxcar City" camps, one for whites and one for blacks, were operational by April 13.

A special WPA grant of $1 million was made available for relief work, and a week later President Roosevelt signed a bill authorizing the Reconstruction Finance Corporation (RFC) to lend up to $50 million for rehabilitation of places affected by spring storms, and the RFC set up an office in Tupelo. As witness David Baker said, "Those who could rebuild, did. Those that couldn't had their homes torn down and something else built in their place. You can't imagine the hammering that was going on. That's all you heard for months."

How much, if any, of the then-generous fund for rebuilding was made available to African Americans is unknown. An editorial in the Tupelo Journal urged citizens to rebuild "our Negro quarters as a model for the nation in neatness and convenience," noting that the town had had "many eye sores" in its black sections that "were not only bad looking but inadequate for living quarters." In general, though, as author Robert Blade points out, "Tupelo's African-American community, all but invisible before the storm, remained that way."

As something of a postscript, one of several historic African-American communities in Tupelo, "Shake Rag," known for its blues and gospel musicians and its proximity to Elvis Presley's childhood home, was leveled during an urban renewal in the late 1960s and its residents relocated.

# ACKNOWLEDGMENTS

My greatest debt is to my longtime friends Robert Blade and Anna McLean Blade for their invaluable help in accumulating information about the Tupelo tornado of 1936. Robert, who authored the important book *Tupelo Man: The Life and Times of George McLean, a Most Peculiar Newspaper Publisher*, helped with library research and generously connected me with people I needed to interview. Anna, my dear friend from childhood who died before this book was published, possessed a tenacious long-term memory and an incisive social conscience; she generously helped in ways large and small to enlarge my knowledge of our hometown and bolster my spirits throughout the research and writing. It is a great sadness to know that she will not read beyond chapter 2.

Thanks to Lyn Martin Schloemer for forwarding me the email about the tornado's uncounted casualties that began this journey. I am grateful also to the survivors of the Tupelo tornado of 1936 who were willing to share their stories: David Baker spent one long September afternoon telling me storm stories, including the tale of his family cat; and the Reverend Robert J. Jamison recounted the loss of his family home in the neighborhood known as "Shake Rag." At the Oren Dunn City Museum, Rae Mathis Guess was exceptionally helpful, especially in selecting photographs of the tornado's aftermath; and Professor Berkley Hudson generously shared his knowledge of Otis N. Pruitt's remarkable photography. Joe Rutherford offered invaluable insights into historical contexts. Many thanks also to Susie Dent, Jim High, Medford "Mem" Leake, and Julian Riley.

*Tupelo, Mississippi, Tornado of 1936*, compiled by Martis D. Ramage Jr., and published by the Northeast Mississippi Historical and Genealogical Society, was essential to this novel, and many of the most bizarre incidents of the tornado leapt into the fiction from those compiled accounts of the storm as well as newspaper clippings, a video of survivors' stories, and other artifacts uncovered at the Lee County Library and the Oren Dunn City Museum, Tupelo, Mississippi. I thank Matt Turi and the Southern Historical Collection, Otis Noel Pruitt and Calvin Shanks Photographic Collection, Wilson Library, University of North Carolina at Chapel Hill, for assistance and permission to publish Otis Pruitt's photographs of the tornado's aftermath.

I am deeply grateful to Carrie Feron, who believed in this book from the get-go and whose enthusiasm and incisive commentary never fail to galvanize the creative spirit. Thanks also to Carolyn Coons and Kim Lewis for their care with the manuscript. As always, Jane von Mehren, agent extraordinaire, provided unwavering support, editorial acumen, and calming energy.

I also thank Elizabeth Spencer for reading the manuscript and giving me the benefit of her considerable writerly wisdom.

Finally, heartfelt thanks to Ruth Salvaggio for the hard questions she asked of this novel.

# HISTORICAL PHOTOS

The following photographs of the aftermath of the Tupelo tornado of 1936 are published courtesy of two different sources: the Oren Dunn City Museum, Tupelo, Mississippi; and the Southern Historical Collection, Otis Noel Pruitt and Calvin Shanks Photographic Collection, Louis Round Wilson Special Collections Library, University of North Carolina at Chapel Hill. Otis N. Pruitt was a remarkable photographer located in Columbus, Mississippi; the Southern Historical Collection contains 88,000 of his photographs, some of which reveal a keen eye for racial dynamics of the early twentieth-century South. The photographs from the Oren Dunn City Museum are from various sources. Some information for the captions was taken from *Tupelo, Mississippi, Tornado of 1936*, compiled by Martis D. Ramage Jr., 1997.

Please be warned that some of the following photos are graphic in nature.

The First Baptist Church of Tupelo received major damage. *Photo by Otis N. Pruitt*

A view of the author's grandparents' house in the upper right. *Photo by Otis N. Pruitt*

Looking southeast from a corner near downtown Tupelo. *Photo by Otis N. Pruitt*

A westward view of the destruction. *Photo by Otis N. Pruitt*

A damaged building. *Photo by Otis N. Pruitt*

A house blown off its foundation and a demolished car. *Photo by Otis N. Pruitt*

A demolished house on Main Street. *Photo by Otis N. Pruitt*

A view of the destruction leading down to Gum Pond. *Photo by Otis N. Pruitt*

A house standing amid the destruction with Gum Pond in the background.
*Photo by Otis N. Pruitt*

Tupelo High School, which sustained major damage. *Photo by Otis N. Pruitt*

The Hill, the African-American neighborhood that overlooked Gum Pond.
*Photo by Otis N. Pruitt.*

Scattered debris from the tornado. *Photo by Otis N. Pruitt*

Residents of the Hill survey the damage. *Photo by Otis N. Pruitt*

Bodies of African Americans, including a child. Some bodies were laid out in the old Hardin's Bakery, some in the alley behind it. *Photo by Otis N. Pruitt*

Residents await news as rescuers assist victims. *Courtesy Oren Dunn City Museum*

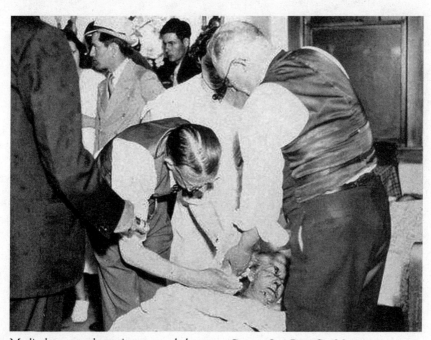

Medical personnel examine a wounded woman. *Courtesy Oren Dunn City Museum*

National Guard personnel unload soup kitchen equipment from a boxcar.
*Courtesy Oren Dunn City Museum*

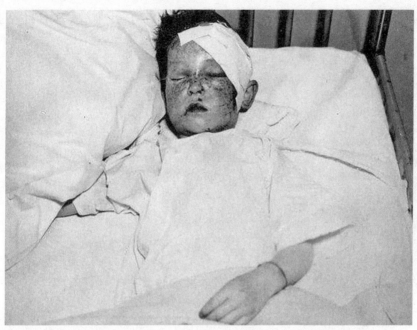

This five-year-old boy lay unidentified in a Memphis hospital until his grandfather recognized him from this newspaper photograph. *Courtesy Oren Dunn City Museum*

Men dredge Gum Pond, searching for victims who were blown into the water and drowned. *Courtesy Oren Dunn City Museum*

A man sits on a piece of foundation amid the wreckage of his home.

*Courtesy Oren Dunn City Museum*

Crosstown, where the Frisco tracks intersect West Main Street.

*Courtesy Oren Dunn City Museum*

A family surveys a severely damaged home in the white area of Tupelo called Willis Heights. This area, like the African-American area called the Hill, took the brunt of the storm. *Courtesy Oren Dunn City Museum*

The author's grandparents' home still standing amid the devastation.
*Courtesy Oren Dunn City Museum*

Victim being loaded into a Tennessee Valley Authority vehicle. Tupelo was the first TVA-powered city in the country. *Courtesy Oren Dunn City Museum*

Victim being removed from a home. *Courtesy Oren Dunn Museum*

Man amid the wreckage on the Hill. *Courtesy Oren Dunn Museum*

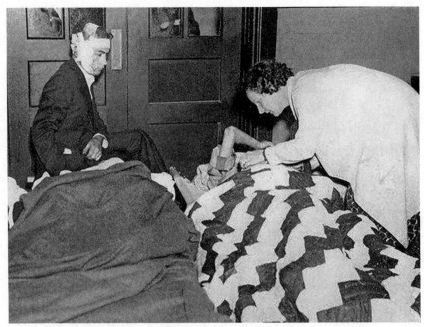

A volunteer, possibly a nurse, attends the injured. *Courtesy Oren Dunn Museum*

Goats, dead and alive, amid the wreckage. *Courtesy Oren Dunn Museum*

# ABOUT THE AUTHOR

Minrose Gwin is the author of *The Queen of Palmyra*, a Barnes & Noble Discover Great New Writers pick and finalist for the John Gardner Fiction Book Award, and the memoir *Wishing for Snow*, cited by *Booklist* as "eloquent" and "lyrical"—"a real life story we all need to know." She has written four scholarly books and coedited *The Literature of the American South*. She grew up in Tupelo, Mississippi, hearing stories of the Tupelo tornado of 1936. She lives in Chapel Hill, North Carolina, and Albuquerque, New Mexico.